The COMPOUND

The COMPOUND

Aisling Rawle

THE BOROUGH PRESS

The Borough Press
An imprint of HarperCollins*Publishers* Ltd
1 London Bridge Street
London SE1 9GF

www.harpercollins.co.uk

HarperCollins*Publishers*
Macken House, 39/40 Mayor Street Upper
Dublin 1, D01 C9W8, Ireland

First published by HarperCollins*Publishers* 2025

2

Copyright © Aisling Rawle

Aisling Rawle asserts the moral right to
be identified as the author of this work

A catalogue record for this book is available from the British Library

Hardback ISBN: 978-0-00-871008-8
Trade Paperback ISBN: 978-0-00-871009-5

This novel is entirely a work of fiction.
The names, characters and incidents portrayed in it are
the work of the author's imagination. Any resemblance to
actual persons, living or dead, events or localities is
entirely coincidental.

Set in Adobe Garamond Pro by HarperCollins*Publishers* India

Printed and bound in the UK using 100% Renewable
Electricity at CPI Group (UK) Ltd

All rights reserved. No part of this publication may be reproduced, stored in a retrieval system, or transmitted, in any form or by any means, electronic, mechanical, photocopying, recording or otherwise, without the prior written permission of the publishers.

Without limiting the author's and publisher's exclusive rights, any unauthorised use of this publication to train generative artificial intelligence (AI) technologies is expressly prohibited. HarperCollins also exercise their rights under Article 4(3) of the Digital Single Market Directive 2019/790 and expressly reserve this publication from the text and data mining exception.

This book contains FSC™ certified paper and other controlled
sources to ensure responsible forest management.

For more information visit: www.harpercollins.co.uk/green

For Dee and Dave

The stupidest questions of all were asked by Mollie, the white mare. The very first question she asked was: 'Will there be sugar after the rebellion?'

'No,' said Snowball firmly. 'We have no means of making sugar on this farm. Besides, you do not need sugar. You will have all the oats and hay you want.'

'And shall I still be allowed to wear ribbons in my mane?' asked Mollie.

'Comrade,' said Snowball, 'those ribbons that you are so devoted to are the badge of slavery. Can you not understand that liberty is worth more than ribbons?'

Mollie agreed, but she did not sound very convinced.

Animal Farm, George Orwell

I

One

I woke up first. There was no particular significance to it, only that I have always slept poorly and generally wake early in the morning. I had no way to tell the time, but I thought that I had slept a while: my limbs were heavy and stiff from a long, motionless sleep. The room was dark and windowless, with only a small skylight directly above my bed, though it didn't smell of sleep, or musk: it smelled fresh and airy, as if it had recently been cleaned. I thought I could detect the slightest trace of air freshener, citrus-scented, or maybe pine. There were ten beds, though only one aside from my own was occupied. The girl in the bed across from me was slowly emerging from sleep. She sat up and looked at me. She was beautiful, but that was to be expected.

'Hello,' I said after a few seconds. 'I'm Lily.'

'I'm Jacintha,' she said. 'Nice to meet you.'

I put my feet on the floor, feeling newly born. I stretched, arms high above my head, and heard my joints pop. There was air conditioning whirring, but I could feel the heat that lurked behind it, thick and cloying. When I looked over, Jacintha was standing. She was wearing underwear and a tank top. Looking down, I saw that I was wearing something similar.

It might have been awkward, but she smiled at me. 'Will we find the others?'

We made our way through the house, exploring as we went. The house was at once familiar and entirely new to me. On either side of the bedroom were the dressing rooms: the boys' to the left, ours to the right. The boys' room held no interest for us, and we went directly to our own. It was enormous: much bigger than the bedroom. It was where we could keep all of our things, once we had them. The room was mostly comprised of storage space: built-in wardrobes, chests of drawers, cupboards and some glittery boxes, similar to one I had used to store my dress-up costumes as a young girl. Running through the centre of the room was a grey laminate-covered table with a bench on each side. Along the tables were lighted mirrors and the little screens. I touched one, but the screen remained black.

While the bedroom had been clean, the dressing room was distinctly untidy: there were clothes strewn across the floor, and make-up stains along the table, with the lingering scent of feminine products still hanging in the air. Jacintha and I looked through the drawers and storage spaces and found mostly clothes, the majority of them cheap and worn: swimsuits that had been stretched to the point of translucency, stained dresses and tired-looking T-shirts. There were a couple of nice pieces, possibly designer – a few dresses, a skirt and a jacket. They were stiff and creaseless, and I thought that they likely had never been worn.

Down the hallway was the bathroom, tiled and pristine. There were two toilets, a urinal running along the length of the wall, and a bath, large and inviting, shaped like an oversized canoe. There was a sleek gold bar on which towels hung, matching gold knobs on the cabinet doors and a similar gold bar over the mirror by the sink. The taps were a fine brass colour, with an impressive number of soaps lined along a shelf, and an artfully arranged stack of toilet roll. On the wall beside the bath was a painting, large and abstract. It was the only piece of art I had ever seen in the house. I know that the place had changed drastically over the years, but the same piece of art stayed, unmoved. The bedroom and dressing rooms had been nice enough, but they were designed for practicality. The bathroom was pure luxury: perfect, except that it had no door.

Jacintha and I went downstairs. There were a number of empty rooms, perhaps four or five. There were some empty boxes left in them, and I thought that the rooms must have been used for storage. There were two more bathrooms, and though they were nice enough, they were clearly the lesser bathrooms.

We came to the living room and paused uneasily in the doorway. While the dressing room had been messy, this room had been trashed. There was no sofa, but there were folding chairs that lay in one corner. There was a mirror on the ground, shards of which reflected the mess around it: a dented wall, a legless coffee table, a shattered vase. Nearly everything in the room had been broken or destroyed, except for the big screen, which hung on the wall, untouched. Like the little screens, the big screen was blank. Neither Jacintha or myself commented on the mess, but we stayed standing in the doorway for a minute or so, waiting to see if the big screen would turn on.

Then there was the kitchen, large and mercifully well stocked. There were granite countertops with the usual appliances, and a small island with three bar stools. The kitchen had an industrial feel to it, designed to accommodate several people cooking at the same time, or cooking in large amounts. Jacintha and I spent a while there, rooting through cupboards and drawers. There was enough food to last for a long time – weeks, at least.

Although it was well built and well supplied, it was incredibly messy; bewilderingly so. There were eggshells on the ground, splashes of sauce on the wall and dishes in the sink. The floor was dirty, the counters sticky. The bins were overflowing and smelled of rotting meat.

'There's no freezer,' Jacintha said.

'The fridge is huge, though,' I said. I opened the chrome double doors, admiring its wingspan, and smiled at her. She looked at me like she wasn't sure about me yet.

There was a large window above the sink that stretched almost the length of the wall. It had a nice effect, though it meant that the kitchen was uncomfortably warm, almost pulsing with heat. Through it, I could spot the swimming pool in the distance. It was only when I saw the blue-tinted water, glinting in the sun, that I fully came to terms with where I was and what we were doing.

'Look,' Jacintha said. It took me a minute to see the girl, curled up as she was, sleeping on the ground at the lip of the pool.

We went out to inspect her. When we approached, she didn't move. I wondered briefly if she was dead. Jacintha crouched down and shook her by the shoulder. For a second, looking down at her, I thought that she looked a lot like myself, and felt a pulse of worry. Then the girl woke, and I could see that she didn't actually look like me: she was just thin and blonde too. She was faintly pink all over from lying in the sun. The girl looked up at us, adjusting her hair.

'Hey, guys,' she said. 'I'm Susie.' Jacintha and I introduced ourselves, and Susie smiled and nodded. 'Those are great names,' she said with energy.

We looked at each other, trying to think of something to say.

'Isn't the pool incredible?' Susie asked.

I said, 'I was just thinking that.'

'I don't know how I woke up here. I don't remember going to

sleep, but that doesn't really matter now, does it? Oh,' she said, looking around her. 'There's so much sand. Wow. It's warm, too. I've only just woken up, and I don't think I've ever been so warm in my life! Where did you two wake up?'

'We both were in the bedroom,' Jacintha said. Susie looked a little thrown, so I said, 'You're the first we've found.' She looked happier, and we set out to find the others.

As we looked for the others, we were able to take in, for the first time, the scale of the place where we would be living. The compound spilled out, varied and brilliant: red-brown earth, yellowed grass in some places, and startling, vivid greenery in others; pebbled paths, small bits of vegetation and amenities, and surrounding it all, separated by a ring of bushes, the desert stretching endlessly to the horizon. Towards the back of the compound, the grass and vegetation bloomed, and an irrigation system spat lazy drizzles of water, the light casting rainbows through the droplets, a casual sort of beauty that contrasted almost garishly with the monotonous plains that lay beyond. The sight of the desert gave me pause; I had seen it before on the television, of course, but it was a different thing entirely to see it before me. The pale gold sand and the flat, barren land seemed as though they had never been tempered by human feet. It was from there that the men would come, and to there that we would be banished, if it came to that.

While the sheer size of the compound was incredible, it was distinctly run-down. It looked a lot like the home of a billionaire, if the billionaire's staff had gone on strike.

Directly in front of the house was a patio, wrapping around the side. To the west of the house the grounds were lush and attractive, with long paths intersecting pretty flower beds. There was a pond glimmering in the distance, and gates and walls that led to nowhere as though someone had started to section off parts, but had given up. At the furthest western point sat an immense maze, green and imposing.

The west was picturesque, while the east was functional. There was a tennis court: no net or equipment, but the ground had been properly marked. There was a small outdoor gym with a bench and a step machine. A little further beyond, there was a ping-pong table which looked fairly new, and a trampoline with rusted springs and tired, sagging canvas.

Curiously, though there were many parts of the compound which were in serious disarray, you could see that there had been a concerted effort to build a boundary. As well as the bushes which had been planted a long, long time ago, there was a simple wooden fence running along the entire grounds, demarcating where our home ended at the expanse of the desert. Previously, I knew, there had been only barbed wire. The fence was an upgrade.

There was much to explore, but I was most interested in the huge, egg-shaped pool, and wherever we walked, I kept turning back to look at it again. The pool was the thing that held the place together: it was what transformed some ill-kept gardens and strange walkways into a residence.

The next girl found us: she was already awake. She was standing in a sandy patch of ground behind the house. She had her hands on her hips, looking out into the desert, so still that we hadn't noticed her at first. She raised her arm in greeting, and I felt her eyes move across us, taking in what she could. Even before we reached her, even from a distance, and with her face partly covered, I could tell that she was beautiful. There was something in the way that she stood, or maybe something about the way her hair fell. Sure enough, when we reached her she dropped her hand, and I saw that she had the kind of face that drove people to madness, with desire or with envy.

'Hello,' she said. 'I'm Candice.' She looked at us expectantly, and we each introduced ourselves. I remembered that I wasn't wearing any make-up.

I couldn't help but stare at her, even as I tried not to look too bothered by her presence. Her hair was long and dark, intimidatingly straight despite the humidity. She had particularly striking eyes of a very light blue, almost translucent; they looked over us carefully, appraisingly. Her mouth was not of a shape or size that was currently in vogue: my own lips were carefully constructed to look full and plump. Her mouth was wide with narrow lips, a decisive slash of pink across her face. There was no part of her beauty that didn't make me question mine.

'Four of us, now. I think I saw someone asleep by that flower arch. This way,' she said, and we followed her.

It took us a long time to find the others – probably a couple of hours. We searched the whole compound, except for the maze, which none of us wanted to enter, even in a group. When all ten of us had gathered together, we headed towards the pool. The heat was relentless, shocking even, and I had no thought beyond getting cool. We stripped down to our underwear and slipped into the water, relief coming at once.

I lay on my back and looked at the sky above me. It was a different blue than I was used to. It was clear, entirely untouched by clouds or smog, with no tall buildings to block out great chunks of it, nor artificial lights to disguise its hues. The compound was rough around the edges, definitely, and needed a great deal of work, but there was something about it that felt fantastically real. Wherever the cameras were, they weren't easy to spot.

We all drifted about the pool aimlessly. We smiled if we caught each other's eyes, but didn't speak. I didn't enjoy the silence: I thought it made it seem as though we were hatching plans of some sort, though I suppose people only wanted to be left to their own thoughts. Towards one end of the pool, Susie was doing handstands. I didn't join in, but I swam towards her and watched. She was pretty good: her legs were straight as an arrow in the air, and when she was done, she did a tumble under the water and returned to the surface, smiling.

I've always been a passive kind of person; it is both my worst quality and the thing that people like most about me. If the others had stayed in the pool for the rest of the day I would have done the same, but apparently they only wanted to cool off, so when the others got out, I got out too, and when everyone sat under the shade of a tree, I did the same, though I dreaded the thought of insects on my bare skin. Were there ticks in the desert? I wanted to look it up, but remembered that I had no phone.

Candice was the last to get out of the pool. I watched her from the shade; we all did. She slicked her hair back in one casual sweeping motion, pressing it close to her skull and away from her face. She dived under the water: sleek, without a splash, only her ankles flashing in the air before she was fully submerged. For a few seconds, she travelled silently under the water, an abstract blur, and emerged at the other side. She walked slowly up the steps, exposing her body one inch at a time, until she was beyond the domain of the water and stood on the deck, dripping and strong-limbed, her hair still in place.

I could imagine just how impressive it would have looked for people watching. It was sort of embarrassing, actually: Candice knew exactly what she was doing, and the rest of us were just bumbling around, trying to avoid the worst of the heat.

When we all had found a comfortable spot to sit, we got to talking a little. A blonde-haired girl named Eloise said that she liked my hair, and I said that I liked her nails. Another girl, beautiful and buxom, who I thought might be called Vanessa, added that she felt as though she might die from the heat. It was all harmless chitchat, as there wasn't much we could really say. Then Candice caught my eye, and said,

'If the boys were to arrive this minute, what kind of guy would you go for?'

The gaze of every girl was resting on me. I wrung my hair out a little, to give myself time. It was a good question. It was the question we needed to get out of the way, before they came.

'Probably the guy who gets me into trouble,' I said. I thought it was a good answer, even if it wasn't necessarily true; I had prepared it in the weeks before I came. I thought that it was open enough that I wasn't hemming myself in before I'd seen anyone, and it made me sound adventurous. Some of the girls nodded thoughtfully as they looked at me. 'And I definitely prefer an older man.'

'Do you have daddy issues?' Susie asked.

'Not that I know of,' I said.

'What about you?' I asked Candice. 'What are you looking for?'

She shook her hair out; it was still wet, and small droplets flew about her, one landing on my ankle. I pressed a hand to my arm: it was warmer than the rest of me. I was burning already.

'I like men who are driven,' she said. 'A man who knows himself. That's what I want.'

The question of what kind of man we each wanted was passed around from girl to girl. Susie liked men who treated her nicely, and who liked to have fun. Susie didn't like men who were boring. Jacintha liked men who were kind, especially to people they didn't know. Jacintha cared deeply about her family, and she wanted a man who was also family oriented. Mia liked men who worked out: it showed dedication, and she appreciated a man who could pick her up above his head. She liked to feel dainty. Short, scrawny guys disgusted her. Becca, who was quiet, and blushed as she gave her answer, said that she liked a man who was kind – that was all. The other girls didn't answer, which I thought was suspicious.

'When do you think the boys will get here?' Mia asked.

We all glanced at each other.

'It can take a while,' Jacintha said carefully. I understood that Jacintha wanted to say that in previous years it had sometimes taken only hours and sometimes days. She couldn't say this explicitly, because it would have broken one of the rules.

There were several rules at the compound. The first was that it was forbidden to discuss that the show was in fact a show, or that we had seen the show before. It ruined the experience for the viewer and the participants, we had been told. The second was that we couldn't discuss our life outside of the compound unless we had been instructed to do so. The third was that it was forbidden to harm another resident. There were other rules, but they wouldn't come into effect until the boys arrived. We all understood that if we broke any of these rules we would be punished.

'We should start getting the place in shape now, in case they're here by tonight,' another girl said. I couldn't remember her name, but she was tall, with sharp features and a faint accent that I couldn't place. I imagined her as a marketing intern, going out for salads for lunch. As I examined her, she turned and looked at me. I pretended to stare at the sky behind her.

'Where to start?' Eloise said. 'The whole place is a mess.'

'The house,' Candice said, and stood. 'The rest can wait. We need to get the kitchen and bedroom in shape first.' Candice held her hand out to me. Her grip was strong, and the muscles in her arms moved subtly as she pulled me to my feet. I was small and soft by comparison. The rest of the girls got up too, and we filed into the house like a line of ants. I kept looking around me, trying to make sense of the space, the condition that it was in. Along the way, we picked up the odd bit of rubbish that we found, left by the residents who had come before us.

We separated into different rooms, and it was a relief not to have to look at all nine of the girls at once. Some went upstairs to clean the bedroom, while a group went into the living room to clean up the mess. I helped in the kitchen, cleaning the surfaces and taking the rubbish out. There was no hoover, and no dustpan either: we swept up the dust using a table mat. The absence of a hoover particularly disturbed Mia, who said, 'I didn't think it would be so poorly equipped. It's primitive, no?'

'We have a washing machine and a dishwasher,' Vanessa said. 'It's not a bad start.'

I picked up a half-eaten apple from the windowsill of the kitchen, around which fruit flies had begun to swarm. The inside of the apple was brown, but not rotten. I reckoned it had been eaten a day ago, maybe less. As I was throwing it out, I saw greasy paper plates and pizza boxes in the bin.

'They had pizza,' I said. No one responded or showed any interest, but it was interesting to me at least. It made the previous residents seem real. I had already begun to see the place as ours: it was strange to think of other people living there before us.

I didn't know under what circumstances they had left – as this year's batch of contestants we hadn't been allowed to watch for the last couple of weeks. The last time I had been able to watch, the rewards were just starting to get really good. One of the girls had gotten a hair straightener that I'd always wanted. 'Salon standard,' I remembered her saying, showing the steaming straightener to the other girls. She had shared it on the first day she received it, but after that had locked it in a drawer and did her hair only at night, when the others were asleep. The other girls would wake up, frizzy-haired, and look at her resentfully.

'I don't understand why they didn't take better care of the place,' Mia said.

'It's not that bad,' Jacintha said. She was standing at the window in the kitchen and pointed out to the garden beyond. 'They planted flowers, see?'

I looked out into the garden, at the brushes of pink and violet among the yellow-green grass. Yes, the place was beautiful, even if it needed work. We could begin in earnest when the boys arrived.

We cleaned the dishes and left the kitchen in some semblance of order. But before we prepared dinner we opted to change for the evening, lest the boys arrive and find us as we were, hair uncombed and faces bare.

In our dressing room, we sifted through the various garments that had been left behind. We were generous with each other, bestowing pieces to the girl they would suit the best, and lavishly complimenting each other every time we tried something on. I found a couple of things I liked, and picked my second-favourite one to wear, a pink gingham romper. I decided I would save the nicest piece – a red dress with a sweetheart neckline – for when I needed it badly.

On the front of each wardrobe was a mirror, meaning that even though we turned our backs or retreated into corners there was no way to avoid seeing each other. As I stripped off my shorts and my vest, I saw flashing limbs in the mirrors: someone's arm contorting to slip into a dress, someone else's thigh, hair being swept over a shoulder. I knew that there were a number of cameras in the room, and that we all were being filmed, but, oddly enough, that was one of the aspects of the day which perturbed me the least. I didn't bother to examine the room to see where the cameras might be. I more or less acted as I had on the outside – with the assumption that we were all being watched in some way or another.

There were very few make-up products, only some different shades of foundation, and two tubes of mascara which we passed around without hesitation. In a different situation I might have thought twice about sharing eye make-up with strangers, but we were in no position to be fussy. Jacintha hovered around when we were sorting through the foundation, and I saw that there was no make-up for dark skin. She met my eye and shrugged. 'It's fine,' she said.

'Sit down,' I said. 'I'll do your eyes.'

I did her make-up with careful swipes, my hand pressed lightly to her cheek to stop her head from moving. When I was finished, she opened her hand and showed me something dark and spider-like.

'Here,' she said, 'Have them. I don't think they've been used.'

They were false eyelashes. I fingered them, feather-light and delicate. 'Are you sure?'

She nodded and passed me the glue. I said, 'If you want, I can try to use the mascara to do winged eyeliner on you.'

As we did our faces, we kept looking towards the door. Though we were looking at ourselves, we were thinking of the boys. Every so often, if someone thought they heard something and emitted a sudden, sharp 'Shhh!', we all fell deathly silent, straining to hear. When nothing came of it, we laughed at ourselves.

Once we were ready, presentable if not glamorous, we went to the kitchen and made a simple dinner of omelettes. There were two bottles of champagne in the fridge, which we divided up, drinking little sips from little glasses. In the absence of chairs, we sat out on the grass, plates in our laps or balanced on our knees. The air was not sweet, but thick and filled with a desert musk, sitting heavily on my skin. It was intoxicating, and I felt my head go light and airy. I smiled genially at everyone, until I remembered that I look clown-like when I smile too widely. I tried for a moderate curling of my lips, like I had just recalled a joke.

We began to chat with more enthusiasm now, imagining different things we could do with the compound, imagining the kinds of boys who might show up and what kind of rewards we might get. After a while of saying different variations of the same thing, I was able to speak without thinking, and observe the girls, trying to fathom what I could from their idle chat. The truth is, we weren't interested in getting to know each other – not yet. We were assessing who was the most beautiful and who might cause trouble. At the same time, we were analysing what our own place in the group might be. Within minutes of speaking to the girls, I knew that I was one of the most beautiful, and one of the least interesting.

I kept smiling and chatting pleasantly while I examined the girls before me, comparing them to myself, and trying to see them as the boys might. Ten of us: myself, Jacintha, Sarah, Candice, Susie, Becca, Melissa, Mia, Vanessa and Eloise.

Ever since I was a teenager, I worried that in a group of people I would be the stupidest one there. It was sometimes the case, and sometimes it wasn't. I didn't think I really was stupid, only that I didn't know much about bookish things: I became uncomfortable when history or geography were mentioned and had an innate fear of politics. I think I have my own smarts though. I can read people okay, though sometimes I get things wrong. I don't think of that as a flaw in my small skill, so much as a testament to the unpredictability of human nature. But with relief, I realised that as long as Susie lived in the compound, I would not be the dimmest person there. I'm not saying that to be disparaging – I don't actually value intelligence that much in a person. Intelligence can be artificial, but charm is always real, and Susie had that in spades.

'I love it here already,' she said to me earnestly, her hand on my arm. 'It's so nice to be somewhere new.' I was curious about Susie's age: I thought that she might be a little younger than me, but it was hard to tell. She had a certain youthful quality to her. I imagined her working as a tour guide, high-fiving children and telling couples that they looked cute together.

Becca was the quietest; she fidgeted with her shorts and looked down at the ground when she spoke. She was pretty in an understated way, particularly when she smiled. She didn't smile often, but looked around her a lot, as though waiting for someone else to step in. She was the smallest of us all, and paler than anyone. She had applied no tan in preparation for coming. She was also the only one with short hair.

Mia was bitchy: I could tell that she was trying to hide it for the sake of first impressions, but bitchiness will out, and more than once I saw her eyes slide sideways or roll upwards when she disliked what someone was saying. I had also seen her openly sneer in another girl's face. Wisely, she didn't try it with Candice, but she didn't go out of her way to be nice to her either. I could tell that she didn't want to be mean: she tried at kindness, and sometimes succeeded. She was generally thoughtful, and was the first to jump up to get people water, or to clean the dishes. She was a self-proclaimed realist.

'I don't like bullshit,' she said, looking around her, meeting people's eyes. 'I'm straight. I expect others to be straight, too.' Her hair was a bright, artificial red, which she moved about a great deal as she spoke, and she had long, well-maintained acrylic nails. She was a lot, but she was still someone you wanted to be around: she had that kind of energy.

But it was Candice who shone, and towards Candice that we all gravitated. She was nice, in an offhand kind of way, and had an air of authority about her that we unquestioningly submitted to. Within minutes of sitting beside her, I found myself thinking, with a quiet, burning intensity, that if I could have been anyone in the world, I would be Candice.

At some point, I heard a girl whose name, I thought, was Melissa, say, 'I have been to a desert before actually, on a family holiday. It was very different.' We stared at her. She looked back at us, uncomprehending.

A voice sounded around us, clear as a bell. I couldn't tell where it came from. Watching the show the voice sounded androgynous, but listening to it in person I thought it sounded distinctly feminine.

'Good evening,' the voice said. 'Please refrain from revealing personal information unless instructed to do so in a task.'

We sat still and looked at each other. It was entirely silent: there were no birds overhead, or sounds from the house, and no men yet. The cameras, which I guessed were all around us, hidden in bushes and stuck to walls, did not whir or click; they, too, were silent.

'I'm sorry,' Melissa said at last. 'I forgot.'

'It didn't mention a punishment,' Mia said.

'I think it was just a warning,' Candice said. She met Melissa's eye. 'Any one of us might have slipped up. Not to worry, Melissa.'

'Let's go to bed,' Becca said, her voice soft and flute-like. 'When we wake up, the boys will be here.' We helped each other up, and went into the house. I kept glancing behind me, as though I would find the boys staggering in through the thicket.

When we passed by the screen in the living room, I saw that

it was still blank. 'Why do you think it hasn't lit up yet?' I asked Jacintha.

'It can't start until the boys are here,' she said. 'It would be an unfair advantage.'

I had already known the answer: it was the same every year. I only asked out of my old habit of prompting people to explain things to me even when I knew the answer. When I was a child, I found that it would make people more likely to want to help me, and it served me just as well as an adult. When we sat at our benches and took off our make-up, Jacintha peeled my eyelashes off and set them gently on my desk. I knew then that we were friends. Some things are that simple, and so it was with Jacintha.

I went to the bed that I had woken up in, and across from me Jacintha took hers, while the others debated over which beds they wanted. I lay down and smelled the air, which was still sweet and fresh, though there was now a slight scent of sand and sweat. The girls murmured around me. Goodnight, we said, our voices soft. Goodnight, goodnight, goodnight.

In the morning the boys still hadn't arrived, and we started to worry.

I opened my eyes – the first to wake, again – and reached for a phone that wasn't there. I woke up properly then, and looked around at all the other girls sleeping soundly. I couldn't see them well in the dark, and I seemed to have forgotten most of their names. The small trace of familiarity from the night before had vanished, and I was reminded that they were strangers to me. In that moment I would have given anything to have gone home.

I padded through the house, checking for any changes. In the living area, the screen was still blank. I walked outside, and fancied that I would see the boys waiting for me by the pool. But there was no sign of them. It might have been peaceful outside – all that flat, pale land stretching out into the distance – but I disliked the extreme quiet, and went into the kitchen, where I made coffee while keeping an eye out the window. Then I made a huge pan of scrambled eggs and wolfed down what I judged to be a moderate amount. I thought of how ugly I must look on the cameras, stuffing my face alone in the kitchen, my hair unbrushed, my face not yet washed. I finished eating as quickly as I could.

When I returned to the bedroom, the other girls were awake. They had been talking, but stopped when I walked in. Mia looked at me with wide eyes. 'There you are,' she said. 'We didn't know where you had gone.'

'I got coffee,' I said.

'Why did you get up before everyone else, though?'

'I don't know,' I said. 'I just woke up.'

'Were you just wandering on your own? That's so weird,' Mia said.

'No,' I said. 'I just made breakfast. I made eggs for everyone.'

'Thanks Lily,' Jacintha said. 'That was really thoughtful.' I met her eye, and felt a profound rush of gratitude for her, as though she had stopped me from falling off a cliff.

After we ate, we took our coffees to the outdoor dining area. There were no chairs, and we stood self-consciously, leaning against the wall, hips cocked.

It was difficult to know how to plan our day. We decided to go back to preparing the house in the morning; we could spend the afternoon relaxing and getting to know each other. Cleaning was hard in the heat, particularly in the kitchen, where the temperature was so extreme that we were forced to take frequent breaks, sprinkling our faces and necks with water.

When we were done, we changed into our bikinis and got into the pool. I noted the relative flatness of everyone's stomachs, and found that, while Sarah had the most toned abs, I was a sure contender for the shapeliest hips.

The pool was enormous; even with the ten of us in at the same time, there was still room left for about fifty refrigerators. We were not as reserved as we had been the day before; we did handstands and splashed each other. Mia and Eloise raced each other, and I swam as deep as I could, keeping my eyes open under the water and navigating around the blurry shapes of the girls' legs.

But where were the boys? As we lay in the shade, snacking on tortilla chips and guacamole, I wondered if they had been hurt. Four years ago one of the boys had broken his leg on the way to the compound and had been stranded for twelve hours before the show's execs got to him. It would have taken less time but he had said, over and over, that he didn't want anyone to come get him and that he could make it to the compound eventually. He was taken home immediately.

I knew I was going to drive myself mad with thinking, and asked Jacintha if she wanted to play ping-pong. It was tucked around the side of the house, and we played for a while – I think probably an hour. There was a ball but no paddles, so we played with our hands. I thought that Jacintha was a relaxed kind of person, but she became tremendously competitive once we started to play. She liked to do victory laps of the ping-pong table while I crouched on the ground to retrieve the ball.

'What time do you think it is?' I asked her between sets. She pointed above us, at the sun.

'It's hard to be sure, but I think around three or four. It's definitely the afternoon.' She came to stand beside me and pointed up, again. 'See?' I nodded, but I didn't understand precisely how she knew. For me, the sun was just the sun. She turned to face me. She wasn't wearing sunglasses, and only minimal make-up, and her face was clear to me. 'Do you think any of the men will be Black? There's usually one, but not always.'

'Maybe,' I said. I thought about it, then said, 'I'm sure there will.'

'If it's all white boys, I'm screwed,' she said. 'The white boys never go for the Black girl.'

'You're stunning,' I said. 'Any of the men would be lucky to have you.'

'You think?' she said, and twisted her earrings around. 'Well, you have nothing to worry about anyway. Is that your natural hair colour?'

I laughed. 'What do you think?'

We went back to the lawn, where the majority of the girls were sunbathing. 'Where were you?' Mia asked. 'Why are you always disappearing?'

'We were playing ping-pong,' I said. She looked like she didn't believe me. What could I say? We were playing ping-pong.

Jacintha and I took a seat a little bit away from her, and Candice came over and sat cross-legged on a cushion beside us. Candice had changed out of her swimsuit and into a crochet dress patterned with pretty greens and blues. She wore her long, thick hair in a high ponytail. I could see the beads of sweat on her neck. 'Don't worry about Mia,' she said. 'She'll lighten up once the men get here.'

Some of the girls had decided that they would make dinner for everyone. They went inside, intent on their task, and I felt impressed by their industriousness. All I could think of doing was getting cool. Eventually lying about got boring too, and

Jacintha asked me to help her sort out some kind of makeshift door for the bathroom.

I've always been useless in these kinds of situations: I don't have any sort of mechanical understanding. I've never assembled furniture myself, and I've never voluntarily looked inside the bonnet of a car. But Jacintha seemed to know what she was doing, and I encouraged her and made affirmative noises. In the end, she just hung a sheet over the doorframe. It was easy to move and provided a degree of privacy that we could live with, for now.

When dinner was ready, we ate tacos outside and covered our mouths as we spoke. I got the impression that everyone was saving their more interesting talking points for when the boys came; I know I was. Jacintha sat next to me, and I was glad that we were becoming friends. She was nice, and smart, too. Already the ten girls had split into two cliques: throughout the day, Vanessa, Sarah, Melissa, Becca and Eloise had kept to themselves, cleaning upstairs and eating lunch by the swings, and at dinner they sat a little apart too. Privately, I thought that the second group – comprised of Candice, Susie, Jacintha, Mia and myself – was the better one. The other girls were boring and had nothing much to add to a discussion. Mia, glancing at them, remarked, 'Vanessa's the only one of them who's pretty, anyway.'

We were slightly more tense that night, and some of the girls were impatient with each other, interrupting or rolling their eyes. We drank more than we had the first night, too, and struggled to find things to talk about. Only Susie remained enthusiastic; I don't think the fact that there was a sort of gag placed on our conversation topics bothered her at all. Susie could talk about anything. 'I don't even want the boys to come,' she said. 'We're having so much fun without them.'

We went inside eventually, to shower and to tend to the burns that we had accumulated. I had a long, red burn running up the length of my arm from when I had fallen asleep in the sun. We lathered aloe vera on each other, until the room smelled sharp and sweet, and we walked around with slow, hesitant steps. I slept poorly, waking constantly. I kept curling my arms under my chin in my sleep, and then wincing myself awake. Eventually I lay like a starfish on my back, listening to the cool rush of the air conditioning and the even breathing of the other girls.

The following morning, the boys arrived.

Two

They had come from the hills behind the compound, south of the tennis court, slipping through a gap in the fence in the early morning. If we'd have thought to go around to the back of the house we might have seen them yesterday, slowly, slowly crossing the terrain and making their way towards us.

They were clearly exhausted: even the ones who were in good shape had cracked lips, were sunburned and covered in brown-gold desert sand. Some of them looked worse: there were three or four who had scrapes and bruises across their faces and arms. One man, huge and hulking, had scrapes all across his chest, a gash on his leg, and an impressive black eye. I wondered if any of the boys had fought in the wars.

It was with some embarrassment that we led them to the grass to sit – they seemed a little surprised that there were no seats, but they didn't complain. We brought them endless jugs of water and had some food ready to give them: toast with jam, bacon, eggs, bowls of baked beans. One man lifted the bowl of beans to his face and poured it into his mouth like it was the final dribbles of milk in a cereal bowl. They'd had some supplies with them, they told us, but it wasn't the same as real home-cooked food. It felt almost indecent, us girls rested and showered, gazing at the boys, dirty and exhausted, their eyes darting around the compound, and travelling inexorably back to us. I thought that the oldest might have been in his early thirties, while the youngest was surely no older than twenty. Even after three days in the desert they were beautiful. But we were beautiful too, and we sat straight and let them look.

'How many of you are there?' I asked, though I had counted already. I had to ask, because it was the most important question.

'Nine,' one of the men said. He had neatly trimmed brown hair and warm brown eyes, and sunburn across his neck and his collarbones.

One of the men who had scrapes across his chest, who had introduced himself as Andrew, said, 'One of the men got lost. He won't be coming.'

Yet another said, 'How many of you are there?'

'Ten,' Mia said, and we all fell quiet as the boys looked at the girls, and the girls looked at the boys.

'We'll show you around,' Candice said, getting suddenly to her feet.

I knew what had motivated her into action; we all did. This was the rule of staying in the compound: it was what made people watch the show, day after day, and what people talked about during the ad breaks: you stayed in the compound only if you woke in the morning next to someone of the opposite sex. If you slept alone, you would be gone by sunrise. There were usually ten girls and ten boys to start with, but now, as the girls outnumbered the boys, one of us would be gone by tomorrow.

'It's too big a group to show around,' Mia said. 'Candice, you take five and I'll take four.'

If this plan was disagreeable to Candice she didn't show it. I went with Candice, as did Jacintha. Eloise and Susie went with

Mia. Becca and some of the other girls cleared the men's plates and brought them into the kitchen to clean up.

Candice took us to the west, the prettier side of the compound, where the maze lay, and the gardens and pond. Of the four men in our group, I remembered only a few of their names. Candice walked slowly, keeping in mind the boys' exhaustion, though they had perked up considerably, and were looking around with interest. We were showing them around like we were showing off our own property, and they were viewing it as though they had never seen it before.

'Was it terrible out there?' Candice asked. 'I wouldn't like to have done it myself.'

Andrew said, 'It was an interesting experience, for sure. We got to know each other pretty well. No, it wasn't terrible, but we were certainly glad to see you all.' I glanced again at the marks on his chest and face. I thought they made him look more handsome. He was of an average height and build, with light, curly hair. When he smiled, dimples emerged deep within his cheeks, softening his appearance and lending him a certain boyishness. There was something about him, though, an ease of movement and a way of holding your gaze that set him apart. Candice walked alongside him, glancing at him now and then. Of all the men, he seemed the most approachable.

'You got a few scrapes, there,' I said. 'What happened?'

'There were some issues,' he said. 'But we worked them out.' He smiled at me. 'It's good to be around women and be civilised again.'

The rest of the boys stayed silent. Whatever had happened, they weren't going to tell us.

'Well, thank God you made it,' Jacintha said.

One of the other men piped up. He was tall and broad-shouldered, like a rugby player. I thought his name might be

Marcus. 'I can tell you this much. You really learn a lot about yourself in the desert. It was difficult, but it was thrilling too. You have to rely on your wits. There's nothing to hide behind.'

Another man, wiry and wearing tortoiseshell sunglasses, possibly named Seb, said, 'A man can be a man in the desert.'

Candice made a polite noise of interest and turned back to Andrew, pointing out the dusty area that we thought must be for boules.

The man with the sunburned neck fell into step beside me. 'I'm sorry,' he said. 'I didn't catch your name.'

'Lily,' I said.

'Nice to meet you, Lily. I'm Sam.' He held out his hand for me to shake. I took it, smiling at the formality.

'What?' he said, smiling back. His eyes were a very warm brown, the same colour as his hair.

'I don't know,' I said. Rounding a corner, I bumped into him a little, and the small act of my arm brushing against his seemed uniquely embarrassing. 'Sorry,' I said. He took a small but noticeable step away, placing distance between us. I pretended to look in the opposite direction.

'I'm, ah—' Sam said. 'I'm conscious that I haven't showered in a few days.'

'That's okay,' I said. He smelled faintly of sweat, and there was dirt and sand clinging to his legs. Perhaps outside, at home, it might have thrown me off, but after days of waiting for the boys in the clean, orderly house, the sight of this man before me, dirty and fantastically real, thrilled me.

He looked around, as though taking in the sights. He stepped closer again. The ground beneath my feet was sandy and gritty, scuffing my white shoes. His arm brushed mine again, the hair on his forearm grazing the underside of my wrist. I hadn't felt so excited since I had come here. He turned to me. 'Do you—?'

He stopped himself. 'I keep forgetting that we can't talk about our lives outside the compound,' he said.

'It gets easier after a couple of days.'

'What do you talk about?'

'The house, mainly. The grounds, the weather.' I shrugged.

We walked in silence for a few moments. I could see the other group on the east side of the compound, Mia leading them around like a tour guide. I could hear her voice perfectly from across the way, loud and nasal.

It was clear that the boys were tired, though they didn't say so. Candice announced that she was hot, and wanted to sit in the shade for a bit, so we paused under a tree. When I glanced at Sam, he was looking above him, his face tilted to the blue sky. In the clear light, I saw lines on his forehead. I wondered how old he was. When he saw me looking, he smiled. 'I think this will be good,' he said. 'A chance to start again, right?'

'Right,' I said. The truth was, I wasn't entirely sure I agreed with him. Neither was I sure that I disagreed with him. I thought that it was endearing that he wanted to start again here. I didn't say what I actually thought, which was that it was a good place for a break.

When Candice felt that the boys were sufficiently rested, we wandered over to the eastern side of the compound, passing the gym. The man shaped like a bodybuilder and with the worst injuries fell into step beside me, and Sam shifted forward, as though to give us privacy. I thought his name was Tom, but I didn't want to ask for a second time. He had closely cropped blond hair and slate-grey eyes. But it was difficult to focus on anything other than his enormous build. He said, 'What did you girls get up to while you were waiting for us?'

'We cleaned, mostly. We were excited for you all to get here.'

He nodded. There was sweat on his forehead, and he wiped

it off unselfconsciously. I had surreptitiously been swiping at my upper lip for the past half hour, when I was sure that none of the boys would notice.

'I imagine you've been making lots of plans for what to do with the place.'

'I guess. Yeah, we've talked about it.'

'I have lots of ideas,' he said. 'Even before we got here I had ideas for what we could do. But,' he said diplomatically, 'I wouldn't want to get in the way of what you girls have planned. You were here first, after all.'

He glanced over at me. His appearance was unremarkable, except for his size. 'We can talk about it when we're all together,' I said.

'We're happy to be here. In the desert it gets so cold at night, you know. You can't feel it here, because you've got shelter. It'll be nice to share a bed tonight.'

I wondered if he was stating it as fact, or if he was providing an opening for me to suggest that we might share a bed. I felt sure, however, that he wouldn't react well to being turned down. When I said nothing, he walked over to Candice.

The boys took a few minutes to test the equipment in the gym, and Jacintha stood beside me and spoke quietly. 'What did you say to Tom?'

'Which one is Tom?'

She made a Tom-like gesture, squaring her shoulders, holding her arms separate from her torso. It was a good impression. In unison, we glanced around to make sure he hadn't seen it.

'I didn't say anything,' I said. 'We talked for, like, a minute.'

'There are ten girls and nine boys. Whether we're here in the morning or not depends on if a boy likes us. Don't shoot anyone down just yet, all right?'

When we had finished the tour, we all sat in the grass. It

wasn't uncomfortable any more: I was already getting used to it. Candice sat beside Marcus, and Susie sat beside Sam. I sat next to Jacintha. Everyone was relaxed, except for Tom, who was looking around him restlessly. 'The fence around the perimeter,' he said. 'That's new, right?'

We couldn't say that it was likely put up in the last couple of weeks by the previous residents, so Candice only said, 'Brand new.'

'That's good,' he said, his eyes following the boundary line. 'And there's the barbed wire, too. It's safe, then? I mean, you've felt safe here, the last few days?'

'It's safe,' Candice said. Tom nodded. I thought then that there was something off about him. While the other boys were staring openly at the girls, Tom was staring out into the desert.

'What about a glass of something a little stronger than water?' Marcus said. 'To celebrate us finally being together?'

I met Candice's eye, who looked quickly away. We had drunk all of the alcohol already. 'There isn't any, yet,' she said.

Irritated, Seb said, 'Have you not been following the instructions?'

'The screen hasn't been on,' Jacintha said. 'We think it was because they needed us all to be here.'

Andrew stood. 'Why don't we check if it's on now?' He offered Candice his hand, and the two of them made their way into the house. A moment later, Candice emerged, her arm waving in the air. The big screen had lit up.

Everyone knew how the big screen worked: it would detail daily instructions for all of us to carry out. We could only be rewarded if everyone took part. If successful, we would receive items for the compound: food, furniture, appliances, or other things that would make our lives easier. There would additionally be Personal Tasks, which were detailed on our little screens; these rewards would benefit us individually. There was no limit to how many tasks you could complete on the big or little screens: every time one was completed, another one would appear. If it wasn't completed in a day, that reward was lost for ever; a new task would appear the next morning.

The quality of the reward for each Communal Task depended on how well we executed the task, while the quality of the reward for a Personal Task in addition depended on how many people were remaining in the compound – the fewer people there were, the more valuable the reward. It was one of the most entertaining parts of the show, actually: they pushed people into couples, and otherwise tried to get you to forge relationships with the other residents, only to see if you were willing to sacrifice those same people in order to get better prizes. When there were twenty people the rewards were pretty basic, but as the numbers dwindled the rewards grew luxurious. In a previous year, a contestant who made it to the final pair got the actual dress that a famous actress had worn to an awards ceremony. Another time, the winner got a watch worth tens of thousands.

That was the other thing: if you won, you got unlimited rewards. Not all of them were as expensive as the watch, but once you were alone in the compound, you didn't have to complete a task to earn a reward – you just asked, and it soon appeared. Your other prize was the compound itself. You could theoretically stay for as long as you wanted, but generally the winner gathered as many rewards as they could carry and left to enjoy their life of fame and further riches on the outside. The minute the last person left, the next group of contestants could enter.

On the big screen, it said, *Task: Every boy and girl must discuss their previous relationships. Reward: Outdoor seating.*

'Easy,' Seb said. There was something about Seb that was easy to dislike. He was wiry, yet seemed to make an effort to take up more space than was necessary, slouching insolently as he sat, legs spread wide, arms draped behind him. As well as that, he had an annoying, moneyed accent, and smirked when other people spoke.

'Did anyone check the little screens?' Mia asked. Several people started to move towards the changing area, but Candice said, 'No one goes anywhere until we get this first task done. We need a place to sit.' She was right: aside from the fact that seats seemed a necessary thing for civilised living, the ground was so hot. Those of us who had started to move towards their dressing room stopped when Candice said so.

We created a rotating line by the pool. The girls stayed in one place, while the men moved to the girl to the left after two minutes. We had no clock or means of measuring time, so whatever girl was not speaking to a boy would call 'switch' after counting two minutes.

We had been waiting for the boys for two days, but the reality of seeing them standing before us was jarring. Even the smallest of them, Evan, was taller than the tallest girl, and they varied in appearance – ranging from trim and toned, to enormously, threateningly muscled. The girls had their backs to the pool, and I felt, as they stared baldly at us, that at any minute the boys might either fall at our feet, or launch us backwards into the pool.

'All right,' Jacintha called, standing at the end. 'Begin!'

In front of me was Seb. He was of average height and tattooed: ink curled from his wrists all the way up to behind his ear. He had taken off his shirt in the midday heat, and I could see the divots of his six-pack. When the men had arrived, I had quietly slipped into my red dress, the nice one, but I wasn't sure, now, if it was the right thing to wear. I felt overdressed, too obviously trying to look alluring. We stared at each other for a good ten seconds, not speaking.

'I'm Lily,' I said.

'I know,' he said. 'We spoke earlier.'

There was another brief silence, and I could hear the others beside me speaking rapidly, as though they couldn't fit all of their relationships into one two-minute conversation. Beside me, Melissa was describing a polyamorous relationship she had been in. 'It's much more relaxed than you might think,' she said.

'When I was fifteen,' I said finally, 'I went out with a boy in my class for three months. His name was José, and we would go swimming together when it was hot. It was a summer fling. When I came back to school in September, neither of us were particularly interested in the other. Then when I was seventeen, I had a brief . . . thing with my teacher. His name was Mr Donovan – Richard. I used to help him file books in the school library after school, and then we started locking the door to the library and staying there for hours. He was married and ended it when his wife found out. Directly after that, I started going out with Louis. He was really, really nice. He was my friend's brother, and we just had a really nice time together. That lasted, I think, less than a year? I broke up with him because I kind of was bored and wanted something different. And then I met Brian, and we went out for three years. We broke up two months ago. He cheated on me with a girl he met on holiday. So, that's me.'

Seb nodded, and though he had studied me carefully while I was talking, he fixed his gaze a few inches to the left of my face as he spoke.

'Amelia when I was fourteen. Then Denise when I was eighteen. Sierra when I was nineteen. Carmel when I was nineteen. Maggie when I was twenty-one.'

I waited for him to say something else, but he continued to look at a point in the distance.

'That's all I get?' I asked. He shrugged. He didn't say anything else for the remainder of the two minutes, and we stood, not quite looking at each other, until Jacintha called out to switch.

Next I was facing Tom, the bodybuilder. He started speaking without prompting, and, like Seb, gave a short list of girls' names, with no other details. Then he spoke quietly and at length about one girl, Amy. He detailed her with surprising tenderness – I could have painted a picture of what she looked like, her doe eyes and petite frame. I thought that he was finished, but then he said, 'She was a very sweet girl. She needed help with everything, but I liked helping her. She used to say that she couldn't last a day without me.'

'It sounds like you still love her,' I said.

'No, I don't,' he said sulkily. He looked away, and I was left with about twenty seconds to recount my own romances.

After repeating the same thing several times, to several different men, it became easier. I could recite it like a list, without thinking. I still felt a faint sting of embarrassment as I spoke, thinking of how I must sound to the people watching, how blatantly unsuccessful I was at relationships. I wished I hadn't said that Brian had cheated on me. It occurred to me around the fifth man that I shouldn't have given Mr Donovan's name, but it was already out now. It was easier to repeat the same spiel without variation than to focus enough to edit details.

The array of beautiful men before us was overwhelming, and yet I automatically found myself filing through them to find the best-looking. I decided that the one called Ryan was the most attractive. He was tall with a spectacularly angular jaw, and blue eyes framed by long eyelashes. But all of this was secondary to his physique – so incredibly chiselled that he seemed to be a teenage dream come to life, the kind of man that girls would giggle at the sight of. Even the boys were glancing at his torso, but Ryan had an easy-going way that showed no hint of self-consciousness. He smiled whenever he spoke, no matter what it was he said. He had no tattoos or piercings, and his chest was clean shaven. I fixed my hair before he got to me.

He hadn't been in a relationship over the last two years but had been deeply committed to the woman he had met after college, with whom he had been in a relationship for a year. Before that, he'd had a number of brief relationships, a fact I chose to ignore. He got through his spiel quickly, and I did the same. As I was speaking, I saw him watching me closely, smiling all the while.

'You've got a great smile,' he said.

'Thanks. You do too.'

'Well,' he said smiling, 'I guess we have that in common.'

The last man I was paired with was Sam. He said, 'You can go first, if you like.'

I gave him my history, and he held eye contact and nodded. I felt more conscious of my words when I was speaking to him, perhaps because he seemed to be paying close attention. He had an intelligent, watchful gaze. When I finished, he said, 'I'm sorry to hear about that. The cheating, and your teacher.'

'It's whatever. It happens to everyone, I think.'

'You were seventeen, you said?'

I had been sixteen, but it didn't matter. I could see that Sam was trying to compose some tragic backstory for me. I didn't want that. I didn't have a troubled past. Nothing bad had ever really happened to me.

'I want to hear about your relationships.'

'It's a pretty short list. I had two girlfriends in school – not very serious. I was with Laura for, oh, three weeks? And then I was with Naya for about four months. Then I was with Shannon for six years. She moved abroad last year, and I've been single ever since.'

We had a few seconds to spare. This was our last chance to reveal personal information until the next task that allowed us to do so. 'What age were you when you and Shannon broke up?'

'Twenty-six.'

He was twenty-seven, then. He opened his mouth, but Eloise, standing at the edge, called that time was up. The girls moved away at once and grouped together to discuss what they had learned. The boys huddled together in turn, glancing over at the girls. I stayed for another moment with Sam. Now that we couldn't discuss our lives outside the compound, it was difficult to think of something to say.

'Are you enjoying your time here?' he asked.

'Yes,' I said. 'The girls are great.' I looked shyly at my feet, feeling like a teenager meeting a cute boy on holiday. When I glanced up, he was looking at me intently.

'It'll get easier,' he said.

I went to the girls, and he went to the boys. When I glanced back, I saw Sam look at me, and then look away. I turned and lifted my hair off my neck, as though to tie it up. I let it fall, then looked over my shoulder to check again. Ryan was watching me, too.

When we returned to the screen, it was lit up green, signalling that we had successfully completed our first task. We went to the delivery area behind the house, and the chairs were there, all nineteen of them. The rewards were delivered through underground vents that connected the compound to the producers' base of operations. I knew this only from online discussions and speculation around the show. They never showed the tunnels or the producers on television, but I knew that the producers were close by and could intervene if needed.

The men carried away two chairs each and settled them along the patio with pride. High on our success, we completed another straight away. Everyone had to jump in the pool, an easy task for which we were each awarded a much needed bottle of sun cream. We lay on the grass afterwards, giddy and laughing. Susie was wiping mascara from under my eyes, and Evan, small and scrawny, was resting his head on my knees.

'We should check the little screens,' Seb said.

'No, no,' Andrew said. 'We'll get nothing done if we all peel away. Let's do one more as quickly as we can, and then we can check our little screens.'

'Andrew's right,' Jacintha said. 'We need a freezer. A lot of the food won't last if we can't freeze it.'

'And we need air conditioning in the rest of the house, too,' Eloise said.

'We need a door for the bathroom,' Becca said quietly.

'Andrew and I will check the screen,' Candice said, getting up. As they walked towards the house, Andrew said something, and Candice put her hand on his arm and laughed.

Ryan came to sit beside me. He gave me a friendly look but said nothing. Evan moved away, taking some unspoken cue. The sun was unforgiving, so it was likely still afternoon, but the evening was approaching. In a few short hours we would all go to bed, and if I slept alone I would be gone. I rolled onto my back. I lifted my head a little and looked at him over my shoulder. Possibly the rule of finding someone to pair up with had been intended as a way to offset the selfishness of pursuing rewards, but lying there, looking at the boys around me, the rule only felt like a cruel exaggeration of our ideas of desire and desirability.

I turned to Ryan. 'Will you put some sun cream on my back?' I said.

'Sure,' he said.

His hands were firm on my back, and while his motions weren't quite businesslike, they weren't salacious, either. He didn't venture below my kidneys. When he was done, he pressed his hands to my shoulders, and said, 'That okay for you?' I turned and propped myself up on my elbows. I smiled at him, showing my teeth, which I had brushed three times that morning.

'Perfect,' I said. 'Thanks.'

Candice and Andrew returned, and stood before us, glancing at each other.

'Well, what is it?' Seb asked. Seb was frequently impatient, even when he was lounging, or floating in the pool. 'Put us out of our misery.'

'For a case of champagne,' Andrew said, and smiled, 'The boys have to rank the attractiveness of the girls, and the girls have to do the same to us.'

I smiled to hide my terror. Some of the men *ooh*ed, as though they were at a football match, and someone had lined up an exciting shot.

Susie said, 'What, *now*? Let us get changed first, at least. We're all soaking. We look ridiculous!' She laughed, but it was clear that she was panicked.

Andrew shook his head. 'Let's do it now,' he said. 'The quicker we do it, the sooner we can be sipping champagne.'

'But we're all wet!' Susie cried. 'And we don't look like ourselves! It wouldn't be right to do it now!'

Mia added, 'We'll just change really quickly. We won't even put any make-up on, honestly. It'll take two minutes.'

Candice said, 'If you go to the changing rooms, you'll see your little screens, and then we'll never get it done. Come on, it'll be quick and painless.' But as we all got to our feet, Susie turned to me, and with tears in her eyes, said, 'If I could only just fix my hair—'

I tucked her hair behind her ears. Before we got into the water, it was straight, but now, after half drying in the sun, it was frizzy and disorderly, almost white, and brittle from too many chemicals. I smoothed down the strands with a careful, gentle stroke. 'You're beautiful,' I said, and it was true.

The girls decided to rank the boys first, both as a method of self-preservation, and to give us a few minutes to wring the water from our hair and erase smudged make-up. The men lined up by the palm trees, and we eyed them, whispering in a huddle. If they were nervous, they didn't show it. Some of the rankings were difficult, and the girls threw their hands up and spoke slowly to convey latent anger. Eventually though, we had it, and lined the men up accordingly. It took us about fifteen minutes to agree upon an order.

In ninth place was Evan, who grinned bashfully, and shouted, 'Personality, ladies; that's what counts!' Evan wasn't a bad-looking guy: he had nice hair, sandy-coloured and floppy, but he was too short. In eighth place was Seb, who was disgruntled to be placed so low down, and moved to take his spot, unsmiling. I thought that he would have been ranked higher if he knew how to vary his facial expressions beyond scowling or smirking. Next was Gav, who was good-looking, but not good-looking enough.

The middle ranking men were harder to place, and we changed our minds even as we lined them up. Sixth was Marcus, who had a strong jaw, though not a lot else stood out about him. Fifth was Tom: there had been some dissent about him. We all agreed that he wasn't classically handsome, but it was proposed that a man didn't need to be handsome if he was that well-built. Fourth was Carlos, who hadn't spoken much, though we all enjoyed his sexy smoulder. 'And we can't forget that he's very tall,' Susie said in hushed tones. He was the only Black man there, and I saw some of the girls glance at Jacintha as they made their decision. I don't know if they thought that Jacintha had some better insight into his attractiveness, or if they thought that she might be interested in him.

In third place was Sam. As he took his place, he smiled, his eyes crinkling, and I thought maybe we had made a mistake in not ranking him higher. In second place was Andrew, who hooted as he stepped next to Sam. I thought that Sam was better-looking than Andrew, but the girls were insistent that he had a confidence that was inherently sexy. In first place was Ryan, who took his spot at the top with a surety that made him all the more attractive.

Then it was the boys' turn to rank us. We stood in a line, reassuring each other while making sure to show our best sides. I let my hair curl around the line of my jaw and rested a hand on my thigh.

The boys reached their decision within two minutes.

In last place was Melissa, who took her place at the bottom of the line and looked at her feet, as though afraid to catch someone's eye. I think it was her nose, maybe: just a little too long. Next was Eloise, who shook her head in apparent rage. She muttered to herself, quiet oaths under her breath that I couldn't hear, but which the microphones would surely pick up. Next, surprisingly, was Mia. She took her place with a martyred expression, and the girls murmured, clearly in dissent. I wondered if it was the red hair: boys didn't always like dyed hair, unless it was blonde. Next was Becca, the quietest girl, though I thought that she had been misplaced; she had a lovely blush to her cheeks, and small, pearly teeth.

In sixth place was Jacintha. It was such a ludicrous misjudgement that I had to stop myself from laughing out loud. She was a true beauty: perhaps as beautiful as Candice. She even looked better after having been drenched in the pool. She walked calmly to her place and held herself with a dignity that shamed the rest of us.

Next was Susie, who pottered over to Jacintha and looked around her, as though uncertain if she was in the right spot. In fourth place was Sarah, who I still thought of as the marketing intern. She was tall and dark-haired, with the smallest waist I had ever seen. There was a waspishness to her that I thought detracted from her attractiveness, but perhaps what was unappealing to me was thrilling to the boys.

In third place was Vanessa, another blonde, who had the body that every man desired: a firm, round ass, and high, lush breasts. I had seen a body identical to Vanessa's a thousand times, but never in real life. For someone who ranked so highly in the boys' esteem, you would have thought that I would have taken notice of her in the last three days, but actually I had to look at her for a minute or two before I recalled her name. She spoke very little, and frequently seemed bored in conversation.

I was placed second. In a different situation I would have been delighted, but the ranking didn't mean much to me if Jacintha was ranked so low. They didn't know beauty, these boys. They saw blurred outlines and thought they knew the picture.

Candice took her place at the top of the line. She walked with a quick, sure step, and waved at the boys, who looked on and clapped.

It was suggested that the boys take a nap, while the rest of us sorted out dinner. 'Don't get used to us waiting on you,' Mia called at their retreating backs. 'This is only because you were in the desert this morning.'

I didn't want to cook dinner. I wanted to sit with the girls, and play with someone's hair, and have someone play with mine. Although the ranking had technically gone well for me, and although we had done the same to the boys, I felt degraded. I saw the boys walk to the bedroom, talking and relaxed, while the women wouldn't meet each other's eyes. I thought that we had lost some crucial bit of power, not from the act of being judged, but by showing that it meant something to us. I wanted to be like the boys, who seemed to have forgotten that it happened the moment they stepped away. Was it that the boys didn't care as much about their appearance, or because they were already so sure of their worth that external opinion meant nothing to them? I didn't hate that I was the second most beautiful: I hated that I had to stand there and be told that everyone else thought so.

We were quiet and thoughtful as we prepared dinner. We were making an enormous vat of spaghetti bolognese; there was a large quantity of meat which had to be used, as we still had no freezer. 'You know I can't eat this, right?' Mia said. 'I'm vegetarian.'

'This is what I'm making,' Candice said, inspecting the meat. 'If you'd like something else, you're welcome to make it yourself.' Candice began cutting the garlic, while Mia looked at her. We glanced between the two of them. I thought that Mia might snap back, but after a few moments she started to cut some mushrooms. Perhaps if things had gone differently Mia might have challenged Candice. But the boys had voted Candice the most beautiful, and it would have been foolish to pretend that the sway she held was limited to boys' perception of her.

At last Susie broke the silence. 'I didn't think the ranking went that badly, actually,' she said. At this, Eloise and Melissa left without a word, dropping their utensils on the counter, leaving their onions half cut. We watched them through the window as they walked to the furthest edge of the perimeter.

'Don't mind them,' Candice said. 'We're going to have a brilliant evening, all of us.' She cut their onions in quick, sure chops, and scraped her work off into the pot in one smooth motion. She glanced at me. 'So, who do you like?'

I knew that there was a significance to Candice singling me out. I wasn't sure if it was because she wanted to be my friend or if she was threatened by me. I think that the simplest way to understand it was that Candice was the most beautiful, and I was the second most beautiful. If we didn't pay attention to each other, what was the point of it at all?

'I don't know,' I said, struggling to open a tin of tomatoes. 'It's too early to tell, isn't it?'

'Please,' Mia plucked the tin from my hands and removed the lid for me. 'It didn't look too early when you had Ryan slathering you in sun cream.'

Candice finished the last of the onions. Her eyes watered a little, and she wiped at them absently. 'I like Andrew, I think,' Candice said slowly. 'I'm going to ask him to share my bed tonight.' She glanced up at all of us. 'But that doesn't mean that any of you can't get to know him. It's far too early to claim anybody.' She went back to her stirring, and she looked so unconcerned, I thought that she probably meant it, too. She didn't mind anyone talking to Andrew; she wasn't threatened. That's what it meant to be the most beautiful.

'We'll need to look good tonight,' Mia said, then turned to me, smiling. 'Lily, would you do my make-up?'

I nodded and offered to do anyone's, if they wanted. Susie gasped suddenly, and I started, sure that she had cut herself. 'The screens!' she said. 'We never checked them!' She ran off, and we watched her for a beat before following her. I caught

Jacintha's hand as we went into our dressing room, and we laughed with excitement at the absurdity of it. My heart raced as I sat at my bench and touched my screen. Distantly, I heard some of the girls exclaim or giggle at the instructions they had been given, but I wasn't paying attention. In fact, I had never felt so disconnected from them.

Task: Tell someone in the compound a secret
Reward: Comb

I touched my hair. I glanced around and saw people looking at their own screens. You weren't obliged to do any task, but once the task expired at sunrise you weren't offered the same reward again. Because there were so many of us, the rewards we received wouldn't be valuable. But as it was, we had fairly little, and weren't in a position to turn down the possibility of anything that would make us more desirable, or more comfortable here. We would take whatever we were offered.

'All right,' Mia said, 'back to dinner.' Most of the girls went back to the kitchen, where we could smell the onions and garlic frying. Becca stayed in the dressing room, cleaning some of the make-up stains that had accumulated on the bench.

'Hey, Becca,' I said.

'Yes?' Becca had a quiet, serious way about her. I wondered what age she was. If she was older than eighteen I would have been surprised.

'When I was eleven,' I said, 'I had a sleepover with my best friend. When she was sleeping, I cut off her hair and buried it in the garden.'

Becca looked confused, and I left without further comment. I went to the post-boxes at the back of the house. There were chutes for every resident, my first name labelled on the massive container. In my chute there was a comb. It was shiny, black, and plastic, like something you might get in a Christmas cracker.

Along with the comb was a slip of paper with the name of

the brand. Once you received your Personal Reward, you had to thank the brand that had sent it. It was the best advertisement brands could get, and it meant that there would always be a supply of things for us to win. I held the comb like a statuette in my hand and looked at the small glass lens fixed on the wall across from the postboxes. 'Thank you, Alsipa, for this,' I said, and smiled.

Sometimes, if the brand really liked you on the show, or if it seemed like a good pairing, they would hire you as a sponsor when you came out of the compound. Contestants would gush over certain rewards in a clear bid to get a sponsorship deal. But Alsipa wasn't a brand that I had ever heard of, and I wasn't going to fawn over a brand if I didn't want to be in a partnership with them.

I sat down on the stairs for a few minutes and brushed my hair, placing the comb gently on the crown of my head and slowly dragging it down, down, down to the hair that hung down my back. There were knots, at first, but I brushed until my hair was sleek and bristling with static. I might have stayed there for longer, but I heard steps coming towards the postbox, and went to the kitchen to join the other girls.

The boys were sitting outside on the grass. They were wearing sunglasses, and it was hard to tell, but I thought they were looking at us through the French doors. Jacintha and I were ladling large portions of spaghetti into bowls, and passing them on to Candice, who would add the bolognese, and then on to Mia, who would add the parmesan. The other girls were bringing out glasses, the case of champagne, and cutlery wrapped in toilet rolls. The men cheered when they emerged, and I saw Sam and Andrew get to their feet to help Becca carry the case.

Tonight would be crucial, and we knew it. It would be humiliating to be the first to leave.

Quietly, I said to Jacintha, 'Which one, do you think?'

She looked out the window at the men who were lounging, confident, at ease. 'Carlos,' she said.

'Do you like him?'

'I'm not sure. I think it's the safest option, for now. Usually the Black couples get together. And anyway, it's not like we have to plan a future together. I just need to make it through the night.'

'The men have the power tonight,' Mia remarked.

Candice, who had been quiet for some time, lifted her head suddenly and said, 'The men do not have the power. Look at them: they're sitting there like kings. But do you know something? I asked Evan to point out to me where they came from, where they had to travel from. It's about five miles away, and it took them three whole days. What power do they have over us? Whatever girl goes out tomorrow won't be leaving because a man didn't find her attractive. It will be because she didn't know how to win a man over.'

The bowls were hot, but we had no dishcloths or oven gloves so we let them cool for a few seconds on the counter before we brought them out. We watched as Susie sat in Marcus's lap and whispered something in his ear. He held her close and smiled at her; she giggled, then ran inside. 'Where's she going?' Mia asked.

'Postbox,' Jacintha said. 'She must have completed her first task.'

There was a rule that forbade residents from discussing the details of their Personal Tasks. This was to help conceal if they were acting on the instruction of their little screen rather than behaving genuinely. For example, last year a girl had been instructed to kiss a boy who had been interested in her for weeks. He was delighted, and thought it was the beginning of a romance between them. Everyone watching had gone crazy for it because we knew that the kiss was only so that the girl could earn a hairdryer.

We carried the dishes of food out and took our places at the seats we had earned earlier that day. We didn't have tables yet, but that would come with time.

We played a sort of musical chairs, moving every couple of minutes to talk to someone new. Ryan sat beside me first, and we chatted a bit about the tasks. Then I said I liked jumping in the pool, and he said, 'The ranking was brutal, but it doesn't mean anything.'

'It was kind of stupid,' I said.

'It was stupid, you're right. But if it's worth anything, I thought that you should have been in first place.'

I was still wearing the red dress. Now it felt like it was the right decision, though it would have looked better if I had blush to apply, or lipstick. We spoke for a little while longer, and I tried to focus on what he was saying rather than on all of the other couples.

'I like talking to you,' he said. 'You're easy to get along with.' Andrew was lingering beside my seat, chatting to Tom, and Ryan gave him a friendly nod. He leaned in close to me, and said, 'Let's talk later, all right?' He kissed my cheek before I could answer and went to Sarah's table.

Andrew took Ryan's empty seat, but didn't immediately look at me. He glanced around at the couples around us, and I did the same. Jacintha was talking to Carlos, but Seb was standing by his shoulder, waiting to cut in. Candice was sitting back in her seat, at ease, as Marcus talked, drumming his fingers on the table. Sam was talking to Becca, who was glancing at her hands and then back at him.

'Amazing,' Andrew said. 'Isn't it?' He turned to me. The look on his face surprised me, soft-eyed and tender, as though he had just witnessed the birth of a baby. There was nothing remarkable about his looks – he didn't have Sam's smile, or Ryan's chiselled bone-structure, but he was nevertheless someone you wanted to look at. 'Can you believe that we're here?'

'It's like a dream,' I said.

'Can I pour you another glass? We earned it, right?'

'Sure,' I said, and he poured. It was fantastically cold, and though I usually didn't care for champagne I liked it that night.

'It's a bit strange, talking to everyone, and not being able to ask where they're from, or what their job is. But isn't it exciting, too? There's something valuable about it, I think. We can get to know each other as we build up the compound. What do you think of it here so far, Lily?'

I wasn't sure whether to talk about how much I loved it, or to reflect on the work we could do to make it better. I wanted to impress Andrew, I knew that much.

'It's going to be spectacular,' I said.

'I think so, too. Cheers to that, eh?' He lifted his glass and looked around at the others, raising his voice so they all could hear. 'To a spectacular home, and the easy life!' Everyone cried out 'To the easy life!' and drank. I looked at the people surrounding me, laughing, leaning close, a hand touching someone's arm, eyes flicking around. You wouldn't have known that every girl there was fighting for her place. Jacintha met my eye and smiled. I smiled back. Sam had appeared beside my seat. I noticed at the same time Andrew did.

'Well look, Lily, I won't keep your admirers from talking to you. I'll see you around.' He walked straight to Candice's seat, and Marcus got out of his seat at the sight of Andrew approaching. Before I had a second to think, Sam stood before me. 'Can I?' he asked.

'Sure,' I said. I ran my hand through my hair. I hadn't eaten much of my dinner, but his bowl was empty. 'Was it good?' I asked.

'Terrific,' he said. 'Thanks for making it.'

I said what I had heard half a dozen girls say in the last hour: 'You needed a good meal after your time in the desert.'

He smiled, and I realised that he probably had been told the same thing several times. 'It wasn't that bad,' he said. 'But tell me, what did you do before we got here?'

'We mostly cleaned. There was a lot of rubbish around. The previous residents had had pizza, probably just a couple of days ago, maybe even this week.' I looked at him. He was nodding. 'We wanted the place to look nice for you when you arrived,' I said, a bit shyly.

'That was very kind,' he said. 'We were impressed, for sure, when we arrived.'

I've always thought that men somehow believe that the art of seduction comes naturally to beautiful women, who delight in deploying these arts to devastate those we encounter. In fact, I had no idea how to seduce a man; I only smiled and asked questions, and sometimes laughed. But the twin aspect of being beautiful is struggling to be taken seriously, and, confusingly, I also addressed that obstacle by smiling and asking questions. Probably I needed new seduction techniques.

I didn't feel like I needed any charms or feminine wiles with Sam. I felt loose around him, and after a while I didn't think too much about what I said, or how I sounded. We weren't talking about anything important, nothing interesting or noteworthy, but I felt that I had a sense of him just from that discussion, from the way he moved and the way he smiled at me and the way he listened so carefully to everything I said, even if it was nothing interesting. His eyes followed everything I did: when I wiped champagne from my mouth, or when I lifted my hair from my neck to try and get some air. I was watching him, too: his large hands, with long, tapered fingers, which he sometimes rested on his biceps, and sometimes splayed flat on the table. When he was looking down at his food, I was looking at the veins that ran along his arms. He didn't look away the whole time that we sat together, though Jacintha was smiling and laughing in the seat next to us, brilliant and shining, and Vanessa was stroking her long, glossy hair.

As we were speaking, the other girls were putting the work in. I saw Becca's serious little face nodding at whatever Gav was saying, and Vanessa touching Seb's arm as she spoke. Curiously, I saw Andrew moving around constantly, talking to everyone, boys and girls. Every time I looked up, I saw his dimples flashing, his white teeth gleaming. He talked a lot, and after listening to him speak I realised that he had a habit of using big words incorrectly.

'Look at that view!' I heard him shout. 'Isn't it just extrapolate?' I thought it might be obnoxious in someone else, but it lent a certain guilelessness that was distinctly charming. The girls were working hard because they needed to secure a bed-mate in order to avoid banishment; Andrew was working just as hard, I think, because he had the compulsive desire to be liked. He charmed with the energy and desperation of someone who thought that they might be gone by the morning.

The evening had started to draw in, and empty bottles of champagne were rolling along the ground. We moved from the seats in the dining area to the grass near the pool. I sat beside Susie and Evan, and Ryan sat behind me, his arm brushing against my side every now and then. 'Isn't it crazy that the boys only came today?' Susie said to me. 'I feel like I've known them for ever.' Evan was biting his lip and looking at Susie as though she was a fish who could free herself from the hook.

The night became loose and hazy: it seemed to take very little for us to get drunk.

'It's because we're dehydrated,' Jacintha said. 'We should all drink more water before we go to bed.' Marcus scooped her up and threw her in the pool. We all laughed, and Marcus jumped in after her. Carlos stood by the side and helped her out. Evan jumped in then, and Susie, too, holding her hair on the crown of her head.

On the grass, Mia started to sing. She had a sweet, liquid voice. She sang a song we all knew, and some people sang along. The temperature had dropped and we huddled close, lying on top of each other, limbs pressed against limbs. Mia sat apart, still singing, with a blank face unlike her usual self. She was beautiful, Mia. I felt sure that she would be here in the morning.

Ryan adjusted himself so that I was lying against him. I closed my eyes. His abs were like rocks against my head. 'This is perfect,' I said, and he stroked my hair. It was smooth to the touch, still, after the rigorous brushing.

Later, I got into my bed and felt the turnings of the universe in my head. I rolled onto my side and pulled the blanket up to my chin. With the boys milling around in the dark, choosing their bed-mates, the room felt enormously full. I was sleepy, but overwhelmingly alert, too.

The bed dipped to my right. I turned, and Ryan was there. We had no light in the bedrooms, but I could distinguish him by the shape of his nose, and that sharp, slashing jawline. There was a brief beat of silence between us, a moment of uncertainty. Then he put his hand on my waist. 'Surprised?' he said.

'Not really,' I said.

I knew that I had done well to have the best-looking boy in my bed. I lay on my back, so I could see him from the corner of my eye. I was reminded again that I didn't know him – didn't know anyone there. I imagined him rising above me, his hands pinning me down, and myself powerless to stop him. But it was only a passing thought. When I glanced over, I saw that he was tense, his large hands clasped across his stomach. The sight of his nervous posture relaxed me. It took me a long time to fall asleep, but when I did, I slept deeply and dreamlessly.

The following morning, when the sun had risen and the birds were circling in the air, there was an empty bed in the compound, and Melissa was gone.

Three

We slept in the next morning. I felt shy around Ryan when I woke up. I worried that I had drunk too much the night before and had come across as silly. The bedroom had a skylight, but otherwise no source of light, and I could only see who was sharing a bed with whom when the sun had fully risen. Andrew was with Candice, Jacintha with Carlos, Susie with Evan, Mia with Marcus, Eloise with Gav, Seb with Sarah, Tom with Vanessa, and Sam with Becca. Despite the fact that I was coupled with the best-looking boy, it felt wrong that Sam should be with anyone other than me.

The charm of the night before was decidedly gone, and the mess of dishes in the kitchen and abandoned glasses in the garden disgusted me. We had coffee and cleaned up a bit, then lay in the shade and chatted a little. When we were feeling more amenable, we turned our attention to the first Communal Task of the day. Now that the threat of banishment was gone, we had time to focus on improving the compound. We reckoned if we stayed focused we could get three tasks done by mid-afternoon, with the option to do more later in the day if we felt like it. We all agreed to leave our Personal Tasks until after the Communal

Tasks were done; easy enough when the rewards were still of such a low value.

Our first task was so simple that we carried it out in a matter of minutes: we only had to name our favourite actor. For this, we got an enormous crate of bananas, which we ate while sitting in the shade.

The next task took longer, but for it we earned a bug zapper. This pleased Susie in particular who told us all, more than once, that she couldn't understand why there were so many insects: wasn't the desert supposed to be *devoid* of life? To earn it, we had to recite a poem in unison. We spent the majority of the morning on that task: we weren't sure, at first, that any of us knew a poem by heart. Carlos knew about ninety per cent of a poem by Keats, but couldn't remember two lines in the second verse, and Mia knew a short poem, but Seb figured if we only managed a three-line poem, we'd get 'an unbelievably shitty bug zapper'. I thought that they were probably embarrassed that they didn't know a poem by heart, and we spent some time walking around and reciting quotes that we could remember, muttering fragments of Wordsworth and Shakespeare, never managing more than a few lines. Only Ryan looked relaxed, lying in the grass, having announced as soon as he had seen the screen that he didn't know a single poem.

Then Becca, having not spoken for several hours, recited a poem by Rilke, short enough that we could memorise it, and long enough that we felt that we would earn something worthy. We cheered her on, and Susie and I tucked flowers behind her ears; Candice kissed her on the forehead. We had her repeat it any number of times, until we all knew it. It took some time: we had no pen or paper and had to rely on memory alone. I can remember it perfectly – the words, and the way that Becca said them, sitting cross-legged in the grass, her face young and open. 'It is life in slow motion,' she recited, and we listened to her in perfect silence, listened to her repeat it again and again until we could say it ourselves.

> *It is life in slow motion,*
> *it's the heart in reverse,*
> *it's a hope-and-a-half:*
> *too much and too little at once.*
>
> *It's a train that suddenly*
> *stops with no station around,*
> *and we can hear the cricket,*
> *and, leaning out the carriage*
>
> *door, we vainly contemplate*
> *a wind we feel that stirs*
> *the blooming meadows, the meadows*
> *made imaginary by this stop.*

When we finished we were triumphant, and though some of us would have been glad of a break we agreed to do one more task before lunch.

The reward for the third task was the biggest yet: a couch. It would be our first piece of indoor furniture, and we all agreed that it was the thing we needed most urgently for the living room. 'A couch really ties a home together,' Evan said, nodding.

The task stated that each resident had to keep another resident underwater for a minute. I thought that it would be easy.

We changed into our swimsuits and got into the pool. For a while we messed around, splashing water at each other and swimming idly around, until Andrew reminded us that we needed to get going: the sun was at its highest point, and we would all burn, whether we were aware of it or not. We gathered at the top of the pool. Tom suggested we divide into the pairs we had slept in: I noticed that he was careful not to use the word 'couple'. Evan would count the time when the girls were under the water, and Jacintha would count when the boys were below.

Ryan stood beside me. In the pool, he was magnificent: he looked like a god. The boys requested to go first, and we let them. Ryan ducked so I could put my hand on the back of his neck. 'All right,' Jacintha called, her own hand on Carlos's head. 'Go!'

Ryan took a breath and went under. I kept my hand very lightly on his neck, and kept my gaze fixed on him, as though he might float away at any moment. Jacintha was counting down from sixty. It was otherwise quiet, all of the girls staring at the men they held under the water. Some of the men's shoulders were visible, but the majority of them had submerged most of their torsos. The seconds went by slowly, and around fifty seconds in, I felt the muscles on Ryan's neck bunch beneath my hand, his head moving. I softened my hold on him a little.

'One!' Jacintha called, and I pulled him up. The pool was suddenly alive with motion, as the men crashed to the surface. Ryan was gasping, as were the others. I felt oddly close to him in that moment. I moved his hair out of his face, and he held my eye as he caught his breath. After a minute, Tom called, 'Ready, Evan?'

'Give me a second,' he said, still catching his breath. I was thrown by how breathless everyone was, even Tom. I inhaled deeply and saw the other girls doing the same.

'Ready?' Ryan asked me. Some of the boys were murmuring to the girls, and I tried not to listen. Gravely, Ryan said, 'It's longer than you think.'

'Ready,' I said.

'On the count of three,' Evan said. 'One, two – three!'

When I had read the instruction on the screen, I had experimentally held my breath and counted to sixty. It wasn't comfortable in the last few seconds, but it was doable. Underwater, with a hand on my head, it wasn't doable. I panicked almost immediately, and though Ryan's hand was gentle, barely there at all, I was seized by the overwhelming fear that I was going to die. I could hear Evan's voice, but after twenty seconds I couldn't keep track any more. I didn't register the decision to rise to the surface; I only knew that one second I was writhing underwater, and the next I was gasping and clinging to Ryan's shoulder. Evan was still counting – he was only at forty-seven – and when I could think rationally, I said, 'Shit. Shit, I messed up.'

'It's okay,' Ryan said, and held me as I continued to gasp. 'Don't worry. Just breathe.'

'Shit,' I said again. Pathetic; I was pathetic.

'You're not,' he said, and I realised that I had spoken aloud. 'Look,' he said. He twisted slightly – I hadn't registered that I was wrapped around him like a vine on a tree. There were several girls above the surface, gasping like me: Candice, Sarah and Becca.

When the minute was up – how the seconds flew when you had air to breathe! – the other girls crashed to the surface, gasping, but grinning too. I looked away. Some of the men started murmuring to each other.

'Look,' Andrew called. 'It's okay, ladies. It's a tough challenge. Take a breath, and we'll go again.'

The girls who had remained underwater were visibly confused. Their partners quietly explained to them that not all of us had managed it. 'Who?' I heard the word echoing around the pool, bouncing off the water. 'Who, who?'

'I can do it,' I said to Ryan. 'It just felt different than I thought it would.'

'I know,' he said. 'I nearly wasn't able to make it either.'

My breathing was regular by then. I looked at the other girls who hadn't managed it. Becca was still breathing heavily. She was clutching Sam's shoulder, and he was talking quietly to her. I took my hands off Ryan and looked away. Candice was composed, but looking at Becca with worry. 'Let's take a few minutes before we go again,' she said. Everyone milled around the pool, but I tried to stand still and inhale as much air as possible. After a bit, Candice nodded at Evan.

'One more time,' Ryan said. 'A minute, and then it's over.' He smiled at me. Ryan made everything seem easy. I took a breath, and felt my chest expand.

'Go!' Evan called, and I submerged myself again. I was calmer this time: I knew that I was safe, and that my lungs were capable of surviving a minute without air. Still, I understood now just how long a minute felt underwater; I tried to sing a song in my head, but I kept abandoning it every few seconds. I thought thirty seconds had to have passed. Ryan's hand on my head was light; I felt his finger stroke my neck, and I knew he was trying to reassure me. But my lungs were burning, and I kept imagining inhaling a mouthful of chlorinated water, how it would feel as it hit my lungs, how I would cough and choke, only to take in another mouthful of water. My hands curled into fists and came up to my chest. I curled myself into a ball, my head tossing back and forth. I made some noise, deep in my chest – it was horrible, horrible, horrible—

Ryan pulled me to the surface and kept lifting me until I was above his head. 'You did it,' he said. I slapped at his shoulders and told him to put me down, but I felt triumphant, fiercely proud of myself. No one was celebrating, though. I saw Candice and Sarah gasping and looking around them. Becca was pressed against Sam, trembling. 'She didn't make it past forty seconds,' Ryan said in my ear. He tutted with regret.

'All right,' Andrew said. 'Why don't we take a break – get some water, maybe get some food.'

Most of the others got out of the pool, leaving only Tom, Andrew, Sam, Becca, Vanessa and me.

Tom looked displeased. He said, 'We have other tasks to do. This is only our third, and it must be – what, two, three o'clock?' He glanced at Vanessa, and said, 'Vanessa, would you mind checking the screen and seeing if it's green yet?'

Vanessa didn't look thrilled with the instruction but swam to the edge and walked inside. I knew that the concrete was atrociously hot – the others had squealed when they stepped out – but she walked unhurriedly, her hips swaying.

To Becca, I said, 'How do you feel now?'

'I'm fine,' she said, her voice scarcely audible. 'I just don't want to do it again.'

'Take a minute,' Tom said, 'And then you can try again.'

'She said she doesn't want to,' Sam said.

'But the couch—'

'Fuck the couch,' Sam said. 'She's not doing it.'

Becca had moved away from Sam, and stood still, with her fingers biting into the skin of her arms. She wasn't looking at anyone, but I didn't yet know her well enough to tell if it was out of embarrassment or dread. Tom said, 'Could you think realistically for a minute, please? Do you think it would make sense to live in a house with no couch? Do you want us to sit on the floor the whole time we're here? How would that look? But it's not just that. It's everything else that we won't be able to get today – we'll have to wait another day before we can move forward. We need a freezer. And we need a front door. There are wild animals out there – they could come in at any minute. When we're sleeping.'

It was funny. Until he mentioned it, I didn't realise that we had no front door.

Vanessa stood in the shade of the house and shouted to us, 'Still hasn't turned green!' She lingered for a moment as though she might come back to us, but nobody answered and she went inside.

Sam said, 'Let's all go and get a drink. It's hot, and we'll burn soon. If Becca is feeling up to it later, we can return to the task then.' His tone brokered no argument. Andrew and Tom glanced at each other, but swam to the edge of the pool and lifted themselves out. Sam stayed for a moment, standing close to Becca, but she told him to go inside. 'I'll just be a minute,' she said. 'I'm fine. Really.' He nodded and followed the others inside. I saw him glance back as he made his way across the lawn.

'I can do it,' Becca said, when they were gone. 'Just – not like that.'

I took her hand. 'I know,' I said. 'It's okay.'

We stayed there for a few minutes, the water calm in the absence of the others. The air was thick and heavy above us, and the sound of voices from the house was far off and muffled, like the buzz of insects. Beside me, I felt Becca breathing deeply, and I did the same. I closed my eyes briefly, and felt the sun on my face, the weight of it on my shoulders. Sam was right: we would burn soon.

I opened my eyes when I heard a splash of water. We turned and saw Tom slip into the pool and swim towards us. Becca let go of my hand.

'Hey,' he said, when he reached us. 'You guys okay? That was pretty intense.'

Becca said nothing, so I said, 'We're fine. We're just taking a breather.'

He nodded. His hair glistened with drops of water. With his shirt off, his muscles seemed almost inexplicably large. I couldn't understand why anyone would need to have that kind of strength in today's world. 'I understand. It was frightening. It's not a pleasant situation.'

'Right,' Becca said.

He looked around him, his neck twisting to take in the lawns and the maze in the distance. 'I know that it seems like the last group didn't look after this place,' he said. 'But they must have done a lot for it to be as grand as it is now. They did a lot of tasks, and put in a lot of hard work, so that we could have what we have here today. I keep reminding myself that. It helps me to be grateful for everything that we have.'

The pool rippled with the small movements of our bodies. I heard a distant sound; either the voice of one of the residents in the house or the cry of an animal in the desert.

'Becca,' Tom said, 'you're going to be fine.' He gripped the back of her skull with one huge hand, and she didn't fight, didn't make a sound as he angled her down towards the water. She took a breath, a wild gasp, and then her face was under. He started to count. I saw her head jerk upwards in what was probably more of a reflex than a concerted effort to get away. He pressed her head deeper below the water.

I grabbed at Tom, but he pushed me away easily with his other hand. 'Stop, Lily,' he said. 'She's okay. It's only a minute.'

'Stop it, Tom – she said she doesn't want to!'

'We both did it,' he said. 'She can do it too.'

I made another move towards her, but he placed a hand out, as though to hold me at bay. He continued to count. She was moving slightly under the water, but not struggling.

'It's okay, Becca,' I said loudly. 'You're doing great.'

At forty seconds, I held her hand under the water. She gripped it tightly, her nails biting into my skin. 'Almost there,' I said. She was kicking her feet. At fifty seconds, she started thrashing. Tom kept a restraining hand on her head and used the other to press down on her shoulders. I could see the muscles in his arms move as he held her in place. The marks down Tom's chest lit up, red and raw. I wondered again what had happened in the desert.

'Sixty,' he said, and pulled her to the surface. Her gasp was that of a dying man come back to life.

She was white all over, her hair clinging to her face, her eyes swinging around.

'I'm sorry, Becca,' Tom said, stony-faced and sombre. Becca stared at him, taking great gulps of air. 'I'll say that you did it willingly. That way, you won't be a target. Otherwise, they'll pick you out as the weak one.'

I could hear cheering from deep within the house: the screen had turned green.

Tom swam across the pool in strong, contained strokes and lifted himself over the edge in one smooth motion. He was like a giant, making his way across the lawn with long strides, not reacting to the hot ground. I could feel Becca shaking beside me. I was horrified by what he had done, yes – and I allowed my uncertainty of Tom to grow into dislike, even fear. I squeezed Becca's shoulder, and let myself seethe with silent rage; I didn't let myself reflect on the fact that I, too, had considered doing the same thing to Becca when it was just the two of us in the pool.

Tom didn't go into the house, but back behind, to the delivery area. By the time Becca and I got out of the pool, his watery footprints had dried under the heat of the sun.

I didn't look at my little screen that day; I had no desire to after the tiring afternoon. Becca neglected to come to the house for several hours, and we abandoned the idea of completing any more Communal Tasks that evening.

The boys were on cooking duty, while the girls stayed outside. Myself, Candice, Susie, Jacintha and Mia sat under a tree and chatted.

'Well,' Mia said, settling back on her elbows. 'What do we think of the boys?'

'I think Tom's kind of sexy,' Susie said.

'He nearly drowned Becca,' I said.

'Did he? I still want to get to know him, though.'

'Evan can't keep his eyes off of you. Stay away from Tom. Stick with Evan,' Candice said.

Susie shrugged and picked up a few strands of my hair, her fingers soft and sweet-smelling, a fine residue of sun cream lingering on them. She plaited my hair with a gentle touch, and I felt myself growing sleepy.

'What do you think of Ryan?' Candice asked me.

'I think I like him,' I said.

'He's gorgeous,' Candice said, but there was something about the way she said it, like she was comforting me.

'You two are good together,' Mia said decisively. 'And a good win for you, getting the best-looking boy.'

'Ryan's lucky to have Lily,' Jacintha said tartly. 'Not the other way around.'

Casually, I said, 'He's pretty nice, I think. He's easy to talk to.'

'What do you think his job is?' Candice asked. We were forbidden to discuss our own personal lives outside of the compound, but we were welcome to speculate on anyone else's.

I thought about it for a moment. 'Doctor?'

'He's not a doctor,' Mia said, so dismissively that I felt foolish for having suggested it.

'What do you think Andrew is?' Jacintha asked.

'Oh, that's easy,' I said. 'He's a project manager.'

Candice laughed. 'Why do you think so? I thought he might be a lawyer, maybe, or a politician. He's good at convincing people to do things.'

'Not as good as Tom,' Mia said. Candice smiled tightly at her.

'Andrew's definitely a project manager. I can see him so clearly, going around the office, making sure everyone's got everything they need, then asking you to stay late. But, like, he'd make you want to stay late.'

Candice smiled at me in a noticeably more congenial way than she had looked at Mia. I felt warm under her regard. She was wearing sunglasses that she must have won in a task. They were cheap and flimsy, and not particularly stylish, but at this point we couldn't be picky. 'I think you're probably right.' She looked thoughtful for a moment, and we waited for her to speak. 'He's very enthusiastic,' she said cryptically.

'You mean in bed?' Susie asked.

Candice frowned at Susie disapprovingly. 'Of course not. What do you take me for? I mean . . . I mean that he's enthusiastic about the compound. About people. He likes to get stuck into things.' I understood what she wasn't saying: Andrew would commit to her, if she could get him interested.

'Do you think that any of the boys . . . ?' I said, trailing off. I paused, trying to decide what I wanted to say, and whether I should say it. I wanted to ask the girls if they thought that any of the boys had fought in the wars. My father was fighting overseas, and I found it difficult, in the safe, ordinary life that I had, to actually visualise it; I had seen images and videos on the television and online, of course, but they had never felt real to me. I preferred personal accounts: my neighbour had once casually mentioned that when he was fighting he went six weeks without seeing a bar of soap. I found it easier to construct an account of what my father might be doing around the image of the bar of soap. Repeatedly, almost obsessively, I imagined him in a number of different scenarios, at last coming across the soap; I imagined, in some iterations, that the sight of it moved him to tears. My father had been gone long enough that I'd stopped expecting him to come home, but I liked to collect the experiences of other soldiers and pretend that they were his.

The girls waited for me to finish my train of thought. Then I remembered that I didn't want to think about any of that. I didn't want to be reminded of the realities of what we'd left behind. I smiled and shook my head to signal to ignore me, and the girls moved on with a speed that made me suspect they knew what I had wanted to ask, and they, too, thought it better to move on.

'Isn't Seb so boring?' Mia said. 'I've never met anyone so dull. He just looks miserable all the time.'

'Who's his bed-mate?' I asked.

'Sarah,' Jacintha said.

'She's boring, too,' Candice said. 'They should stick together.'

'It's hard to keep track of everyone,' Jacintha said.

'Oh, I have nicknames for everyone,' Mia said. 'It's the only way to remember all of the names.'

'Go on,' Candice said.

'"Sleepy Seb". Because he's a boring prick.'

We nodded our agreement.

'Vanessa's "Big-Tits", obviously.'

'Come on,' Candice said. 'You're objectifying her.'

'If she had a personality, I wouldn't have to objectify her.'

There was something almost comforting about Mia's meanness. Most people kept the ugly part of them hidden, and worked hard to never have it be seen. Probably everyone who came on a show like this was a shitty person in some way or another. I almost admired that she was upfront about it.

'What about Evan?' Susie asked, smiling with equal parts nervousness and girlish excitement.

'"Man-child",' Mia said. Susie's face fell. 'Sorry. He's always doing fucking cannonballs into the pool, though.'

'What about me?' Candice asked.

'Oh,' Mia said, after a pull from her bottle of water. 'I don't have one for any of you girls. I know you well enough.'

We smiled and pretended that we believed her. She got to her feet and said that she wanted to apply more sunscreen. Candice watched her go, her lovely face pulled into an expression of disdain.

'I'm going to talk to Marcus tonight,' Jacintha said. 'Carlos is nice, a bit too shy, maybe, but I want to see if there's something there with Marcus. He's sharing a bed with Mia at the minute. Do you think she'll mind?'

'She'll mind,' Candice said. 'But don't let that stop you.'

Evan stepped out of the house and called that dinner would be ready in twenty minutes. We went inside to change for the evening.

I noticed that the girls were buzzing around their screens a lot, and that there were a few products on the counter that I hadn't seen before: Mia had a scrunchie, and Candice had a make-up brush. I had been vaguely embarrassed of having the comb, but when I saw the other new products I placed it on the bench, not caring who saw it.

It was difficult to discern what was an instruction – a means to get some Personal Reward – and what was just normal getting-to-know-you carry-on. Sometimes it was obvious, like when I was coming down the stairs, and Evan stopped me to tell me that my tits looked great in my dress. He had flushed red from his hairline to his neck, and then moved on without another word. But when Carlos lifted me onto his shoulders and gave me a piggy-back to the dining area, was that a task? Or when Sam picked up one of my braids and smiled at me – was that real? Either way, I had blushed, as though it had meant something more.

When we finished dinner – a half-hearted effort at chilli con carne, and an even more lethargic attempt at a vegetarian option for Mia – Gav suggested that we explore more of the compound. We wandered and found a set of swings in a dusty expanse close to the southern perimeter. I pushed Jacintha for a while and enjoyed watching the elegant arc of her flight through the air, her pointed feet reaching higher with each push.

'All right,' I heard a voice say, and then arms were wrapped around me, depositing me on the empty swing beside Jacintha. I turned my head and saw Ryan. He drew my seat far back, until I could kick my feet and not touch the ground. Then he let go, and I was sailing through the air, in tandem with Jacintha. Marcus was behind Jacintha now, giving her gentle nudges in the back. I felt a small thrill every time Ryan's hand pressed against my back, and I let my hair fly around me and stretched my legs out. Jacintha swung next to me, arcing upwards as I was falling down. We reached out and brushed hands every time we swung past each other. The boys behind us were silent as they pushed us, but Jacintha and I giggled and exclaimed, the night filling with the sounds of our glee. When I felt brave enough, I jumped off. I landed on my feet, more or less steady, and looked over my shoulder at Ryan, who was watching me and smiling. He came to my side, and took my hand, and we walked off together, my empty swing still travelling through the air, up and down.

We walked to the west until we reached a pond. It was beautiful: willow trees with swaying vines, and sweet-smelling flowers growing towards the water. There were ducks in the pond, swimming idly back and forth, and there were fish too; glints of orange and gold flashing beneath the water. We sat down on the bank.

'Today was fun,' he said lightly. He was so easy to talk to – he never seemed to think too deeply about anything.

'The underwater task was a bit intense,' I said. I hesitated, and then said, 'I know you weren't there, but Tom got a bit . . . forceful at the end.'

'Oh, Tom? He's a good guy, really. He's forceful for sure, and he's got a temper, but he's just trying to keep things running smoothly.'

'I don't know why he feels he should be the one to take charge,' I said.

Ryan shrugged. 'We kind of sorted it out in the desert. More or less.' I was curious to know the particulars, but I felt instinctively that now wasn't the time to ask.

There was no moon that night, but it was so beautiful, with the dusky purple flowers and the swaying vines, that it wasn't missed. He sat close and kept my hand in his. In the dark, my hands looked lily-white.

'It's hard to believe we only met yesterday,' he said. 'I feel like I know you. You were so sweet on that swing, Lily. You looked like you didn't have a care in the world.'

He towered over me, his chin tilted towards me. He was so incredibly handsome; he looked like every actor I had ever wanted, and the men I always pretended not to notice.

'I'm glad you picked me,' I said. 'I wasn't sure.'

'I was sure,' he said, and leaned his head down and kissed me. He tasted like chlorine and aloe vera. It was quiet, save for the occasional ripple of the water before us, and the hum of cicadas. He pressed me gently into the grass, stroked my hair, and whispered that I was beautiful. I thought that it must have been a great moment of television. I could imagine people watching at home, smiling softly, pleased for us.

We went to bed a while later. Ryan didn't kiss me again, only got into bed quietly beside me. It was dark, but I could hear people moving around: not just taking their places in beds, I thought, but shifting to different beds, too. There were surely people who had shared beds last night who had found someone else that they preferred.

When I thought that the bathroom was empty, I peeked around the sheet we used as a door. I saw Sam there, brushing his teeth. 'Sorry,' I said. 'I'll wait.' I started to replace the sheet, but he shook his head and gestured me in, his toothbrush still in his mouth. I had brought my washbag, but I didn't particularly want to remove my make-up in front of Sam. Instead, I took out my toothbrush, too. Sam reached over and squeezed a pea-sized glob of toothpaste on my brush, and we stood facing the mirror, brushing in silence. He brushed quickly and vigorously; my method by comparison seemed lethargic. There was something about Sam that seemed to fill the room: I was aware of his every movement. I spat as daintily as I could. I kept waiting for him to finish and leave so that I could take off my make-up, but he continued brushing. I spat one last time. 'Goodnight,' I said.

He spat, too. 'Wait a second,' he said. He reached over and brushed the corner of my mouth. 'Toothpaste,' he said.

'Oh,' I said. I think I blushed. 'Thanks.'

'Sure. Goodnight, Lily.'

I walked back to the bedroom and returned to my bed. I turned on my side so that I faced Ryan and saw from the occasional flash of white and blue in the dark that he was watching me, too. We might have looked like lovers, gazing at each other with that tenderness that comes out at night – but I was looking at him to see if he would leave, to make sure that I was safe. It had happened before: residents creeping out of bed in the middle of the night and swapping with another, sometimes returning later in the night, and sometimes leaving their bed-mate vulnerable. I felt his eyes on me and knew that he was thinking the same. It would have been easier for us both if I had just said, 'I'm not going to anyone else's bed – I want you.' Instead I said nothing, and woke often, checking to see that he was still there.

Four

In the flare of morning light, I could see the other couples in bed: Andrew and Candice were sleeping next to each other, each keeping to their own side of the bed. Jacintha was with Marcus, his arms wrapped around her. Mia and Carlos were sharing a bed now, lying so far apart that they were both hanging partly off the mattress.

I slipped quietly out and into the girls' dressing room, where, in the absence of air conditioning, the heat hit me at once, cruel and abrasive. I sat at my desk and brushed my hair, trying to erase any semblance of sleep from my face. I pressed on my screen, and my Personal Task lit up.

Task: Skinny dip in the pool
Reward: Lip balm

I moved through the house, tying my hair up as I went. In the kitchen, I found Tom sitting by the arch where the door should have been. He had brought one of the dining chairs inside and was facing the outdoors. He turned back to look at me when I came in.

'Hey,' I said.

'Morning,' he said.

'Couldn't sleep?'

'I wanted to keep an eye out. It's not safe without a door. Any kind of savage animal could walk in.'

I had been planning to do my task quickly, before anyone else woke up, but there was a direct view of the pool from where he sat.

'There's a spider in the bathroom,' I said. 'Would you mind getting rid of it?'

'Of course not,' he said, and got up at once.

I walked quickly towards the pool, taking my clothes off as I went. I hesitated at the lip of the pool for only a second, then jumped in. I gasped at the cold, as painful as it was refreshing. I pulled myself out and dressed as quickly as I could. When I glanced up, I was startled to see Tom back in his seat. He didn't react when I saw him watching me, but he didn't look away either. I didn't want to walk by him, so I moved towards the swings we had found last night. I kicked my feet off the ground and swung for a while. It was shaded, and I felt cool and clean. When I heard the others up and about I went inside for coffee.

The house was in general disarray again. The kitchen was messy, grimy counters and dirty dishes in the sink. The sheet doubling as the bathroom door now lay in a crumpled mess on the floor. I saw Jacintha and Gav arguing about the best way to keep it in place and left them to it.

I changed into my day outfit, shorts and a bralette, and went about cleaning the kitchen. There was hand soap and a sponge, but no gloves, and no washing detergent. After a few minutes, Becca appeared beside me and silently dried the dishes I had washed. I had seen her this morning, in bed with Sam, sleeping curled in a ball while he had been lying on his back, close to each other, but not touching.

Gav entered and rooted through the fridge. There was still plenty of food, but not a lot that we could eat for dinner. 'How are you lovely ladies this morning?'

'Fine,' I said, and Becca said something I couldn't hear.

He took out a carton of orange juice and drank from the carton. He drank in long gulps and made an *ahh* sound when he finished. He put the carton back in the fridge. 'Sorry,' he said. 'I'll use a glass next time.'

'Please do,' Becca said.

'I got a razor this morning,' he said. 'Man, was I delighted. All I had to do was tickle Susie until she cried.'

He didn't understand why we were staring at him. He opened his mouth, then closed it.

'Good morning,' the voice said. 'Discussion of Personal Tasks is forbidden. This is the last warning before action is taken.'

A handful of others piled into the kitchen. It was obvious who was at fault from the stricken look on Gav's face.

'Idiot,' Marcus said.

The first task was to talk about pets we'd had and how they died. For this we got a long tube of glue. I wasn't particularly excited about that reward, but Jacintha shouted with glee when she saw it. She ran to the bathroom, and I followed her. 'Here,' she said, holding one side of the sheet. 'Hold this up – put it right there.' I did as instructed, and she glued the sheet to the frame of the door. I could only see her vague outline through the sheet as she continued to apply glue liberally.

'So,' she said. 'You and Ryan?'

I looked down the hallway to check that we were alone. 'He's great,' I said.

'Did you . . . ?'

'We kissed.'

I could hear her smile. 'Good for you.'

'Did I see you with Marcus in bed last night?'

'Yeah,' she said. 'We had so much fun yesterday. He's a really funny guy.'

'What about Carlos?'

'Carlos is great, too. I'm keeping my options open.'

'That's smart.'

She moved the sheet aside and looked at me. 'You should keep your options open, too.'

'What do you mean?'

'I've seen Sam looking at you. He seems nice. And he's gorgeous.'

'So is Ryan.'

'I know, but it's only been a couple of days. Don't limit yourself.'

I wondered if she thought that Ryan didn't like me. It stung to think so, but I saw the sense in her suggestion. 'I guess it probably wouldn't hurt to get to know him,' I said.

She looked at her handiwork. It wouldn't last for long: it would likely have to be fixed and reglued at least once a day. But it was a degree of privacy, for now. I had seen Evan's bare bottom as he used the toilet and had been shouted at by Sarah when I stumbled into the bathroom stall in the middle of the night to find her there already.

'Talk to every boy here if it keeps you safe,' Jacintha said. 'Now isn't the time to be sentimental.'

We made better progress that day: we completed four tasks that afternoon, and earned toilet cleaner, a ladder, scissors, and a new towel for each of us. The tasks were easy, and we were happy as we did them, though a little deflated when we looked at our spoils, all sickeningly practical. We had lunch outside – bread and tiny portions of ham or cheese. After lunch we napped in the bedroom, still the only room in the house that was cool.

Jacintha climbed into my bed, and Ryan went into hers. Carlos came into the room, looking for Jacintha. I held my finger to my lips and pointed to her sleeping form beside me. He nodded, and hung around for a couple of minutes, as though hoping she would wake up. Then he said, 'Don't tell Mia I was here,' and disappeared.

I didn't sleep, but I enjoyed the cool air and the quiet. Before I went to sleep, I thought about how easy everything had become. At the same time, everything here felt new and exciting. I felt, now that I was fully removed from it, that there was nothing for me back home, only the same drudgery, day after day. I didn't know what might happen in the compound in the following weeks, but I knew that there would be opportunities for more. One simple, even fun task, and something new would appear. What tedium I would have to go through to get the same things at home: standing on my feet for hours, faking smiles, pretending to have energy and enthusiasm. When I slept, I dreamt of prizes falling from the sky, and all of us standing in the desert with our arms outstretched, waiting for them to reach us.

When I woke, the rest of the compound was in the living room, sitting on the brand new, enormous, L-shaped couch, facing the big screen. They stopped talking when we entered.

Task: Choose one person to banish from the compound
Reward: Freezer

'Look,' Andrew said, and put his hands on his hips. 'This isn't going to be easy. But we need to be quintessential about it.' In the corner of my vision, I saw Jacintha roll her eyes.

Mia said, 'It'll be worse when we've become friends and

forged relationships. As it is, we don't really know each other. We should do it quickly, and not make a spectacle about it.'

We had no pen or paper yet, and debated for a while on how to vote. In years past, they usually had writing materials by now. Instead, we went to the edge of the compound, to the dustiest section where no trees or flowers grew. We spent a while looking for rocks and sharp, pointed pebbles; once we had one of each, we scratched the name of the resident we wanted to banish on the rocks using the pebbles. We all spread out, as though we might try to peek at each other's answers. We then placed our stones in the designated circle.

When everyone had voted, Tom entered the circle and turned the rocks over, revealing the letters etched on each. We crowded around him, all trying to get a glimpse. Becca received six votes and Gavin had the rest. No one felt the need to speculate, or justify themselves. Gav had broken one of the rules in a moment of carelessness, bringing us closer to some unnamed punishment, and because of Becca we almost didn't have our L-shaped couch.

'I knew it,' he said morosely. 'I knew it would be me.'

We stood around uncertainly for a few moments. I wondered if Gav would kick up some kind of fuss. They often did on the show. I couldn't think of anything more humiliating than being the first to be voted out. But Gav just said, 'I think I'll get a glass of water first.'

We went back to the house, unsure of what to say. Gav went to the kitchen and ran himself a large glass. He drank it in three long pulls, his throat bobbing, his eyes on the ceiling. We watched him, all seventeen of us, piled in the kitchen.

'Okay,' he said when his glass was empty. 'I'll go now.'

We went out with him. When we reached the southern perimeter he looked nervous.

'It's not like coming in,' Tom said quietly. 'There'll be

someone waiting for you along the way. They'll show you where to go.'

Unexpectedly, Gav reached forward and seized Tom in a tight, fierce hug. 'Thanks, man,' he said. Tom said nothing, but he let Gav cling to him. I looked at Eloise, who had been sharing a bed with Gav. She was pulling at her sleeves nervously, but she was also looking around at the other boys, as though sizing up who else she could share a bed with.

There was no real entrance or exit in the fence separating the desert and the compound, but the boys had made a gap to slip through when they first arrived. There was the barbed wire, too, presumably to keep out animals, and Gav crossed over it carefully, then turned and looked at us as though he thought we might change our minds.

'Bye, Gav,' Andrew said, and some of the others chorused in for a goodbye. 'We'll miss you.'

He looked distinctly disappointed.

'Bye,' he said, and went on his way.

We went back towards the house, going along the back so the boys could pick up the freezer. The freezer was a huge win for us, a major improvement to the compound, but we didn't celebrate; it wouldn't have been right.

Gav had left quickly and quietly. He hadn't taken anything with him, not even the razor. We all agreed that it was a classy move.

With Gav gone, there would be someone sleeping alone, and therefore another person would be gone in the morning. Sometimes people were banished in twos, but generally viewers liked when the residents voted for one person to be banished, which meant that the rest of the day was fraught with tension about who would be left to sleep on their own. Once again there was a surplus girl, and we were left on the back foot. We all shuffled around the compound for a bit, until Mia spoke decisively.

'Let's go for a swim,' she said. 'We need to cool off.'

When we were changing into our swimming suits, I looked at my screen.

Task: Talk to Sam
Reward: Necklace

I paused, re-reading it. It was strangely simple, and I wondered why it had come about. The instructions were occasionally random, but occasionally deliberate. Sometimes they paid attention to what the viewers wanted, and sometimes it was malicious, an attempt to stir up drama. I debated whether or not to do it as I fixed my hair and applied more sun cream. I liked Sam. I wanted to talk to him. It was possible that I liked him maybe a little more than I should, and I didn't want to get sucked into anything. If I rocked the boat this early with Ryan I mightn't get such a good opportunity again.

Vanessa walked into the dressing room, carrying some kind of gold fabric. She stripped unhurriedly and put on the garment. She turned slowly in the mirror, observing herself from different angles, watching us watching her. It was very small, made of bronzes and golds, and shone as she moved. My own bikini was blue with polka dots. Beside her, I looked pathetically childish.

'Where did you get that?' Mia asked.

'Task,' she said. 'It's from Trench and Co. It's eye-catching, right?'

None of us had received clothes yet. I wondered what she had to do to get it.

Susie came in from the bedroom, placing clips in her hair. She looked at us sadly. 'I always think I look pretty until I see the rest of you.'

'You look like Princess Leia,' Jacintha said to Vanessa.

She turned again, and we watched, mesmerised. She didn't praise it too much, like other people did when they were looking for a brand deal. She just looked damn good in it. I could imagine all the people at home who would be reaching for their phones, searching Trench and Co. I would have bought it too, if I was watching. It was the best possible reward she could have gotten at this point, not just because it showed off her body, but because it was small and easy to carry for whenever she had to leave, and because people would associate her with the outfit, making it easier to land a brand deal when she left.

She scrunched her hair up by her ears. 'Should I do the hair, do you think?'

'No,' Candice said. 'Your hair is nicer down.'

Vanessa moved her hair around a bit, and then left.

Mia picked up her bronzer, then put it down again. '*Fuck*,' she said.

Some of the boys were in the pool, and some of them were scattered around the compound. When I got there, Vanessa was sitting on the edge of the pool, while Evan and Seb were treading water before her. Like Princess Leia herself, Vanessa's stomach had no crease when she sat.

Mia, Candice, Jacintha and I walked into the water and stood at the top of the pool for a moment, unsure of what to do. The boys made no effort to come near us. Mia waded deeper in, then did slow, methodical strokes for the length of the pool. She had good technique. I thought that she must have had a lot of swimming lessons in her life.

Candice settled into the side of the pool, and put one arm on the edge, relaxed. She nodded at Jacintha. 'Purple's your colour,' she said.

'Thanks,' Jacintha replied. 'I like your hair today.'

'Oh, thanks. Look, I don't know about you guys,' she said. 'But I don't trust Mia.'

Jacintha and I glanced at each other. 'Why?' I said.

'I think she's two-faced. You don't think so?'

Mia was swimming back towards us. She paused when she got to Vanessa, Evan and Seb. 'Hey guys,' she said. 'Want to race? I'm really fast.'

Evan said, 'I'm really fast, too!'

'Seb?' Mia said.

'Sure,' he said.

'Vanessa?'

'No, thanks. I don't want to get my hair wet.'

'No problem. You can be the judge.'

As they set off on their race, Candice gave Jacintha and me a significant look. 'See?'

Jacintha said, 'Nothing wrong with that, really.'

Candice shook her head. 'She only pretends to be friendly.' She looked at me. 'You know that on the second day she was saying that there was something shady about you?'

'What's shady about me?'

'Nothing. She's just being mean. But then she'll be sweet to your face.' I wondered if Mia actually did think that I was trouble, or if she was threatened by me. I knew that she felt inferior to Candice – we all did – but she knew better than to make trouble with her. I supposed I was an easier target, passive as I was. If I was Candice, I would have swum straight towards her and asked her what she meant by talking about me behind my back. But I didn't say anything. I just watched them, along with Candice and Jacintha. I wondered if the viewers would say that I was gormless, or wise to not rise to the bait.

They had almost finished the length. Evan was a little behind, but Seb and Mia were neck and neck.

'Hey, I hope I'm wrong,' Candice said. 'It's just a feeling I have.'

I found Sam in the living room, sitting on the couch with Carlos. When I took a seat, Carlos glanced between us and got up, saying he wanted to go for a swim.

The living room had windows with no blinds, and the room was warm, but not enough to be uncomfortable. I sat so I was facing him, my legs propped against the cushions of the couch. He was lying on the couch, and though his legs were stretched before him it was big enough that our legs were close, but not touching.

'Just us,' I said.

'Just us,' he said.

'How's Becca today?'

'Fine, mostly. She was rattled by the challenge yesterday, and by Tom. The fact that a couple of people voted for her earlier didn't help, either.'

'I didn't vote for her,' I said.

'I didn't think you did. People think that she's weak, but they don't know her.'

'I mean,' I said, hating the way my voice sounded, high and slow. 'You don't really know her either.'

'You're probably right. I keep thinking that I know people in here, and then I remember that I don't know where they're from or if they're a twin, or an only child, or even what their job is. It's strange, not being able to talk properly.'

'We can talk properly,' I said. 'You can't tell me about your personal life, but I bet I could guess a few things.'

'You think?'

'I bet I can guess what your job is,' I said. 'You don't have to say anything. I'll tell by your reaction if I'm right.'

'Go ahead.'

'Vet.'

He said nothing, but he was smiling a little, as though I was doing something cute. I tucked my legs under me. Although I was enjoying myself, enjoying sitting next to him and speaking easily to him, I paused for a moment, listening, as though I might hear the voice warning us about breaking the rules. But there was no sound except for that of distant conversations. As long as he didn't directly speak about his personal life we were fine. I couldn't pretend that walking the line of rule-breaking didn't add to the overall enjoyment of the conversation. 'Contractor.' I was met with silence. 'Dentist. Therapist.' He put his arm on the back of the couch, so his hand was an inch or two from my head. 'Software engineer. Solicitor. This is boring. Am I close?'

'No, not at all.'

'Gardener.'

He shook his head, smiling. 'But that sounds nice.'

'Do you really like Becca, then?'

I looked at him and he looked back at me, his gaze steady. 'Becca's nice. I like her, yeah.'

'Yeah, I like her, too. She's great.'

'What?' he said, his mouth curling at the side.

'What?' I said, smiling, too, though I didn't know why.

'Why were you making that face?'

'I wasn't making any face!'

'Okay,' he said. 'Where's Ryan?'

'The gym, I think. He got a dumbbell this morning,' I said.

'You don't want to watch him work out?' he said, grinning now.

'Shut up,' I said, and pushed his leg. It didn't move. 'I'm not, like, married to him. I hardly know him. Actually,' I said, reckless, giddy, 'I kind of thought that you might have offered to share a bed with me that first night. I thought that we got on well.'

'Did you?' he said. 'You haven't spoken to me for days.' There was something dry about his tone that I didn't like.

'Well,' I said. 'You've been with Becca.'

'And you've been with Ryan.'

'Right,' I said. I felt that I had soured things. I had been so excited, when I had sat down beside him and it was just the two of us. 'That doesn't stop us from talking to each other.'

'You're absolutely right. I guess it's kind of interesting that you're only talking to me now, when a girl is going to be banished tonight.'

'So?'

'So, the last time that we spoke properly was the last time a girl was going to be banished. I guess it's starting to feel a bit transactional, no?'

I wanted to get up, and walk around the compound, and then return with some breezy answer. 'That's not true,' I said. He was right – but it didn't take away from the fact that I wanted to speak with him.

'Well, you have nothing to worry about. You've got plenty of interested parties. You won't be going any time soon.' His tone wasn't particularly nice, and I wanted to storm out of the room, as though he had suggested something vulgar. I felt angry that our nice moment had been ruined, and just as angry that he had seen right through me. I didn't want to be confronted by my selfish decisions. I wanted to be absolved through his regard for me.

'Why are you being so mean right now? You're not like this.'

'Maybe I am,' he said. 'You don't know me either.'

'Can't you just be *nice*?'

'Is this you being nice?'

'Fuck you,' I said, and got up. I didn't go to my postbox. I went back to the pool, though I had only just dried off. I dove straight in, arms over my head, back arched. I stayed underwater for as long as I could, trying to ignore the sound of other people's laughter. When I came to the surface, I floated on my back for a while, then treaded water in place, focusing on keeping my expression pleasant.

I searched for Ryan, but couldn't find him. I looked in the tennis court, empty of rackets or balls, and by the dumpster, and at the swings, but didn't see him anywhere. Andrew spotted me by the gym, and said, 'Hey, Lily. You looking for someone?'

'Ryan,' I said.

'Ah,' he said, grinning. 'And here I was hoping you might have been looking for me. He's just finished up here. I think he went to take a shower.'

'Oh, cool. Maybe I'll see him around.'

'Hey, will you do me a favour?'

'Of course.'

'If you see Candice,' he said, 'will you tell her I'm looking for her?'

'Sure.'

'Did you see her . . . ah, speaking to any of the boys today?'

'I don't know,' I said. I shrugged. 'You'd have to ask her yourself.'

He looked disappointed. I wanted Andrew to like me, so I said, 'If I see her I'll tell her to go find you.'

He smiled. 'I'll find her first, don't worry.'

When I got to the bathroom, Ryan was just pulling back the sheet, steam billowing behind him. There was a towel wrapped around his waist – we had recently earned a luxury towel each with our names embroidered along the edge. He looked surprised to see me, and I realised – too late – that I must have looked strange, waiting for him outside the bathroom.

'This is a nice surprise,' he said. 'Were you planning to accost me in the shower?'

'No,' I said, though my cheeks heated. He laughed at the look on my face. 'What's up?'

'Nothing. I just was wondering where you were.'

'You're not worried about tonight, are you?'

I looked up at him. There was no point in lying. 'Of course I am.'

'You have nothing to worry about, as long as I'm here,' he said, and kissed me on the forehead. He smelled of the body wash that we all used, a giant container of it left behind by other residents, mild and grapefruit-scented. He had smelled differently last night, when I was curled around him. I wanted that: I wanted to be close to him.

'Kiss me,' I said. He put his hand on my back and pulled me close, and as his lips touched mine, I felt an immense sweep of relief: not because it was a particularly special kiss, or because I wanted him, but because I knew that he wanted me. As long as Ryan wanted me, I was safe. I only had to keep a firm hold of him until the final five, when couples no longer mattered, and no one was banished if they slept alone. But it could be a long time until then, weeks or months, and I needed to be sure that I had someone who would stick by me.

Ryan changed into his swim trunks, and took my hand and walked around the compound with me. Everyone was busy, even if it looked as though they were idle. In previous seasons of the show some people had stayed with the same person from the first night, and others changed, looking for the right person, whether as a strategic choice or out of genuine interest. Strategic pairings rarely lasted long. Sharing a bed was not simple, even if you only slept. I liked Ryan: I liked sleeping next to him. But still, there had been a couple of times I had woken up in confusion to find a mouth breathing next to my ear. When I thought of having to share with Seb or Evan I felt vaguely disgusted. There was nothing wrong with them; I just didn't want them.

There was something sad about seeing some of the girls trying to keep their place in the compound. Tom, peeling an orange and sitting in the grass, didn't even look at Susie as she told him about her favourite brands of perfume. When he had finished his fruit, he got to his feet and left. The sight of her sitting alone might have been terrible, except that Evan came to her side almost immediately. He took her to the trampoline, lifting her up in a gentlemanly fashion. He bounced with great enthusiasm and some skill, performing tumbles in the air, artistic backflips and ambitious triple bounces. Susie bounced lethargically beside him, arms limp by her side.

The sight of them reminded me of how desperately I had wanted a trampoline as a child. We lived in a densely populated area where I could see trampolines dotted across neighbouring gardens. Seized by an envy which nearly overcame me, I spent weeks pooling all of my money, every coin I had, given to me by a kindly relative or left over from my last birthday. I gathered all of it, and presented it to my mother triumphantly. She opened a toy catalogue that had been my personal bible, particularly around birthdays and Christmas. She showed me the price of a trampoline, and then told me how much I had. 'Do you see?' she had said. 'Do you see how you're not even close?' The fact that the trampoline seemed so out of reach only increased my desire for it. I hated to go outside and see my neighbours happily bouncing through the air. I abhorred their spinning and tumbling.

Then, a few months later, for my birthday, there it was, outside, on our ordinary, plain little patch of grass. I screamed. I remember it so clearly: I stood in the doorway and shrieked with excitement. I bounced for hours that night and for every night that week, until the top of my head ached and dew started to coat the nylon. I ran around its circumference, my feet so quick, so light, and catapulted through the air; backflips, tumbles, belly flops – all of these fantastical contortions that had been previously unavailable to me.

But after about three weeks I lost interest. I didn't particularly want to go on the trampoline any more. Since I knew exactly how much it had cost – the number rattled around constantly in my head – I felt an immense sense of guilt that I had tired of it so quickly. I made a point to go out a couple of times a week, but it felt, more than anything, like work. More time passed, and my mother asked me nearly daily, with a sort of savagery, if I had been out on the trampoline that day. I'd tell her that I was going out, definitely. 'You'd better,' she'd reply.

The dreariness of it, then. The tumbles and the flips felt like a tax I had to pay. I regarded my bouncing neighbours with disinterest. Within a year, I no longer played on it at all, and within a few years the springs became rusted, and my mother threw it out when a skip appeared on the street. I was glad to see it go: there was something about it that made me weary – how fiercely I had wanted it, and how quickly I tired of it. I wanted to recount this memory to Ryan, but it wasn't allowed, and besides I don't think it would have meant anything to him.

When we passed by the ping-pong table I saw Candice talking to Carlos, but by the time we had circled back around the compound she was sitting with Andrew, under his arm. He was stroking her hair, her eyes closed.

Ryan made a point of saying hi to the others. I knew that he was showing everyone – myself included – that we would be sharing a bed together that night. In previous years, fights had occasionally broken out in the middle of the night as a boy tried to usurp the place of someone else. I didn't generally like possessiveness, but you had to be definitive about your choice on the show. People changed their minds quickly, and if you got too relaxed someone might swoop in and steal your bed-mate. I knew that Ryan was being primitive, in a way, but I can't say that it didn't please me.

Later, in bed, I could hear the sounds of movement long into the night. Someone would be banished at sunrise, and not a minute before. I didn't know if the sounds were caused by people finding comfort in each other, swapping of beds, or if there were girls begging quietly to not be left alone. Whatever it was, the following morning Eloise was gone, and the numbers were even again.

Five

The next day we realised that we were running out of food. When we had arrived we had roughly estimated that the kitchen's contents would last us two weeks, but we had vastly underestimated just how much the men ate in a day. We now had only two loaves of bread, both of which were hard but still edible, a couple of dozen bananas, some vegetables, a bottle of honey and a large bar of chocolate. It was unclear how things had dwindled so quickly. I secretly suspected that someone had been getting up in the night to eat.

The lack of food worried us and led to the calling of a meeting. It was Andrew who gathered us all together. He was wearing a shirt and trousers, a little too overdressed for the heat, and I wondered if he had changed for the occasion.

'First of all, thank you to Sarah and Vanessa for alerting us to the dwindling food supplies. The most important thing that happens in the compound is co-operation, so we're all going to have to pitch in to make it through the next day or so, and to make sure that this doesn't happen again.

'Vanessa and Sarah, I'm going to put you in charge of food. This will involve divvying up the portions to last us until tomorrow. We're going to have to do as many tasks as we possibly can today in the hopes that one of the rewards will be food. Even then, we're going to have to be careful. Going forward, Vanessa and Sarah will be in charge of inventorying the food and dividing the portions.' At this, Sarah looked around, as though daring us to argue. We all stayed quiet, waiting to hear what our roles would be.

'While we're sorting this out, we need to establish a better way of maintaining the compound. The place is getting dirty and disorganised. At present, there's sixteen people living here. I'm dividing the jobs into eight categories, and I'm going to need volunteers for each group. Let's call them departments, for the sake of clarity. Raise your hand if you'd like to volunteer for a department.'

Generally, in seasons past, everyone fended for themselves, pitching in as they could, although inevitably some people pulled their weight more than others. While I didn't relish the idea of having an assigned job (hadn't we come here for a break from all of that?) I was slightly smug at how organised and competent we all must have appeared. I thought of the contestants from five years ago, who the media had called the Sloppy Seven. When they first arrived, they had been moderately untidy, but grew progressively worse as they fell out with each other. Then there were only seven residents left, but none of them seemed to like each other, and, in a breathtaking display of mutual passive aggression, they all stopped cleaning entirely to try to smoke each other out. They lived in genuine filth – overflowing toilets, maggots on the counters, mice in the beds – until one day they collectively decided to leave rather than to fix the mess they had made. When the next set of contestants arrived and saw the place they had cried. Two of them left immediately. It was a real hoot.

I don't know if the others were thinking of the Sloppy Seven, too, or if they just agreed with the familiar structure of industry, but no one protested against Andrew's proposed departments. As Andrew was speaking Tom stood quietly beside him, once or twice jumping in when Andrew had lost track of who had what job, and I suspected that Tom was likely responsible for thinking up the division of labour. I wondered, had it been Tom who proposed the idea, in his stoic, serious way, if we would have questioned it; Andrew had presented the idea with such enthusiasm and confidence that it felt like we were all collaborating on a fun project rather than being instructed to carry out manual labour.

The departments were as follows: Food Organisation and Preservation: Vanessa and Sarah; Food Preparation: Candice and Carlos; Cleaning (Kitchen and Living Room): Becca and me; Cleaning (Bathroom and Bedroom): Mia and Seb; Communal Task Managers, and Reward Distribution: Tom and Andrew; Yard and Pool Maintenance: Ryan and Marcus; Safety and Wellbeing: Susie and Evan; Repairs and Construction: Jacintha and Sam.

Andrew and Tom's roles placed them in a leadership position, a decision which no one questioned. It made sense to me at the time: Andrew presented a compelling argument, and Tom had gravitas to make it seem like he knew what he was doing. I thought that Candice looked a little put out, and the truth was that if I had to vote for someone to lead operations at the compound, it would have been her. But she hadn't volunteered for the role, so I kept quiet.

With the responsibilities thus divided, our home became infinitely more liveable. I hadn't really noticed how run-down the place had been getting until we began living in a structured manner. It meant we didn't have as much leisure time, but Tom and Andrew organised a schedule so that we would always, without fail, finish a minimum of five Communal Tasks, with an aim of finishing seven if time allowed. They took to their new roles with a committed zeal that encouraged the rest of us to take our own roles seriously. If I was in the kitchen and someone else was there, I tried to always have a sponge at hand so that I looked busy.

Andrew was boundlessly enthusiastic and liked to give pep talks before tasks. 'Just think about all the things we could achieve,' he liked to say, gesturing around him. Even when he wasn't organising a task, he was always 'on', walking around the compound, checking on everyone. 'Everyone okay?' I often heard him call, his upbeat voice echoing across the grounds. 'Having a good time? Yes? Excellent.' He was easy to like. There was a boyishness to him; running alongside his earnest desire to help others was his love of games, jokes, and general fun. There was a part of his charm that sometimes veered into ridiculousness, but we mostly chose to ignore it to preserve the peace. Over dinner one night, he said that potatoes were so much more expository with butter. I'm not sure what precisely he had meant to say, but the people sitting beside him nodded, and I nodded too. The word wasn't right, but there was hardly any point correcting him when we all knew what he meant. Potatoes were better with butter.

Tom, on the other hand, was more practical, and didn't like small talk. Tom didn't like most kinds of talk, actually. But he was more reliable than Andrew: if you asked Andrew for help or advice he often spoke a great deal about what could be done, and then got distracted on the way to fixing the problem. Andrew left you motivated but no further on with what you had wanted to achieve. Tom generally tried to solve the problem on the spot, and if he couldn't do it himself he delegated it to someone else. He was good at that: people generally liked it when Tom came to them and asked for their assistance. He often went to Jacintha, who had a quick mind and could turn her hand to anything.

Sam had similar skills to Jacintha, but Tom very rarely went to him to ask for help.

Tom only occasionally delegated jobs to me. I didn't mind. I didn't want any more work to do.

That first day after the meeting we had a breakfast of bananas and coffee, and completed our first task quickly and painlessly: in exchange for a shelving unit, we had to swap our clothes with a member of the opposite sex. Because Ryan was so much bigger than me, I swapped with Seb, who, with a hangdog face, took my leggings and T-shirt and gave me his shorts and T-shirt. The shelves were of a decent size, and Andrew and Tom decided to place them in the hallway, by the entrance. Some people put their shoes on the lower shelf, and others put sunscreen and hats and aloe vera on the other shelves. It gave our entrance a homey feel, even if the absence of the door took away from the general effect.

Then we were instructed to compliment each resident of the compound, in exchange for a net for cleaning the pool. We were placed in an assembly line, the boys standing still and the girls moving to the right each time. I moved along, giving and receiving compliments without much thought, eager to get to Ryan.

'You have gorgeous hair,' Ryan said when I reached him.

I had my compliment for him ready to go. 'You have the best body of anyone here,' I said.

He smiled widely at that, looking the most pleased I had ever seen him. 'I work out,' he said modestly, as if it was something I didn't know, as if I didn't see him lifting weights for hours a day and doing press-ups before he came to bed.

Jacintha nudged me, and I moved on to the next person. I wasn't looking forward to complimenting Sam. I had seen him that morning, on the way to breakfast, and had given him one of my curated, customer-service smiles, but he hadn't looked at me at all. I didn't like the way that we'd left things.

When I'd received the necklace from my chute after our conversation, I'd initially felt guilty. But when I checked the brand I saw that it was Dorian, a luxury brand that everyone knew and admired. Already the prizes were becoming valuable and worth the risk. 'Thank you so much, Dorian, for this beautiful necklace,' I said to the camera. 'It's perfect. I can wear it with any outfit.' I felt that I had sounded stiff, so I showed it to the girls in the dressing room, making sure to mention the name of the brand. Mia had admired it, fingering the cool metal. 'Real gold,' she said. Candice had met my eye in the mirror. 'Good girl,' she said.

I decided I would give Sam a nice compliment, and we could smooth things over. But when I reached him, he spoke before I could.

'You have nice skin,' he said, voice so flat and empty that it entirely negated the meaning of the words. And what kind of compliment was that, anyway? At once, my good will left me. I stayed standing there for so long that Jacintha had to nudge me again.

'Can't think of anything?' Sam said, impassive. My compliment that I had prepared for him had been that I liked that he fixed things without anyone asking. Andrew liked to loudly announce that he was getting to work whenever he was presented with a job, and Jacintha sometimes complained that she got stuck with all of the most menial tasks. Sam generally fixed the problem before anyone else had noticed it. But I felt irrationally cheapened by the fact that he had given me such a superficial compliment. I had expected it from Ryan, because I knew that he liked me most of all for my beauty, and that, to me, was okay: my beauty was what I prized the most too, and the only thing about me which I expected to draw a response. But for some reason, from Sam it felt like an insult.

'You're tall,' I said, and moved on.

We did one more task (we had to reveal our favourite alcoholic beverage in unison in exchange for bleach) and then took a break for lunch. Although we had finished the three Communal Tasks faster than ever thanks to Tom and Andrew, we were disappointed that none of the rewards involved food. The remaining bread was divided into sixteen pieces and drizzled with honey. It wasn't unpleasant, but it wasn't filling either. We finished quickly but were reluctant to return to the tasks. We sat in the shade sleepily until Andrew and Tom called us to the front yard.

'All right, everyone,' Andrew said. 'Two more tasks, and then we can take a break.'

'Two tasks and then we're done, right?' Sarah asked.

'That's what I'd like, for sure,' Andrew said. 'But we need to get food.'

For our next task, we got a roll of tape in exchange for revealing the names of our grandparents. For our fourth task, we got an extra pillow for each of us, in exchange for climbing onto the roof of the house. This one took a while, and Andrew and Tom let us look at our little screens while they arranged the mechanics of us getting up.

My Personal Task was to dance in front of at least one other person in exchange for a pair of shoes. I considered the task, and what they wanted me to do: what the viewers or producers wanted to see. It might have been that they wanted something sexual, a dance for Ryan, maybe, or something to catch the attention of the other boys, something to mark me as a provocative presence in the compound. Or it was just as possible that they were trying to present me as a comic figure, and that the viewers would be laughing at me, dancing for a pair of shoes like a jester in the court of a king. For the first time since I had been there, I considered not doing a task.

At last, it was arranged that the men would climb on top of the dining chairs, and from there, hoist us girls up. There would be one person already on the roof, who would pull us up one at a time if necessary. Tom would take that role; he was by the far the strongest resident, but he wasn't particularly tall. Carlos, the tallest, boosted Tom onto the roof, steepling his fingers together as a step. He grunted when Tom stepped into his hands, and it looked as though it would be too much – but Sam stepped in and helped to push Tom upwards. Carlos then lifted Becca from the ground – she was so tiny even I could have lifted her – and rather than offering the steepled fingers, he simply lifted her towards Tom, who leaned off the roof and plucked her up as though she were a rag doll. If anyone else noticed how uncomfortable Becca was in Tom's grasp no one mentioned it.

We all went, one at a time, first the women, and then the men, until only Evan remained. I wondered at first if it was wise, but Evan was lithe and agile, and launched himself from the chair to the waiting hands of Carlos and Tom.

Once we all were up there, we got as comfortable as we could and looked at the view before us. It was beautiful, in its own way. Beyond the compound, there were great stretches of desert plain, but far, far beyond was a blur of vegetation, trees and bushes. I thought that there was some red plant growing there, and said so, but Carlos, who was sitting beside me, looked at me in confusion and said, 'Those are bushfires.'

'Oh,' I said.

'It's the heat,' he said. 'They might have been burning for hours, or even days. They won't reach us, though.'

We stayed up there for longer than we should have, our voices overlapping, chatting about nothing in particular. It was easier now, to talk without revealing personal information. It limited your conversation, but if you just emptied your brain and said whatever came to mind, it was enjoyable in its own way.

At some point, Vanessa and Sarah went down and stacked the dining chairs on top of each other as a makeshift ladder. They brought the chocolate we had been saving, dividing it amongst each of us with benevolent expressions, like nuns bestowing blessings. I had eaten that exact brand of chocolate a thousand times, but it tasted better than I ever could recall.

The sun was setting, and it, too, was as I had never seen it before: a fantastical dusty purple sky, splashes of rich oranges, all pressing against that endless stretch of flat plain. There were mountains to the south-east, cast in a rich indigo glow.

Candice and Carlos scrambled down and brought our dinner up to us, too: a selection of potatoes, cooked as many ways as they could manage. There was salt and some butter, and some people drizzled honey on theirs, though I didn't try it myself. Sitting together on the roof was the nicest time we'd had since coming to the compound, I think because we were somewhere familiar but different: we had by now explored everything within the perimeter, and there was a novelty in being on the roof that was, in some small, vital way, intoxicating.

It was easier to come down off the roof, but the boys made a fuss of depositing us individually. It was dark, and we were still in a fine humour. Ryan had his arm around my shoulder, and on my other side Evan was chattering in my ear. The others went to go into the house, but I walked over to the pool, which was now a silvery blue, lit by lights I hadn't realised were there. The light rippled and refracted with the slight movement of the water.

'Jacintha,' I called softly. She was nearby, talking to Marcus. It was obvious that he liked her from the way that he was smiling at her. Carlos was talking to Evan, but was glancing frequently at Marcus and Jacintha. I was glad that Marcus and Carlos were fighting over her: it made a mockery of her being placed sixth in the attractiveness ranking. Jacintha had told me that she'd put the ranking out of her head, but I thought about it all the time.

She came over, and I said, 'Dance with me.' She laughed, her teeth flashing white, and put her arms around me. I moved without any insecurity, and without thought. I was a good dancer, and I knew it. I twirled her around, and we both were laughing, dancing without inhibition. After a minute or so, we stopped laughing and became serious, our dancing growing wilder, our limbs thrashing through the air. She gripped my hands and I gripped hers, and we spun each other around, and I knew that if one of us let go suddenly the other would go careening into the pool; but I knew, with a surety that was like balm on a burn, that neither of us would do that.

When we slowed, we leaned against each other, panting. I felt giddy and dizzy, my mind blissfully empty: I had forgotten where we were, what was going on around us and beyond us; I had forgotten, even, that it was all for a task. I sensed movement behind me, and heard a voice call, 'Don't look!'

Of course, I turned, as did Jacintha, and saw Susie a few feet away, squatting above the ground, her skirt lifted. 'Don't look at me,' she wailed. 'I had to!'

It was cold, as it always was at night in the desert, and there was steam rising from below her. Susie was shitting on the concrete. I knew it must have been for a Personal Task, but it didn't make it any easier to see.

Before we went to bed, we checked the screen one last time. It said:

Task: Banish one person from the compound
Reward: Pasta

We all agreed, every single one of us, that we wouldn't complete the task. We were wrapped in a warm, companionable glow and when we went to the bedroom none of us went to sleep, but instead stayed awake for hours, sitting on each other's beds, laughing loudly at every joke, exchanging flirtatious looks and friendly smiles. Some of the girls had a pillow fight, and some of the boys were roughhousing. Jacintha and I watched them fondly, while Candice plaited my hair the way I liked it. I still wasn't sure if Candice singled me out amongst the other girls because I was competition, or because she actually liked me. That night, I felt disposed to be generous and kind to everyone, and when Candice told Jacintha and me that she was glad to have found friends like us I believed her.

I also felt an underlying smugness that we had resisted being goaded by the producers into banishing someone. Time and time again I had seen contestants on the show throw their friends and lovers aside for the sake of a reward, for something that would make their life easier. Right then, lying against Jacintha, with Candice working through my hair with gentle hands, and watching the boys, beautiful and strong, posturing for the equally beautiful girls, I felt confident that we would never get so brutal and senseless as to cast each other aside for material gain. Besides, the big screen would reset in the morning. There would be more opportunities for food tomorrow.

When I woke up the next day, Sarah and Vanessa greeted me in the kitchen with sombre faces and handed me a banana and a cup of coffee. 'Thanks,' I said. 'I haven't seen you guys up so early before.'

'We needed to make sure that no one stole any of the food,' said Sarah. 'We've been here for hours.'

I looked at the crate of bananas. There were maybe two dozen left. The bread was gone. The vegetables, too.

'You didn't clean the kitchen last night,' Sarah said. 'We take our job seriously. You need to do the same.'

'Sorry,' I said, immediately chastened. 'I meant to. I'll do it now.'

'Get Becca, too,' Sarah said. 'Don't let her get away with not working, Lily. There's no room for laziness here.'

Sarah had, apparently, found a personality in the last few days. I preferred her as the girl who no one remembered very well.

'Okay,' I said. 'Sorry. I'll get her now.'

'Have your coffee first,' Vanessa said.

Becca was still asleep, as was Sam. They weren't touching, but they were facing each other in bed, their heads on the same pillow. This small intimacy between them sickened me. I didn't want to wake them, but I knew I couldn't let anyone else see that we hadn't done our job. Everyone had worked so well yesterday. I was filled with shame at neglecting our duties.

'Becca,' I whispered, touching her shoulder. Her eyes opened.

'Lily?'

'We need to clean the kitchen,' I said. 'We forgot to do it last night.'

She stretched like a kitten, and I was tempted to let her sleep and do it myself, but she said, 'Okay,' and swung her legs off the bed.

'Becca?' Sam asked, his eyes still closed.

'Go back to sleep,' she whispered. She grabbed a hoodie from the foot of her bed and put it on. She was one of the few women in the compound who was openly self-conscious about her body. Of course, we all loathed how we looked in some way, but most of us were better at hiding it.

We cleaned in silence, as we always did. I found it soothing; Becca, it seemed, did not enjoy the inane chatter that we had all become partial to. I thought there was something fortifying about her quietness. Once we finished, Vanessa and Sarah appeared again and produced a coffee and a banana for Becca. We talked a bit, sitting on the counters, or leaning against the fridge. It was the most open and chatty I had seen Vanessa and Sarah. Having a purpose clearly suited them.

Andrew emerged, his hair messed from sleep. 'I wish we had a clock,' he said. 'It would make things so much easier. I can never wake up early without an alarm.'

'I can wake you when I get up if you want,' I said.

'Would you mind, Lily? It would be much more civilised if I could start the day nice and early.'

'Sure. No problem.'

'Thanks.' He turned to Sarah and Vanessa. 'How are we doing on supplies?'

'Not good,' Vanessa said. 'We have enough breakfast for everyone, and maybe a very small lunch, but there'll be nothing for dinner.' Sarah handed him a coffee and a banana, and he hesitated, then said, 'Keep it. Save the banana for later, and give my coffee to Candice. She'll be up shortly. Thanks, guys. It's nice to wake up to the smell of coffee.' He smiled at us and his curls fell across his forehead, giving him an air of innocence. 'Feels like home, right?'

A little while later, we all met in the living room. It was Tom who spoke rather than Andrew, his face drawn and serious. Whatever else about Tom, when he entered a room you looked at him. 'We're going to have to be ruthless today,' he said. We were quiet. 'We need to do as many tasks as it takes to get food.'

It looked as though Tom was going to speak further, but Andrew interrupted, eager to get a word in. 'We can do this, guys,' he said. 'We'll put in the effort, and we'll reap the rewards. And look, if we have to work into the night, so be it. We've got to eat.'

The first task was for every man to lift their bed-mate over their head. It wasn't a great start to the morning. Evan couldn't manage it, as he was now sharing a bed with Vanessa, who was curvy and buxom. Vanessa flushed as he struggled to raise her up, but it was clearly Evan's fault: I didn't think that there was any girl there he could have lifted, not even Becca. He managed it after a half a dozen attempts, his arms shaking and Vanessa shouting down at him not to drop her. When she was back on the ground, Susie smirked at her. 'Big breakfast?' she asked.

Vanessa turned to her coolly. 'Wasn't that you last night, shitting in the yard like an animal?'

None of the girls spoke for the rest of the morning lest a fight break out. We were all on edge; I was so hungry I felt liable to snap at anyone.

The big screen read,

Task: Choreograph a dance to the song 'Uptown Girl' by Billy Joel. Everyone must sing and dance in unison.

Reward: Lawnmower.

It was the biggest reward that had been offered, except for maybe the freezer. I didn't really care – at this point, all I was thinking about was food. Beside me though, Ryan murmured, 'This is really going to make Yard Maintenance a lot more effective.'

Urgently, Tom called out, 'Who knows the lyrics to "Uptown Girl"?'

It took us a long time. Myself, Becca and Evan knew bits of the lyrics, so it took us sitting for what was probably an hour to get all the words right. Candice and Susie worked on organising the choreography while Tom paced impatiently. We would have a verse figured out, but, with no paper to write it down, we sometimes forgot the words we had just remembered. Eventually, when we had a couple of lines, Andrew would shout it out, and have a group of people repeat it over and over.

Candice and Susie kept the choreography simple, but still it took us hours. We were slowed down considerably by a small number of residents, namely Marcus, Seb, and Jacintha. Jacintha was particularly uncoordinated, and I could see that she was getting frustrated with herself, shaking her head in annoyance when she muddled the moves. I tried to be supportive, but she was shockingly bad.

Halfway through, Sarah stopped and said, 'Isn't there a key change in this song?'

Tom looked as though he might snap somebody's neck.

'That's just the Westlife cover,' I said.

'Are you sure, Lily?' Tom said.

'Positive.'

Finally, we finished. Any giddiness that we had at the beginning of the task had disappeared: any enjoyment we got from the song and dance evaporated after the tenth time we tried, unsuccessfully, to get through it. When we at last managed the routine in unison we were tired and irritable. The men loped to the delivery area to look at the lawnmower while the girls went to the pool. Jacintha and I sat under a tree, away from the others.

'I'm the most pathetic dancer,' Jacintha said. 'Fuck. I really messed that one up.'

'It's over now,' I said.

'But people will remember how much I set us back the next time we vote to banish someone.'

It was true that people were likely looking for reasons to banish someone now that food was so scarce. But I knew no one would banish Jacintha: at least, not yet. 'That's not true. You're the department of Maintenance and Construction. That's, like, the most important one, except for Tom and Andrew's department. I just clean dishes,' I said, shrugging.

'Maintenance and Construction,' she repeated, with an irritated jerk of her chin. 'I haven't even made us a proper door, yet.'

We were interrupted by the sounds of whooping coming from the side of the house. We all turned to look. Ryan came around the corner of the house, riding the lawnmower. Despite myself, I was impressed. It was enormous, oddly sleek, and a shiny red. Andrew was on the back, standing, his arms spread wide and crying out with happiness. We laughed fondly at them, like mothers watching their children in the playground.

Candice said, 'Ladies, that was all us. We put together one hell of a show.' Susie, standing at the edge of the pool, laughed happily, then jumped into the water, crying 'Cannonball!' The water splashed the rest of us girls, and we complained, but then the boys cannonballed into the pool too. After some urging on their parts we joined them. It was easier to just give in. Marcus, who had been almost as lousy as Jacintha at the choreographed dance, took her in his arms, twirling her around. She resisted at first and then relaxed, laughing and throwing her arms around his shoulders, the two of them swaying in the water, him dipping her so that the back of her head touched the surface of the water but never quite went under.

After two further challenges (name fifteen capital cities – a tin of white paint; reveal who we voted for in the last election – baseball hats for everyone) we were exhausted and starving. We'd finished the majority of the food. There were still one or two bananas left, but we were all sick to death of them.

'I know everyone's tired of them, but think about it,' Candice said. 'The bananas were the first food reward we got. And we must have got about two hundred of them. The next food reward we get will last us for a long time.'

Andrew blamed himself for not having us do the task from last night in exchange for pasta. He sighed a lot, and muttered to himself, pacing around the living room, then sat in front of the screen for a while. Eventually he slapped his legs and got up, calling, 'Let's go again, folks! I'm feeling good about the next task. We are seriously on the crust of something here!'

No one was particularly eager to do this next task. It was for another stupid reward, a pair of garden shears. Only Jacintha was up for it. 'I can use them for the hedges,' she said. I gave her a look, but for her, I said, 'We'll do it quickly and have it over and done with.' Luckily, it was a task that required no physical labour: we simply had to reveal our phobias. It took us two minutes to complete, but when we went back to the screen, it had not yet changed colour.

'Did we miss someone?' Mia asked. We puzzled over it for a while. We wondered if we hadn't spoken loud enough. We read the instruction again: *Everyone must reveal their phobia.*

Tom was frowning, confused. 'Let's do it again,' he said. 'Everyone speak clearly.'

My phobia was being buried alive. Ryan's was snakes, and Jacintha's was a fear of small holes. After we had all spoken again, the screen still hadn't lit up green.

'It's obvious, isn't it?' Candice said. 'Someone's lying.'

There was silence, during which we all looked at each other. I started to feel nervous. Was my phobia really being buried alive? Did I have a greater fear? I decided, after a few moments, that I had told the truth.

'One more time,' Andrew said. 'Everyone, there's no need to be embarrassed. We're a family here.'

Everyone said their fear a third time, while listening carefully to spot the liar. It was Marcus: his fear was not spiders, as he had said, but the cold, dark void of outer space. He looked straight ahead as he spoke, and no one said anything, but I saw Jacintha smile softly to herself, as though charmed by his confession. The big screen lit up green, and the new task appeared:

Task: Spit in your bed-mate's mouth
Reward: Sun-loungers.

There was a chorus of disgusted groans, and exclamations of dissent.

'They know that we're desperate,' Carlos said.

'We should just wait until morning,' Seb said. 'That's fucking gross, man.'

I thought that Tom looked inclined to agree, but Andrew was clearly torn. Waiting until morning was another night without food. 'They won't let us die,' he said with certainty. 'But . . . I suppose, they did offer us food last night and we didn't take it. No, they won't let us die, obviously, but we could certainly get very uncomfortable.' We watched him, and he sighed, and said, 'Let's take a break, anyway.'

Candice said, 'Everyone be sure to have a glass of water. There are a couple of bananas left, too.' By the time we had drunk our water the bananas were all gone. Ryan had managed to get one for me. I gagged a little at the smell but ate it anyway. The two of us sat outside in the grass, a light wind rippling through the green. I sighed. Ryan ran his hand through the grass, a couple of inches long, no longer yellow-tinged. It was now a muted green. Ryan had been watering it, and this, added to the work of the sprinklers, had improved it in only a few days. 'I'll cut it tomorrow,' he said, satisfied. 'We're always sitting in the grass. It would be nice to have sun-loungers.'

I looked at him. 'You're not serious. You'd spit in my mouth? You'd let me spit in your mouth?'

'If it was you, sure.'

'You're disgusting,' I said, but his statement pleased me.

'Come here,' he said, smiling at me.

'No,' I said.

'Come here,' he said again. I inched forward. He kissed me gently, deeply, stroking my jaw with one hand and my ribs with another. His tongue slipped between my lips and mine did the same. It was a nice kiss, but I found that I couldn't entirely relax into it. I kept thinking about what I looked like, kept wondering from what angle the camera was capturing our romantic moment.

'Now,' he said. 'Was that so bad?'

'It's not the same. You didn't . . . you know. Spit.'

'It's the same thing, sweetheart.' He grinned at me, his eyes flashing. 'I bet you're conservative in bed, too.' He stroked my neck, a little firmer now, along the column of my throat.

I pulled back a little. 'Wouldn't you like to know,' I said. Perhaps I had known him only a few days, but we had shared a bed and a hundred other intimacies. People often had sex in the compound. The cameras couldn't legally show the actual act, though they gave a fairly good idea of what was going on. When I watched the show I had always said to myself that I would never have sex for the whole world to see. But it felt different, now, living it. I was no longer sure about what I would and wouldn't do.

'I'm going to get another glass of water,' I said. 'I'll be back in a minute.'

He lay back on the grass, relaxed, and watched me go.

In the kitchen, I saw Sam, and said nothing to him. I couldn't deny that I was aware of his presence, but I was determined not to show it. Jacintha came in with her shears. She was pleased with them, and turned them this way and that way so that they glinted under the lights. Sam poured himself a glass of water and leaned against the counter. I poured myself a glass of water, too, and stood beside him. I wanted him to go; I would not be the one to leave the room first. He didn't do the courteous thing and move out of the way. I drank my water at the sink, and let him hear my gulping. I exhaled a loud sigh when I finished, just to annoy him.

'Sam,' Jacintha said, 'if I cut enough barbed wire I should be able to make a trap.'

Sam thought for a moment. 'Who's in charge of Pool Maintenance?' I didn't like the way that sounded, like their only job was to clean the pool. Ryan spent a lot of his day on the lawnmower.

'Ryan and Marcus.'

He nodded. 'Jacintha, you get the barbed wire.' He turned to me. 'You tell Ryan we need his pool-cleaning net. Meet me at the pond in a couple of minutes.'

'He's Pool and Outdoor Maintenance,' I said.

That night, we had duck for dinner.

After Sam caught the first one, the other ducks seemed to know their fate and started to flee, but Jacintha and Ryan caught them and held them in the giant pool net. They squawked and resisted with surprising power, but Sam took the barbed wire and wrapped it around the net. The ducks didn't stop struggling, but they didn't flap their wings with such zeal any more.

Taking the ducks out of the bag one by one was difficult, and I helped Sam by holding their wings while he grabbed their beaks and necks. Once he had a good grip, he gave a mighty wrench, and the duck was dead. I watched in abject fascination as each duck went from writhing and flapping to limp in his hands in the space of a second. We were methodical – me trying my best to restrain them and Sam snapping their necks, one at a time – and when each bird was dead, I placed it into a bin bag gingerly, as though it might come back to life and fly back out.

Jacintha and Ryan struggled the whole time: the more ducks that died, the more violent the others became, tearing their wings against the barbed wire. Once or twice a duck flew out, and Ryan had to grab it, and inevitably was bitten, pecked or whacked in the face, for although the birds were not particularly clever they knew how to make a fuss. Each time, Sam took it calmly from him and snapped its neck before it had time to escape again. There was something about Sam in those moments – it wasn't that I admired his killing of innocent creatures, but I was fascinated by the easy, clinical way he did it before handing the carcasses to me so gently. I found myself examining him closely, the way he twisted his mouth while making a quick jerk of his wrist. I was unable to look away. Ryan might as well have not existed to me.

I remembered that some days or weeks before, I had stopped myself from considering the boys' possible participation in the wars. I thought of it again as I watched the quick, clean, detached way in which Sam killed the ducks. But it didn't repel me; it made him more real. For a moment I stopped thinking of Sam solely as a fellow contestant on a television show, in which he was suspended somewhere between reality and social experiment, and thought of him fully, truly, as a man standing before me, impressive, attractive, intelligent – someone I realised I liked a great deal.

No one had any reservations about eating the ducks: only about the best way to skin them and cook them. Even Mia stayed quiet. Some of the boys had ideas, and voiced them loudly, but Candice held up her hand, and said, 'Carlos and I are Food

Preparation. We'll handle it.' She tied her hair up in a long, sleek ponytail and asked Jacintha to fetch the garden shears.

It was surprisingly tasty. We ate with fierce satisfaction: we were not at the mercy of anyone – we could fend for ourselves. We sat in the outdoor dining area and arranged our seats so that we sat in a circle. We spoke only a little, eating as quickly as we could while glancing around us, as though suddenly seeing all the possibilities of the compound. What else could be eaten? Jacintha remarked that there had once been an orchard but the previous residents had picked it clean. It would take some time to restore it, but it could be done.

We licked our fingers and put our hands on our stomachs: we weren't exactly full, but we were brimming with pleasure. Most of us had helped in some way. Candice and Carlos had plucked, disembowelled, washed and cooked the ducks, and Vanessa and Sarah had gathered the grease and fat to store in a jar, now the only thing in our fridge. They had frozen some of the duck meat too, and though we would have gladly eaten every bite that night we saw the sense in it. Susie, who I would have thought was squeamish, surprised me by taking the duck feathers and cleaning them with meticulous precision. After we ate, she went around the circle and presented everyone with a single, pristine feather, smiling bashfully, as though we might refuse it.

Six

The satisfaction of our dinner the night before evaporated in the morning when we woke, hungry once again. I went to wake Andrew, as he had requested, but when I leaned over him and said his name he jolted awake and stared at me with horror. He looked at me with wide eyes, as though I were a stranger. 'You asked me to wake you,' I said.

He rubbed his face. 'Of course. Thanks, Lily. You're more reliable than any alarm clock.' He looked around the bedroom. 'Have you checked the big screen?' I nodded. 'No food?'

'No,' I said.

He nodded wearily. I could see him thinking. 'We should probably wake the others,' he said. He looked at Candice, who was sleeping still, her hair splayed out around her, her mouth slightly open. She was beautiful in sleep, her face dewy and her lips like rose petals. As Andrew watched her, I saw his face soften. 'Maybe just a few minutes more,' he said quietly.

For breakfast, Vanessa and Sarah handed me a coffee only, and even then it was only half a cup. I was desperate for something more substantial, and imagined buttered bagels and bacon-topped pancakes. Sarah and Vanessa didn't take their eyes off me the entire time I was in the kitchen, as though I might try to tackle them to get to the remaining duck in the freezer.

Task: Each man and woman must eat a handful of grass
 Reward: A whistle
'They're mocking us,' Tom said.
'It's cruel,' Mia said. 'It's just cruel.'
But we had no choice: it was the first task of the day.
'I know it's difficult,' Andrew said, 'but I'm positive that the next task will be food. A couple of seconds and this task will be over.'

We sat in the grass, and each took a handful. 'Check for insects,' Ryan said, and Susie gave a tearful gasp. Evan had left Sarah's bed and returned to Susie's bed that night, and he sat beside her now murmuring encouraging words.

Well, we did it, and what more is there to say? It was grass. It was disgusting.

We went back to the screen.

Task: Every man and woman must participate in a three-legged race.
 Reward: Nails

At this, Mia erupted. 'I'm done with this shit,' she said. 'Fucking bullshit. We're *starving*. A whistle? Nails? This isn't a joke. This is our lives!'

She walked away, and some of the others went after her. I was too tired to follow. I lay down on the couch, and felt the velvet press against my legs. Andrew was still staring at the screen. 'I don't understand,' he said. 'I thought by now they'd offer us food. Maybe we haven't been doing a good enough job? We've done something to displease them, maybe.' Tom went outside to see if there was anything around the compound that we could eat. Andrew continued to pace in front of the big screen.

The delivery area and the dump were side by side; both functioned through the use of vents that were assumed to connect to the production team's base. The amount of rubbish we amassed in a day was literally staggering, mostly due to the wrapping or containers our rewards came packaged in. As Becca and I were in charge of kitchen maintenance, we took the bins out, and generally we had to go out to the dump five, six times a day.

I was heading out there with a bag of rubbish, my arms aching almost as soon as I left the house, when I heard the boys' voices. I hesitated before rounding the corner. I could make out Seb's drawl, and Tom's quiet baritone.

Seb was saying: 'Funny the way they go around in revealing clothes all day, then when they get into bed they act all frigid.'

Tom said nothing, and Seb continued. 'The way they go around. They want you to notice.'

'You have to be a gentleman,' Tom said. He spoke in a weary kind of way, like he was talking to a child. It was clear to me that Tom didn't like Seb. Seb, somehow, didn't seem to understand this.

'Of course, man, of course. I'm just saying the girls are beautiful, is all.' He was quiet for a moment, and then said, 'Susie's been hanging around you a lot. What do you think?'

Tom took his time before he answered. 'If she were out in the wild, she'd be killed within the hour.'

'She's a twit,' Seb said excitedly. 'It's people like her who give the rest of us a bad name. People will look at her and think that we're all that stupid. Her and Lily. They're just here because they're nice to look at.'

Tom said, 'Lily looks like a lot of other girls, just better. The hair, the teeth, the skin. Some girls don't do it very well, but Lily has it down. You have to work hard to look like that, and I respect that. I do.'

'I was surprised that Ryan went for her. I thought he might go for Candice. Lily, though – she'll put out easier. You can tell just from the look of her.' I glanced down at myself. I was wearing a floral sundress, similar to what many of the other girls wore every day. And yet at his words, I felt a flash of shame flood through me. I wondered if Ryan had thought the same thing when he had chosen me.

Seb went on. 'Candice should learn when to stop talking. There's something about her – like, she's kind of stuck up. She thinks she's better than everyone else.'

'Listen. You can't talk about the girls like that. You can think whatever you want, but keep it quiet. People don't like to hear that kind of thing, even if they've had that very thought themselves.' I could hear him move, as though he was getting to his feet. 'I'm going to go and see if there are any plants we can eat. You're in charge of Bathroom and Bedroom Cleaning with Mia, right? Why don't you find her and see if she needs any help. I think I saw her in the nicer bathroom.' I wasn't surprised by Seb's comments, but I was shocked at Tom's defence of me. It was true that I looked a lot like the other girls here: there were six blondes, and many of the boys frequently confused me for Susie. I watched Tom walk away, towards the back of the house, and Seb stayed for a while, dragging his feet before he left, speaking under his breath about the bathroom drains and about Mia. Although Mia and Seb, judgemental and mean, were practically the same person, neither of them liked the other.

Jacintha and I were lying on the grass, chatting about nothing, trying not to think about food. It was always easy being with Jacintha. When I was with the boys I was constantly considering how I looked, measuring the way they looked at us, calculating their intentions, their shifting levels of desire and interest. With the other girls I was mindful of everything I said, careful not to talk too much or too little; with so few forms of entertainment at our disposal, several of the girls occupied themselves with repeating what they had heard said that day, and the recounted version was not always in line with the original. With Jacintha, I spoke as I liked, and was entirely at ease, and had the comfort of knowing that she felt the same with me. We talked about the heat and how we wished it was cool, and then we talked about which of the boys we thought would be the worst at raising kids, and then we talked about the heat again. I stretched on the grass, my eyes closed against the flare of the sun. Insects hummed around me, one treading a slow trail up my arm; I was too idle to brush it away.

'It'll be so nice,' I said drowsily, 'when we're in the final five, and we can talk about whatever we want.' There were several changes to life in the compound when you made it to the final five. The instructions from the big screen were for competitions rather than Communal Tasks: the prizes were essential for living comfortably, but whoever lost was banished. The other big differences was that in the final five, all rules were off: you could talk about your personal lives, talk about your Personal Tasks, and there was no penalty for harming other residents. The producers only stepped in if someone's life was in danger. For the first two seasons, there had been no violence whatsoever, and the residents had lived fairly peacefully with only minor disputes. In the third season, however, one of the girls had attacked another girl, nearly taking an eye out. The producers at once added the rule that violence of any kind was forbidden – but viewership had sky-rocketed after that particular episode, and so, the following season, they adjusted the rules to allow for controlled conflict among the final five. It was a great opportunity for vendettas to be addressed and other such things.

'Mmm. And the rewards.'

I opened my eyes and looked at Jacintha. Excitement flared within me, not just at the prospect of the rewards, which were markedly more valuable late in the show, but at Jacintha admitting that she was looking forward to it, too. It felt like a vulgar thing, to admit to how much it thrilled me: the promise of material things, the rush you get from obtaining something new, something better than you had before.

'I keep thinking about the Personal Rewards,' I said. 'The ones you get at the end, particularly if you win.'

Jacintha's eyes were open now, too. 'It does sound nice,' she said lightly. 'I guess I'm mostly here for a good time, though.'

I changed the subject, not wanting to seem quite so shallow. I propped myself up on my elbow and looked at her. 'Carlos seems to like you,' I said. 'He's always hanging around you.'

'He is gorgeous,' she said. 'He just doesn't talk. I can't get anything out of him. I'm still keeping my options open, anyway.'

A shout rang out from inside the house. Jacintha and I got to our feet, our midday fatigue forgotten. It was coming from one of the rooms that we rarely used, as it was one with absolutely no furnishings or function. In truth it depressed me, the sad, grey little room, without so much as a carpet on the floor, and I made a point of never visiting it.

That day, however, it was filled with raised voices, and I half ran, half walked to get there.

'. . . greedy little *bastard*,' Candice was saying. 'You disgusting *pig*.'

Seb was sitting in the corner of the grey room, a jar of strawberry jam in his hand. The jar was huge, the kind you got if you were preparing for the apocalypse. My mother had a whole room of similar-sized jars, along with tins of dried food. The longer my father was away, the fuller it got.

Seb had other things, too. A packet of almonds, and a roll of doughnuts.

'I earned it,' he said. 'It's for *me*.'

'Bastard,' Candice said. '*Bastard*.'

The jar was half full, and there was jam on his face and on his right hand. There was no spoon or fork, and I supposed he had been eating it with his fingers.

'Stuffing your face,' Candice said, 'While the rest of us are starving.'

'We ate last night,' he drawled. 'We aren't actually starving.'

'And what did you have to do with it?' she snapped. 'Did you take out the ducks' organs, Seb? Their guts, and livers, and hearts? Did you get your hands bloody?'

By now, most of us were there, watching. Andrew was hovering close by, and I thought that he might be afraid, as I was, that Seb would get to his feet and strike Candice.

'I'm sick of this,' Seb said. 'We can get what we want from the little screens. We've been doing stupid tasks for days and not a morsel to eat. How do we know that they will actually give us food again? We have no guarantees. But I've noticed, yes, *I have noticed*, that if you speak about something that you want, sometimes you'll get offered it as a reward on your little screen. But the big screen? That's just so people can laugh at us. Don't you see? They're all laughing at us!'

I no longer thought that Seb would go for Candice, but I wondered, with genuine trepidation, if she would attack him, rules or no rules. But when she spoke, she was calm.

'We're going to do the Communal Task now,' she said. 'And we'll do as many tasks as it takes until we all eat again.'

'I'm not doing it,' Seb said.

'You are,' she said. 'You will. Who has the rope?'

Evan ran out of the room. We waited in silence until he came back. Seb continued to spoon jam into his mouth with his fingers. I had never felt so disgusted by another person in my life.

Evan returned with the rope. He placed it into Candice's hand, and Seb stared her down, though he sat on the ground. Seb was pathetic, but he was strong and tall: he wasn't frightened of her. Candice made no move towards him.

'Tom?' she said.

Tom stepped forward and took the rope from her hand. Seb's eyes swung from Candice to Tom, like the pendulum of a clock.

Ryan and I won the three-legged race. He had taken long strides with his arm around my waist, lifting me a little when I couldn't keep up. We would have been faster if we'd had more food in our stomachs. As it was I was out of breath when we crossed our makeshift finish line, and my leg was cramping. Jacintha and Carlos were only inches behind us, and we might have engaged in some good-natured taunting under different circumstances, but none of us were in the mood. When we crossed the finish line, Ryan let me lean against him, but I only stayed in his arms for a few moments, until I felt that I could stand on my own, then stepped away. I couldn't deny that I was increasingly unsure how I felt about Ryan. He was gorgeous, but there wasn't much else that drew me to him. There was a part of my brain that couldn't quite understand that I wouldn't want a man so aesthetically perfect, but I found myself tracking Sam and Becca's journey to the finish, her arm wrapped around his waist, tiny and slim compared to him. I admired the veins that stood out on his arms, the appealing slope of his shoulders.

We watched each couple cross the line, and then finally Tom and Seb, who finished last by quite a margin. Seb had struggled, at first, and their legs were bound with a great deal more rope than the rest of us had required, and far tighter too. Three quarters of the way to the finish line, Seb had fallen to the ground, crying out. Tom didn't hesitate: he kept walking, slowly, slowly, moving his left leg, to which Seb's was still bound, and dragging the other man along after him, though Seb shouted and wailed. His leg was bent at an awkward angle, and I saw his arms scrape against the concrete, leaving blood in a trail behind him, as red as strawberry jam.

As soon as Tom lumbered past the finish line, Seb limp on the ground behind him, the rest of us went back into the house. Candice and Andrew reached the living room first, and before I had caught up I heard Candice's laugh, like the ring of a bell. I could hear it as I moved from the kitchen to the hall: she was still laughing when I reached the living room. Andrew and Candice were wrapped in each other's arms, Andrew grinning into her hair, his lips pressed against her forehead. I thought that they looked like a couple in love. *Task*, the big screen read:

Banish a resident of the compound.
Reward: Meat

Once Seb had limped away into the desert plains, we went out back to get our reward. There was a case of meat – lamb and beef and veal and mutton. Enough to last us for weeks, maybe months, depending on how many people we decided to keep in the compound.

We were safe for now, but we knew what it was like to be hungry. The fear still lingered, though for lunch we ate lamb cutlets until the juice ran down our faces and our stomachs were straining against our waistbands. We had food now, yes, but we knew that we needed more.

Andrew was wearing the new whistle around his neck, and we understood that when he used it we were to meet in the living room. On another day there might have been some eye-rolling at his carry-on, but we were too jubilant to complain. We carried out tasks for the rest of the day with committed zeal, and when we were asked to banish another person in exchange for bread we voted quickly and painlessly. Before the sun was down, Sarah was out on the desert plain, too. She had cried when she read her name on the stones. 'But the food,' she said. 'I'm Food Organisation and Preservation!'

'I can do it,' Vanessa said to her, crying as well. 'I can do it.'

It worked out well, to cast out a boy and a girl: that way, no one had to sleep alone. That night, everyone had a huge slab of meat, any kind or cut we wanted, and we stuffed our faces with bread until our jaws ached. Mia took pains to assure us that her vegetarianism had just been a phase she was going through. Vanessa ran into the kitchen as soon as she had eaten and put some bread in a cupboard, freezing the rest along with the meat. She used a padlock that we had earned the other day to lock the freezer. It had been a hard day, but we had put the work in; we knew we wouldn't be hungry again for a long time, and we feasted like kings.

Seven

In the days that followed, we relaxed a little, spending more time by the pool, sitting down for long, leisurely dinners, and taking extended naps. Tom was the only one who remained highly strung. When the sun rose each morning he went out to sit by the front entrance. One morning I slipped out the back door, walked around the house, and appeared silently before him. He gave an almighty lurch in his seat, nearly falling to the ground. I had never seen him so discomposed. I watched neutrally as he straightened himself in his seat again.

'Morning,' I said.

'Morning. I'm glad to see you, actually – I have a favour to ask.'

Despite myself, I was pleased. It felt nice to be needed. 'What can I do?'

'I was wondering if you might speak to Sam.'

'About what?'

'We need to get back to doing tasks. We've been getting complacent since we got the food delivery. Sam's in charge of Construction and Maintenance. People trust him. If he would say something to the others about needing to get back on track, they'd take it seriously.'

'Why don't you say it to him?'

'He might pay it more mind if it came from you.' I considered his words. I wasn't sure if he was taunting me, hinting that he knew I liked Sam, or if it was simply because Tom was intimidated by Sam, and wanted someone else to speak to him.

'Why don't you get Andrew to say it?'

He picked up a stray piece of rubbish from the ground. I felt a dim flush of shame. Cleaning was my department, not his.

'Andrew and I aren't in charge, you know. We all have a say in how things are run. Otherwise it wouldn't work.' I watched him place the piece of plastic in the recycling bin by the entrance, then sit back down, his arms braced on his knees. The sun was in his eyes, but he looked at me directly. 'Would you mind mentioning it to Sam, then?'

Sam and I were hardly close, even if we were on slightly better terms after killing the ducks together. Becca was Sam's bed-mate: it would have made more sense to ask her. I wondered if Tom knew that she loathed him.

'I'll say it to him,' I said.

I woke Andrew, as was now our custom. He turned to Candice and kissed her lightly on the lips. She smiled and opened her eyes. Becca and Sam were still sleeping. Ryan was, too: he generally woke close to noon. We sometimes had to delay doing a task until he woke, but no one ever gave him trouble for it; no one really criticised Ryan – even the bitchier girls only ever said that he was indisputably gorgeous. He slept like the dead and could nap at any time of the day. I wondered if he'd had a stressful job, and if this time on the compound was a rare break, or if he was naturally easy-going.

My little screen said:

Task: Wear another girl's clothes without asking.

Reward: Mug

I mulled for a moment. A mug was a fairly basic prize at this point in the show. But, I consoled myself, rifling through the other girls' clothes, it would likely be a very nice mug.

Mia was closest to my size, but I didn't dare to cross her, though she had been nice enough to me recently. Instead, I took a dress from Jacintha's wardrobe, a beautiful blue midi-length tea dress, and twirled around in front of all the mirrors, and laughed a little. I then slipped on her sandals, a bit too big, but not too bad. I looked good. I had been collecting more and more rewards from Personal Tasks, and had started to look similar to how I would have on an average day at home.

I saw Jacintha later, fixing a drip in the bathroom sink, and watched her do a double take. I chewed my cheek, but said nothing. She frowned at me, but then I saw something shift in her expression as she realised that it must have been for a Personal Task. She didn't look thrilled, but she let me pass by without comment.

The mug was unexpectedly gorgeous: wide-brimmed, lilac, with silver clouds painted along its circumference. I put it in the cupboard, thinking gleefully about how drab the other mugs looked beside mine.

Everyone must have been doing a number of Personal Tasks that day, for they were all acting strangely. I found Marcus in the kitchen, holding his hand in the freezer. When he saw me he smiled painfully, but didn't otherwise move. Vanessa sat down beside me at the edge of the pool and, apropos of nothing, said hello to me in five different languages.

There was time now, too, to be with our bed-mates, and I sought Ryan out early in the afternoon, when we usually would be doing Communal Tasks. I found him doing chin-ups on a bar that the boys had installed over their dressing room. He was shirtless. 'Looking good,' I said.

'Thanks,' he said, touching back on the ground. He picked

up two enormous cartons of protein powder called Strong Stuff and used them to do bicep curls. He continued that way for a long time, his face blank with concentration, the cartons rising and falling, and I wondered if he was angling for a sponsorship deal with the brand.

When he was done, he pulled me into the bathroom, still doorless, and kissed me against the sink. I sighed into his mouth, and he gripped me tighter. Then he was lifting me and carrying me into the shower. I giggled, and he kissed my neck hungrily. He cupped my breast, and I shivered. When he lifted my dress, I stepped back, and said, 'Wait.'

'What's wrong? Don't you want to?'

'No. I mean, I do, but . . .'

He looked confused, and I leaned up and kissed him. He kissed me back, deeply, and then took his own shirt off. I had seen his bare chest every day in the pool, but it was extraordinary up close. I stroked his abs and felt his muscles twitch. He gripped my thigh and kissed me again and again, his hand creeping up higher, until I pushed him away once more.

'I thought you said you wanted to?'

'I do, I just—' The truth was I would have, if we had been on the outside. But I was worried he wanted to sleep with me for a Personal Task. It happened very rarely, and generally the public were outraged, but it still happened. A couple of years ago, an odious man named Brian had received a pool table for convincing a woman who was not his bed-mate to have sex with him. They had fallen asleep afterwards, but he got up in the middle of the night to assemble the pool table.

Ryan pressed his forehead against mine. 'I want you,' he said. He did want me, I knew that. I had known it for a while. I wanted him too, and though I kept thinking that the viewers must want me to be with him, there was still a part of me that wasn't sure. 'There's no door,' I said. 'Anyone could walk in.'

He sighed, and kissed my neck lightly, then let me go. 'You're right,' he said. 'Sorry for jumping on you like that. You've been driving me fucking crazy.'

'I have?'

He groaned. 'Are you serious? Seeing you in your bikini, day after day, sleeping next to you every night. Christ.' He rubbed his face. 'It's enough to drive any man crazy.'

We went out of the bathroom, heading towards the kitchen. I saw Sam walk up the stairs.

'Would you make me an iced coffee?' I asked Ryan. 'I want to change into my evening clothes.'

'Sure,' he said. I went upstairs slowly, so as not to seem that I was chasing after Sam. He was in the nice bathroom, putting hooks onto the wall for our bath-towels. Some of us had been complaining about certain residents throwing their towels on the ground wrinkled and damp. The towels were monogrammed, so it was easy to see who the culprits were, though it didn't stop anyone from doing it. I watched Sam from the doorless doorway, listening to the measured thud of his hammer against the nail. There was something soothing about it. I would have liked to have watched him for longer, but he glanced up after a few moments. I felt caught, as though I had witnessed something private.

'Hey,' I said.

'Hey.' He placed the hammer down on the lip of the bathtub and looked at me.

I had thought that we'd patched things up between us when we killed the ducks together. It only struck me then that it wasn't necessarily that we were on better terms – only that it had become clear to me how attracted I was to him. Watching him fix the bathroom wasn't helping matters.

'Builder,' I said.

'What?'

'Were you a builder, before?'

He smiled at me, his brown eyes warm, and I felt that things were well between us again. 'You've never tried to guess what my job was,' I said.

He shrugged. 'It doesn't do to get caught up with titles and the like. We're all equal here, at any rate.'

I wondered if he was right. If Tom wanted Sam to encourage the rest of us to work, was that the formation of some sort of hierarchy?

'Tom wants your help to get everyone back on task,' I said.

He looked surprised. 'He asked you to ask me?'

I nodded. He picked one of the towels up from the ground and hung it on the hook. I handed him another towel, my hand briefly brushing against his.

'What do you think?' I asked.

'I'm not sure,' he said. 'People are upset about the four banishments. A reprieve might be healthy. These things take their toll, I think.'

'There's still things we need,' I said, gesturing to the space behind me. I wanted better shampoo, and tea towels, and a lamp for the bedroom, and more food, and more clothes.

'Right,' he sighed.

I didn't know what Sam had been before coming here, where he lived or what job he had, or what kind of family, but I knew that he was an impressive guy. I think the same things that attracted me to Sam were the things that intimidated Tom: he was strong and smart and capable. Even though I couldn't really picture Sam outside of the compound, I knew that I wasn't the kind of person he would be with outside of the show. I wondered, though, if I might be the kind of person that he would consider being with here, even if only for a brief period.

I also knew that downstairs there was Ryan, who wanted me, and I knew that we made sense together – we were precisely the sort of couple who I would have paired together if I had been watching. And yet, I was fairly sure that Ryan's interest began and ended with his physical desire for me. I couldn't blame him; I felt the same way about him.

'Would you have sex in the compound?' I asked.

He looked up. 'What?'

'I know some of the other couples are doing it. I'm not sure about having sex with the cameras there – but, on the other hand, don't we do everything else with the cameras watching us?'

'I don't know,' he said. 'I hadn't really considered it.' He picked up another towel. 'You're thinking about it, I take it?'

'I'm not sure,' I said. 'I'm weighing the pros and cons.' I was hoping for a reaction from him. I needed to know if he thought about me, if he desired me in any way at all. I felt sure of Ryan's desire for me and it made me feel assured, and even powerful, at times. Wanting Sam but not knowing if he wanted me – it was as intoxicating as it was infuriating.

Sam's gaze rested on me for a moment, then he looked away. 'I wouldn't feel that you had to sacrifice anything for the sake of viewers, or for the sake of securing your place. If we're sacrificing more than we get, we're defeating the purpose of being here.' He paused, collecting his thoughts. 'Listen. I've been meaning to talk to you. I was hoping to get a chance to apologise for the way I spoke to you a while back.'

'That's okay,' I said.

'I didn't feel good about it. I didn't mean what I said, about our conversations being transactional. Or maybe I did, but that's okay. We're forced to be transactional here; that's the nature of the way we're living. I don't blame you for wanting to keep your options open.'

The sound of raised voices drifted up the stairs. We fell quiet and listened. It was Andrew and Tom, arguing in the living room. I had known that it was a matter of time before they fought: they were both strong-willed, but opposite in nearly every other way.

Sam and I went down to see what the fuss was. Walking down the stairs, I was conscious of Sam behind me. I let my hand skim down the length of the banister, my nails freshly painted, my fingers long and slender.

Tom and Andrew were standing in front of the big screen, squabbling. Tom wanted to do a task, and Andrew was saying it could wait. They didn't notice us standing at the door.

Andrew was nodding slowly, his hands on his hips, the picture of a sympathetic supervisor. 'Look, Tom. I see where you're coming from. But there's no need to rush everyone. We'll get to it when we get to it.'

'We still don't have a *door*.'

'We're not going to get a door from this task.' He gestured at the screen, which read:

Task: Every man and woman must reveal their professions.
Reward: Table

After reading the instruction, I looked at Sam. He met my eye briefly, before we both looked away. 'Let's put it to a vote,' Sam said. The boys looked up, startled.

'All right,' Andrew said after a pause. 'I vote to leave the task until later, after the sun has set.' He put his hand in the air and looked at Sam and me expectantly.

'I meant let everyone vote,' Sam said.

Andrew put his hand down. 'Right,' he said. He blew the whistle. Tom looked at him with irritation. It was unclear if Tom was irked by Andrew using the whistle, or if it bothered him that he didn't have one.

Eight people agreed to do the task, and six voted against. I voted against. I was curious about everyone's jobs, but I had heard Vanessa suggest that I was an influencer, and I liked the idea that that was my reputation.

When I compared everyone's actual jobs to my original guesses, I'd got only one correct: Andrew was the office manager at an IT company. Some of the jobs surprised me. Candice, who I thought might have been a model or a minor actress, worked in human resources at an insurance company. Ryan was a lifeguard, which explained his strong tan and physique. Sam was an architect. He met my eye when he said it, and it confirmed in me that I had made the wrong decision, that I should have tried harder with Sam rather than settle for Ryan. But I wondered, looking away in confusion, if I only felt this confidence about my preference for Sam now that I knew that he had a better job than Ryan. I liked to believe that such things had no bearing on my judgement, but I couldn't be sure. By that logic, I wondered if Sam liked me less now that he knew what I did for work. I looked at Ryan, who was joking with Marcus and Carlos. By all accounts, we were better suited: all beauty and no brains.

Some people's jobs were unsurprising. Jacintha was a student, completing a Master's in engineering. I had known that she was smart and felt vaguely proud of her.

I was reluctant to reveal my own job, the least interesting and the least impressive. When it was my turn to speak, I said, in an off-hand way, 'I'm in retail. I sell make-up in a department store.'

'I knew it,' Mia said.

Mia was a social worker; unexpected, as she didn't seem to like people that much. Tom worked in finance, which was a shock to no one. Susie was a waitress, and Evan was, to everyone's surprise, a professional golfer. Carlos was a personal trainer and Marcus worked in media. Becca was a student, though she phrased it as, 'Reading history at university.'

Vanessa revealed that she worked as a brand ambassador for a popular alcoholic beverage. Susie said, 'Like, you're one of those girls who goes around with expensive shots at the bar?'

'No,' Vanessa said, not looking at her. 'I am a brand *ambassador*.'

It was the most revealing information we had found out about each other and, all in all, I preferred not knowing. It felt strange to me that Evan, who spent half of his day on the trampoline and the other half inventing new cocktails, was a professional athlete. I had thought that Ryan was maybe a football player, or a boxer. It was hard to believe that he was a lifeguard: he didn't even like going in the pool that much. I'd had an idea of everyone in the compound, and, all in all, I would have preferred to have gone back to my preconceptions of everyone.

We voted again on whether or not to do another task that evening. We agreed it was enough for the day and went back to doing our Personal Tasks. I received new clothes, which were sorely needed.

In bed that night, Ryan pressed up against me and kissed me for a long time. I let his hands wander and tried to be quiet as we carried on. I was shy, though there probably wasn't much need for it. I had heard noises in the dark for a number of nights, and had attributed it to people shifting in beds, or getting up to use the bathroom. But that night, there were the distinctive noises of breathy whispers and moaning, and the sounds horrified me. I sprang away from Ryan when I heard Jacintha and Carlos moaning in the bed across from us.

'No,' I said. 'I'm sorry. No.'

He rolled away, and we went to sleep shortly after. I couldn't stop wondering what everyone's Personal Tasks had been, and how many of them had been sexual.

The next day, I looked at the others with a critical eye: their hair seemed shinier, their clothes nicer, their tans brighter. But perhaps I was imagining it.

The next couple of days unfolded in a similar way. We did one or two tasks a day. We got some useful things: a huge sack of peanuts, a beanbag, aloe vera, toothpaste, fruit. But mostly we focused on our Personal Tasks, which were getting better and better all the time. It was a happy period. We drifted around the compound, moving from the sun to the shade, showing each other our rewards, careful not to reveal what we had done to get them. If anyone received food or drink as a reward we always shared it. Evan had earned an inflatable bed, and he spent probably five hours a day floating around on it, a fluorescent drink in his hand. When he wasn't using it he gave it to Susie, and when she wasn't using it the rest of us took turns.

Tom still tried to coax us to do tasks, but Andrew insisted we needed to relax. 'We're here to have a nice time,' he reminded us more than once. 'We don't need to constantly be insouciant.'

We were free now to spend time in our couples. Better again, there was time to discuss the couples in detail with the other girls. All the girls gathered for discussions on the patio with cups of iced coffee, except for Vanessa, who had made it clear that she was 'not a girl's girl,' and instead spent her time in the gym with Tom and Ryan. Vanessa and Tom were coupled up together, and so far as I could tell the only thing that they had in common was their commitment to high-intensity weight training. I wondered if they went to bed and talked about protein supplements.

I thought that Candice seemed the most settled in her couple: she had exclusively shared a bed with Andrew since the first day, and they were undeniably close, talking and touching often. But Candice stayed coy, and only said, 'I'm happy, and that's all you're getting out of me.'

Susie was with Evan again. She wasn't sure about him, even though she had fought to get him back from Vanessa. The truth was, none of us thought that they were a good match. Evan clearly liked her, but Susie wasn't showing much interest in him. 'I can't stand to see him with anyone else, though,' she said. 'When I saw him get into Vanessa's bed I could have killed him. Obviously Vanessa's gorgeous, but she isn't any fun. She hardly talks to anyone. *I'm* fun. But,' she said, sadly, 'I don't really like him. I thought Tom might be fun, but he usually walks away if I try to talk to him. I guess I'm not insouciant enough or whatever.'

'Susie,' Candice said firmly. 'That is not how you use that word.'

In the absence of Vanessa telling us about her relationship with Tom we speculated about Vanessa's relationship with Tom.

'Tom's starting to be a pain in the ass,' Mia said. 'He never shuts up about that fucking door.'

'It's because of what happened in the desert,' Candice said. We looked at her.

'What happened in the desert?' I asked.

Candice was quiet for a few moments. I knew her well enough now to know that she wasn't pausing to build suspense: she was judging if it was worth her while to reveal valuable information. For the sake of sisterhood, she said, 'He was attacked by a wild dog.'

'I thought that the men got into a fight,' I said.

'They did,' she said. 'That was a separate event.'

'What happened to the dog?' Becca asked.

'What do you think? He killed it. But it got a nice bite out of him first. That's why he's so insistent that we get a door. He's afraid of an animal getting in.' I tried to imagine killing a dog, even a wild one. I couldn't picture it. Candice nodded at Jacintha. 'How are things in your couple, anyway?'

She sighed. 'I'm back with Carlos, but I think I'd rather be with Marcus.'

We all tried not to meet anyone else's eye. Mia was currently sharing a bed with Marcus. I thought that Mia might have looked shame-faced: she had taken Evan from Susie's bed, and now Marcus from Jacintha. But Mia had her face tilted up to the sun, eyes closed, unperturbed.

I thought about Sam. I couldn't imagine charming him into leaving Becca. If Sam changed beds it would be entirely of his own volition.

'I'll talk to him later – but I don't want to create an awkward situation,' Jacintha said delicately, trying not to offend Mia.

Mia, however, had no qualms about offending anyone, and said, 'Obviously it's his choice, but things are going well with Marcus and me. Actually, we had a *lot* of fun together last night.'

Candice rolled her eyes. 'Nice, Mia. Classy.'

Jacintha said, 'What about you, Becca?'

'Sam's a good guy,' she said. We watched with interest as she blushed. 'But – I don't know.'

'What?' Jacintha said encouragingly.

'I'm not sure if he likes me, is all.'

Jacintha stayed quiet, but Candice frowned and said, 'He seems protective of you, no?'

'Men are generally protective of me because I'm small and quiet, I guess.'

And beautiful, I thought to myself, but didn't feel the need to share the thought aloud.

'Still, it's a good sign,' Candice said.

'The thing is, I see him looking at other girls sometimes.'

'I've never seen him look at me!' Susie cried.

'Me neither,' Mia said.

'Well . . . not girls, then. Just – one girl.'

I pulled at a loose thread on my shorts, trying not to look at Becca.

'Things are so uncertain here,' Candice said when the silence had grown uncomfortable. 'It's hard to tell what's real and what's fake. It gets harder every day, actually.'

'What about you, Lily? How are things with Ryan?' Susie asked.

'Good,' I said, looking up. 'Really good.'

That night I was woken by a violent crash. When I opened my eyes Andrew was already out of bed and running towards the door. It was too dark to see properly, but I knew him by his height.

'What's happening?' I said. 'Is it a fire?' I groped beside me for Ryan, but his side of the bed was empty. Panic seized me, and then I was on my feet, bumping into a neighbouring bed and moving with my arms thrown out. I reached the door from memory and went to leave, when I felt an arm come around my waist, stopping me. 'Let me go, Ryan,' I said.

'It's me,' Sam said, and dropped his hand. 'Stay here until we know what's happening. It's not a fire. There are alarms for that.'

'But—' I said, but he only squeezed my arm and moved past me.

'Stay here,' he said. And he went.

I groped back towards my bed. 'Ryan?' I said. 'Ryan?' I could hear other voices, and see shapes moving around me. People were panicked. My mind kept thinking *intruder*, but of course there was no possibility of that, miles away from civilisation.

'Ryan?' I called again.

'Here,' he said, and I felt his hand wrap around my wrist.

'Where were you?'

'The bathroom,' he said. 'What's going on?'

'I don't know. There was some kind of noise from the front of the house.' Before Ryan could respond, Andrew and Sam were back. They left the door open, and a crack of light poured in from the hall.

'It's all right,' Sam said. 'No one's hurt.'

'But what happened?' I said.

'Some kind of animal got in,' Andrew said. 'It's gone now.'

'What?' Ryan said. 'Are you fucking kidding?'

'Well, we don't have a door,' Carlos said drily from the other corner of the room. 'It's not the most surprising thing in the world.'

'Tom was right,' Vanessa said, her voice loud and righteous. 'He said that this would happen!'

'Listen,' Andrew said, placating, 'It's late. We're not going to get anything sorted tonight. We should get some sleep, and tomorrow we'll try for something resembling a door.'

'I'll get something to block the entrance for now,' Sam said. Andrew nodded and Sam left.

The rest of us got back into bed, but I couldn't sleep: I was looking at the beds, trying to make out the shapes of people. Sam was gone, yes – but so was Tom. I slipped out and went towards the kitchen. I could hear Sam and Tom's voices inside and hesitated, listening. The big light in the kitchen was on, the one that we rarely used because of its ugly fluorescent glare, and the hum of it filled the room.

'Damn lucky I didn't get another bite taken out of me,' Tom said.

'What was it, anyway?'

'A fox, I think. You know what they're like: they don't like to attack, they just root around for food and make a mess. I came in just as it was leaving. If I had been on the lookout, I could have caught the thing,' he said. 'I'll stay up for a while, and make sure it doesn't come back.'

'If you want. I'll move the cabinet in front of the entrance. It'll do for now.'

'I can do it,' Tom said.

'It would be easier with two sets of hands,' Sam said.

'I can do it,' Tom said again. He paused. 'Who's there?' he called.

I stepped in. 'Only me,' I said. The kitchen was indeed a mess: there was broken glass on the ground, cutlery thrown around, ripped kitchen roll, a couple of toppled chairs – one broken, missing a leg. Whatever it was had got at the sack of peanuts, too, clearly, as they were all over the floor. There was a pale liquid shining on the tiles, and the smell told me that it was urine. And yet, I didn't entirely believe the scene before me. I had heard no shouting or animal noises, nor any sound of a struggle. And Tom, who had been so concerned about this very thing happening, looked perfectly composed. I stepped further inside and Sam said, 'Watch your feet, there's glass everywhere. Hold on—' and then lifted me off my feet and placed me so that I was sitting on the counter. He stepped away and I looked at Tom.

'Thank God you were up,' I said to him.

'We need to get back to the tasks,' Tom said heavily. 'It's the only way to keep everyone safe.'

'Yeah,' I said, holding his eye. 'Imagine if it had been something more dangerous. Like a wild dog.'

'You should get back to bed, Lily,' Tom said. 'You sleep so little as it is.'

'I'll walk you back to the bedroom,' Sam said.

In the hallway, Sam steered me not towards the bedroom but to the bathroom. He turned on the light above the mirror. 'Are you okay?' he said.

'I'm fine,' I said. 'Why?'

'Don't try to get a rise out of Tom,' he said. 'He's got a temper like you wouldn't believe.'

'What happened in the desert?' I asked him. Sam would tell me. I knew he would, if I asked.

'Tom . . .' he said, and then stopped. 'Tom was attacked by a dog. It bit him, pinned him to the ground. He was on his own, and he screamed for help, but there was no one there. When he found the rest of us, he was nearly hysterical. He wouldn't sleep; he was too afraid that there was something else out there that would attack. He was jumpy and started fights. He calmed down as soon as we arrived here, but he's still not someone you want to mess with. Leave him alone, Lily, and don't go looking for trouble.'

'I can look after myself.'

'I know you can. I just worry about you, that's all.'

We said nothing for a minute, and I couldn't help but admire him in the soft light, the scrape of stubble on his cheeks, the perfect cupid's bow. Already I was dreading the moment we would leave the bathroom and go back to our separate beds.

'Things will get difficult once it's down to the final ten,' he said. 'It's a good idea to keep your head down until then.' There were no rule changes in the final ten, but the rewards became notably better, and people grew more competitive. There were fourteen of us now.

That wasn't what I had expected him to say. 'I know that,' I said. 'Why are you telling me now?'

'People will try dirty tactics to stay. I think it's probably already started.'

'You think I can't fight dirty?'

'I don't want you to. You don't need to, Lily. Better to leave with your dignity than stay to the end and make a fool of yourself. At least, that's what I've been telling myself.'

I heard a movement from the bedroom. We both looked towards the door, but no one appeared. 'You go back to bed,' he whispered. 'I'll follow you in a minute.'

I walked down the long hallway with a light step. I didn't see anyone along the way, and once I was back in the bedroom it was too dark to see if anyone was missing.

Motivated by the animal invasion the night before we returned to our previous schedule of five tasks a day. We spent the first day doing relatively easy tasks; they went by quicker now that we were down to fourteen. Among other things we got a huge vat of coffee beans, and I thought that if we had that we would get by for a long time.

Two days after the animal invasion, the first task of the day read:

Task: Temporarily banish one resident of the compound until sunset
Reward: Wood

It was the task which rattled us more than any other. No one wanted to be banished, but at least if you left you left to be brought home, with someone waiting for you. It was very different to be cast out – wandering around the desert, exposed – and how long was it until sunset anyway?

Jacintha argued that we should send someone out half an hour before sunset since the task didn't specify how long they had to be gone for. Mia disagreed.

'If we do a poor job, we get a poor version of the reward. If we send someone out for half an hour we'll get a stick of wood, but if we send someone out for the day think about how much we could get. We could build a door for the entrance and the bathroom, and more besides.'

No one wanted to go, but Mia was right. We knew we would have to commit. We discussed it for a while, voices overlapping, nearly shouting over each other. Andrew blew his whistle and we fell silent.

'It's not an easy decision,' Andrew said. 'But that's why Tom and I are in charge of Task Organisation and Reward Distribution. We make the hard choices for all of us.'

I glanced around. Nobody made any sign of protest or disagreement. It was true that no one actually wanted to be the one to make the decision.

'We'll send someone out now,' Tom said.

Andrew nodded. 'It would be too cruel to put it to a vote. When the person returns, it wouldn't be right if they looked at everyone else with condensation. We need to be able to live in harmony. We'll draw lots. The person with the shortest straw goes into the desert.'

I had never been in the desert: I had woken up in the house, in my bed. I suspected I had been drugged, transported and dumped when I was unconscious; I had signed a waiver which gave permission for a wide range of things that might happen before, during and after my time in the compound. Still, I feared the desert, the same as everyone else, and as we picked our straws my hands trembled. I thought that Tom looked pale.

It was Susie. She looked in confusion at the straw in her hand, a little stump. 'I'm sorry, Susie,' Evan said, and she stared at him.

'But,' she said in confusion, 'I'm not going. You won't send me out.'

'Vanessa,' Andrew said, 'Would you fetch some food, and as much water as you can fit in a bag.'

'Not meat,' Tom said. 'Just bread. The meat will attract unwanted attention.'

'Wait,' Susie said, and her knees were knocking together. 'Wait. I'm not— you won't really send me out there!'

Andrew and Tom had already started to walk her to the southern perimeter. I walked behind them, as did Jacintha. Evan trailed a few feet behind.

'There's shelter to the east,' Andrew said. 'Get there as quick as you can. You'll need to get into the shade and out of the open.'

Susie started to cry. 'Which way is east?' Andrew pointed, and Vanessa ran up to her with a bag. Susie put it on her back, and looked at Jacintha and me as though we might step in.

Tom put his hands on her shoulders and looked at her with

a gentleness which changed his face entirely. 'The desert is cruel, but it's beautiful. You'll be back in a few hours, and you'll feel like a new woman. You'll be reborn.'

Susie was sobbing in earnest now. Jacintha came forward and hugged her, and I did the same. 'We'll have a party for you when you come back,' Jacintha said. 'We'll be so happy to see you, Susie. Think of how nice it'll be, when you're back.'

'Please don't make me go.'

We were silent. When it became clear that no one was going to change their mind, she turned and ducked under the barbed wire. She tottered away, the bag on her back engulfing her small frame. The sun flared white overhead, and we shielded our eyes and watched her go.

'Find shelter, Susie,' Andrew called. 'We'll be back at sunset.'

Jacintha and Sam were discussing how they could make doors; it wouldn't necessarily be simple. They needed doorjambs and hinges. We could manage without a handle, probably, but there would be no point in having a slab of wood blocking the entrance.

There were no Communal Tasks to do, as we had to wait until Susie returned, so we kept to ourselves. I didn't want to do a Personal Task: it felt wrong, when Susie was out there on her own. I spent time with Ryan instead. I had been worrying about us a little. Though he still seemed interested in me I knew that I would have to do more to keep him until the end. I hadn't gone further than kissing and some fondling with him, but I was anxious that he would stray from my bed if I didn't offer something more. We lounged by the pool, and I stroked his chest, trying to initiate something, but he just smiled at me and closed his eyes. Eventually he fell asleep, and I tried to think of what I could do.

I went to the girls' dressing room and looked through my clothes. While I had received a lot of clothes and jewellery lately, none of it seemed to be enough. I was tired of the outfits I had: everyone had seen me wear them at least once. I often changed several times a day depending on the heat, and sometimes just for something to do. I wondered, then, how long we had been there – weeks, surely. I felt sure that if I took the time, I could figure it out fairly simply – but it was an effort I didn't want to expend just then, and I let the thought drift away.

I again contemplated the thought of having sex with Ryan to secure my place. I hated thinking of an editor watching on in a remote office, arranging shots of bare legs sneaking out of blankets. I hated the thought of the viewers watching me. I hated the idea of Sam seeing me or hearing me. I knew that Mia had slept with Marcus and suspected Jacintha had slept with Carlos, but I wasn't sure who else had slept with their bed-mate. I worried that everyone had, except for me, and people at home were laughing at me – the frigid bitch.

When Candice came into the dressing room, she found me sitting on the floor, biting my nails and staring at myself in the mirror. She dropped down beside me.

'What is it? Has something happened?'

'No,' I said. 'Only I'm worried about me and Ryan.'

'Oh, darling,' she said. 'You have nothing to worry about. You should see the way he looks at you.' She stroked my hair, and I leaned against her.

'I know,' I said. 'That's what I thought. But I just tried to, you know, have a moment with him by the pool, and he was completely disinterested.'

'I'm sure he wasn't. He's a red-blooded man. They're always interested.'

'He fell asleep.'

'You'll have to work a bit harder, is all.' She looked at me consideringly, then went to her wardrobe. It was full to the brim: she clearly hadn't been neglecting her Personal Tasks. She pulled out a red dress and pressed it against my body. 'There,' she said. 'That should do it. Put it on, and I'll fix your hair.'

I slipped it on, gratified that it fit. I looked at myself in the mirror, turning to see myself from different angles. She was right: it was perfect. I sat down and closed my eyes as Candice brushed my hair. She told me what colours she wanted to use, and what her preferred style of contouring was. I was generally particular about how my make-up was done, but I only nodded and let her do what she wanted. Candice knew what she was doing. She dabbed a couple of products on my skin, and wiped a silver shimmer over my eyelids. 'Look up,' she said, and I did. 'Tilt your head like this.' She put her hand on my chin to steady me. Her face was very close to mine. I could see the ring of grey in her blue eyes, and the blush she had placed across her cheekbones. She leaned closer still, though she was looking at me differently now. The air between us became suddenly charged, I felt her breath on my cheek, and we watched each other for a moment. I waited for her to lean in and kiss me. I could see that she was considering it. I was considering it too. She looked at me calmly but appraisingly. When she leaned back, I knew her thoughts as if they were my own. You survived a sunrise banishment if you shared a bed with someone from the opposite sex. There was no safety to be won from being in a same-sex couple. She finished my make-up, and we let the moment go.

On my way to find Ryan I stopped by the living room, where I knew Sam would be. Even down the hallway I could hear the low pitch of his voice, the slight rumble of his laugh. There was no mirror in the hallway, but I could picture how my hair moved across my shoulders, how my gold necklace glinted against my tan; I could feel the tips of my eyelashes brush against my eyebrows. I wanted to see Sam. I wanted him to see me.

He was talking to Becca. I paused in the doorway, trying to think of some excuse to enter the room. I needn't have bothered: they were thoroughly engaged in conversation, and didn't glance my way when I stepped in. They were sitting in armchairs that faced one another, Becca shaking her head, more animated than I had ever seen her. They seemed to be talking about politics. Of course, we weren't allowed to talk about our personal lives, and before we had come we had been told that it was better not to speak about life outside the compound; it would be too easy to let a personal detail slip, which would in turn lead to punishments. They were speaking obliquely however, skirting around mentioning anything too obvious, in the same way that Candice and I skirted around saying outright what it was we wanted to receive as a Personal Reward.

'I think if ordinary people stopped working together to make things easier for the people at the top, and started working together to effect change that would benefit them— you're laughing at me,' she said.

'I'm not,' he said. 'I'm really not. Only you remind me so much of myself when I was younger. I had ideas then, too.'

Becca looked at him sitting across from her, elbows resting on her knees. I don't think that there was any attraction there, but she looked at him with a sort of directness which nevertheless spoke of intimacy. 'I think you still have ideas now,' she said. 'Only you let other people do the talking.'

'I've never known anyone to willingly give up power. Things would have had to get very, very difficult.'

'You don't think it would be worth it?'

'It's not that. I guess I can't think of a system to replace what we have. Pointing out that something is broken doesn't count as a solution.'

'I'll never understand why you let Tom and Andrew take charge,' she said scornfully.

I might as well have been invisible. It was incredible how quickly the value I had placed on my appearance evaporated. I looked stupid standing there, dressed up with nowhere to go. I tried to slip away, but Becca looked up and saw me. Sam looked at me too, then, and looked quickly away. I crossed my arms, my hands gripping my elbows.

'Hey, Lily,' she said. 'What do you think?'

'Of what?'

'Systems of government.'

'What, like, here?'

'No,' she said slowly, staring at me like I was stupid. 'In real life.'

Becca had never spoken to me in such a disparaging way. I wondered if Becca's lively conversation with Sam had made her feel that she was intellectually superior, in the same way that being dolled up by Candice had given me the strength to arrive in a room and expect to be admired. Becca was the only one among us who wanted to think about the world on the outside. I wondered why she was here if she couldn't fully commit to life in the compound. Sam was looking at me now, too. I kept my arms taut, resisting the urge to let them swing behind my back. 'I don't know. I never really thought about it.'

'You don't think about the society we live in?'

'Becca,' Sam said.

'We're not supposed to talk about the outside,' I said, my voice small. I wasn't fooling them: they knew I had nothing to say. It was hard to remember how powerful I had felt only minutes ago, standing in front of the mirror. I had never felt more foolish.

There was a brief silence in which Sam took a sip from his beer. When he placed it down Becca reached for it, and Sam moved the bottle out of reach. You had to be at least eighteen to be on the show, but I don't think anyone believed that she was really that old.

'You look beautiful,' Becca said to me. Her tone was conciliatory, as though by praising my looks my ignorance was cancelled out.

'Thanks.' I touched the necklace at my throat, then let my hand drop. 'I was just passing by. I'll talk to you guys later.'

When I walked away, I heard Becca say something low, and Sam replied, 'That's not fair. You don't know her.'

I wandered into the kitchen, where Tom had resumed his usual sentry duty near the door. He turned and looked at me.

'You looking for Ryan?'

'Yeah. I guess he's still outside.'

He stood to let me pass by, but I didn't move. I had been thinking about the fox invasion from the other night. Everyone in the compound thought I was empty-headed, but I wasn't entirely brainless. I noticed things. There was something off about his story, but I knew that Tom wasn't the kind of person who would like to be criticised or made to feel embarrassed, particularly by a girl.

'It'll be a relief when we get the wood,' I said. 'We can build a door, and you won't have to stand guard any more.'

He nodded. 'I think everyone will feel better knowing we have some protection.'

'What colour was the fox?' I asked.

'What?'

'From the other night. What colour was it?'

He looked at me evenly, in that blank way of his. 'Red, of course.'

Even I – I who had nothing to contribute to the kind of intellectual conversations that Sam and Becca engaged in – knew that there were no red foxes in the desert. I thought about the urine on the floor that Becca and I had cleaned. A good laugh, he would have had. The two of us, cleaning up his piss.

'It's good that everyone's back on track,' he said. 'With the tasks. We're working together again. We're making progress.'

'Right,' I said. I thought of Susie, out in the heat of the desert, without shade or company. My mind skittered away from the image of her out there alone, not wanting to think about it.

I walked past Tom, and as he stepped out of the way he said, 'You look lovely, Lily.'

'Thanks,' I said. With effort, I kept myself from glancing behind me to see if he watched me go.

I found Ryan in the garden. He was still asleep, so I lay down beside him and glanced behind me. Tom was no longer at the entrance.

After a while, I was jolted out of my reverie by a hand on my thigh. 'My God, you are stunning,' Ryan said.

'Really?' I said.

'Come here,' he said, and lifted me so that I lay on top of him. I melted into him, and some part of me felt reassured. He wanted me; yes, he wanted me. We kissed, and I gave in to it fully. His hands stroked me, but after a few minutes he groaned and pulled away.

'Let's go inside,' I said. 'There's no one in the bedroom.'

He bit my earlobe. 'I want to,' he said. 'But we're not going to do that.'

'Why not?'

'Because you don't want to. No, don't say anything. I know you, Lily. I've shared a bed with you for weeks now. I know the thought of having sex in a room full of other people upsets you, and I get it. I won't put you in that position.'

'Are you sure? I don't want to be a disappointment.'

He laughed. 'You're far from it. I want more than that from you. I want us to be together, now and when we're out of here. You know that, don't you?'

'Yes,' I said, though I hadn't given any thought at all to life after the compound. 'Yes, I think so.'

'I want to be your boyfriend, once we're out of here.'

'Can't you be my boyfriend now?' I said, teasingly, though I was serious. I was too stupid for Sam, and didn't Ryan and I make sense? Weren't we the kind of couple who always got together on the show?

'There's no real point,' he said. 'It wouldn't be the same. This isn't real, this compound life.' My face must have fallen, because he said, 'How I feel for you is real, Lily. None of that is fake.'

'I know,' I said. 'I feel the same.' He kissed me again, and then we both lay back in the grass, and the sky above us was a perfect, cloudless blue. Across the way Evan was miserably drinking cocktail after cocktail, until he abruptly leaned forward and vomited a fluorescent concoction over the deck. We watched him clean it up, blubbering all the while. No one moved to help.

We waited for Susie at the southern perimeter at sunset, but she didn't appear. We began to feel uneasy. Evan was pacing, a bleak look on his face. Jacintha, too, was upset. 'We shouldn't have left her out there. It wasn't worth it. Why did we agree to it?'

'We need the wood,' Tom said. 'I know it was a difficult decision. But we'll all be safer this way.'

'What if we've killed her? What if she died out there?' Jacintha asked, openly distressed. She looked around at each of us, and when she met my eye, I dropped my gaze to the ground. I didn't know what to say.

Andrew put an arm around Jacintha's shoulders. Attempting to console her, he said 'They don't let anyone die here.' It was true, of course, but people got hurt all the time, every season.

When Susie finally made it back to us, it was dark, and the temperature had dropped.

She ducked under the barbed wire, and we stood close, but didn't touch her.

'Are you all right?' Evan said. 'Are you okay?'

'I think so,' she said in a faded voice. 'Well – yes, I think so.'

We backed away and looked at her in the dim light. She was burned all the way from her face to her feet, which were encased in strappy sandals; she had blisters and blood on her heels.

'What happened?' I said.

'Nothing, really. I walked for a long time before I found shelter. It was just a couple of trees, it wasn't much at all. But there was a . . . nest of snakes. One of them came up close and just looked at me for a long time. I thought if I dropped the bag with the food and water, it would leave me alone. It was stupid, really. I left the bag, but as soon as I turned around, it started to follow me. I started running, and I thought, well, I guess I'm going to die. But after a while it stopped chasing me. I think it probably wanted me to get away from the nest or whatever. I thought there must be another source of shade, but there wasn't, and I just walked and walked, and I got lost, and I thought I wouldn't make it back. You can't really tell from here, but the compound kind of blends in with the landscape, and I thought . . . well. Anyway, I'm back.'

I expected tears, or hysterics. But she looked at us dry-eyed, smiling a little.

'Oh, Susie,' Evan said, and his voice shook. 'I'm so sorry. I'm so sorry, Susie.' He didn't move to embrace her again; none of us did. She looked strange. She didn't look like herself.

'There was nothing out there, for miles and miles. I kept wondering how you boys found us, but you had each other, I suppose. I forgot – I'm so stupid – I forgot which way was east, and I just kept walking, and I thought that I would pass out. It was so hot – you think it's hot in the compound, but it's not. Out in the sand, with no shade and no water, the heat just overwhelms you, it's all you can think about. It was more horrible than I thought it could be.'

'I'm sorry, Susie,' Evan said, and hiccupped.

'How could you do that to me?' Susie said to all of us. 'Why would you do that?'

We brought Susie inside and put her to bed after some food and drink. We lathered her in aloe vera and checked on her regularly. She didn't speak to us, but she called out in her sleep all through the night.

When we went out to look at the reward, there was enough wood to build a thousand doors: enough to build another house if we wanted.

II

Eight

We knew that Susie would be next to be banished. She had not been the same since her time in the desert: she'd become withdrawn, and buzzed like a bluebottle around the house, refusing to go outside except for Communal Tasks. We waited for the next banishment, watching on as she grew increasingly agitated, jumping at loud noises and frequently lying curled up on the ground, as she had been when we first found her by the pool. We tried, for a while, to help her, and for a while she let us. She had me do her make-up, while Candice styled her hair. As more time passed, though, she made it clear to us that she wanted to be left alone and became almost violent if approached. She put on an outfit entirely gifted from a popular fast-fashion brand and wore it every day, until her clothes began to smell and were stained and rumpled beyond recognition.

Don't worry, we said to each other with a look. *She won't be here long.*

Perhaps a week after she had been in the desert, the big screen offered an ornamental vase in exchange for a banishment. We didn't even vote: we just found Susie and escorted her to the perimeter. She seemed to know what was happening before we had reached her, and ran around the house, hiding in different places and sobbing loudly. Evan eventually coaxed her out, but she became the only resident who had to be removed by force.

Evan and Ryan led her gently to the perimeter, but the closer she got to the boundary the more upset she became, thrashing and crying out.

Evan stopped her. He was nearly as upset as she was. 'You don't want to stay, do you, Susie? You haven't been happy here for this past while.'

'I don't want to stay!' she cried. 'I want to go home!'

Still, she wouldn't take another step forward, and Evan rubbed her arms and asked her what she wanted.

'I want—' she said, and faltered, overcome with tears. 'I want my things!'

I went inside to fetch her belongings. There was a lot: armfuls of clothes, of course, but also a fridge magnet with a picture of a dog, hairspray, fluffy socks, a fake plant, perfume, primer, toner, an eye-shadow palette, make-up brushes, a small teddy bear, and a poster of a popular singer. For lack of anything else, I put her things in a bin bag.

Flanked by Evan and Ryan, she had no choice but to pass through the gap in the fence. Once she was beyond the perimeter, she froze in place. She held her arms around herself and shook her head. She was shaking all over, in what might have been mistaken for rage, but which I knew was fear. I had never found out what age she was, though I thought she must have been eighteen or nineteen. As she paced before us she looked no older than a girl.

She tried to climb back over the fence, but Tom stepped forward, his face spelling impatience.

'Wait,' Jacintha said, pointing at a spot in the distance. It was a car, approaching with alarming speed across the desert plains, dust and sand billowing in its wake. The sight of it stunned us all, even Susie, who stared, clutching the bin bag of her belongings to her chest. The car parked a hundred yards or so away from us, and a man and a woman got out and approached Susie. They were plainly dressed in shorts and T-shirts, sunglasses and hats. The sight of them, ordinary as they were, felt hideously alien and disconcerting. The woman put her hand on Susie's arm, and she followed them back to the car, wordlessly.

Of course, with uneven numbers, it meant that a boy would be gone by the next morning. It was the easiest banishment by far: when the rest of us went to bed, Evan was waiting by the door with his bag already packed.

We actually forgot to collect the vase from the delivery area. When Carlos went to get it the next day it was fractured and broken, shards missing, and a crack running through what was left.

Susie's banishment was the most difficult, but it meant that we had built up a kind of immunity to the harshness that was necessary to live in the compound. And so, a few days later, in exchange for a Persian rug, we banished two people, Mia and Marcus. The vote was difficult: people were conflicted, and it took a while before we came to a result. For the first time, I received a single vote to banish me. It hurt, but I knew that it had been Tom; I had voted for him too.

It hurt to lose Marcus. There was nobody who disliked him, only that we loved the other boys better. It was not so hard to say goodbye to Mia, who had become difficult and recalcitrant in her final days, getting into arguments with the boys and ignoring the girls. I think that everyone wanted her gone, though we were frightened to suggest it. We sat in tense silence in the living room in front of the big screen, not looking at each other. Then Candice said 'Mia,' coolly and without explanation, and that was that; we didn't even bother with a vote. She cursed us viciously as she left, her fingers slashing through the air as she told us what she thought of us. Then she went around each room of the house and packed whatever took her fancy; some things we had won in Communal Tasks, and other things that had been there when we had arrived. No one offered to walk her to the boundary, even though she was laden down with bags filled with rewards, stooped over like an old lady; we stayed huddled inside, as though afraid that she might come back.

Jacintha didn't leave the bedroom for a day when Marcus left. Carlos hung around outside the door, waiting for her to come out.

We were down, then, to ten residents: myself and Ryan, Jacintha and Carlos, Sam and Becca, Tom and Vanessa, and Andrew and Candice. The challenge was generally staying in your couple until you reached the last five; this was often the period couples began to bicker and get sick of each other. As a viewer it was fun to try to spot which couple was faking it and which were genuine. As a participant I found it no easier to discern which relationships were genuine. The others smiled to see Ryan with his arms around me, lying in the shade, and I often marvelled at how well we must have looked together. I think I would have been happy enough with Ryan if I didn't spend my hours waiting for a chance to run into Sam.

Jacintha and Sam had managed to make a door for the bathroom, and they were still working on the door for the entrance, waiting for the right parts to arrive. But as we had a considerable supply of wood, Tom decided to make a shed. The problem was that Tom worked in finance and had never built anything beyond a birdhouse. Sam and Ryan took pity on him and helped. The shed, when it was finished, was undeniably rough, but huge: about three times its original plan. Inside it we stored the excess wood, as well as miscellaneous items that we had earned in Communal Tasks. The boys were delighted with themselves, and spent a long time finishing it, and a longer time congratulating themselves on it. They congregated there often, and it irked me.

When the boys were in the shed, the girls usually gathered by the patio and drank iced coffees and complained about the boys. Vanessa still never joined us, and sometimes we complained about her, too.

'I'm happy it's just us,' Candice said. 'It means that the four of us are closer.'

Jacintha had been withdrawn since Marcus left, and often our iced coffees on the patio were the only times when I really got to talk to her. She rarely spent time in the house, and instead hid herself away in different parts of the compound. I often saw Carlos trailing around, looking for her. I found her one day by the tennis courts, staring at the synthetic green. I sat beside her and, after a few minutes of silence, rested my head on her shoulder. She didn't move, and after a while I lifted my head to look at her. 'I'm sorry that Marcus had to go.'

'He didn't have to go. He was voted out.'

Her tone was sharp, and I looked at her properly. She didn't look good: if anything she looked worse than when we had first arrived. She was wearing no make-up, and a basic outfit of shorts and a cotton T-shirt. I thought that she must have been neglecting her Personal Rewards.

'What about Carlos?'

'I don't like Carlos. Everyone keeps asking me what about Carlos? Everyone seems to forget that I liked Marcus. I really, really liked Marcus.'

'I guess it's just because Carlos seems to really like you.'

'It's because he's Black and I'm Black. I wish he'd just leave me alone.'

I tried to think of something to say. We had spoken so little recently. 'I'm sorry I haven't been here for you,' I said.

She sighed, and pressed her knee against mine. 'I'm sorry I've been hiding. I'll try to make more of an effort.' We got to our feet and walked around the edge of the compound, filling each other in on what we had been doing for the past several days. I mostly spoke, first about Ryan, and then about the rewards I had gotten. I kept waiting for her to jump in, but she stayed quiet, and when we had finished our circuit of the compound, she went inside, and I went to the pool.

I tried not to take her reticence personally; I understood that she was missing Marcus. I tried to think of how I would feel if Ryan left without me. Problematically, I felt equally panicked at the thought of Sam leaving. It was harder still because I liked Becca; she seemed to me to be one of the least conniving people here, and she had a quiet intelligence that I appreciated. It was easy to fantasise about being with Sam, but not so easy to consider how that would leave Becca vulnerable. I liked Becca, but I wasn't sure that many other people did: if Sam left her, she would surely be banished the next morning.

A few days later, when the other girls were on the patio drinking coffee and the boys were in the shed talking about whatever boys talk about in a shed, I cleaned the kitchen before checking my little screen for a Personal Task. As the original department system accounted for sixteen people we had fractured off some of the roles, but mine was the same. I didn't mind doing it; it steadied me. Someone else was assigned to clean the bedroom and bathroom, but there were grey areas of the house which I also had taken upon myself to do.

If I didn't force myself to do my chores before looking at my screen it was too tempting to do nothing but Personal Tasks, and Andrew had made it clear that, while they were necessary, an over-dependence on them was selfish.

The task was simple, as they often were.

Task: Use the outdoor shower
Reward: Pyjamas

This prospect pleased me immensely. I had, in recent days, earned a couple of lovely items of clothing. Each time I collected a new garment from my post-box, I was amazed at just how much it suited my exact taste. I felt seen: I felt like the producers knew me, anticipated my desires as they manifested. I already had two pairs of pyjamas, but would have liked another just the same.

I took my towel and went outside to use the shower. Around the front I saw Carlos and Jacintha, in the garden. Jacintha was sitting cross-legged and making daisy chains, and Carlos was lying on his side, watching her as she worked. There was no one else around, and the compound seemed oddly quiet, the slap of my flip-flops against the concrete like gunfire.

Before I rounded the corner to the back of the house, I heard the sound of running water. I wasn't bothered by the possibility of glimpsing someone showering. I had become used to seeing the others in various stages of undress, and no longer even had any qualms about using the toilet when someone else was in the bathroom. We had become close, all of us, even if we didn't truly know each other.

I didn't stop when I heard the shower running, but I should have when I heard the moaning. A second before I rounded the corner I knew what I would see, and yet still it shocked me: Ryan and Vanessa, wrapped around each other, her naked back pressed against the wall, her face tilted towards the sky. Her mouth open, catching drops of water.

I don't know if they saw me – I stood there for longer than I should have before I ran off, my flip-flops slippery under my feet, hitting clumsily off the ground. I went to the northernmost part of the compound, an unremarkable patch of trees and grass. I knew that no one would come here and I wouldn't be easy to find even if they did look for me. I tried to arrange myself next to some bushes, so that I wouldn't be easy for the cameras to notice, and though I knew that it was futile, I took some small comfort in pretending that I had some control over the situation. *Stupid girl*, I thought to myself, my head on my knees. *Stupid, stupid, girl.*

I stayed there until the sun had moved a hand's width across the sky. I wanted to stay until it was dark, but I heard Andrew's whistle and moved obediently to the living room along with the others.

'Where were you?' Jacintha asked. I shook my head. Ryan stood beside me, glancing sideways at me. Did he know that I had seen him?

'So, guys,' Andrew said. 'This one's kind of wild, but I think it'll be funny. We're all friends here, right?' A couple of people tittered, and others stood stiffly. I looked past Sam and read the instructions.

Task: Every resident must kiss each other
Reward: Barbeque

'No,' I said immediately. 'I don't want to do it.'

'It's only fun, Lily,' Tom said.

'It's stupid,' I said. 'I don't want to do it.'

'A barbeque,' Andrew said. 'Think about it!'

'If she doesn't want to do it,' Sam said, 'let's just leave it. People shouldn't be made uncomfortable by the tasks. We have everything we need now.'

Ryan said, 'It'll be funny. We'll get a laugh out of it.'

He hadn't seen me, then.

Sam was looking at me, trying to be discreet about it.

'Fine,' I said. 'Let's do it.'

Andrew and Tom debated where to carry out the task – I think they both wanted to do it in the bedroom for further intimacy, but wouldn't say so. Candice interrupted. 'We'll bring the beanbags outside to the lawn, beside the pool.' It was the best idea: the sun was softening, nearly disappearing for the day. On the beanbags, in the grass, we would be like teenagers again. At least, that was the intention.

Outside, I settled on my beanbag, trying to look relaxed. Jacintha was on my right, and Ryan on my left. He took my hand, and I let him. 'Who wants to go first?' Tom said. There was silence. We all looked at each other, and I'm sure to an outsider it might have seemed like shyness, but we were no longer shy with each other. We looked at each other as a player might eye their opponents on the field.

'I will,' Andrew said. 'It's all a bit of fun, anyway.' He laughed, and the boys laughed, too, but the girls were looking at Candice. She was smiling.

He came to her first. He kissed her deeply, and she pressed her hand against his head, keeping him there, and then gently pushed him away after a few moments. He then went around to each girl and bestowed a chaste, friendly kiss. When he took his seat, the men cheered. Candice raised a brow. She was the picture of elegance, wearing a long dress with her hair twisted behind her head. 'What are you doing? You're not done.'

He grinned. 'You want another kiss, Candy?'

'The boys,' she said. '"Every resident must kiss each other", it said. Not "every boy must kiss every girl".'

Jacintha and Vanessa started to laugh, and I joined in a little, though I didn't feel like it. The boys looked everywhere but each other, and Andrew frowned at the ground for a few moments. Then he sprang up, and said, 'No problem. Lads: pucker up, if you will.'

He went to Tom first. He clapped his hands on his cheeks, as though to keep Tom's face from moving, and gave him a loud smooch, his lips making an exaggerated smacking sound. 'All right, all right,' Tom said, trying desperately to hide his discomfort. We all were laughing now, and Andrew sauntered around the circle, a showman entertaining his audience, making jokes and professing his undying love for Sam before they locked lips. Because Andrew made a joke of it, it was easy for him and for the men who he kissed; but every other man was visibly nervous, and when they kissed each other, it was an awkward, clumsy affair. In a way, it made me feel sorry for them.

Candice was next. Every eye in the circle was glued to her. She went to Andrew first, too, and sat on his lap, and kissed him so sensually that we called out to get a room. She went around the circle then, boy, girl, girl, boy, boy, giving kisses that were not over the top, but not prim either. When she got to me, she said, 'Hello, gorgeous,' and kissed me, long and heated. I was a little surprised, but not a lot; it was like something she would do. It was a fantastic kiss, and when she broke away, she stroked my arm seductively and blew a kiss over her shoulder to me. The others had gone crazy at the spectacle, cheering and hooting. It wasn't a competition, but Candice still somehow managed to win.

No one else was nearly as remarkable as Andrew or Candice, and as the two of them sat together, holding hands, I thought that they would certainly win it: they would be the ones who got to stay here, in the end.

Some of the other kisses did stand out. I dreaded Tom's, though I tried not to show it. He hovered in front of me for several seconds, and I met his eye, but with difficulty. He leaned down and pressed his lips to mine. I felt his tongue push into my mouth. I pushed him away. The others cheered.

Next, I watched Ryan go around the circle, acting the gentleman, even with Vanessa. When he reached her, Vanessa looked at the ground, then flicked a glance up at him; I wondered if I would have realised, from her look alone, that he had been sleeping with her behind my back. I looked at Tom, and wondered if he knew, too. He was looking at her possessively, but he always did that.

When Ryan got to me, he stroked his thumb across my jaw, the way he knew I liked. He tipped my head back so that I could look into his eyes. I looked at him with all the coldness, all the disgust I could muster. I could see the precise moment that he knew that I knew. Still, he dipped his head towards mine, slowly, as though I might pull away, and I kissed him as I had always kissed him. When he pulled back he scanned my face, uncertain now. I smiled at my feet in the same demure way that Vanessa had.

Jacintha went next, then Sam. Everything depended on Sam, I thought. He kissed Becca sweetly, but briefly. He kissed the boys with the same detached seriousness with which he kissed the girls. When he got to me I saw him hesitate a little as he knelt before me, and then his lips were on mine. He kissed me a little longer than the others, but not long enough to draw any attention. But I wanted to draw attention, so I slowly, deliberately ran my tongue across his lower lip, then very lightly bit down. I felt his eyes open. He pulled away but didn't move for a moment – only a moment, but I felt it like an age – and when he turned and moved to the next person, I felt the urge to grab him, to cry at his feet and to grab at his hair. I felt mad; I felt ready to make a fool of myself, which, I suppose, was the intention of these challenges.

I waited until the end. I wanted Ryan to have to wait, and I allowed my eyes to flick over to Sam's every couple of minutes. More frequently than not, when I looked over at him he was already looking at me. By the time I rose from my beanbag, night had fallen, and we could see each other only from the lights of the pool, a rippling, blue glow around us.

I went to Vanessa first, and kissed her, only our lips touching. She tasted of watermelon. I was surprised, when I kissed her, to find that her lips were naturally plump: I had thought that it was filler. She was just naturally beautiful, Vanessa.

I went to Ryan next, and knelt between his legs. I leaned in slowly, as he had, and he whispered, 'Lily,' but I didn't want to hear anything from him. I kissed him for a few seconds, and let him feel the nothingness of it, then rose and moved on to Jacintha. I moved from person to person, delivering light pecks. I hesitated before Tom. He looked at me impassively, watching my hesitation. I didn't want to kiss him, but the worst thing that I could do would be to show that I didn't trust Tom.

I left Sam till last. I floated over to him like a butterfly landing on the brightest flower. I knew his features in the dark. His face, the little of it that I could see, was serious as he looked at me, but searching, too. I placed my hand on his cheek, and kissed him, soft but deliberate, and I felt his lips meet mine, expecting, I think, just a moment pressed together; but I placed my other hand around his neck, and kissed him deeper, and his hands came around to cup my face, and then he was tilting my head to kiss me deeper. There was some cheering, but that quieted too, when we didn't let go of each other, and our lips met again and again. Silence fell around us, thick as the cover of night. Eventually I pulled back, and saw his eyes stay on mine as I rose above him.

We disbanded shortly after, and when I saw Ryan stepping towards me I slipped away quickly and quietly, the inky darkness swallowing me. I went to the orchard, where the grass was high and the leaves swayed in the rare summer breeze. I could see the house in the distance, a lovely glow of whites and yellows. I waited there for a while, shivering. I told myself that I was hiding from Ryan, but I knew that I was waiting for Sam, because he often checked on the vegetables before we went to bed. I stood shivering, my head swinging around at every sound, but he never came. I went inside before it became embarrassing.

That night, I felt the bed dip beside me later than usual. Ryan had been in the shed for a long while, putting off our conversation. It was dark, but I knew it was him.

'Lily,' he said. I kept my back to him. He put his hand on my shoulder, and I jerked so violently that he lifted it, and didn't touch me again. After a minute, I felt him turn. I didn't sleep at all that night. I stayed in bed until I was sure that the sun had risen, and when I stepped outside the compound with my coffee I could see bushfires burning in the distance, raging and writhing, miles away from us, but moving closer, inch by inch.

Nine

Ryan found me in the wasted orchard the next day, sitting beside the bare trees, knees hugged to my chest. I had been walking around all morning, wanting to avoid him, and wanting him to find me.

He wore a sombre look that irritated me no end.

'Lily, I'm sorry,' he said. He didn't seem inclined to give an explanation, and I wasn't going to ask him for one. It was obvious enough, anyway: if he wasn't getting it from me, he would look elsewhere. Like everything else here, it was a game, a competition, no matter how relaxed and 'genuine' things looked: what wasn't yet clear was whether Ryan was the one who had fumbled the play, or if I was the one who was now at a loss. In a lot of ways, it wasn't about the fact that he wasn't faithful to me – it was about how it made me look, and how it would impact the rest of my time here.

'How many times?' I said.

'That was the first time,' he said. He looked at the ground. 'The first time with Vanessa.'

I stared at him. 'Who else?'

'Mia,' he said.

I wanted to tear at his face until my nails broke and my fingers bled. Mia hadn't spoken to me for the last week that she had been here. I thought that I had offended her in some way.

'I want to kill you,' I said. 'But probably Tom will do that for me.'

'Lily,' he said, and looked at me sadly. 'Tom sleeps around, too.'

'What? With who?'

'Sarah,' he said. 'And Mia, too.'

I turned and picked at withered leaves, just to hide my face and give my hands something to do.

'I still love you,' he said. I didn't turn. I shredded leaves and thought about the sound of people moving in the night. I wondered if he had ever had sex with her in the bedroom, then returned to me by sunrise.

'Aren't you going to say anything? I said I love you, Lily.'

There was silence for a long time, and when he spoke again, his voice was cold. 'And what was that with you and Sam last night, during the task?'

I turned to him, then. 'Are you fucking serious?'

'He's been sniffing around you from the first day. Well, he didn't claim you. I did.'

'*Claim* me?'

'The first night, when I came into the bedroom he was standing at the foot of your bed. Did you know that? I'm sure you did. Well, I knew what he was about. So I told Andrew to pretend there was something important he had to ask him. When his back was turned, I got into your bed. And I fell in love with you so quickly, Lil. Long before I said it. Don't you know that?'

'You won't share my bed again,' I said. 'If you come near me tonight, I'll kill you.'

I went to the patio, where the girls were drinking their coffee, and he went to the shed, where the boys were already waiting. The girls were wearing sunglasses, but I saw Jacintha register something amiss as I walked towards them. She held out her arms, and I went to her, and she stroked my hair as I cried. I told them what he had done, leaving out any mention of Sam for the sake of Becca.

Candice was troubled. 'I thought that you two were so strong,' she said. She frowned, and while I knew she was talking about my situation, she was thinking about her own.

'Tom, too,' I said. 'Vanessa, Sarah and Mia.'

'Shit,' Jacintha said. 'Sarah was Vanessa's best friend here.'

'Did he mention anyone else?' Becca asked.

'I think three girls is enough, no?' Jacintha asked.

'No,' Becca said. 'I mean, did Ryan mention anyone else cheating?'

'No,' I said.

'If Ryan was sleeping around,' Becca said, 'Anyone could be, really.'

Eyes flickered around the circle.

Jacintha turned to me and said, 'Oh, honey. I'm sorry this happened to you.'

Becca said, 'We should banish him. When the next challenge comes around.' We looked at her. Her face was set, serious.

Candice said, 'I agree.'

I hated Ryan: I wanted him struck from the earth. But the thought of him being banished was a blow that I wasn't sure I was ready for. He had been my person for weeks now: he was my safety net, and my comfort.

'I don't know,' I said. 'Isn't that petty?'

Jacintha looked at me with a trace of pity. 'Where is Ryan now?'

'In the shed,' I said.

'In the shed,' she said. 'With the other boys.'

'So?'

'So, what do you think they're talking about?' Candice said, impatient. 'I'm sorry, Lily, but they won't be singing your praises in there. You're the one who broke it off with him.'

'He cheated on me!'

'Lil, I *know*. But that's not what they'll be saying. You told him you wouldn't share a bed with him? That puts him at risk. They'll get rid of one of us before they get rid of one of them.'

I couldn't keep up. There was a part of me that was stuck on the other day – was it yesterday? The day before? – when he had asked me to be his girlfriend, and I had lain with him in the sun. But they were right: things moved quickly here. We were becoming less sentimental with every passing hour. We were looking for reasons to get rid of people.

'Fuck,' I said, and Jacintha stroked my hair. I leaned against her. It felt good to be close with her again.

'The next challenge,' Becca said. 'I'll tell Sam to vote him out. He won't mind; he hates him. And the four of us vote for him too.'

'That's five votes,' I said. 'We need at least one more.'

'I'll talk to Carlos,' Jacintha said. 'He'll do as I say.'

'Six votes,' Candice said. 'I can't say it to Andrew: it'll tip off the others. But six votes will do. Fuck Ryan; he doesn't deserve to be here.'

We glanced behind us, to make sure they couldn't hear.

'But,' Candice said, 'if we vote Ryan out, Lily will be vulnerable that night. We can't have you kicked out Lil, for something that he did.'

'She'll have to find someone else to share a bed with,' Becca said, and I looked at her sharply. She was so young, Becca. I had yet to find out what age she was.

'Who?' Jacintha said.

'Tom, of course,' Becca said.

The thought of sharing a bed with Tom filled me with dread. I knew I wouldn't sleep for a minute, his massive form lying inches away. The girls were looking at me expectantly, and I knew that they were right. If someone had to go, let it be Vanessa.

'We'll need to try and get the vote done as soon as the task comes up on the screen,' Jacintha said. 'We can't let the boys talk to each other.'

'The sooner you talk to Tom, the better, Lily. Do you want me to find you an outfit?' Candice said.

'I'm not going to *seduce* him,' I said. 'Jesus.'

'It's all right,' Jacintha said. 'There are other ways.'

'I don't like Tom,' I said. I didn't say what I really meant, which was that there was a part of me that was frightened of him. I didn't say it, but I think that the girls somehow understood.

'Don't worry,' Candice said, and stroked my hand. 'He's next.'

The producers must have known what we were about, because after a simple task in exchange for teabags, the screen read:

Task: Banish one person from the compound

Reward: Tennis racquets

We had received a net for the tennis court in a Communal Task, and balls that one of the boys had won in a Personal Task. The racquets would mean that we could play proper games.

'We should get it over with now,' Candice said.

Andrew sighed. 'I don't know. The banishments are always hard, but worse now that there are only ten of us.'

'I fucking love tennis,' Jacintha said, and Andrew brightened.

'Yeah?' he said, smiling. 'Me too. Willing to take me on? I'm pretty good.'

'Sure,' she said. 'Let's get the racquets, and we'll play.'

He looked at the position of the sun low in the sky. We generally didn't do tasks in the evening any more, but it was too tempting an offer to let pass us by. He pointed at the shadow of a nearby tree. 'When the shadow of that tree reaches the red bucket. That's when I'll blow the whistle.'

When he walked off, Jacintha said, 'That's not long, Lily: it might be an hour, but it could be a half hour. I need to go and talk to Carlos and make sure his vote is secure. Go find Tom. Quickly. People will be planning to make sure they don't sleep alone tonight. Get to him before someone else does.'

'I'll find Vanessa, and make sure she's occupied,' Candice said. 'Becca, go to Sam and tell him to keep quiet about the vote.'

I didn't see Tom anywhere, but I couldn't be spotted rushing around looking for him. I walked casually around the perimeter of the house, and then to the gym, and eventually found him in the grey room. He had put up shelves. It was amazing how much better the room looked, actually. There was a chair and a desk, giving the room the feel of a home office. He had placed some things on the shelves, and on closer inspection I saw that they were all his own personal items – a model of a ship, a potted cactus, a print of a gangster movie, a toy soldier. When I found him, he was sitting quietly in the swivel chair, gazing at them.

'Planning on moving in?' I asked. He looked up and smiled.

'Can I help you with something?'

I realised that I had been stupid: if I revealed to Tom that I knew that they were going to vote me out, and instead was planning on voting Ryan out, he would tell the others. I didn't need to talk to Tom; I needed to talk to Sam.

'Go on,' he said. 'If you ask nicely, I might think about saving you.'

I left without another word and I saw the look of surprise on his face before I turned my back on him. I went from room to room. Sam. Where was Sam? I couldn't trust Becca to convince him to keep me: in a way, it would be against her best interests. I saw Jacintha in the living room with Carlos, and she nodded at me as I passed. Carlos was accounted for, then. The swelling in my chest eased a little, but adrenaline pumped through my veins, urging me to move faster. Sam. Find Sam.

I found him by the back of the house. He was mending a part of the fence that was broken. Outdoor maintenance was technically Ryan's jurisdiction, but when something went wrong people usually asked Sam or Jacintha to fix it. When I got to him I was panting. He turned and saw me.

'What is it?' he said. 'Are you okay?'

'Did Becca find you? Did she tell you?'

'Tell me what? What's happened?'

Silently, I cursed her. 'They're going to vote me out,' I said. 'The boys are going to get rid of me. I don't want to go. Please, Sam. I don't want to go back.' Without warning, I burst into tears. He pulled me into his arms at once, my head tucked under his chin, and I let him murmur soothing words in my ear. I might have stayed where I was, but the sun was moving, and the shadows grew longer. I pulled away and looked up into his face.

'It's okay, Lily,' he said, and wiped the tears from my face. 'Of course. I'll vote for Ryan; of course I will.' He pressed his lips against my forehead. 'You have no idea how glad I'll be to see him gone.'

There was more I wanted to say to him, and more, I think, that he wanted to say to me, but the whistle shrilled, and I jumped.

'It's okay,' he said. 'I promise.' I felt relief, but also a sense of vindication, of triumph: he wanted me there. It meant something; it had to mean something.

We went to the northern circle together, and Ryan looked at us and shook his head, as though I had done something disgusting.

'All right,' Tom said. 'We all know how this works. We'll make it quick and painless.'

'We don't want to say goodbye to anyone. But we have to be practical here,' Andrew said. 'We have to consider the value we can bring to this place – and our lives here – by doing tasks.'

We went to the barren, dusty plain to cast our votes. I looked at everyone scratching the initial on their rock, my eyes settling on Becca, whose head was bent, and working away at her rock. I had been a fool to kiss Sam like I had yesterday; I hadn't thought of Becca, watching on. Stupid, stupid, stupid.

We placed our stones in the pile. Crouching down, with a rock labelled R in my hand, I prayed that there were enough people there who liked me enough to keep me.

Andrew and Tom bent down and read the initials on the rocks. After counting, Andrew looked up.

'Ryan,' he said.

Beside me, Candice squeezed my hand – not a supportive squeeze, or a gentle caress: she took my hand in victory.

I hated Ryan for what he had done to me, but when I saw the look on his face it didn't please me as much as I thought that it might. I saw Tom looking over the stones again, double-checking. The boys all looked at each other. I knew that Ryan must have asked them all to vote for me, and probably Vanessa too. I wondered if he'd thought to ask the other girls. I knew what they were thinking: which of the boys had turned on Ryan, and why? We all went forward to look at the stones: six Rs, and four Ls. I saw Becca look at the stones, then walk away from the group, keeping her back to us.

Ryan was staring at the pile, unmoving.

'Better get going before it gets dark, Ryan,' Candice said. She walked past him and into the house.

We usually gave the person space to gather their things in private, but when we reached the house, Ryan said, 'Lily, can I talk to you?'

I went into the bedroom with him, but he just stood there and looked at me, and I began to gather up his things. The boys' dressing room was to the left of the bedroom, and I had been in only once, before the boys had arrived. It was disgusting now, with clothes all over the floor, shaving cream and toothpaste on the sink. I opened Ryan's wardrobe and started to cram everything into a bag, the same one he had come with, that he had travelled with across the desert. He appeared beside me.

'Please,' he said. 'Let's talk.'

'Would you still want to talk if I had lost the vote? You'd be watching me go out into the desert without a word.'

'That's not true,' he said. 'It's not. It's not true.'

I looked at him. He was incredibly, undeniably gorgeous. I could see why I had gravitated towards him at the beginning – I liked beautiful things – but there was a part of me that was ashamed by the shallowness I had shown in betting on him with so little thought.

'Wrap up,' I said. 'The desert is cold at night.'

Only the men went to see him off. Jacintha, Becca, Candice and I went to our dressing room and burned a candle to clear the negative energy. 'Justice,' Candice said, over the flickering flame.

I don't know where Vanessa was, only that she wasn't with the boys, nor with us.

When the boys arrived back, Candice blew out the candle. 'Did you talk to Tom?'

'Not properly,' I said.

'You need to find him now,' Jacintha said. She glanced outside. We would be going to bed soon.

I didn't want to speak to him in the house – I wasn't sure how our conversation might go, but I knew that I didn't want an audience. I can't say how, but I felt certain that if I waited alone by the pool, Tom would show up. I was right: I was there for only the length of a brief birdsong before I saw a movement to my left. He had, incredibly, a cigarette, which he smoked with clear relish.

'Where did you get that?' I asked.

'Personal challenge.'

'What on earth did you have to do to get it?'

He gave me a look. It was silly to even ask, I knew. I tried to think of something else to say, to get him relaxed, to make him trust me a bit more, but I couldn't come up with anything. I grappled for a few moments with my own uselessness.

'That was a clever thing that you did,' he said. 'Ryan walked right into that one.'

'You would have done it, too.'

He nodded and pulled from his cigarette. 'I didn't think that you were that cold, though. He was your man from day one.'

'Don't you know why I did it?' I said.

'That's your own business.'

'I did it because he cheated on me. With Vanessa.'

He looked at me, his face blue under the lights of the pool. 'That's not true.'

'It is.'

'Liar.'

'I'm sorry, Tom. I saw them. Just yesterday.'

He was quiet, thinking, piecing things together. I didn't feel sorry for him; he had done the same, and worse.

'It was in the shower, out the back. He had her pressed against the bricks, and he was biting her neck.'

'Be quiet.'

'She had her legs wrapped around his back: she has such lovely, long legs. Probably the longest of anyone here, I'd say. I kept thinking that her back must be sore, the way she kept moving against the wall.' There was a terrible, vindictive thrill to finding myself capable of rattling Tom, but I still had to quell the fear that I would push him too far.

'Be quiet, I said.'

'Did you notice scrapes across her back? Or maybe a bruise on her neck?'

He stepped towards me, and I glanced towards the house. There would be someone nearby to hear me shout, surely. But he only threw his cigarette on the ground and looked at me. We were very nearly nose to nose. He was not tall: we were almost the same height.

'Tom,' I said. 'I don't want to be the one to go tonight. I've been faithful.'

He stared at me a while longer. The pool lapped lightly beside us. I thought of Becca, on that day weeks ago, maybe months ago, when he held her under the water.

'Will you help me?'

He continued to look at me in silence, and then said, 'Say please.'

'No,' I said. 'I won't beg. I'm only asking you to help me, just this once.'

He nodded, a brief bob of his head. 'I think that you have this idea that I don't like you. But I was one of the six who voted to get rid of Ryan. I kept you in.'

'What?'

'Ryan was bad news,' he said. 'He had no drive. I think in a day or two people will have forgotten that he was even here.' He picked up his cigarette and went inside. I saw him pause outside the door to put his cigarette in the bin.

The girls waited in our dressing room for Vanessa to go to bed, before Jacintha said, 'Well?'

'He'll do it,' I said.

'Don't worry if you're on your own at first,' Candice said. 'The banishment isn't decided until sunrise. A lot can happen in a night, here. The dark will help.'

I went into the room, guided by the dim light filtering through the open door. When the others came in and closed the door the light was gone, and it was with great trepidation and terrible loneliness that I went to my bed, now empty. I lay down, and felt my heart thumping against the mattress, so loud that I thought the others must have been able to hear it.

I looked around and saw the faint outline of the other four couples in their beds. No one said goodbye to me, but no one ever did as nothing was certain until the night was finished. And it was easier, too, in the night, to pretend not to know what was happening. You slept, and forgot.

I wished I could see properly. I sat up and looked at Tom's bed until my eyes adjusted to the dark. Vanessa was there, lying on her side. Tom sat up too: I could make out his bulky figure well enough. He raised a hand, palm facing towards me. *Wait*, I think he meant. Or was he waving, in a mockery of a farewell? I looked to the other beds. I thought of what Candice had said. *A lot can happen in a night, here.*

I looked to her bed, and though I couldn't see anything

but a mass of bedclothes, I could hear faint whisperings and noises that a man and woman make in the night. I thought that Jacintha and Carlos were talking, or maybe they were asleep. I couldn't see anything from Sam and Becca's bed.

The girls' encouragement seemed a distant thing now. I felt entirely alone, more than I ever had in my life. If Tom was telling the truth, someone I'd trusted had voted against me. I knew Carlos the least, but I thought that he had voted for Ryan as he had stood apart when the boys had said their goodbyes. Jacintha I was confident of. Candice, too, I thought I could trust. Sam had surely voted Ryan out.

Of course it would be Becca. If I was gone, she wouldn't have to worry about Sam straying. I can't say that I blamed her. I would have done the same, if I had thought about it.

I tried to imagine what it would be like to go home. The endless talk of the wars, and the masks that we wore in the cities and big towns, and the dreary grey skies, and evenings in front of the television. I couldn't stomach the thought of waking every morning and hating it, all of it: the flavourless brown cereal that was supposedly good for gut health, the coffee that hadn't had time to cool, the walk to work, that stupid hill that I hated – the feeling in my thighs just before I got to the summit, and knowing that I'd make the same walk the next day over and over. And the standing around, day after day, waiting for something to do and then resenting being given work to do. The chitchat, the mould on the wall of the breakroom, the hole in the ceiling above the staff toilet, the insects that gathered there, and then the commercial sheen of the display counters. Going home and dreading doing it again the next day, and still never having enough money. And what was the point of it anyway, if I was never going to be able to afford nice things, or have anything worth owning – when we all would probably be dead in twenty years, maybe thirty if we were lucky? What did it matter to wake up at the same time every morning and wear the same clothes and try to eat more protein but less sugar, when an earthquake or a tsunami or a bomb might end it all at any minute? Or maybe we would all continue to boil, slowly but surely, in the mess that we pretended was an acceptable place to live.

I don't know how I slept, but I slept. I knew from watching the show that when a person was banished at dawn they were woken by a vibration in the mattress; if you didn't rise immediately, the mattress heated to the point of burning. When the mattress moved, I gasped wildly, thinking that the sun had risen and I was being banished, but a hand pressed against my mouth and I realised that I was safe. Nevertheless, I stayed tense until the hand was removed.

'Shh,' he said. 'It's okay. It's me.' I turned onto my other side. Sam was lying beside me.

He was beside me. I would be okay. Yet my limbs were trembling, my fingers clutching at the sheets. 'Lily?' he whispered.

'I thought I was going to be banished,' I said, my voice barely there. 'I thought I was gone for sure.'

He hesitated, and then reached out, his hand touching mine. His hand was warm and calloused. It shocked me, how nice it felt; just his hand on mine. 'I couldn't stand to be here if you were gone. It wouldn't mean anything if you were gone.'

I put my arms around him, and he held me tightly. My relief at the fact that I was staying was equal to the joy I felt that it was Sam beside me. I said his name over and over, quietly, like a sigh. At last, I stopped trembling. I felt solid and secure, pressed against him, his hand warm and heavy on the small of my back. I heard him give some small, happy sigh – could feel it against my neck. I think I knew exactly how he felt from that small sound alone. I wasn't afraid to close my eyes: I knew that he would stay where he was, that he would be there in the morning.

I pulled back to look at him. I couldn't make out much, but still: it was Sam. I could see the slight motion of his chest rising and falling. I put my hand on top of it. Then I leaned forward and kissed him. He was warm, and tasted sweet. I moved my leg so that I was pressed fully against him. I made a noise low in my throat, and his tongue licked against the top of my mouth. I moved my hand from his chest to his underwear.

'We don't have to,' he said.

It touched me to hear him say it. I had told myself, before, that I wouldn't have sex on the show – but I realised, with his body pressed against mine, that I wanted to do it all differently with Sam: I wanted it all to feel real. With Ryan I had been constantly overthinking us being together, weighing up my own desires against my desire for safety; but with Sam I let myself be motivated purely by instinct. I pulled off my T-shirt, let it fall to the ground behind me. 'I want to,' I said. His hand reached forward and stroked the softest part of my arm. I kissed him again, but he made no further move. I drew back again, worried that he had come to me only out of sympathy. 'You'd rather not?'

He gathered me close to him and whispered my name against my lips. I cast a glance up towards the ceiling, and he bit my neck. I couldn't believe how good it felt: I couldn't believe that this had been available to me, that Sam had been available to me, and I was only experiencing it now. I didn't know what time of the night it was, whether the others were asleep or awake still. I could only think about Sam, his hand stroking me, the urgency of his lips. He pressed his forehead against mine, and I clutched urgently at his shoulders, as though I could pull him closer still. He made a noise I had never heard him make before, and I felt, in having heard it, that he belonged to me in some small, essential way.

I woke again when it was still dark. Sam was awake too: I could see the white of his eyes, the soft shine of his pupils as he looked at me. I looked back at him, then, feeling as though I was in a dream, I reached out and moved the piece of hair that fell across his forehead. He watched me as I pushed it back. I left my hand there and traced the line of his eyebrow. I felt perfect, untouchable happiness. I didn't need to speak, or to communicate with him in any other way to know that he felt the same.

Sam fell asleep shortly after, but I drifted in and out of sleep for a while, until a movement across the room woke me fully. There was a weak cast of light from the early dawn drifting through the skylight, and I looked over to see Tom stepping down from his bed. He walked over to Becca's bed, where she lay next to Vanessa. Tom had kept his bed empty: I supposed he thought that I would come to him. He touched Vanessa's arm, and she opened her eyes and stared at him. He jerked his head towards the door, and she slowly got out of bed. She walked towards the girls' dressing room; he followed behind, a hand on her back. I waited a few seconds and then slipped out of bed, walking quietly to the door of the bedroom, where I could hear them talking.

'You've packed your things?' Tom asked.

'Yes,' Vanessa said, her voice small.

'You can keep the things I gave you, even though I earned them.'

There was a beat of silence.

'You aren't going to say thank you?'

'You're forcing me out. Sorry if I don't feel particularly grateful.'

'Do you know,' he said, 'if there weren't rules in place, I'd knock some manners into you. You're a slut, Vanessa, and now everyone knows it.'

I heard him take a step back towards the bedroom. I stepped back, too. 'You're not going to walk me to the boundary?' she asked, her voice high. I thought about how frightening it would be to go into the desert with only the dim light of early dawn.

'No,' Tom said. 'I'm tired. I'm going to bed.'

I stepped deeper into the shadows and let him pass by me. He walked back to his bed and stopped briefly by the bedside locker. There was a stuffed teddy sitting there, which Vanessa had won a few weeks ago: a cheerful-looking polar bear. Not daring to move, I watched Tom lift it and consider it, its white fur glowing in the dark room. In one quick motion, he ripped its head off, and dropped it to the ground. Then he got into the bed where Becca lay alone, curled on her side like a question mark. I knew that she was awake: I could see her fist, tiny and white-knuckled, clenched around the blankets.

Ten

With Vanessa gone there were eight of us left in the compound. It made carrying out Communal Tasks very easy, and for a time we gathered five, six, seven rewards in a day. Even if it was only a simple reward, we received a vast amount of it now, or a very high-quality version. The compound was now truly thriving. We had enough food to last us for months — it was good food, too: marinated meats, a range of vegetables, fruit, snacks, and dried goods. We had so much food, in fact, that we used one of the empty rooms beside the kitchen as a food pantry. We visited the pantry often, not just when we were hungry, but to look at all that we had amassed. Anyone would have been impressed. We now had an impressive array of alcohol, which we kept in the kitchen: beer and wine and champagne and gin. And there were no longer only tasks to do to pass the time: we had a functioning tennis court, a blue plastic slide that led into the pool, goalposts for football, a basketball hoop, a dance floor, a karaoke machine, mats and pouffes for yoga, and enough beauty products for a salon. It was up to each batch of contestants what they wanted to leave behind and what they wanted to take back with them. Looking at the compound, I thought that I would want it to stay just as it was. But I had the feeling, too, that if – when – I had to leave, I would be reluctant to leave behind all of the things that I had earned.

Sam and Jacintha were committed to their roles maintaining the house, and now helped Carlos with Outdoor and Pool Maintenance, too. We had working doors for the bathroom and the front of the house, and we'd used some of the leftover wood to secure the fence that marked the perimeter. There was still a great deal of it left, most of which was stored in the shed. The shed, though I didn't like it – it was too much the boys' domain – was now our Cave of Wonders, as more and more rewards spilled in; the spare rooms on the bottom floor had filled with things and still there wasn't room. We kept a lot of our rewards, therefore, in the shed, and at any time of day there was usually one person there, looking over the things that we had received. It was a varied collection: tools, lamps, a drum set, yards of fabric, a snow globe, a toy plane, a stuffed bear's head that we all hated but didn't want to throw away. I wasn't immune to its draw – in fact, I went three or four times a day myself, to look at the gleam of the lawnmower, or the hardwood deck chairs, or the sports equipment, or the boxes of fairy lights that we couldn't find the right place for. There was a chocolate fountain we kept for special occasions, and fancy wine glasses that we kept for the same reason. Of course, there never actually were special occasions, as every day was the same as the last – but there were days when we needed a boost, and it felt like the same thing.

I felt shy with Sam following the first night we spent together. I worried that he had come to my bed out of a sense of obligation, and that he felt that I had thrown myself at him in an effort to keep him from straying. I wandered around the northernmost part of the compound for most of the morning, cursing myself for making a simple thing complicated, and yet unwilling to face him. When my feet grew blistered and red, I walked back to the house and ate a bowl of cereal in the outdoor dining area. A few minutes passed, and he came and sat beside me, sliding over a cup of coffee. I thanked him and said no more: absurdly, I felt as though I might cry.

He said nothing either, and the silence became protracted. I could see some of the others in the distance, Andrew engaging Carlos in a water fight while Jacintha watched on.

'Lily,' Sam said. I looked at him. The sun was in his eyes, and his expression was grave. 'I need to ask you something.'

'Okay,' I said. In the distance, Andrew pushed Carlos to the ground and sat on his chest. Jacintha had drifted away. I watched them as you might watch dogs in a park.

'Do you regret last night?' he asked.

'No,' I said. 'Do you?'

'Of course not. But, Lily – I'm older than you. You were in a vulnerable position. I don't want you to think that that's what I intended to happen.'

'I wanted to,' I said. I looked away, towards the pool. 'I wanted to since the night with the ducks.' When I glanced back at him, I saw that he was gazing intently at me.

'I think that the way we're living now,' he said slowly, careful not to break the rules and mention that we were part of the show, 'preys on the idea of desire. It amplifies it to the point of absurdity. You have to find someone to share a bed with, or you're out. You have to make someone want to share a bed with you, or you're out. And then they throw these tasks and rewards at you, and you keep living in this uncertain state, lurching between wanting and having. I think that must affect all of the decisions we make here, don't you?'

I didn't understand what he was getting at, and tried to hide my uncertainty.

'What I mean to say is – I liked you before all that. I liked you immediately. You were quiet, but I could see you taking everything in. I thought you had everyone figured out from the first day. But I know how things get here. I don't want you to feel like you have to do anything with me to keep your position here. I'd make sure that you were safe, no matter what the circumstance is.' I thought briefly of Becca, sharing a bed with Tom. He had been cold with me all day, walking past me when I had said good morning and watching myself and Sam get coffee with a look of disdain. There was no jealousy, I knew; Tom didn't want me – only he was displeased that he had offered help, and was turned down.

'You think I slept with you to keep myself safe?'

'No – no, I don't think that. I'm saying that for me, it's real. That's all.'

A slight wind lifted my hair and brushed against my neck. Across the compound, beyond the boundary, the desert sand shifted in the breeze. 'It's real for me, too,' I said. He looked at me, and smiled, shyly at first, and then more fully, wrinkles forming by his eyes. He took my hand and kissed it.

He led me to the garden and showed me the vegetables which were starting to sprout and would be ready to eat in the coming weeks. Jacintha and Sam had planted a large number of crops over a wide span of land; they were sure that not all of it would make it, Sam said, so they were overcompensating. Even with an irrigation system, the climate was too unforgiving for much to grow, but they checked on it constantly. He seemed almost shy as he told me about it.

'Whenever they're ready, I'll give you first pick.'

'Thanks,' I said, oddly touched. 'What can I eat first?'

'The lettuce, maybe, if it ever does come to be something.' He met my eye, at once bashful and intent. 'I have this very strong desire to feed you the food that I've grown. Isn't that strange? I've never had that thought before.'

I sat beside him in the dirt, careful of the crops. 'I should have chosen you on the first day.'

He smelled earthy, but not dirty. He put his hand on my knee, and I felt the same thrill that I had felt the first day, when we had walked beside each other and his arm had brushed against mine.

'It's okay,' he said. 'Everything was uncertain then.'

We were quiet for a little while. I could hear the faint call of distant birds. There was a small amount of ash near the perimeter, blown over from the bushfires.

'I used to see you walking around the compound,' he said. 'I'd be in the orchard, or doing something in the house, and when I caught sight of you, even just for a second, I'd feel out of breath.'

I felt a vague sense of shame, knowing that Sam had been available to me. 'I always go for the Ryans. They make me feel safe, but I still end up getting hurt.'

'Do you think,' he said, then stopped and smiled in a self-mocking kind of way. 'Do you think that you would have come to me, if I hadn't come to you? If Becca had gone, would you have come to my bed?'

The question saddened me, because I knew that it was justified, and that Sam knew that it was justified, too. It wasn't that I didn't care for Sam – but rather than fixing a situation that made me unhappy, I tended to hang around and wait for someone to fix it for me.

'I don't know,' I said.

Sam pulled me against him and stroked my hair. To my infinite relief, I had received peroxide and hair dye in a Personal Task, and my hair was a fresh, bright blonde again. I'd had to insult Carlos's mother to earn it; he had looked hurt, and baffled, but I would have insulted his mother a thousand times over, and the mother of everyone in the compound, if it meant having my hair back as it had been.

'Things will only get more competitive the longer we stay here,' he said. 'Particularly the final five, if we make it that far.'

'We'll make it to the final five,' I said. 'We'll be the last two, me and you.'

He smiled a little but shook his head. 'I don't care about making it to the end.'

I looked at him in shock. 'Well, why are you here, then, if you don't want to win?'

'Lily,' he said, almost sadly. 'I stayed for you.'

'Sam,' I said. It was strange – even as I rejoiced in the realisation that he could now be mine, I wanted more: I wanted to know that he wouldn't grow bored and find someone else. I thought, in a brief moment of unease, about the trampoline that I had wanted so desperately as a child – that maddening, all-consuming desire to possess something that I didn't have – and how quickly I had tired of it, how soon after I was looking for something new to covet.

'Listen,' he said seriously. 'I'm not going to be another Ryan. I won't treat you badly, and try to be rid of you if it suits me. Things will get more brutal here, Lily, but I would leave before I had to hurt you in any way.'

'Neither of us are leaving. Look at this place – look at what we've done. Why would we leave?'

He was quiet for a long while, and I let my eyes wander along the boundary, the fence and the sparse, dry bushes that surrounded the compound, and back to the shed, our Cave of Wonders. Even Becca, the least materialistic of all of us, couldn't resist its draw, though she preferred to call it 'the warehouse'.

'Maybe we could do it,' he said finally. 'We could stay here and build a life for just the two of us, at least for a while.' The longest anyone had stayed had been six weeks after everyone else had gone. We could do that; that, and more.

'Of course we could. That's what all of this has been leading up to.' I thought of all the rewards we would have won by the time the others had left: how well stocked the compound would be, how easy it would be to spend our days here.

Just then, the irrigation system started up and we were cast in a light shower of artificial rain. I wondered if it was set on a timer, or if the producers had turned it on to create a romantic moment for us. Within seconds, my hair was damp. Sam smiled at me, and I smiled back. He moved a piece of wet hair behind my ear and stroked the line of my jaw.

The whistle blew, piercing through the silence.

'Why aren't you in charge?' I asked. 'You'd do a better job of it than Tom and Andrew.'

'I'm happy to help out where I can, but I don't want to be the one to make the rules,' he said. 'I don't think that we necessarily need anyone in charge, right now; I think they both like to feel needed, Andrew particularly. I'm not sure what they even do, Andrew and Tom.' The whistle blew again, high and shrill as a bird's cry. We went inside.

I had enjoyed life in the compound from the beginning, and if anyone had asked me I would have said it was the relationships I had forged that I enjoyed the most. It wouldn't have been a lie, but it wasn't entirely the truth either. Up until this point, what I'd truly enjoyed doing most was completing the Personal Tasks. Seb had been right: if you spoke about something that you wanted, you were often offered it as a reward. This meant that we spent a great amount of time sitting around talking about material things. Sam wasn't partial to those kind of conversations, but I could sit speaking with Candice for hours under the shade of a tree. It would have looked greedy to simply sit around and say, 'I want, I want, I want,' and so we tried to work our wishes into our general conversation.

'It's so warm,' I would say. It was surely the statement that we uttered the most, but it didn't stop us from saying it again and again, day after day.

'Boiling,' Candice would say.

'We should go inside, to the bedroom, where there's air conditioning . . .'

'Mmm. Shame to go in, though. It's such a beautiful day.'

'It would be easier to sit out if we had a fan, I suppose. A little hand-held fan.'

'You're right. A battery-operated fan.'

'That would be incredible. We could bring it with us everywhere.'

'Not too big or heavy. Just a little thing that you could hold in your hand.'

'And not the black ones that look like a television remote. The white ones are nicer, don't you think?'

'Much nicer. I love the colour white. Actually, I was thinking just this morning about how a white linen dress is the most elegant thing a woman could wear. Don't you think?'

And so on.

I loved that part of it. It was so simple, really. When I thought of all of the hours of work I would have had to do at home to earn enough for a high-quality white linen dress, I wanted to laugh. Two days' work, it would have cost me. In the compound, I only had to drink a mouthful of expired milk, and it was in my postbox within minutes.

All of that's to say that, despite how much I loved the Personal Tasks and rewards, it wasn't the best part of life on the compound any more. Now that was Sam. When I had watched the show, I sometimes thought that they were liars, the couples mooning around, hand in hand, talking about how in love they were. But I saw now how it was. When I woke in the morning and saw his face resting on the pillow next to mine, I thought I would die if we were ever separated. I knew he felt the same: if we were occupied in different parts of the compound, he would always find me after an hour or two. I told myself it was the first flush of love: that we had spent weeks wanting to be together. I didn't let myself think that it was the nature of the show to isolate us so that the connections we formed were all-consuming. It would have been a miserable, lonely experience otherwise.

The fear of loneliness affected everyone, even Tom. I had been napping in my bed one afternoon, to escape the worst of the heat, when I heard him puttering about in the boys' dressing room. From where I lay, I could see his reflection in the mirror, combing his hair. He was looking well. His hair had grown to a fashionable length, and his clothes had improved in recent weeks. He had a gold signet ring on his little finger which he twisted as he eyed his reflection. I wondered if he sat with Andrew and manifested his rewards like Candice and me, or if the small screen simply anticipated his wants.

I watched him with curiosity. I had never seen him take such care in his appearance. He looked almost nervous. He sprayed a generous amount of cologne in the air around him, then stepped out of the dressing room and into the bedroom. I closed my eyes and pretended to sleep. I heard him go down the stairs, and into the sitting room.

'Oh – hi,' I heard him say. I crept out and sat at the top of the stairs.

'Hey,' Becca said.
'What's that you're doing?'
'Crochet. I'm making a headband.'

I rolled my eyes. Of course Becca would make her own headband, rather than try and get one from her Personal Tasks. We scarcely spoke to each other at all since Sam moved to my bed. We no longer cleaned together: I did the morning and afternoon, and she did the evening and night shift. I tried not to miss her quiet, calming presence: she had tried to get rid of me – but it was difficult to think of Becca as conniving, or vindictive. Sam checked up on her often, and although she was cool with him they still spoke every day. Despite myself I worried at times when I saw Sam and Becca speaking together. I had trusted Ryan implicitly, until the very last minute.

'Nice,' he said. 'Colourful.'

There was silence for a little bit, and I wondered why Tom was bothering. Everyone knew that Becca hated him.

'I got new sheets this morning,' he said. 'Egyptian cotton. Eight hundred thread count.'

'Okay,' she said.

'I put them on our bed already. They're a pale orange colour – I'm not sure how you feel about orange . . .'

There was another silence, and I thought that I would have liked to have been a viewer at home, seeing their conversation from all angles. I would have killed to have seen Becca's face.

'It should be more comfortable, anyway.'

'Nice sheets won't make me comfortable in that bed.'

'Things don't have to be so . . . strained between us. I want to look after you.'

'And why do you think I want you looking after me?'

'I just – just mean that . . .' he said and stopped. It was incredible to hear Tom discomposed. If I had been a viewer, I would have rewound to hear him stutter again. I would have played it over and over. 'I mean that I want—'

'And while we're on the topic,' she interrupted, her voice

quiet but sharp, 'I'd like you to stop bringing me breakfast in the morning. I can get my own breakfast.'

'Becca,' he said, in an oddly stern voice, as though he was chiding her for bad behaviour. 'You know I only want—'

'I'm not interested in what you want. Now, could you leave, please? I want to work in peace.'

I thought that he would go outside, but he stepped back into the hall, and started up the stairs. I didn't have time to move: he saw me sitting on the top step. I could smell his cologne from here. I smiled at him. He turned and went outside, and I didn't see him for the rest of the day.

The girls no longer met on the patio for iced coffee, and I didn't see Jacintha as often as I once had. I spent so much of my day with Sam now, making up for lost time, and while I knew that she didn't care for Carlos, I sometimes saw them engaged in serious, urgent conversations. They would stop speaking if anyone approached, even me. I hadn't spoken to her in a while, and I wondered, with a feeling of terrible sadness, if she no longer wanted to be my friend.

I found her by the swings one afternoon, and sat next to her, pushing myself off the ground and swaying lightly.

'Hey, you,' I said.

'Hey,' she said curtly.

'You okay?'

'Fine.'

I swung for a bit, not high, just enough that the tips of my feet brushed against the ground. It was too hot to be out, but I'd grown more tolerant of the extreme temperatures. My skin had been porcelain when I arrived, but now I had a light tan all over. There were times when I looked in the mirror and didn't immediately recognise myself. My hair had grown an extraordinary amount, so that it now hung down to my waist. It was frizzy and damaged from the heat in the first couple of weeks, but after earning products and sprays it was now luscious and full; my skin was glowing, and the teeth-whitening strips that Vanessa had left behind made my smile whiter than I had thought possible. I now had an extensive wardrobe of clothes – things I never could have worn at home: crochet bralettes, tiny denim shorts, fabulous dresses that we wore in the evening, linen trousers, scarves that we wore as tops. It was a pleasure to dress every day. I used Vanessa's old wardrobe space to hold my shoes.

When I glanced over at Jacintha, I saw that she was staring at me. 'What?'

'I said, where have you been?'

'Oh, just in the gym with Sam.'

'I hardly see you any more.'

'That's not true. We did two tasks together this morning.'

'You know that doesn't count, right?'

'Is something the matter?'

'No. I just need someone to talk to, is all.'

I dug my feet into the ground to keep the swing still. 'What's going on?'

'It's Carlos,' she said. 'I just don't like him like that.' Her voice cracked, and there were suddenly tears on her face. 'I miss Marcus. I wish he hadn't gone.'

I went to her and hugged her. I rubbed her back and said soothing words. When she pulled away, she wiped her face and looked away, to the house. 'Carlos asked me last night to be his girlfriend.'

'What did you say?'

'I said I didn't know. He was nice about it, but I can't lead him on. I don't know what I'm doing here any more.'

Part of me wanted to tell her to forget about Marcus and stay with Carlos until we made it to the final five, but I wasn't sure that I would have listened if she had told me to stay with Ryan. I held her hand. She glanced north, to the sparse line of vegetation. 'How long do you think we've been here now? I've lost track. I don't know why they don't give us a clock, or a pen and paper. It's cruel. Don't you think it's cruel?'

'We don't need those things. Just like we don't need phones or televisions. We're better off without them. And besides, we have so many other nice things.'

'I don't know if I do have nice things,' she said. 'I have *things*, sure. Do you know, they keep sending me wigs? Long and straight. One of them was pink.' She touched her hair, which she usually wore naturally. 'I wore a black one for a little bit. I keep dropping hints for things – a bonnet, conditioner that works for my hair, darker concealer. But then I kept getting gifted these clothes – stuff I'd never wear. When I put the stuff on, I don't look like myself.' She looked at me steadily. 'I look like a Black version of you.'

'I'm sorry, Jacintha. I'm sorry they did that.'

'There wasn't even a Black person on the show for the first three seasons. I don't know how much this feels like progress.'

I didn't know what to say. I felt a surge of guilt that I hadn't spent more time with Jacintha recently. She was my first and truest friend there. I squeezed her hand. 'You know I'd be lost without you here, right?'

'I don't know,' she said tiredly. 'I don't know if I get the point of it any more – to build up relationships only to see them leave, and worse, to be secretly happy when they go because it means more for yourself.'

'That's not how I see it. I think that we learn to value each other, is all.'

She said nothing. I pointed at the flowers that were blooming a little bit away. 'Look,' I said. 'You did that. You and Sam. You've made this place so beautiful. This is our home, now.'

She looked at me for a long time, her eyes scanning my face. 'This is not our home, Lily.'

Later, I checked my little screen.
Task: Break or destroy another resident's Personal Reward
Reward: Dressing gown

I checked that there was no one else in the southern wing of the house, then went into the grey room. The room was now more or less a shrine to Tom's possessions, and I looked with interest at the things that he had earned in the last few weeks: a shaving brush, one of the old-fashioned ones that look like a make-up brush; a cleanser; sun cream; a belt; boots; cologne; a bottle of whiskey, and a leather wallet with his initials stitched along the side. I checked the wallet. It was empty, of course. There were also items in the room which belonged to all of us. We had earned a gold frame that no one presently had use for, and had put in the shed until we earned a print to place in it. But it was not in the shed: it was there, on Tom's desk, still empty. Looking around, I saw a few other things that we had earned in Communal Tasks, placed on his shelves as though they were his.

I found his collection faintly ridiculous, and yet it was the part of him that made the most sense to me. I liked having things, too.

On the top shelf, there was something long and white. I picked it up and dropped it immediately in revulsion. It was a bone.

'From the beast that tried to kill me,' Tom said from the doorway. I jumped, and cursed myself for reacting. 'I kept it with me. It wasn't easy to get, I can tell you that.'

'The beast? You mean the dog?'

'Not like any dog you've ever seen.' He stepped inside. 'What do you think of my room?'

'It's not your room. We all live here.'

'Of course, of course. You know what I mean.'

He opened a cupboard and took out a record player. It had a vinyl record on it already. He lifted the needle and set it down, carefully, reverently. Music spilled out. It was beautiful, a clashing of cymbals and a frenzied whirlwind of reeds and strings, one note rushing past another.

'Do you know classical music?' Without waiting for my answer, he said, 'I'm a big fan. It was a real treat for me when I got the record player. I'd had the vinyl for weeks, but of course it's no use without the player. Some people think that classical music is soothing, but I find it incredibly exhilarating. I like living here in the compound, but I have to say it became a lot easier when I had this record to listen to. I had to sleep with Mia to get it. I'd like another record, though. God knows what I'll have to do to get another one as good as this.' His eyes lifted to mine.

'Good evening,' the voice said. 'It is forbidden to reveal Personal Task details. Punishment will be administered before the sun rises.'

I saw Tom look around him, his eyes wide, as though the punishment might come at once. Or maybe he was looking at his possessions, to make sure that they were still safe. He left, nearly at a run, and when I couldn't hear his footsteps, I took the needle from the record player and lifted it, so that the music stopped. It was deathly quiet without it. I kept pulling until the needle broke, and came off in my hand.

Everyone was restless, pacing in front of the big screen, as though it would give some indication as to what punishment would be inflicted on Tom. 'It won't be all of us, though, will it?' Becca asked, sitting on the couch. 'It will just be Tom who's punished?'

I wondered, not for the first time, if Becca had watched the show before. 'If just one person breaks the rules, only that person is punished. If two or more people are involved in rule-breaking, every resident is affected.'

The others drifted out, and then it was just Becca and me, alone. 'What will it be, I wonder,' she said, her brow furrowed in thought. She sat with her hands folded neatly in her lap, looking somehow studious, as though she was puzzling out a maths question, or drafting the opening of an essay.

'Becca,' I said, interrupting her thinking. She looked at me. 'Has Tom tried anything with you?'

'No,' she said. 'But he let me know that if I try to betray him, I'll regret it.'

This was the first time we'd spoken alone since Sam had switched beds to be with me. I felt that, as the jilted one, Becca was obliged to hate me, while I was obliged to be demurely magnanimous. 'I'm sorry that I put you in that position,' I said. She gave me a blank look, and it occurred to me that Becca disliked me long before I had taken Sam from her.

Andrew came back into the room, eyes on the screen. 'You know,' he said, 'I reckon that if everyone's milling around anyway, we might as well do a Communal Task. It's not a big one, but we can get it out of the way.' He blew the whistle, and the others trickled in.

Task: Every resident must reveal the details of their first kiss
Reward: Yoghurt

'We don't even need yoghurt,' Jacintha said.

'Always better to have it than not,' Andrew said. We almost always did a task if food was involved, as we all remembered the hungry days. Nevertheless, no one looked enthusiastic. Andrew glanced out the window, to where the sun hung low in the sky. 'I'll tell you what,' Andrew said. 'I reckon it's probably closeish to five o'clock. Why don't we go out to the beanbags, sit in the sun, and have a beer? And while we're at it, I'm going to tell you about poor Kiley, the girl who was unfortunate enough to be my first kiss.'

We brought the beanbags out, and it was surprisingly perfect: the beers, the sun, Andrew making everyone laugh. He erased the tension so easily, so artfully, that everyone was loose and relaxed within minutes. Everyone except Tom, who kept twitching and surreptitiously looking around, as though waiting for his punishment to present itself.

As we told each other about our first kisses, I thought about how much I loved it here, and how proud I was of the life we had built together. We didn't even go in to get our reward or check the big screen until it got dark. That's how nice it was.

When we did go back inside, the screen read:
Task: Banish a couple from the compound
Reward: Hot tub

I tried to keep my face blank to hide my excitement. Tom and Becca. It would solve all of my problems. With the two of them gone, I could live peacefully here. I wouldn't have to look over my shoulder for Tom, and Sam wouldn't have to check on Becca all the time.

Andrew said, 'I don't know about this one, guys. It's late; we could just go to bed, and there'll be a new task in the morning. We've had a nice evening. Why ruin it. Right?'

Candice nodded thoughtfully and said, 'I mean, the more people there are, the longer we all get to stay here.'

'How great would it be to have a hot tub though?' I said and laughed. The others looked at me, considering.

'Lily,' Sam said quietly. I ignored his look and continued.

'When it's hot during the day we could cool off in the pool, and then at night when it's cold, we could unwind in the hot tub . . .' I trailed off. Candice and Andrew shared a brief look.

'All right,' Candice said. 'Let's go to our voting spot.'

'We don't need to vote,' Jacintha said. 'Carlos and I will leave.'

We stared at her, mute with shock. 'No,' I said.

'It's okay,' she said. 'He and I have discussed this already. We've been looking for a time to go. This makes sense.'

'We've had a nice time,' Carlos said, 'but it's time to go now.'

'Now, hold on,' Andrew said, looking alarmed. 'Let's talk this through.'

'Jacintha,' I said. 'You can't go. What are you talking about?' I was crying. Not a couple of tears glistening down my cheeks, but an ugly cry – my face involuntarily scrunching, gasping noises coming from the back of my throat. Panicked, I said, 'We don't need to do the task! We don't need a hot tub!' She wrapped her arms around me and hugged me tight. We stayed that way for a few heartbeats, and I cried into her shoulder.

'Please,' I said. 'We started together. Don't go.' Although Jacintha and I had only been together for minutes before we found the other girls, I had always felt that we had been closer because we had woken together.

'I'll miss you,' she said, and her eyes were wet but she wasn't crying. 'I'll find you after, on the outside, all right? I promise.'

Before I knew what was happening, the others said their goodbyes, and Sam held me as I continued to weep.

Carlos said, 'If it's okay, we don't want to be walked to the perimeter. We'll let ourselves out.'

It was by far the hardest farewell of the compound – not just for me, but for everyone. Sam and Jacintha had been friends too, and he hugged her tightly while she told him how to keep the pests away from the roses, and when to change the soil in the basil plant. Andrew and Carlos had been close, and though Andrew tried to be businesslike, I thought that his eyes were wet when Jacintha and Carlos walked off. I saw Becca watching Andrew's discomposure with interest.

I went to the living room and sat on the couch. Sam sat beside me and held my hand. When the screen turned green, I sobbed anew. Soon we heard a scraping and grunting from outside and knew that Tom and Andrew were moving the hot tub around to the front of the house. I stayed on the couch with Sam while he rubbed my back. I told him about Jacintha before he had arrived, how she had fixed the sheet to the doorframe, and how she had wiped my make-up the first night. I talked about her for a long time, and he listened quietly. When I was done, he said, 'We could leave too, if you wanted?'

I shook my head and cried harder. 'What good would that do?'

After a long time, I heard the sound of water bubbling, and male voices. Sam got up and opened the window blind. Andrew and Tom were sitting in the hot tub, arms around the rim, looking pleased with themselves.

'Those two think they're personally responsible for every reward,' Sam observed. Andrew saw Sam at the window and waved. Sam opened the window and called out, 'Having a nice time?'

'Join us,' Andrew called. He spotted me behind Sam and said, 'Come on, Lil, you too!'

I shook my head, and Andrew looked slightly chastened. He stood and said, 'I suppose it's time for bed anyway. It's been a long day.' When he stepped out he was pink all over. He grabbed his monogrammed towel and headed back into the house. Tom stayed where he was. The hot tub had purple lights, and he was cast in their glow.

Sam closed the blind. 'Let's go to bed,' I said. He nodded, and kissed me lightly, but I pulled him down for a longer, deeper kiss. He kissed me again, and asked if I wanted a glass of water first.

'I'll get it,' I said. 'I'll be up in a minute.'

I went into the kitchen, where Becca was sitting at the table, drinking herbal tea. Since she shared a bed with Tom, she usually tried to stay up as late as she could. I said nothing as I filled my glass of water. Probably she knew that I had been aiming to banish her and Tom, but I didn't particularly care any more.

Apart from the sound of the water from the tap it was very quiet, until the sound of Tom's screams tore through the silence. I ripped the curtains open and saw him struggling to climb out of the hot tub. When Andrew had got out he'd looked slightly flushed. Tom was lobster-red. The water was bubbling angrily, and the more he moved, the more he splashed himself and screamed anew. Eventually he threw himself over the top and landed in a heap on the deck, a raspy groan escaping his mouth, his hands scarlet and twitching. There was literal steam coming off of him. Andrew came running through the house. When he reached Tom, he put a hand under him, then promptly ripped it away, wincing at the heat of Tom's flesh. I went out too and turned off the hot tub. I looked to see if there was a trace of anyone having been there, or a remote mechanism. For the first time I felt frightened of the producers. What else could they do?

The others came out. Candice got the first-aid kit, and Sam helped Andrew carry Tom to bed. I found the aloe vera, and left it by Tom's bed, but after that I went to the wardrobe and put away some of the clothes that I had been leaving on the bench. I didn't feel inclined to fuss over him. Becca remained in the kitchen, drinking her tea.

Eleven

Tom stayed in bed for the entirety of the next day, and most of the day following that too. It meant that we couldn't do any Communal Tasks. Not that anyone particularly wanted to. We kept to our couples, and I saw hardly anyone apart from Sam for most of the time. We brought our beanbags to the pond, and spent long hours there, retiring to the shade when the nylon material became hot to the touch. We talked a lot about how it would be if it was just the two of us at the end. Sam was shy about the idea, but I had been thinking about it constantly. From the way that he spoke, I gathered he assumed we would stay for a week or two after everyone else had left, as a way to enjoy spending time together. I didn't tell him, though I hinted, that I wanted to stay as long as possible. Before I had even come here, I had fantasised about making it to the end. When I watched the show and saw the people building up the compound, or changing things, I planned what I would do in their place. It was different when you were actually there, of course. Although I had adjusted to the heat, I was tired often, even when I had done nothing all day. Still, I had no desire at all to leave.

When Sam was gardening, or fixing things around the house, I had plenty of time for Personal Tasks, and consulted my little screen often. I got some fake plants, which I put in the bedroom, though Andrew pursed his lips a little. I got nail varnish, the kind I sold in the shop but could never afford myself, and put on coat after coat after coat. I found Candice and did her nails too, out on the patio. When I finished, she held out her nails and admired them. She smiled at me then, and said, 'I always knew we would be good friends. I'm sad that Jacintha is gone, though. I liked her a lot.'

I nodded, not trusting my voice, and she looked at me with sympathy. 'I know it's been difficult,' she said. 'But things will be better soon. There are only six of us left. One more gone, and then the rules will be lifted.'

I nodded again. It was exciting, even if the idea of talking about our lives outside the compound felt disconcerting.

'Listen,' Candice said, and lowered her voice. She took my hand in hers and held it tightly. Her fingers were long and slim, the varnish on her nails smudging as they pressed against my skin. 'Andrew and I have been talking. We're going to be here until the end, but neither of us wants to win and live here alone. That's kind of sad, I think. We're going to stay as long as we can and win as many valuable rewards as we can, and then, when we've had enough, we'll go. But we both agreed: it wouldn't be right to kick everyone else out. We have enough things here to last us for months and months, probably. We wouldn't have to do any tasks; we wouldn't have to banish anyone. We could just live here in peace and have a simple life. We want you and Sam to stay. Just the four of us. What do you think?'

Up until that moment, genuine friendship with Candice had seemed out of reach, but now it felt like a gift I could hold in my hands and admire, like one of our treasures in the shed. I knew too we would work well together as a group. Candice and Andrew were the opposite of Sam and I, in the best way: whereas I was passive, Candice was authoritative, and while Andrew had great vision for the compound, it was generally Sam who was able to realise his ideas; Andrew couldn't hammer a nail into a wall, but Sam had built the shed, almost entirely by himself. 'That sounds incredible,' I said honestly. 'We wouldn't have to worry about anything if it was just the four of us.'

'Exactly. And we get on well too. We could be like a little family. More fun that way. And if anyone wants to leave and go back to their old life, there's nothing to stop us. But we won't banish anyone. We'll live free, without the screens.'

'It sounds perfect,' I said.

We looked out on the gardens, which were blooming and magnificent, and the shed, tall and proud, and the pool, glinting and glimmering. *Mine*, I thought.

That evening, when the sun had sunk beyond the horizon, and a chill had started to creep in, I heard Tom's voice calling for me. I was lying on the couch with Sam, and he said, 'I'll go with you.'

'Don't bother,' I said. 'He's asked me ten times today for aloe vera. I'll be back in a minute.'

Tom called my name again, and I was surprised to realise his voice was coming from the grey room. He had been recuperating in the bedroom until now. I hesitated for a minute. I had forgotten about the record player. But he must have heard my step falter, as he stepped outside and saw me. 'Come in,' he said.

His skin was pink now, though his hands remained raw and angry. He was pointing to his record player. 'Do you know what happened here?'

'No. Did you get tired of listening to that same shitty song over and over?'

I didn't see the blow coming. Before I registered the sting of the slap, I registered the heat of his hand. I staggered, clutching my cheek.

We stared at each other for a moment. The slap had surprised me, but I think it had surprised him, too. He took a step towards me, and I didn't wait to see if he was approaching with a pacifying or threatening gesture. I spat at him, and he glanced down at the glob of my saliva that had landed on the collar of his shirt. He struck me again, this time knocking me off my feet. I felt a tooth move in my gum. I gagged.

'You're an idiot, Tom,' I said. 'It's against the rules to hit another resident.' I started to laugh then, loud and not at all like my usual laugh, but it felt good, so I laughed louder. His expression stayed flat, though I knew that it bothered him. 'What will they do to you this time, do you think?'

He crouched in front of me, then reached out and touched a lock of my hair that had come from my ponytail. He twirled it around his finger, gently, almost tenderly, and then took it in his fist and ripped it from my head. I screamed: at the pain and at seeing the lock of my hair in his hand.

Strangely, it seemed to disturb him almost as much as it disturbed me. He stared at the piece of hair, then let it drop to the ground. He put his hands in the air. 'I shouldn't have done that,' he said. Although his demeanour was placating, my body screamed out with terror, and I let out some cry of distress, skirting backwards. He took a step towards me, frowning. Suddenly Sam was there, and Tom was thrown against the wall. I tried to say *stop: don't*, but I made some strange babbling noise instead. Sam punched Tom in the face, once, twice, three times.

'Stop!' I said. Where were the others? Didn't they hear us? Didn't they care?

Tom groaned. His head had hit the wall, and he looked strange, his eyes rolling back in his skull. He brought his hands up to try to strike Sam, but they appeared pathetic, cooked as they were. Some sense seemed to come to Sam at last, and he stepped back and let Tom stumble away. He came to me, hands gripping my arms, his eyes wide. He gingerly touched the stinging point on my head where my hair had been, and I gasped at the pain of it. When he pulled his hand back, I saw that there was a trace of blood on his fingertips: not a lot, just a smudge. I wasn't really wounded, I reminded myself. Only a chunk of my hair was lying on the ground beside me.

'Are you all right? Lily, are you all right?'

The voice said, 'Good evening. Fighting between residents is forbidden. Punishment will be administered to the compound before sunrise.'

I gripped Sam's shirt, my hands shaking. Tom groaned in the corner. Andrew appeared, white-faced under his tan.

'What did you do?' he shouted. He looked unlike himself; he looked wild. He wasn't looking at the boys: he was looking at me. 'What did you do?'

All six of us waited in the bedroom for whatever punishment would be doled out. We were all thinking of possibilities, but not speaking them aloud. I was remembering a few years ago, when a group had to go naked for a whole week. The punishments were there, of course, to keep us in line, but they usually also had some entertainment factor for the viewers.

Tom sat on the edge of his bed and jumped at every noise. His face, which had already been pink and tender, was now bloody and puffy. Candice sat on my bed and dabbed my swollen face with antiseptic. When she was done, she used her nicest products on me, her moisturiser and eye cream and serums. I hadn't looked in the mirror; I couldn't bear to think of how I looked.

Candice glanced at Sam and shook her head. 'You shouldn't have hit him. I know why you did it, but still. We're all in a mess now. God knows what will happen.'

'Don't be angry with him,' I said. I worried, even through the fear of the punishment, that she wouldn't want to share the compound with us any more.

'I'm not angry with him.' She turned to Tom. 'It's his fault, of course.'

'Andrew,' Tom said. 'Tell your woman to be quiet.'

'Watch it, Tom,' Andrew said. He stood up from his bed, and took a step toward him, but no further.

'Let me be clear,' Candice said to Tom. 'Your hours here are numbered. Tomorrow, the next day, the day after – there's going to be a banishment. And when you're gone, Lily and I are going to turn your stupid little man-cave into a yoga studio.'

'You wouldn't last a day without me, sweetheart. Don't you know I'm the reason we have most of the things in this compound?' It was rare to see Tom so openly cruel, or so ruffled. He was frightened; he was very, very frightened.

Candice laughed, and Andrew frowned. 'They're Communal Tasks, Tom,' he said. 'Everyone worked for them. You and I helped organise the process, that's all.'

'Tell me the truth,' Tom said. 'If we hadn't come, how long do you think you girls would have lasted here? Well, Candy, what do you think?'

'Two punishments in three days,' she said. 'Because you're too much of an ape to follow basic instructions.'

'Don't call me an ape.'

'Look at Lily. Does that make you feel good – seeing the blood on her face, you *sick fuck*?'

He looked at me. 'I shouldn't have hit you, Lily. I know that. But let me ask you all something. What does everyone think that Lily brings to the compound? Why is she still here? I've seen her do some of the girls' make-up, sure. Is that going to help us last the rest of the year here? Any idiot could do it, anyway. We all know the reason that she's still here is because there was a list of men who wanted to fuck her. Well, now it's just Sam, and how long will that last?'

Candice reached Tom before Sam could. She slapped him, hard enough that his head snapped back. 'Don't you dare talk about her like that,' she said.

Tom stepped forward. Andrew pushed him away, a violent shove, and Tom reacted worse to the push than to Candice's slap.

'Everyone needs to calm down,' Andrew said. 'We're in enough trouble as it is.'

Becca spoke, sitting cross-legged on the bed furthest away from everyone. I think it was Sarah's bed, once. She had been sitting quietly for the whole altercation. 'Why should the rest of us be punished when it was only Sam and Tom who fought? I say they both sleep outside and be banished at sunrise.'

Andrew lost his temper for the second time in one night. 'Jesus *Christ*, everyone!' he yelled, and hit the wall behind his bed. The sound wasn't particularly loud, but it filled the room just the same. 'Can't we just make an effort to get along? If we play our cards right, we could be here for a long time. But not if we're at each other's throats! What's happened to all of us? Can't we just live in peace?' His voice rose until it was booming around the room, his face red, the veins on his neck standing out. 'We need to do better!'

Candice spoke calmly. 'Tomorrow we'll do as many tasks as it takes until there's a banishment. There are too many of us here to live comfortably.'

When Tom spoke again, he was composed. 'I agree,' he said.

Candice only turned away from him and went to bed.

I lay stiffly for a long time. Whenever I was near sleep, I imagined my loose tooth falling from the gum and down my throat, and would jolt awake. Every time I woke, Sam's arms would tighten around me, and he would murmur something reassuring in my ear.

I don't know if I next woke from the sound of someone else moving, or the distant shouting, or if some primitive part of me responded to the threat of danger. My feet were moving before I realised I was awake. Sam was gone; so was Tom. I knew what was happening before I was outside: I could see it, and I could smell it. As I ran through the kitchen, there was a sea of red and orange out the window, and I felt the heat as soon as I stepped out the door.

I think they had only meant to set the shed ablaze, but the grass was so dry and caught fire quickly, spreading quicker than I had thought possible. I watched the scene unfolding before me with a horror so profound I scarcely knew myself. The grass was ablaze, the gardens and the crops, even the hedge surrounding our compound.

Tom was standing by the shed, trying, I think, to find a way to get to it. Andrew ran out of the house, a streak of white, screaming, 'Get away! Get away from the shed!'

The two of them were pulling at each other, Tom nearly insensible. While they were shouting, Candice ran from the back of the house with the fire extinguisher. I knew that there was another one, but it was Evan and Susie who had been in charge of Safety and Wellbeing, and they had moved it around a couple of times. I stood frozen, overwhelmed, as the blaze engulfed the orchard and swept towards the area where Jacintha and I used to lie in the afternoon shade. I saw the controls for the irrigation system, and ran towards them, the heat terrible, lacerating, overwhelming. Then I felt hands on my arms, gripping me tightly, and Sam was there, his brown eyes reflecting the red flames. 'It's not safe,' he was saying, loudly, insistently. 'You need to get back.' I struggled free somehow, and reached, at last, the tap that turned the sprinklers on. I hadn't realised just how quickly the metal had heated, and as soon as I touched the tap I cried out, snatching my hand back to my chest. But by then, Sam had understood what I was doing. He pushed me aside, his hands bunched in the sleeves of his shirt. With one quick wrench, he turned the tap, and the sprinklers came on, water showering us. In the lazy heat of an afternoon, the sprinklers had seemed perfect, luxurious, but now, with the fire crackling and roaring closer and closer, they provided a near-irrelevant drizzle. 'There's a hose by the delivery area. Go back to the house,' Sam called, and then he was gone, racing back the way we had come.

I made my way towards the shed again, where the largest fire was still raging. 'There are sandbags,' Candice shouted. 'Out the back, they just delivered them!' It was the only time that we had something delivered that we didn't earn. They knew they had done wrong: the fire had burned beyond what the producers had intended. Or maybe it was their intention, but they still worried that we would die.

I ran, Becca alongside me. The sandbags were heavier than they looked, and we had to drag them together.

I'll never forget Tom's face as he stood before the shed,

engulfed in great swathes of red flames and falling apart before his eyes. More than once, I wondered if he would try to brave the fire and salvage what he could. He didn't, of course, but he didn't help the rest of us for some time, only stood there, looking as though he was staring into the face of death.

In the gentle morning light, the sun shone on a ravaged, ruined compound. The house was fine and the maze, the furthest western point, was entirely untouched, but nearly everything else outside had been destroyed. Ash covered everything, a thousand times worse than what had been blown over from the bushfires: the place was black and grey, stripped entirely of colour. Beyond the house, it was no longer clear what land was our own, and what belonged to the desert.

III

Twelve

For a long time, the only person I spoke to was Sam. Everyone kept to themselves, and the desire to work together – or even to live together – had dissipated in the fire. Each of the six of us was angry about what had happened, for different reasons. Once the fire had been put out, bitter, bitter words were exchanged. Becca made it clear that she blamed Sam and Tom. Candice had stood, covered in ash, her hair singed and her face streaked, and said such terrible things that even Tom turned away. Though they didn't say it outright, I think that Candice and Andrew blamed Sam and Tom, too. Tom, on top of the injuries from his first punishment, was burned anew; his face was blistered, his hands scarred and misshapen. Sam was too upset to talk to anyone. Even with me he was quiet and withdrawn.

I was entirely aware that it was my own fault. I didn't, and wouldn't, excuse Tom's violence, but he had hit me because I had broken his prized possession. Sam wouldn't have struck Tom if it hadn't been me lying on the floor. During that fight, when vicious words had been exchanged, I kept expecting Tom to point out that it had all started with me, but he never did. Sam felt guilty for his part, but, more than anything, I think he was upset to see the garden gone: Jacintha's herbs, their vegetables, and even the flowers planted by the previous tenants; it was as if they'd never existed. But Sam's grief over the loss of the garden and vegetation was nothing compared to Tom's devastation over the destruction of the shed and all that was in it. Aside from the finger-pointing, I think that the real reason that we didn't talk to each other was because we were all ashamed of what had happened, and what had become of the compound. There had been days when I felt as though I knew the other residents as well as one can know a person – but there were some when I thought the only thing I knew for certain about the others was that we all wanted the compound to be as nice as it possibly could be, and to stay. It was easy to let anger fester, and to pin the blame on someone else, but the fact remained that the compound was left in our care, and it was now laid to waste.

Sam and I hid out by the tennis court, which was around the back and therefore had not been burned, though it was now an insipid grey, covered in ash. Andrew and Candice stayed mainly in the bedroom. Whenever anyone entered, they stopped talking. I never knew where Becca was. Tom stayed mostly in the grey room, emerging every so often to look for Becca. Sometimes he called her name, but she never answered. I was never sure if Tom genuinely liked her, or if he felt obliged to look after her because they were in a couple together.

It's difficult to say how long we carried on in this manner; I really couldn't tell you. The big screen showed a different task each day, but we never did them, and it never turned green. I don't think any of us even did Personal Tasks. I know I didn't.

I didn't clean any more, and everyone else had given up on their roles too. The dishes in the sink grew dirty, and then mouldy, and then the rest of the house followed. It was as if by letting the kitchen go to ruin, we had dropped the facade of civility: the shower drain clogged with hair, the toilet seat broke and stayed broken, and the floor became sticky and stained. I left all of my clothes on the floor, and didn't care much to notice anything else lying around. There was something sort of thrilling about it, actually: you spend so much of your life adhering to all of these rules and ideas – keep everything orderly, keep busy, look presentable. When we stopped following these basic tenets, I realised how meaningless they had been. We got on fine as we were.

We were a lifeless bunch, but I felt no pressure to entertain, or to be entertained. I knew from watching the show that there were often weeks, particularly before it got down to the last five contestants, where things slowed down and became dull and dreary. There were times when you watched, waiting for drama to start, desperate for something to happen. But just because nothing happened, it didn't keep you from watching the following night. At some point, you stopped waiting for something to happen. The dullness almost became the point: the monotony was soothing, even, like watching livestock drifting across a plain. And then, when something dramatic did happen, it was an adrenaline-jolting surprise to your system, a jarring reminder that no one ever really knew what these people might do. You came to crave it again and again, that shock factor, the surge of conflict, the possibility of violence. From my years as a viewer, there was a part of me that knew that at some point, drama would happen again – its origin either organic or manufactured – but the fact that I was living it rather than viewing it didn't make it any easier to snap out of the stupor. Reality had become a slippery thing: I wasn't certain on what part of my life I was an active part of, and what was a result of the machinations around me. But that, to me at least, felt no different to how it had been on the outside.

For the first time in my adult life, I stopped doing my hair and make-up, and usually wore shorts and a sports bra under a silken dressing gown. There was no point in being shy with Sam. I had seen myself the day after the fire – covered in ash, my face swollen and bruised, my eyes red, and a small but noticeable bald spot where Tom had ripped the hair from my head. I looked so terrible that I gave up without another thought. My hair, my face, my splotchy skin – they were too bad to consider rectifying.

Those weeks in the compound remain hazy to me, and I don't remember what Sam and I spoke about or if we spoke much at all. I think we played some games, making up silly rules as we went. I remember playing tennis with fruit instead of a tennis ball: the first to burst the fruit lost. It was childish, but it was diverting. Sam was playing along for my sake, I knew. I suspected that he would have done anything I asked him, then, partly because he wanted me to be happy, and partly, I think, out of guilt over his role in our punishment.

One day, as I was making ice pops in the kitchen, I looked out the window and saw Sam standing in the remains of the garden, tall and broad-shouldered, almost exactly as he had appeared on the first day. He was trying to make a new fence for the perimeter using some of the leftover wood, but the wood splintered when he tried to hammer it into the earth. He threw it towards the desert in frustration and sat on the ground for a long time, looking out at the sand. After a while, he went and picked up the piece of wood, and left it spiked loosely into the silt, a rough marker of where the boundary line lay.

It occurred to me then that he would leave, too, and soon.

I worried that if I addressed it I would only highlight the problem: Sam was ready to move on from the compound, while

I couldn't. The uncomfortable truth was that when Sam left, he would return to a life where he was of use to the people around him. He was a smart guy, and had an important, meaningful job; he cared about the environment and sustainability – whereas I struggled to remember what went in the recycling bin. I was stuck in a dull job I didn't care for, and I couldn't scrape together the money to do anything meaningful, like travel, or go back to school. It was my own fault: whenever I had any money, I spent it immediately, mostly on the fast-fashion brands that Sam despised. What he didn't realise was that there would never be a better opportunity for me than this one. I couldn't see myself ever owning a house. Not, at least, until my mother died, and even then I wasn't sure; she didn't like me very much.

One day, sitting in the shade of a wall, I watched Candice emerge from the bedroom with something clenched in her hands. She went to the dump – now overflowing and stinking – and hesitated before it, perhaps reluctant to be confronted so viscerally by our own filth. Then she let go of what was in her hands, letting it drop to the scorched earth. There was no breeze to move it, and I thought at first that she had dropped a mouse; but I saw, upon closer inspection, that it was a chunk of her own hair. I looked at her retreating form and saw that she had cut it carefully enough, though it wasn't a particularly flattering style on her. I knew how much Candice had loved her hair, and felt puzzled over what I'd seen, until I realised that it was strange enough to suggest a Personal Task. Candice, I saw, wasn't ready to give up yet.

Good for her, I thought, and dozed for the rest of the afternoon.

We might have continued in this way for longer still if not for Becca, who found Sam and I passing a lemon between us on the tennis court. I was startled when she appeared, as though I had seen a ghost. In truth, I had almost forgotten she still lived there.

'Is everything okay?' Sam asked.

'I want to do the Communal Task.'

I squinted at her. 'Why?'

'Why not? We need to get back to stocking the house with essentials. We're running out of toilet roll. We have no shampoo, only soap.'

I wanted Becca to leave. Childishly, I turned away. Sam sighed.

'There's so much that we need,' he said ruefully, 'it seems fruitless to even try to begin again.'

Becca didn't say anything, but she didn't go, either.

'What's the reward?' I asked.

'Coffee,' she said.

We got Andrew and Candice, and Becca got Tom. We brought them to the living room, where the screen loomed. It was one of the cleaner rooms in the house, as we never went in there any more. No one wanted to see the screen. I sat in my usual place on the L-shaped couch, and Sam sat beside me, his arm around my shoulders. Andrew and Candice sat on the other end, a mirror of us. Andrew stayed perched at the edge of the couch as though eager to slip away. I was reminded of Candice's suggestion that the four of us live together. She looked at me and smiled, as if she was thinking the same thing.

She was fine with doing a task, but Andrew shook his head.

'Why not?' Becca said.

'I don't want to.'

Andrew's unwillingness made my own reluctance return. It wasn't like him, but I took it as proof that we had entered a new phase of our time there, where we no longer had to be productive, or work together towards some goal. I waited for someone else to say *let's just leave it then*. I was tired: I wanted to curl up in my bed for a while, maybe have Candice brush my hair.

'Do it for me,' she said, smiling.

'We're skipping this one,' he said. 'I don't feel well. I feel sick. Leave me in peace.'

Tom, who had been standing in the corner, said, 'I say we do it.'

It had saddened me to see the difference in Candice – her shorter, uneven hair, her tired eyes – but it truly shocked me to see Tom. The burns he had sustained from both punishments, as well as the beating from Sam, had left his face scarred and puffy. His hair had grown long, and he had a full and scraggly beard. I would hardly have recognised him, if not for his enormous bulk. I suspected that was the part of himself that Tom was unwilling to sacrifice. Becca, by contrast, looked like a baby seal sitting on the ground, sleek and clean.

'I don't want to,' Andrew repeated. 'Can't we just live in peace for a few more days? We can do one tomorrow if you feel so strongly about it.'

'We need to keep the house stocked. We'll run out of supplies without knowing it,' Becca said.

'Becca's talking a lot of sense,' Tom said. 'Maybe you should give up your role of Task Organisation and Reward Distribution and let Becca do it with me instead.' He was attempting a joke, but no one laughed.

Sam was quiet. I glanced at him, and then at the screen, re-reading the instruction.

'Let's do it,' I said. 'We'll put it to a vote.'

Everyone's hands went up, except Andrew. I noticed that Sam put his hand up last. I was nervous now, clenching my jaw, and gripping the bottom of my dressing gown.

Becca read the instructions, as though we hadn't all been looking at it for the past several minutes. 'Task,' she read.

Reveal your sexual partners since entering the compound
Reward: Coffee

'I'll go first,' she continued, her voice low and melodic. 'I haven't slept with anyone since I've come to the compound.'

Tom looked out the window as she spoke, his neck flushed red.

'Sam,' I said.

'Lily,' Sam said, and kissed my neck.

'Andrew,' Candice said.

'Candice,' Andrew said.

Tom said, 'Mia, Vanessa and Sarah.'

Candice looked at him with unbridled disgust. He didn't look at her, though he must have felt her glare.

The screen remained as it was.

'Someone's lying,' I said. I looked at Becca, her knees underneath her chin, gazing at the screen.

'It's obviously Tom,' Candice said.

'And why do you think that?' Tom replied evenly.

'You probably didn't sleep with anyone,' Candice said. 'You're as innocent as Becca.'

Becca. She was sitting on the ground, running her fingers across the fibres on the rug. I couldn't help but recall the morning I'd woken her up to help in the kitchen, and how Sam had said her name, half asleep. They had shared a bed for far longer than we had. I glanced at Sam: I couldn't help it. He was already looking at me. I don't know if it was because things worked so differently in the compound, isolated as we were, bound to a small group of people, but at precisely the same moment that I wondered if Sam had been sleeping with someone else, I also wondered if I hadn't fallen in love with him. I wasn't sure if the feeling had been rising in me steadily, or if it came to me in the panic that he might leave me. He met my eye steadily. Neither of us looked away until we heard Tom's voice, soft and snake-like, thrashing through the silence.

'Don't you know who's lying, Candice?'

Candice looked confused. The expression sat strangely on her face.

We all turned to look at Andrew. He was looking at the ceiling.

'Eloise,' he said, 'and Carlos.'

The screen turned green.

Andrew lifted himself from the couch and left. I heard the front door swing shut behind him.

'But that's not true,' Candice said. 'We've been together since the beginning.'

'I'm sorry, Candice,' Sam said. She glanced at him, irritated.

'I'm going to sort this out,' she said, and rose from the couch. She followed after Andrew; I could tell from the distance of their voices that she'd caught up with him by the pool. After the quiet of the previous weeks, hearing snippets of their conversation, their heated and raised voices, seemed wrong to the point of obscenity.

'Did you know?' I asked Sam.

'I wasn't sure, but I'd suspected.'

I thought for a moment. 'Did you know he was bi?'

'Oh, sure,' Sam said.

Becca smiled at me from her spot on the floor. It wasn't a particularly nice smile. 'Did you think that everyone here was straight, Lily? We're all here living the perfect, hetero life?'

'Easy, Becca,' Sam said. I threw her a dirty glance, but didn't say anything. Since we weren't yet in the bottom five, I couldn't reveal personal information without punishment, so I couldn't say that I was queer, too. In retrospect, I fancied Candice nearly as much as I had Ryan.

Tom was looking at Becca too, frowning slightly, either because he was surprised by her comment, or because he was considering the possibility that she wasn't straight, either.

Sam stood, pulled me up with him and led me to the shower. We unpeeled our clothes and stood under the spray. It felt good. I closed my eyes and imagined that we were standing in a rain shower outside my house. I could see the red door, could imagine the curtain twitching at the window and my mother peeking out. When we were ready, we could open the door and go inside. Sam asked me what I was thinking about, and I lied and said I was thinking about how tomorrow I would make an effort to clear away some of the mess in the front yard.

Candice woke me in the middle of the night. I jerked at the touch on my elbow, and Sam stirred beside me. She lifted a finger to her lips. I nodded, gently lifted Sam's arm off me and followed her out of the room. She brought me to the dressing room, where one of the lighted mirrors had been left on. The room was otherwise dark. She sat at the bench, and I sat beside her.

'Candice,' I said. 'I'm so sorry.'

She began to weep. I put my arms around her and hugged her tightly, stroking her hair, murmuring kind words. She pulled away after a few minutes and wiped the tears from her eyes. Despite the tears, despite the questionable haircut, she was still the most beautiful woman I had ever seen. 'I'm sorry I didn't get to know you better, Lily,' she said.

'I know you, Candice,' I said. 'I know you well.'

'Oh, no, you don't,' she said, and laughed, still a little tearful. 'I spent too much time with Andrew. I spent a long time making sure that he chose me, and then longer still making sure he kept me. Well, it's all a joke now isn't it? I'm sure that's what everyone's thinking now. Candice, the joke!'

'You're the best of us,' I said. 'You're the best of us, and he knows it. Everyone knows it.'

'How did I let myself become so pathetic? When the jobs were assigned, I didn't mind that I'd be doing the dinners. At the time food was scarce, and I thought I was the right person for the job; I'm crafty, and – well, I can say it now. Everyone knows that there's power in being in charge of a scarce resource.'

I said nothing, and she picked up a bottle of nail varnish that I had left on the bench. It was a siren red colour, loud and brassy. She examined the colour and put it down.

'But then I looked at myself, as though I had woken from a dream. What was I doing, cooking dinners while Andrew decided what we do and how we do it? And what did he know about anything? You know that in bed he would talk with me for hours, under the blankets, asking for advice? There was nothing he could do without talking it through, or looking for advice or reassurance. I liked it, to tell you the truth. It made me feel as though I was pulling the strings. But in actual fact he was creeping out as soon as I'd fallen asleep, and into someone else's bed.'

'I know how you feel,' I said. 'With Ryan, I thought I would kill him when I found out.'

She took my hand and gripped it, hard. 'I know you did, Lily. I know you did. The best thing we did was banishing that bastard. The worst part of it all, is that I know that if I wanted to, I could banish Andrew – I could ask him to go, and he'd leave without a word. But I can't – I won't do that to him. Isn't that absurd? Isn't that ridiculous? I've loved him now for months – from the very beginning!'

'Candice,' I said, and squeezed her hand. 'He loves you, too.'

She looked at me for a moment, and kissed me softly, briefly on the lips. 'Go back to bed, Lily,' she said. 'It's very late.'

I rose, but didn't want to leave her. 'Make sure to come back before sunrise,' I said.

'I'll remember,' she said.

I wasn't surprised, in the morning, to find that Candice had taken her things and left, though it hurt like a knife to the guts. I knew that she would go, because I knew that Candice would rather not participate at all than be the person who people would laugh at. I even wondered – for a second, just a second – if the compound was worth staying in without her. I missed her, not just because I liked and admired her, but because when she left she shattered some illusion that I had held on to from my time as a viewer: that the show was, in fact, about love – or, at least, about finding someone who you could live with. I had been comforted by the thought that Andrew and Candice were 'the real thing'. Somewhere along the way I had let myself forget the most obvious thing: that it was a game.

There were now five of us left: me, Sam, Tom, Becca, Andrew. It was a big deal, to make it to the last five. You were more or less guaranteed fame. Things got competitive in the final ten, but they often turned brutal in the final five, when all rules lifted. Some of the rules that had been in place were a nuisance, such as not being able to discuss Personal Tasks, but some of the rules had protected us, like the no-fighting rule. More than once in the past physical fights had broken out almost instantly once the sixth person left. The producers only stepped in if they thought that someone was in serious danger. I wondered if Becca had known that Andrew had slept around, and if that was why she had encouraged us to do the task.

In her absence the compound became a different place to us.

While we had been despondent after the fire, we were worse after Candice left. Andrew became useless, hiding in the bedroom, lying in bed, speaking to no one. When he withdrew, I realised how much we depended on him; even if he wasn't particularly useful, he was always an encouraging and enthusiastic presence. When he did come out of the bedroom, it was mostly to talk about Candice; how much he had loved her, and how he loved her still.

Thirteen

Now that we were no longer obligated to sleep next to someone, we scattered further still across the compound. I saw Becca very rarely, perhaps once every couple of days. Tom kept mostly to the grey room. Though I saw little of them, their presence was like wasps buzzing at the corner of my vision: I couldn't relax until they were gone. Once or twice I complained to Sam that I wished that they would just leave, and he looked bemused. 'Don't you reckon they're thinking the same about us?' he said.

One day, not long after Candice had left, Sam and I were walking along the southern side of the grounds. The barrier between the desert and our land was still intact there, and I liked to think that lent an air of civility to the area.

'What are you thinking about?' Sam asked me.

I had been thinking of my mother, which had then made me recall a girl named Trish from a long-ago season of the show. Everyone loved Trish: she was a fantastic dancer and would sometimes get the other residents to put on performances in the evenings to keep them all occupied. She was funny, too, and liked to play pranks on the boys. After maybe three months in the compound she became increasingly withdrawn, until it got to the point where she spent her days crying, not leaving the bedroom and not speaking to others. Usually, in a case such as that, the big screen would frequently suggest banishments, hoping to get rid of the 'problem' resident. But none of the residents wanted to vote her out, and those watching at home didn't want her to go either. Even though she was a wreck, she had once been the undeniable star of the show: there are some people who are so compulsively watchable that you feel yourself surrender some small bit of your personality to them. I remember how I used to try to copy her easy laugh, the delighted boom of it.

To try to remedy the situation, Trish was offered a previously unheard-of reward on her little screen: a phone call with anyone she wanted. She called her sister and spoke to her for hours. She cried again when she had to give the phone back, but afterwards she was much more composed; she participated in tasks and interacted with the others. She tried to be fun and engaging again, but you could see the strain, and it didn't make for good viewing. She was gone a week later.

I wondered what it would take for me to be offered a call with my mother. We didn't even get on, but I found myself thinking about it constantly, how I would give anything to speak to her, even for just a few minutes. But Trish had been given the opportunity to restore herself because she had previously been vivacious and interesting. There was no former glory for me to return to. I was now as I always had been.

'Just thinking about my mother,' I said.

Sam stopped me abruptly. He put his hand to his face in astonishment. 'I forgot. We can talk about our personal lives now.'

I smiled at him. The change in rules wasn't particularly

interesting to me. I knew Sam well enough. 'Anything I should know?'

We walked in silence for a few moments. 'I'd prefer to tell you on the outside,' he said, surprising me.

'Oh,' I said. We kept our pace slow. I saw him glance at me. 'So it's bad.'

'No, nothing bad. I just think it'll be easier to be real when we're out.'

'What do you mean "real"? Like you're not being real with me now?'

'No, I mean – I don't know.'

'You should know, Sam.'

'I'm being real with you, Lily. But, up to a point.'

'Up to a *point*?'

'You know what I mean. It's not possible to be completely real in here.'

It was almost word for word what Ryan had said to me. It confused me no less when Sam said it. Of course, the situation was unique, but did we not feel as deeply here as on the outside? The situation was constructed, a production – but were *we* not real?

'So you've been faking how you feel about me?'

'No, Lily, no. But, this – the way we communicate, the way we got to know each other – that hasn't been real. I didn't know what your second name was for a month. And now that we can talk without punishment, I don't know if I want to. I want to talk on the outside, when we're not on display.'

I never even thought about the viewers any more. Obviously, I knew in some distant way that they were there, watching. When you were beautiful, really beautiful, you moved through your day with an exquisite self-consciousness. Now that I didn't put an effort in, and wore my dressing gown every day, that feeling was dulled. It seemed absurd, in a way, that people could be watching me.

'It'll be easier to talk when the others are gone,' I said.

We walked on in silence for a brief while. I could almost feel him thinking deeply. Sam was the type to turn over conversations in his mind, to consider things from different perspectives. It was one of the qualities I liked most about him, and one of the things that made me feel inadequate. I lived in constant fear that he'd find out how shallow I was, how little time I spent considering the ways of the world.

'Lily,' he said suddenly. 'I've been putting this off. I don't know why. I really don't. But I think we should go. Today. Let's just pack our bags and go.'

I tried not to react. 'Don't be ridiculous, Sam – why would we leave now?'

'Because it's all fucking – fake! How can you go on living like this? Pretending that everything is okay?'

'Isn't that what we were doing before, on the outside?'

'But on the outside it was real! It mattered what we did – we weren't just . . . entertainment! There's no point,' he said. 'No point in being here.'

I didn't want to say it out loud: the prizes. 'We've almost won,' I said.

'Won what? What is there here that you want?'

'Look, I know you think that I'm being superficial – but the better we do here, the easier things will be on the outside. We'll have more prizes, more opportunities, more fame . . .' I paused, trying to decide how much I wanted to admit to. 'But even besides that, why would you want to go back to that, what we had before?'

I could see that my words hadn't fully landed with him. He didn't get it. He was silent again, for a long time. We were walking very slowly now.

'Ask me something,' I said. 'It'll make it easier.'

I thought he wasn't going to say anything, and we'd remain locked in silence for the evening. But he said, 'Do you have any brothers or sisters?'

'No,' I said. 'I'm an only child. What about you?'

'I had two brothers. They're both dead.'

He still wasn't looking at me. In the sky, birds idly circled.

'I'm so sorry, Sam. What happened?'

'They died in the war,' he said. 'My father was a veteran, and when the war broke out, he encouraged us to enlist. My brothers died within a year, two months apart. My father still wanted me to join up, even after we'd buried them both. I wouldn't. We fought about it – we never agreed on politics – and eventually I moved to a different city, and we cut ties. I got a job that I had thought that I wanted, and I met new people, and explored a new place, but I was terribly, horribly lonely. I hated my life, but I didn't know how to fix it. It felt like it was out of my hands.'

I looked at him. Wasn't that how I felt, too?

'I didn't want to go home, but I hated where I was. I went back and forth constantly in my head between the two places, until it felt like I was nowhere at all.'

'What did you decide to do?'

'I came here,' he said.

'Oh,' I said.

'What about you?'

'What about me?'

'Why did you decide to do it?'

'Why? Because everyone wants to do it, and I got the chance.'

'And?'

I knew that this was my chance to make Sam understand, to try to get him to stay. I struggled for words, struggled with the enormity of it.

'I wanted to be here because . . . there's nothing else for me. I've tried that life – meaningless job, no money, feeling tired *all the time* – and I'm not going to *get* anything from any of that. It won't bring me any happiness. I got a gold necklace in here – look at it. Real gold! Just from talking to you! Do you know how long I'd have to work to earn something like that? And who wants to work anyway? If you make it to the end here, you can have whatever you want, and you don't have to deal with all the other bullshit . . . I don't have any real talent. I'm pretty, but not the prettiest. I'm not smart. I'll never have a better opportunity than this.'

I turned to Sam, to see if he understood. My heart was beating so hard it bordered on being painful. He was facing away, towards the desert.

'You got a reward for talking to me?'

'A long time ago.'

'When? Which conversation?'

I felt a sort of heaviness settle over me. All of my inadequacies were rushing to the surface, all of my faults that I had tried to hide were now being revealed. 'Near the beginning. When I tried to guess your job, and we argued.'

He nodded. When he turned, his face was grave.

'What are we doing here any more?'

'You mean – us?'

'No, not "us" as in our relationship. I mean why are we still here? Why are we still living here?'

'We're waiting for the others to go.'

'Do you really think Tom will go?' I knew that Tom wouldn't give up easily, but that was a problem I could deal with later.

'If we left, things would be different with us. I'd never see you.' I didn't like to draw his attention to our life outside, where he would surely realise that it made no sense for us to be together. Here we were limited by the circumstances the producers placed us in. There, I was limited by my own lack of ability, my lack of drive and general feeling of apathy.

'We would, Lily. Of course we would.' He paused, seemingly confused. 'Isn't that what we've been working towards?'

I said nothing.

He looked around him, his face pinched in sadness. 'Do you really want to live here, in this . . . wasteland?'

'It's no worse than what's out there! Is that what you want to go back to? Constantly living on the periphery of disaster, just waiting and waiting and waiting for it to finally reach us, doing stupid, dull work to pass the days until then? We're safe here – we're removed from all of it.'

'It's still there, Lily. It's still happening. You think that because we can't see it, it's not going on?'

'Don't talk to me like I'm stupid.'

'There's no actual future for us here – it's just a twisted game. Christ – look at this place! I shouldn't have let myself get so complacent – only I kept thinking I couldn't leave you here, with Tom, and with everything. But now . . . Lily, I don't think I can spend another night here!'

He was standing in a sandy patch of ground, where part of the desert had crept in. He looked like a statue, strong and tall and still. I had known that this moment was coming, but it terrified me just the same. 'What's brought this on?' I asked. 'We were having a nice day, up until a few minutes ago.'

'I just realised that I can ask you personal questions, and tell you about myself, but I don't know what to talk about any more! I've gotten so used to these inane conversations, saying the stupid thoughts that are in my head at that exact minute, but not being able to talk about where I've been and the people I've met – not being able to tell you about *my life* – and not knowing that about you, either!'

'Go, then,' I said. 'If you really want to.'

'I'm not leaving without you.'

'Well, I'm staying. And you want to go. So go.'

'Lily.'

'I'm serious. I'm not going to hold you back.'

'What can I say to change your mind? What can I do to take you with me?'

I said nothing. He picked up a stone. Rather than aim it into any of the vast, untouched space around us, he threw it at the house. It crashed through the window of the living room, glass shattering. I expected someone to come out and make a fuss – Tom was surely in the house, Andrew too – but there was no sign of movement.

'Shit,' Sam said, and rubbed his face.

I walked forward a little, watching out for broken glass. 'You shouldn't have done that. The place is damaged enough as it is. That's another thing that we'll have to fix.'

I felt his eyes on me. I turned. 'You know,' he said, 'all of this, all of these *rewards* – they're just . . . stuff. The house, the Personal Rewards – having them doesn't make a difference.'

A faint wind licked at the back of my legs. Now that I knew that he would leave me and this would be the end, I wanted to cling to some bit of dignity. I felt the return of awareness that we were being watched, that people were forming opinions on our actions just as we carried them out. Even as I looked at Sam's face, the small details that were so dear to me – the bridge of his nose, the faint red line that crossed his cheekbones from too much time in the sun – I was thinking of the girls who had appeared on the show before, who had been strong and inscrutable as their men left them. The girls who made a fuss and cried and begged never won any sympathy; in fact, whatever impact they'd had before diminished the moment they fell to pieces over a boy.

No one liked to see that – people preferred us fierce and fearless. I understood it: I didn't like to be reminded either of just how quickly I could fall apart. Just the same, if we'd been alone and no one was watching, I think I might have fallen at his feet and told him that he needed to be patient with me, he needed to give me time, that I would be better, I only needed time.

'I'm sorry you feel that way,' I said coolly. 'I suppose we're not really that similar. I never thought we would be compatible, you know. That's why I chose Ryan.'

He looked out at the desert sands, and then back to the house.

'I'll fix the window,' he said. 'I'll fix it, and then I'll go.'

It didn't hurt, not really. I knew it would hurt later, but I had expected it even before we got together. Still: I turned away so he couldn't see me, just in case.

'Fine,' I said. 'I'm going for a swim.'

I changed into my bikini – it was lying on a chair, still damp from my last swim – and floated on my back for a while, gazing into the sky until my eyes blurred, until the blue became a single, fixed point above me. I sat on the steps of the pool then, still half submerged, and watched Sam fix the window.

I loved him; I loved him, and it was terrible, because I knew that he was right, and that things had gotten out of hand here. I couldn't bear to see him go, but I couldn't fathom leaving. I didn't want him to see just how small and insignificant my life had been before. If my greatest accomplishment had been getting onto the show, then everything beyond that would be a disappointment.

There was a moment, as he carefully hammered a nail into a scrap of wood, when my blood ran cold with terror at the thought of living here without him. But I had so nearly won. It wouldn't be the life I'd wanted, with Sam sharing my solitude, but it was still better than the dim, pale existence I had at home. Tom said I was useless, and probably the others thought so too, but I knew that I could do it. I could make something of myself here. I could win. People would think back on the show, this year, this iteration of the house, and say, 'Wasn't that the one with Lily?' That was worth something. Even Sam would have to think so.

Sam finished and went into the house. I got out of the pool and took my time, making a serpentine path to the front door through the blackened trees and mounds of debris. I stayed off to the side, out of sight. Andrew and Sam were walking out of the house. I watched Andrew grasp Sam close to him, his shoulders shaking.

'I'll miss you, man. I'll really miss you,' he said.

Sam said nothing, but he hugged him back. Unlike nearly everyone else in the compound, Sam had never warmed to Andrew.

'I should go, too,' Andrew said, stepping away and releasing him. 'I know I should go, and be with Candice, but – I'll go soon, very soon, and I'll see you then, won't I Sam, yes? We'll all see each other. We'll meet up regularly, I'm sure. Sam, will you find Candice, when you're out? Or call her – I forgot for a minute that you can pick up a mobile and call someone; isn't that funny? If you could get her number, and just tell her that I think about her every minute, *every minute*, and that I'll be out soon.'

Still Sam said nothing, and Andrew continued, his arms swinging by his sides in an uncharacteristically nervous gesture.

'Well – that's you off, then! I'll look after Lily, don't you worry. Are you sure you're going? Do you really need to leave?

When I heard the window break, I thought: I must sort myself out and get back to taking care of the house. You know, I really do think we can get it back to the way it was before the fire.'

'I'm going, Andrew. Maybe I'll see you after.'

'Of course, man, of course. Well – goodbye, then. I won't walk you out; I'm going to check on the big screen, and see if maybe we could earn something to help us get organised. I'll see you for a drink sometime, right?'

'Sure, Andrew.'

Andrew left, walking around the compound, inspecting scorched lumps of metal, perhaps wondering what reward each of them had been before the fire. I watched Sam go around the side of the house to look at the window he had covered up. He stayed there for a while, and I thought that he was likely waiting for me to come back. I stepped forward to approach him, but then Becca appeared, walking across the dusty stretch of ground towards him as though she knew that he had been looking for her. I moved around the corner so that I could listen to them, out of sight. He told her he was going, and she listened and said a few affirmative things. I couldn't see her, but she sounded cool and unbothered.

'I can't persuade you to go?' he asked.

'I'll go soon,' she said.

'Becca,' he sighed. 'I don't know why you want to stay. But it isn't worth it.'

'I'll miss you,' she said. 'You were the only person here I liked.'

'Tell me something. Why do you want to win?'

'I don't care about winning. I just need Tom to lose.'

I thought he might be running his hands across his face. 'Oh God,' he said. 'What am I thinking, leaving you and Lily here with Tom!'

'We can look after ourselves. We're not children. And anyway, nothing will happen to us. They always step in before things go too far.'

'That isn't comforting.'

'I know what I'm doing,' she said. 'I reckon I'll be home by the end of the week.'

'You know what day it is?'

'Sure,' she said. 'It's Tuesday September twentieth.'

September. The entire summer had passed, then. I had never imagined staying this long. But everyone would understand, when they watched what was happening. It wouldn't make sense to leave when I was nearly at the end.

'How do you know?'

'My first Personal Reward was a notebook. I've been using Susie's lip liner as a pencil.'

'You're incredible, Becca.'

She was incredible. My first reward had been a hairbrush. I didn't have a single thing that was of any use. I had never even considered finding a way to mark the time – I just accepted that I didn't know it.

'Thanks,' she said. 'Well – goodbye.'

'Goodbye. Take care of yourself.'

Becca rounded the corner, glanced at me with disinterest, and moved deeper into the compound, towards the maze. Suddenly I was seized by such terror at the thought of never seeing him again that I wanted to stay where I was and hide, if only to avoid the final parting. But I heard him call my name and I went to meet him.

We stood shyly before each other, as though we were strangers. His skin had darkened in the past months, and though he had a lot of scruff, just short of a beard, his hair was still neat and well cared for. I felt a wave of shame over how I looked. I touched my hairline self-consciously, wondering if my bald spot was still visible.

'Don't watch me, when you're out there,' I said.

'Okay,' he said. 'If you want.'

'Where do you live?' I asked.

He named the place, a city about three hours' drive from my own. 'And you?'

I told him, and he said, 'I could visit. If you were up for it.'

'I don't know,' I said. 'Maybe.' He looked so incredibly, profoundly hurt, that I said, 'What we had here was perfect, don't you think? I don't want a lesser version of it, on the outside.'

He didn't answer. After a moment, I saw that he was crying.

I put my arms around him and rested my head in the crook of his shoulder. He held me tightly, and I could smell him, smoke and cedar; I felt the light tremors that ran through his body. He pulled away first and looked at me like I was still beautiful.

'Sam,' I said.

'Don't mind me,' he said. 'I'll be fine.' A minute later, he was composed again, and wiped a hand across his face. We stood silently for a moment, and then I said, 'I'll walk you to the perimeter.'

He took my hand and slung his bag over his shoulder, and we walked together towards the boundary. His bag looked light: he hadn't taken many of his rewards.

There was a part of me that didn't really believe that he was going; I thought that he would reach the boundary, see the desert before him and change his mind. But we were approaching the edge now and his step was steady.

'Take this with you,' I said, and reached into the pocket of my dressing gown. I gave him the duck feather that Susie had given each of us the night we killed our own dinner. He took it and smiled a little, tucking it into the pocket of his shirt. He looked out at the vast expanse of land, the sand and the dirt, cooked and bleached under the white sun, and I said, 'What happened in the desert?'

He took his time before answering. 'We were dropped off individually. We didn't know where the others were, or where we were. I found Carlos first, and then Gav. Remember Gav? Well, he was useless. He kept leading us in the wrong direction – the same wrong direction, over and over. We found the others by pure chance. Tom had been bitten by then – he was attacked on his first night. All of us had found at least one other person by then, except Tom; he'd had to sleep alone. He was frantic when he found us. He kept talking about the dog, the attack, how he had killed it. He had broken its neck, he said, and then broke all four of its legs for good measure. I might not have believed him, but he kept a bone from its carcass. He didn't let it out of his grasp the whole time we were wandering.

'On the second day, we were low on food and we were starting to worry that we'd run out before we found the compound. We'd been walking aimlessly for hours arguing with each other and no one was making any decisions. It was felt that we should vote for one person to take the lead. Tom felt strongly that it should be him. He kept holding up that bone, as if it meant something. He got into a fight, and some of the other men had to intervene, including myself.'

We were nearly there, now. The sun was hot on my neck; I had no sun cream on and would surely burn.

'Who did he fight with?'

'Andrew. They both thought that they should be the one in charge. It was vicious. They were swinging and tearing at each other. Tom was already in bad shape from the dog, but Andrew was merciless. Then we heard the voice, telling us that violence was forbidden. We were all stunned by the sound of it – no one could tell where it came from. I think we had forgotten, with the heat and the exhaustion, that we were being watched. We took some time to compose ourselves, and then we voted on who would lead us to the compound.'

'Who did they elect?'

'Me,' he said. I smiled, but I wasn't surprised. 'As soon as we reached the compound, it was like their fight completely went out of their minds, but none of us forgot it. I remember hearing some of the girls fret over the men that first day. There was one less of us, and one more of you, remember? And they thought that they were at a disadvantage because of it. My God, if you could have imagined how glad we all were to see you all, waiting there calmly, the house looming behind you. We were entirely at your mercy, though I don't think any of you realised it.'

'The other man, the man who never made it here. What was his name?'

He had to think about it, his brow furrowed, eyes searching before him. 'Alexandre,' he said at last.

'What happened to him?'

'On the second day, before Andrew and Tom fought, there was a suggestion that we split up and try two different paths. It wasn't a popular idea, but Alexandre said he'd go and scout a different direction anyway. I think he wanted a break from the bickering, to be honest. We waited for him for a long time – half a day – but when night fell it was too cold to stay out in the open and we had to move. Some of us wanted to wait. We put it to a vote. The majority said they wanted to move on. We didn't come across him again,' he said.

I wondered if he envied Alexandre, who never made it here at all.

We were now standing at the boundary. I didn't know how to say what I wanted to say, but I knew what I wanted him to say to me. I had told him that I didn't think we would work on the outside, and while it was true, I desperately wanted him to tell me he'd wait for me. Isn't that what people said, when their loved ones went off to war, or when they left on some long journey – that they would wait for them?

'I don't want to leave you this way,' he said.

'It's okay,' I said. 'Hardly any of the couples ever actually make it.' I didn't mean to be cold, though perhaps that's how I came across. The situation had gone beyond my control so quickly, and it was easier to pretend that I knew what I wanted. But I knew that if he had asked me one more time to go I would have gone, without a fuss. *Ask me*, I thought. *Ask me again.*

A faint wind rippled across the desert, shifting the sand. 'Don't stay too long,' he said.

He didn't kiss me goodbye, only moved through a gap in the barbed-wire boundary, and was gone. I thought: I deserved that. I watched him get smaller and smaller, but I could feel the top of my head burning, my hair scorching to the touch, and my neck was already tender. I went and sat in the shade, then walked around the compound for the rest of the evening. I stayed in a room at the back of the house that we had been using to store bed linens. It smelled of laundry detergent and must. I didn't see anyone for some time, and that was fine with me.

Fourteen

A few days later the water stopped working. It was Becca who told me; she was waiting in the kitchen when I woke up. It was a shock to see her. In a whisper she told me it wasn't just the drinking water but the showers too, indoor and outdoor. It was frightening to think of, but somehow thrilling, too. The past week, or weeks, probably, had been nothing but endless dreariness. The water being turned off was at least something to focus upon.

'Have you told the boys?' I asked. I knew she hadn't: they were asleep still. Without realising it, I had fallen into my old habit of asking questions I already knew the answer to.

'No.' She hesitated, and then said, 'I have water, stashed away.'

'Where?'

'If I show you,' she said, 'You can't tell the others.'

'Okay. Fine.'

'I'll need you to swear. This will only work if the boys don't have access to water.'

'I swear. Jesus.'

She started walking towards the maze, and I trailed uneasily behind her. While the edges of the maze had been burned, the general structure still remained. I didn't want to go in – I had entered only a few times before, and I'd never stayed long. The maze had been a popular spot some years back – but two years ago, couples started to go there when they wanted to have sex without being noticed by the others. At first it was just one couple, and it was quite romantic, the two of them sneaking away, meeting there in the middle of the night – until other couples started doing the same. It was awful; couples trying to find their way out would have to pass other residents naked in the bushes. As viewers we couldn't see everything, of course, but we saw enough. Residents in the following seasons had avoided the place entirely, and we had instinctively done the same. Becca, I supposed, hadn't seen that season, and didn't know the sordid reputation of the maze, or she did but was unfazed by it. She took the maze's turns quickly, with a light step, and once or twice I thought I'd lost her. Eventually she stopped at an entirely unremarkable hedge, identical to all the others. She stepped *into* it, and I saw something glinting there, though I wouldn't have noticed if I hadn't been staring. She re-emerged with a gallon of water, her tiny arms struggling with its weight. I sat on the ground and took a lengthy pull from it. She sat down beside me and drank from it when I was done.

'How long will it last?' I asked. It seemed an enormous amount, but I knew how quickly it would go in the heat. It was blessedly cool in the maze, the enormous hedges providing much-needed shade, and I sagged against one of them as I tried to think of what this would mean.

'Not long. Three days, maybe four.'

'Did you check the big screen?' I said. She nodded. 'And the reward is water?'

'Of course.'

In the final five, the screen stayed stuck on the same task until it was completed. Crucially, they weren't tasks any more, but competitions. Whoever came in last was banished. Like any task, we didn't have to complete it, but we didn't get a reward unless we all took part. I had never seen anything as extreme as the water being turned off, but I supposed that after weeks of inactivity they needed to trigger a strong response. Six or maybe seven years ago, after a particularly dull stretch where the five residents were living happily with no conflict whatsoever, the producers had released a box of rats into the kitchen and offered the reward of rat poison. For days it was like watching a horror movie; so many shots of them screaming, crying, literally shaking in fear. They were finding rat carcasses in every corner of the house for weeks afterwards.

'What's the task?' I asked.

'A hundred-metre race.'

I could see her plan, now. There was no question about it: the boys would win under normal circumstances. I was fast, but not as fast as Andrew and Tom. I didn't need to be the fastest, however. I just needed not to be the slowest. Becca knew that too, of course.

'We need to wait them out,' she said. 'Without water, they'll get weak in a day, two days tops. You and I will be fine. Either they go home just to get some water, or they do the challenge. If we wait until they're dehydrated we can beat them.'

'How dehydrated?'

'That's up to them.'

'Why did you tell me where the water is, though?'

'Are you asking me why I'm sharing water during a drought?' Her tone was distinctly arch, and I gave her a blank look in response. I understood that Becca didn't particularly like me, but had limited options. It would be risky to pull it off on her own, and she knew that to have a shot at Tom being banished both of us needed to beat him.

'Look,' Becca said. 'I don't mind sharing. I just don't want Tom to have any. If I tell Andrew, he'll tell Tom. You won't tell Tom.'

'Girls?' Andrew called from somewhere beyond. I jumped. 'Lily? Becca?'

We sat quietly, and eventually he moved on. I heard him head towards the tennis court, the call of our names becoming dimmer.

Becca whispered, 'Are you still thirsty?'

'No.'

'Good. See where the sun is now? Wait until it's directly above the skylight in the bedroom before you have another drink.'

'I don't think I'll remember how to get here.'

'You don't need to. I'll be here. I'll hear your step and come and get you.'

'You're going to stay here?'

'I can't risk the boys finding me. If we're all together they'll force us to do the task. I'll need you to bring food to me, though – at least twice a day. When you're here, I can give you water. Pretend to be as thirsty as the boys, and don't let them see you come. That's the most important thing.'

'Okay,' I said. I was eager to go; the maze was eerie, even in the daylight.

'Lie low today,' she said. 'By tomorrow they'll be desperate.'

I left the maze and sat on a stump where the orchard used to be. When it grew too hot I moved to the tennis court. Eventually I had to use the bathroom, and went into the house. Andrew was sitting on a chair by the front door and jumped up as soon as I walked in.

'Oh, thank Christ, Lily, there you are. I was looking everywhere. Where were you?'

'Just around.'

'Sam would have killed me if anything had happened to you. *I* would have killed me if anything happened to you. Look, I've got some bad news. The water's been turned off. Did you already know?'

'No. Do you think you can fix it?'

'No,' he said, and ran a hand through his hair. 'They've turned it off. I guess they want us to do a task and get rid of someone.'

'Huh,' I said.

'Here's the thing. I know I've been kind of MIA for the last while. It's just – well, it's been hard without Candice. But you get that, now. I know how you must be feeling without Sam. I have to be honest, I woke up a couple of mornings ago, and I kind of thought – well, what's the point, right? What am I doing? But the water going off woke me up. I mean, Jesus, look at this place. This was paradise not so long ago. We've let it go to shit, and it's my own fault, I know it is. But I think we can get it back to something like it used to be. And I know that doing tasks in the last five means getting rid of someone, but we've been put in a position where we don't have a choice. I don't want anyone to go, I really, really don't, but we can't make it without water.'

His explanations sounded a lot like an apology. He knew that us girls would lose, too.

'Sure,' I said, and he smiled at me, relieved. 'I'm going to use the bathroom,' I said, and he nodded. I was nearly down the hallway when he called my name. I turned. He looked apologetic.

'The thing is . . . if the water isn't working, it might be best if we don't use the toilet. I can dig you a hole outside, if you like?'

When the sun was above the skylight, I returned to the maze. I got lost at once and drifted around for a while, until Becca appeared and led me to the right spot. I wondered if she'd let me wander on purpose.

'Did anyone see you?'

'No, no.'

'But you spoke to them? They know the water's gone?'

'I spoke to Andrew. He knows.'

'Did he ask to do the task?'

'No, but I think he was leading up to it. Do you mind if I take a drink?'

'Sure. It's hot, right?'

'Yeah. It's hot.' I took measured sips. It was her water, and I was only allowed to share it out of her good grace.

'It's okay,' she said. 'Go ahead and have another pull. We need to stay strong.'

I took one more gulp, and then set it down. There was a lot left. It looked like it would last us days, but I remembered that the water had only been gone for a couple of hours. I wanted to wash, but not in front of her. Sometime while we had slept the pool had been drained and, bizarrely, so had the pond. The fish that had lived there lay on the muddy ground, like nuggets of gold.

'Do you think I could take a small bottle of it with me?'

'Absolutely not. If they see it they'll have questions. They might follow you here. Did you bring me food?'

'Oh. Shit. I forgot. I'm sorry Becca. It honestly slipped my mind.'

She looked at me, clearly deliberating whether I had intentionally decided not to bring the food in an attempt to weaken her, or if I was genuinely that empty-headed. 'Remember next time, please.'

'Right. Well I guess I'll see you later, then.'

'Don't you think you should stay in the maze until it gets dark?'

'I don't want to be a bitch,' I said, 'but I really, really don't want to stay in this maze. So I'm going to go, and I'll see you later.'

I figured I could last until nightfall without another drink, but it was difficult. I went to the kitchen to see if any other beverages were left and found Tom looking through the fridge. I tried to slip out without being seen, but he said, 'Come here for a minute.'

I stepped back and saw him look me over. 'You know the water's off?'

'Yeah, I know.'

'So, are we doing the Communal Task, or what?'

'I don't know. Maybe.'

'Maybe? You don't want to take a shower? Or have a drink?'

'I was thinking of just leaving, actually,' I said.

'Bullshit,' he said.

'It's not like we'll last long without water. And obviously either me or Becca will lose the task. That means that either I'll get banished, or I'll be alone without another girl, with just you two. If I leave now, it's painless.'

He studied me closely. 'What's stopping you then? I'll walk you out now, if you want.'

'I'm still thinking it over,' I said.

He took a step towards me, and I took a step back. Andrew appeared in the doorway just then holding the dustpan and brush. We had never earned a hoover. He looked dishevelled. 'I was just cleaning the bedroom,' he said. 'It was pretty, uh, disgusting. But it's better, now. I think we should all go back to sleeping in the same room. We've gotten so distant. I don't even know where Becca is,' he said.

'Do you know where she is?' Tom asked me.

'No,' I said.

Tom looked at his feet. 'Do we know if she's all right? She might be hurt.' I thought he sounded both genuinely worried and embarrassed that he was worried.

'She's not in the house, anyway, and she shouldn't be out in the sun,' Andrew said. 'Neither should you, Lily. You're red around your shoulders. Have you been sitting out in the open?'

'Sometimes,' I said.

'Better you stay inside, in the house. Without water, the heat will be so much more dangerous.'

'Andrew's right,' Tom said. 'Better to stay inside.'

Becca and I knew what we were doing, but so did they. They weren't going to let me run loose, and go missing like Becca. They needed all of us in order to do the task.

'I think I'll just stretch my legs,' I said.

'Don't go far,' Tom said.

I wandered to the pool, and sat at its edge, letting my feet dangle into its empty space. It seemed enormous now, emptied of water. It was ugly, too – another gaping sore on the face of our compound. I looked west, towards where Becca was hiding with the water. I thought that Andrew would be the one to break. If things went well, he would leave in a day or two out of sheer desperation, leaving Tom, weak and dehydrated, to do the task. And hadn't Becca said that she would go once Tom had? At the end of this task, it could be just me alone in the compound, and I would be the winner. My pulse raced in excitement, and I felt almost vindicated for not going with Sam. If he had known how close I was to making it to the end – if he had known that I could best Andrew and Tom!

The problem was knowing whether or not I could trust Becca. There were no other options that I could see: as long as Becca had the water I was at her mercy.

I saw faint shadows of movement in the kitchen window, and knew that Tom and Andrew were standing there, watching. I stayed within view of them, and plaited my hair, and sang quietly to myself.

When I returned to the house that night, the kitchen was clean, the counters gleaming, the food all put away, the floor swept and washed. It looked so nice that I wanted to cry. It was absurd, the difference that the clean kitchen made. It felt like getting a second chance at life. The thing is, I'm actually a clean person. I like things neat and tidy; I just didn't see the point recently. Motivated by the cleanliness of the kitchen, I thought that I would sleep in my bed that night: change the sheets, get rid of all the clothes that were now lying on what had been Sam's side.

When I went into the bedroom Andrew was already there. He was sitting on the very edge of his bed, as though he had been about to get up. 'Hey,' Andrew said. He looked poorly, pale and drawn.

'You feeling okay?' I asked.

'I could definitely do with some water. My head is pounding, and it's only been a day. Are you feeling okay?'

'Yeah, I'm just really thirsty, too.' I actually was thirsty: I shouldn't have stayed out in the sun for so long. My mouth was dry, and my throat, too. Swallowing felt strange.

He gazed drearily at the blank wall. 'I know that humans can survive without water for three days. Does that number change, though, if you're in the desert? I mean, obviously they're not going to let us die.'

'When we ran out of food,' I said, 'they let us get pretty uncomfortable before we ate.'

He nodded. 'I guess that by tomorrow we'll be in a bad way. Christ, I'm uncomfortable already.' He looked at me for a moment. 'Where did you go, earlier?'

'The tennis court, and then the boules area.'

'I think we should get Tom and find Becca. We need to do that task tonight.'

'Okay,' I said. I tried to appear tired but willing. 'Lead the way.'

We went to Tom's room – the grey room. Andrew knocked. 'Buddy?'

'What?' Tom said from behind the door.

'We're going to look for Becca,' Andrew said. The door opened and Tom appeared. The light was dim, but he looked as bad as Andrew. The room was clean – pristine really – everything neat and orderly, but there was a faint smell that I realised, after a beat, was the smell of an unwashed man.

'She hasn't come in for food?' he asked us. Andrew shook his head. 'All right, let's go.'

It was cold outside. I rarely left the house after dark, and then usually only with Sam. I missed him. I missed him so much that I considered going home right then and there. I should have: I felt a sort of lightness in my head at the thought of it. But then something like tiredness came over me, and I thought, *a couple more weeks won't make much of a difference.* I had stayed for the summer, but I would leave before winter came.

Someone – Jacintha, I think – had installed lights around the house, but in the dark their illumination didn't go very far, and only a few metres past the house was pure darkness. 'Hold on,' I said. 'Let me check if there's a torch in my room. I think Sam might have got one a couple of weeks ago.'

Tom turned to me. I could only see half his face, but the irritation there was easy to read.

'A torch would have been very useful a couple of weeks ago, Lily. You're only telling us now?'

'I'll only be a minute. Don't go without me.'

I went into the kitchen and ducked low, so that they couldn't see me through the window. They were standing just outside, and I knew that they would be able to hear me. I had closed the door behind me, but despite Sam and Jacintha's best efforts it was imperfect and noise slipped through easily enough. I crawled as quietly as I could to the cupboard where we kept the dried foods and snacks. It creaked as I opened it, and I paused, listening for the boys, but only heard the song of the cicadas thrumming in the night. I opened the door of the cupboard the rest of the way and grabbed a fistful of chocolate bars, then closed it quickly, wincing again at the creaking. I put the bars in the pockets of my robe and returned to the boys.

'No torch?' Andrew said.

'No,' I said. 'I must have imagined it.'

'Are you afraid of the dark, Lily?' Tom asked.

Before I could answer, Andrew said, 'Lily, why don't you come with me and check to the west of the pool; Tom, you can check to the east.'

'Let's all split up,' I said. 'We'll cover more ground.'

'Are you sure?'

'Yeah. We'll probably find her in no time.'

'Okay. Call out if you find anything.'

We separated, and within seconds they were out of sight. I heard them call Becca's name, Tom to the left of me, Andrew to the right. I wanted to stay there badly, where the house was within view and I could track the boys' locations, but Becca had been on her own now for long enough. I called her name loudly, and then walked quickly and quietly towards where I thought the maze was.

I had underestimated just how dark this part of the compound was at night. With the house behind me there was nothing to illuminate the way but the dim light of a crescent moon and the pale, tired glow of distant stars. I kept stopping and listening for the boys. I heard Tom far off, to the west, but Andrew was maybe only a couple of hundred feet away. I wondered if Becca thought that I had abandoned her and was hunting her like the others.

Somehow I got lost. I swung around and saw the illumination of the house, white and brilliant in the distance, but once I turned around again I saw only darkness. I had thought I was approaching the maze, but worried now that I had missed it entirely. The boys were no longer calling Becca's name, and I had no frame of reference now as to how close they were. I wanted to call out myself, just so that someone could know where I was. I was gripped by a sudden terror that I had ventured past the perimeter and into the desert.

I heard movement and froze, my mind conjuring images of snakes and other wild creatures. Where was Tom? Was he frightened, too?

'Lily,' a voice said. A hand grabbed my shoulder and I screamed, my hands thrown out, encountering nothing.

'It's me,' Andrew said. 'Calm down, Lily, it's only me. Here, take my hand. I knew we should have gone together. It's okay; there's nothing wrong with being afraid of the dark.'

'I'm not afraid of the dark.'

'I used to be, when I was a boy. I'm not afraid here, because I know you're here and Tom is somewhere, and Becca too.'

'Where are we? Can you tell?'

'Put your hand out – there, can you feel? It's the swings. To the left is where the vegetable garden used to be. A little further south is the maze.'

'How do you know? It's so hard to tell,' I said, and with the right amount of artlessness led him towards the maze.

'Do you think she might have gone into the maze?' Andrew asked. 'We've searched everywhere else.'

'I don't know. Becca?' I shouted, and waited, letting the silence echo. In clear tones, I said, 'I don't think that we should go in tonight. Maybe in the morning, when we can see where we're going.' I put my free hand, the one that wasn't holding Andrew's, into my pocket. There was the tiniest rustle of the wrappers.

'I think you're right,' Andrew said, resigned. 'We should go back. Even if she was standing in front of us, we wouldn't be able to see her.'

I moved my foot across the ground, to cover the noise as I took a hold of the chocolate in my pocket. I could still hear the rustle, just slightly. Could he? 'Let me call her one more time,' I said, 'just in case.'

Was she in the same spot deep in the maze, hoarding the water, not making a sound? Or was she hiding by the entrance, peeking out at us, laughing as we stumbled through the dark?

'Becca!' I shouted, and at the same time I dumped the food from my pocket and left it on the ground. Even over the sound of my voice, there was a noise as it hit the ground. I moved backwards, to try and cover it, but I felt Andrew tense.

'What was that?'

'What?'

'That noise.'

'What noise?'

'Guys?' We both jumped, my nails digging into Andrew's hand. 'It's just me,' Tom said. 'You find any trace of her?'

'It's too dark,' Andrew said. 'We'll come back in the morning.'

Tom moved restlessly, his huge, barely visible silhouette

shifting back and forth over the sandy ground. 'I don't want to leave her out here,' he said.

'She chose to hide,' Andrew said.

Tom was quiet for a few moments, and then said, 'All right. She'll come inside by the morning, I'm sure.'

He moved quickly, and I felt sure now of what I had suspected – Tom was frightened of the desert.

I glanced behind me. I couldn't see the maze, but I knew that it was there. Andrew kept a hold of my hand, and I felt it spasm a little. He walked far slower than he should have. I could make out Tom's broad shoulders moving ahead of us and watched him as I would have tracked a bull in a field.

When we got to the light of the house, I saw that Andrew looked paler than before. There was sweat on his forehead, though it was freezing out. 'Are you okay?' I said.

'I'm good. Just a headache. We'll find her in the morning, don't worry.' He stopped in the kitchen, and Tom leaned against the counter, feigning casualness to hide his fatigue. 'We should all sleep in the bedroom,' Andrew said.

Now that I knew how to navigate my way to the maze in the dark I had been intending to slip out later to get some water. It would be a dreadful night without any. My lips were cracked and my mouth was gritty. I knew that if I insisted on sleeping separately they would get suspicious. But they were weaker than me, and would surely fall asleep first.

'I think that's a good idea,' Tom said. 'We need to get back to working together.'

Suddenly, Andrew's head whipped around, and I thought that Becca had appeared, or a creature from the desert. But he was looking at the fridge. 'There's nothing in there,' I said. 'We drank all the juice and milk.'

He went past me, not to the fridge, but the freezer. He took out the moulds that we had once used to make popsicles. And then he pulled out lumps of ice. His eyes were shining. 'Lily,' he said. 'Get your hairdryer.'

After minutes of us staring at the hairdryer, watching slow, steady drips of water drop into the bowl below, we each took a small sip, and it was glorious, though nowhere near enough. If we wanted more, we would have to stay up for a long time, and as it was we were very nearly swaying on our feet. It seemed ridiculous that we hadn't thought of it before: despite how long we'd spent here, away from the rest of society, we still weren't terribly good at fending for ourselves.

Andrew took out every bit of ice there was and placed it in the bowl. 'We just have to wait. When we wake up there'll be enough to get us through the morning.'

We each took a small, unsatisfying nugget of ice to tide us over. We left the bowls mournfully and went to bed. Tom closed the door so that no light slipped in. I lay stiffly, the thirst a beast I tried to ignore. Though it would be difficult, I would still sneak out later when the boys were sleeping deeply. They were exhausted: it wouldn't be long. But my own eyelids began to droop, and I let out a fervent prayer that Becca had found the chocolate by the entrance. Sleep had nearly claimed me when Andrew spoke, his voice clear and articulate. 'Lily, would you mind waking me when you wake up? I want to check on that ice as early as I can.'

'Of course,' I said. 'I'll wake you first thing.'

'Thanks,' Andrew said, and his voice was warm, almost like he was smiling a little. 'Just like old times, right?'

I felt something close to pity for Andrew. He must have had a comfortable life before coming here. It hadn't occurred to him that I might be trying to trick him or hinder him in any way. Andrew still believed, I think, that if you played by the rules and worked hard then you'd be rewarded. I don't know what I believed at that point; I could only think in the short term. Find Becca, get the water, hope that Tom left. I would deal with whatever happened after when I had to.

It was a long night. The air conditioning droned on, and I kept imagining that it was sucking the moisture out of the room, out of my mouth, even. At intervals it turned off, leaving us in deafening silence. I heard every twitch that the boys made, every shift in bed, and though we lay in darkness I imagined I saw them moving about like ghosts in the night.

Fifteen

When I woke, I felt hungover. I had been accustomed, over the previous months, to drinking bottles and bottles of water every day, in addition to coffee and whatever other drinks we had. I'd had only a few mouthfuls of water yesterday. My tongue felt huge and ungainly. I had slept longer than usual: I could see the sun, clear and bright, through the skylight. I figured it must be around ten, maybe eleven.

I swung my legs off the bed, my limbs stiff, my muscles aching. I didn't fully understand dehydration, never having experienced it myself until now. I thought of Becca, and reckoned if I moved quickly I could bring her some food, drink some water, and be back before the boys were up. I moved quietly through the room, and was at the door when I heard Tom say, 'Where are you going?'

I turned. He was lying in bed with his eyes open just a crack. 'I'm going to dig a hole in the back and take a shit. Do you want to come?'

'Wake Andrew first.'

'Do it yourself.'

'He asked you, didn't he?'

I walked to Andrew. I said his name, but he didn't move. I looked at Tom nervously. I shook his shoulder, and he remained still. 'Andrew,' I said, louder this time. '*Andrew.*'

He groaned and opened his eyes. He mouthed something, but I couldn't hear what he was saying. 'Is he dying?' I asked.

'He's not dying,' Tom said. 'Just get the melted ice.'

I fled to the kitchen, my feet sliding on the cool tiles. The two bowls were half full. It wouldn't be enough to get us through even the morning. It might bring some relief, but it wouldn't sustain us. I carried them carefully, aware of every drop in each bowl. I wondered why Tom hadn't come with me to inspect the bowls, but when I returned I realised he was nearly as poorly as Andrew. He was sitting up, but the veins stood out eerily on his face, and his skin looked oddly thin. I went to Andrew first, who said, 'We need to divide the bowls between us.' His voice was hoarse, but he looked more alert now.

'Drink,' I said. 'I'll have some after you.'

'Half a bowl each,' he said, turning to Tom. 'That way there'll be some for Becca when we find her.'

He took a drink and made a whimpering sound in the back of his throat when it touched his lips. After a moment he offered the bowl to me. I shook my head, and he took another sip, and offered it again. 'Finish it,' I said. I saw that he was conflicted, so I leaned close and whispered, 'I'll take some of Tom's.' He smiled and finished the bowl.

I brought the other bowl to Tom. He had his feet on the floor, but didn't seem strong enough to raise himself out of bed. I stood over him, and brought the bowl to my lips and drank – just a little, though my body cried out for me to drain the bowl dry. He watched me, and took the bowl from me when I had taken my small sup. He drained the bowl quickly and handed it back.

'We need to find Becca,' he said.

'God, I'd love a shower,' Andrew said, and stood slowly. 'What time is it, do you think?'

'Noon,' I lied. I wanted them wary of the midday sun.

'Fuck,' Tom said. 'There's no way that Becca's dead, right?'

'No one has ever died on the sh— in here,' Andrew said. He was right. It had never happened. People did die after the show though – there was a long list now of people who'd taken their lives after they returned home – but that was a separate issue.

I knew that I needed to make it seem as though I wanted to find her, and the only place we hadn't properly looked was the maze.

'I'll go and look for her,' I said. 'I'll check the maze.'

'I'll go,' Tom said. 'You rest. Anyway, she was my bed-mate. I should find her.'

'I'll go with you,' I said.

'No, you stay here with Andrew. There's some fruit left – a couple of apples and some pears. See what kind of juice you can get from them. We need electrolytes as well as water. I won't be long.' Without turning, he took off his underwear and put on a pair of shorts. We were past the point of privacy now, and it didn't particularly bother me as it might have a few months ago. He put on shoes and left.

Andrew and I went to the kitchen. He rooted around the freezer for more ice, but found only small chips. He offered me some, and we chewed on them meditatively for a few minutes. I gathered what fruit was left from the pantry, and Andrew sat in the chair.

'I'm sure I know another way to get water,' he said. 'If we had our phones this would be so much easier. I'm sure I saw something in a movie, once . . .' I worked on pressing what juice I could out of the fruit. There was maybe an inch of liquid, and the rest was just pulp and husk, which I pressed to my lips, smearing them with what moisture remained. When I glanced back at Andrew he was dozing in his chair, like an old man. I left the glass of fruit juice beside him and slipped out as quietly as I could. I had stepped only a few feet beyond the door when I saw Tom returning. I stayed where I was, shielding my eyes against the burn of the sun, and watched him walk towards me. I knew that he was weak: I had seen it in his movements this morning. Yet he looked strong enough as he walked across the terrain. If we were to do the task now, Andrew would be gone, and Tom would stay.

'Nothing?' I said.

'I couldn't see her in there. I can't imagine she'd venture in, anyway. It's overgrown, and not at all navigable.' He wiped the sweat off of his forehead and looked at it with concern. 'We need to stay inside,' Tom said. He looked a little shaky. 'When we were in the desert, we kept in the shade during the day, when the sun was the most brutal. We should stay inside while we wait for Becca. She'll come find us in a couple of hours, I bet. If we're feeling a bit off now, she'll be feeling much worse, out in the open like that. We sit tight in the bedroom, where there's air conditioning, and by this evening she'll be back. We'll do the task, and we'll have water again. And I'll tell you another thing,' he said, 'If there was ever any doubt about who's getting banished, it's certainly gone now with Becca running off and leaving us in this mess. When she comes back she'd better have her tail between her fucking legs.'

We stayed in the bedroom until the sun had disappeared beyond the horizon. I felt terribly weak: the simple act of getting off the bed was more challenging than I cared to admit. Still, I kept thinking about Becca. The chocolate bars would have been only enough to last her for a couple of hours, presuming she had found them at all. It was too long to leave her without food, but I was parched now, in pain, my head pounding, joints aching, eyes dry. Some foods helped a little, like vegetables, but others that seemed harmless, like yoghurt, left my mouth drier than before, sorely regretting having tried it.

The boys were weaker still. Andrew lay in bed, staring blankly before him. Every so often he became very still, and I would call his name in a panic. He caught my eye once, around the evening time, and, seeing my worry, smiled, placating. 'They won't let us die,' he said.

When the sun was setting, I couldn't stand it any more. I said I was going outside to relieve myself. The boys didn't show any sign that they'd heard, but when I was outside, I heard a sound behind me and saw Tom standing in the doorway.

'You should go back to bed,' I said. 'You're very weak.'

'I am feeling weak, you're right. But you're not. I can see that you're uncomfortable, but you're not ill like Andrew and I are. You look like Andrew did last night. Which means you've had water at some point.'

'You've been with me all day,' I said. 'When would I have had the chance?'

'All day today,' he said. 'But not yesterday.' He stayed standing in the doorway, though I feared the moment he would step beyond. There was a shovel near me, leaning against the wall.

'I had energy drinks,' I said. 'Left over from a Personal Task. They're gone now, but they kept me going for a while.'

He looked at me for a few moments. 'But you need water now. I can see it. Your stomach feels hollow, even though you've eaten, right? And you feel light-headed, like you might pass out.'

I didn't answer. He stepped out of the door. As he stepped

close beside me I flinched, and he saw it. But he only took the shovel and handed it to me. 'Just beyond where the flower arches used to be. That should be a good place to go. It's private, but close enough that I can hear you shout if you feel like you're going to faint. I'll stay here and keep an eye out for Becca.'

'Thanks,' I said. The shovel was heavy, and my instinct was to drop it. My muscles felt good for nothing.

'We haven't always gotten along, have we, Lily? I got a little caught up in some things that didn't really matter. Losing the shed was hard for me. I built it with my own two hands. And losing all of our rewards . . . it was a hard blow to take. But the most important thing now is that we work together. If we only look out for ourselves – well, we're no better than animals. We'll find Becca, and we'll do the task, and we'll have water. Becca will go home, and the three of us can live together peacefully. We don't need to live on top of each other. I could build another shed. But it wouldn't be a shed, it could be a kind of . . . guesthouse. And you wouldn't have to worry about running into me or being uncomfortable or anything like that. That sound good?'

'Sounds like you have it all planned out.'

'Well,' he said, looking at me. 'I'm sure we're all starting to make a plan at this point.'

'What would you do if you won?'

I didn't expect him to answer, but he replied instantly, as though eager to tell me. 'I'd get yards and yards of barbed wire. And I'd build a fence around the compound, much better than the other one. I'd make sure nothing and no one would be able to disturb me. I'd stay here for ever. No one could make me leave. Not ever.' He looked away, then flicked a look at me. 'What about you? You want to be famous, is that it? Get some nice brand deals for yourself?'

'I don't know,' I said. 'I just want a rest.' I didn't want to give Tom the satisfaction of telling him that his plan didn't sound so different from my own.

He jerked his chin to the plain before us, a dismissal. 'You go and do your thing, and I'll wait for you here.'

I went beyond, to where the flower arches used to be. A few weeks ago, weeds and rushes and flowers would have brushed by me as I made my way across. But it was empty now, and I had to focus all of my concentration, every drop of energy that I had, on walking across the flat plain and keeping my balance, making sure that when I walked I was steady, with no weakness showing.

When we returned inside, I immediately got into bed. I had grown so soft. I just wanted to lie there and let the issue resolve itself. They wouldn't let us die, but I *could* die.

Without meaning to, I fell asleep. I woke, horrified, unsure of how much time had passed. I had no way of knowing if it was deep into the night, or if only a few minutes had gone by.

How long had Becca gone without food? Andrew and Tom were asleep, too. I didn't hesitate this time. I took my jumper off the ground where I'd thrown it, and left.

My feet were light on the ground, but they still might have heard me. I stopped more than once on the way to the kitchen, listening for the sound of the boys waking up, but the house remained entirely silent.

The door to the cupboard creaked again, loudly, as I filled my pockets with all the food that they could hold. I felt terrible, but in a dimmer way than I had earlier. I brought a lighter, the only light source that I could find. Its light was weak, and flickered as I moved across the grounds, but it focused me. There was adrenaline crashing through my veins, urging me to move swiftly. Fear overtook exhaustion, and I managed to run at a reasonable pace across the grounds, though I made strange gasping noises, not like I was out of breath, but like I was being strangled. The light went out as I ran, and I held my hands in front of me, waiting for the touch of the hedge maze. I crashed into it at last and groped for the entrance. Finally, I found it, and said, 'Becca!' softly. I lit the lighter again, and glanced behind me. There was nothing there, only darkness. Far beyond, there was the light of the house, warm and inviting in the distance.

'Becca!' I said again. She would know the sound of my step, she had said. I found the entrance and entered the maze, clutching the lighter, terrified that it might set one of the hedges alight, and there would be another fire. The walls seemed impossibly close. 'Becca,' I said again, truly frightened now. I kept glancing at my feet, thinking that I would see her little body curled up, unmoving and white in the moonlight.

A hand grabbed me, and I jumped, crashing backwards into the hedge. The lighter fell at my feet, extinguished. 'Be quiet,' Becca's voice said.

'Becca,' I said, reaching out, but she swatted my hands away.

'Be quiet, I said.'

We stood in silence, listening. There was nothing, no sound at all. I picked up the lighter from the ground. I could only see the whites of Becca's eyes, and the vague outline of her hair. Speaking with barely a whisper, she said, 'Follow me.' She put her hand in mine and led the way. How she knew where to go in the dark I don't know. She had a dancer's step, light and precise, and I tried to mimic her.

We got to the spot, indistinguishable to me from any other, and she sat us down, and moved the branches so that we were half exposed and half within the hedge. The twigs and leaves scraped at my face. I moved out a little more and lit the lighter.

I could see her then: the light seemed enormous in the small space. She didn't look good, but she definitely looked better than Andrew or Tom.

'Water,' I said.

She nodded, then said, 'Did you bring food?'

'Yes,' I said. 'Is there water left? Is it gone?'

She said nothing for a beat, and I took the food out of my pockets and dumped it in her lap. She turned and crawled a bit away. 'It's here,' she said. 'See?' I could see it, dimly, the gallon bottle. There was water left: not a lot, but enough. She gave it to me, and even as I drank it in great, noisy gulps, I marvelled at the self-control it must have taken to leave any. She was tearing at the food, stuffing it into her mouth, and we were like two rats, I thought, hiding in the shadows and gorging on what we could.

She pulled the bottle gently from me. There was maybe a fifth left. 'That's enough,' she said. 'I know it's hard. But we need to save it.'

'Until when?'

'Tomorrow they'll either do the task or decide to go home,' she said. 'One, or both. I'm betting Andrew is holding out on the producers stepping in?' I nodded. 'I almost feel bad for him.'

I was panting. My face felt numb. My hands were shockingly cold.

'Are you okay?' I said. 'Why didn't you come into the house? I thought you would freeze to death out here.'

'I'm fine,' she said. 'It was a long night, but it was fine.'

'Becca, this is ridiculous,' I said. 'Let's go in and do the task. It's freezing out here. You can't stay here again. They'll lose now, easily.'

'Tomorrow,' she said. 'You can have more water, then go to sleep. In the morning, you'll be in better shape, and so will I.

I'll sleep inside tonight, maybe in the back room, and we'll see whether they choose to do the challenge or just leave.'

I listened for the sound of footsteps, or some animal or beast. Becca looked calm enough. Her face was very white, and there was a smear of chocolate around her mouth.

'How old are you, Becca?'

'Seventeen,' she said, and then: 'No. Eighteen. I turned eighteen a few weeks ago. I lied to get on the show. Well, everyone lies a little to get on the show, don't they? I don't think it matters much anyway, the difference of a couple of weeks.'

'I suppose so.'

'Time feels different here, doesn't it? I don't know if I'll go back to the old way of living by every minute and hour, will you? I know enough to get by, just by the place of the sun in the sky and the waxing of the moon.'

It was the most I had ever heard Becca speak, though we had spent weeks together cleaning the kitchen.

'Didn't you lie, to get on the show?' she asked me.

'Not really,' I said. 'I probably made myself seem more interesting, but I think everyone probably does that. I guess I lied about having more hobbies and stuff. At home, I used to just stay in bed all day on my days off. I left that out.'

'I almost exclusively lied,' she said. 'I don't even like men.'

'Why are you here?' I asked. 'Why did you come on the show?'

She was quiet for a few moments; there was only the sound of our breathing and the soft whisper of leaves moving about our feet. 'I used to make fun of the people who came on the show. My friends and I, we'd laugh at how vapid everyone was. The things that people will do for the sake of something pretty. I guess I came on as a joke. I thought I could go home and do an exposé, maybe start a career in journalism or something. I suppose it was just as vain to think that I could gain attention by getting cast and then criticising the show as it would be to come here looking for genuine fame. But I didn't realise how – immersive it would be. I never particularly cared about the prizes. But Tom – I couldn't understand how everyone was all right with him still being in the compound, how we let him order us around, coming when he and Andrew called, like dogs. I wanted to humiliate him – but it became more difficult, when we became bed-mates. He was so close all the time, and I knew how quickly he could become violent. I'd wake in the night and find him staring at me. Sometimes he'd stroke my face. When he was punished – when he was burned in the hot tub, and then when the shed burned – I thought that would make me happy; I thought that would be enough. But I don't want to go home before he does. I don't want to go home; not while he's still here, collecting rewards. I want him banished in the most humiliating manner possible.'

We were silent for a short time. 'Aren't you going to ask me why I came on the show?'

'No,' she said. 'I don't need you to explain it. You're the kind of girl the show was made for.'

Before I could register what was happening, I was being pressed against the ground, a hand on my throat. The world went white. I thought I was dying: I screamed and felt relieved to hear my voice. Not dead then, but I was choking. My brain told me that I could overpower Becca, even if she'd had more water: she was a tiny thing, but my body was panicking, flailing. I gripped the hand that was struggling to find the right grip on my throat, and felt hair along the fingers, a signet ring on the pinky finger.

Tom loomed over me, one hand on my neck, the other holding Becca down, her face in the dirt.

'I knew it,' he said. 'I knew it, I knew it.'

Becca managed to twist her head. She wasn't looking at him; she was looking at me. She was mouthing something, but it was too dark to see what. I saw Tom's hand move backwards, and then the sound of a sharp *crack*, and Becca's head smacked sharply against the ground. His hold on me loosened, and I scrambled forward towards the water hidden in the bush. I heard Becca make some sound behind me, and I thought that she must have fought back in some way, and then I had it: I had the water, and I was getting to my feet, clutching it to my chest. Tom was on me in a second, pinning me to the ground again, his knees on my chest, the air whooshing out of me. I could breathe, but I thought my ribs would break if I drew in another breath.

He opened the bottle, his hands fumbling, and tilted his head up towards the sky, his mouth stretched obscenely open, and emptied the contents of the bottle over his face. It rained down his face, into his mouth, into his eyes, and he made a keening sound as the drops hit his tongue, writhing like a snake in his mouth. Some of the water fell down onto me, and even though I was struggling to breathe under Tom's massive weight, still my body cried out to try and catch some of the liquid that was falling. I was thirsty, so thirsty, and the bottle was empty now; Tom, emitting wild gasps, had finished it all. I rolled him off me in a huge lurch, and he didn't fight it.

I grabbed Becca, pulling her to her feet with what little strength I had, and ran down the path lurching left and right. Becca was the only one who knew the maze, but she was running wildly next to me, jerking us down different pathways, glancing back every couple of seconds. I didn't know if she was leading us out of the maze, or leading us further in, or if she was running in a blind panic, her only goal to flee from Tom.

I glanced over my shoulder; the moon had come out from behind a cloud, and a distant ray dimly lit the path behind us. Tom wasn't anywhere in sight, but there was a splotchy, dark trail behind us. I stopped and looked at Becca. There was a steady gush of blood running from her nose and onto the ground. I could actually hear the drops hitting the dirt. I pulled off my jumper and threw it at her. 'You need to stop the blood,' I said. 'He'll find us.'

She held the jumper to her face. Her eyes swung wildly around. There was something about the look on her face – that raw fear – and I wondered what had passed between them in the weeks that they had been sharing a bed.

'They can't let us die,' I said, but my voice shook. Becca looked at me for a beat, then at the maze beyond us.

'If you take five lefts, three rights, a left and two more rights, you'll reach the entrance,' she said.

'I won't find it on my own,' I said.

'We need to separate. He needs both of us to do the task. I'll take a different route. Go, quickly!' She pushed me towards the left path, and then she ran to the right. I wanted to call her name, but I couldn't risk being caught. I could hear footsteps, but couldn't tell whose they were. I ran left, and the moon moved again behind the shadow.

Left, left, left, left – but where the fifth left should've been there was only another right turn. I paused, my heart knocking painfully against my ribs. While I was standing, trying to decide what to do, I heard a sound behind me. I froze, my limbs locking. If this were the wild, I thought, I'd be dead.

Andrew came around the corner, and I sagged with relief, slumping against a hedge behind me.

'Lily, thank Christ,' he said. He took my arm and pulled me upright. 'Are you all right?'

'I'm fine,' I said, but my voice was hoarse. 'I just— Andrew, are you all right?'

'I really need water,' he said. 'I feel incredibly ill.'

'It's okay,' I said. 'Lean on me. We'll get you inside. It's going to be fine.'

He leaned on me, and I was pressed further into the hedge. I tried to shift a little out of the way, but he took my shoulder. 'Don't you feel sick, too?'

'I do,' I said, my voice barely there. 'I feel really sick.'

His face was close to mine. 'Why did you go out on your own, Lily? It's dangerous out here.'

'Andrew!' came Tom's voice, at once close and far away.

Whispering urgently, I said, 'We can't let him know that we're here.'

He squeezed my shoulder. 'It's okay,' he said. Then he shouted, 'I'm here! I'm here with Lily!'

I tried to wrench myself free from him, but he held tight. His fingers dug into my skin. I pushed against his chest, and he said, 'Stop, Lily, stop. We need water, all right? Stop.'

Tom came around the corner, carrying Becca. She was limp in his arms. I tried to move again, but Andrew held me tightly, my arms pinned behind my back.

'She's fine,' Tom said. 'She's fine, she just – needs a rest.' He placed her on the ground with great gentleness.

She sat up, and shivered, her arms tight around her. There was dried blood on her face, and scrapes on her arm. She clutched her leg and moaned.

'What did you do?' I said to Tom, my voice trembling, though I wished for strength. 'You – you psychopath, what did you do?'

'I didn't do anything,' he said. 'She ran away from me and tripped.'

'And why was she running, do you think? Andrew, *let me go*. You're hurting me,' I said. He complied, and I knelt beside her. 'What happened?' I asked her.

'He grabbed me and I ran away. I fell and twisted my ankle. I must have passed out.'

'But you didn't hurt her, Tom?' Andrew asked.

I turned to him. 'Look at her! Of course he hurt her. And he would have hurt me, too, if he had caught me. He pinned us down and took the water – the last of the water, every drop!'

'Well,' Andrew said, in a strange voice, looking at me. 'You did hoard the water, the two of you. You snuck out here and left us sick and dehydrated.'

'We wouldn't have let anything happen to you,' I said.

He sighed. He sounded exhausted. 'We need to do the task. Now. It's not ideal, but we all need water, fast. We can't put it off.' He said, 'I'm sorry, Becca, I don't think I'm strong enough to lift you.'

'Wait,' Becca said, but Tom bent over and picked her up again. 'No!' she screamed. 'Put me down. Put me *down*!' Tom let her down roughly, and she leaned against me, her legs trembling.

'Jesus fucking *Christ*,' Tom said. He grabbed his hair in a strange mix of rage and exasperation. He twisted towards Becca, spittle flying from his mouth. 'What is wrong with you? Don't you realise that you're the ones who put us in this mess? All I've ever done is look after you!'

Behind me, Andrew suddenly fell to the ground. It shocked me to see: there was something horrifying about it, the limp way that he fell, the fact that it was Andrew. Curiously, no one moved to help him.

'I'm fine,' he said. 'I'm fine. Just – let's just do the task.' He got back to his feet, unsteadily, and leaned against the hedge. 'Is there really no water left?' His words were slurred.

'I'm sorry, man,' Tom said. 'We'll get you sorted as soon as the screen turns green.'

Becca was sobbing quietly.

'Becca,' Tom said. 'We need you to lead us out of the maze. Can you do that?'

Becca's blood was drenching my shirt, and I felt that I might pass out at any second; still, Tom's condescending tone in that moment somehow struck me as one of the worst moments of that night.

She leaned on me, limping, and led us through the maze. The boys followed closely behind, Andrew stepping on my heels every now and then, apologising each time.

Sixteen

We went to the dusty patch of ground where we had done all our tasks, back when we still cared to look after the compound. Tom marked out what he thought was one hundred metres, placing a stone as the finishing line. I was pleased to see him stagger a little at one point, though I found it infuriating that even in the state he was in he had to be the one in charge. For a brief time it had felt like Becca and I held the power – yet we were back, now, to our old routine, because Tom had found us, and Tom was stronger than we were.

We were all panting before we'd even begun. We stood at the starting line that Tom had drawn in the sand, and stared at the stone, one hundred metres away from us. It seemed impossible. Not one of us was in the condition to race. Becca, who an hour ago had been the strongest, was now clutching her leg, blood dripping down her face.

'We don't need to do an amazing job,' Tom said. 'We just need to do it. It'll be over in a few minutes.'

Andrew nodded, though his head didn't remain still after, but seemed to float around a bit, drifting up and to the side. I thought that it must be killing him not to be the one to give a pep talk.

'You okay, Becca?' Tom asked.

'Let's just do it,' she said.

Tom looked at us. 'We know from before that if someone cheats then it doesn't count. We really, really don't want to have to do this over. Does everyone understand?'

The other two nodded, and Andrew's head again dipped all over the place. 'Lily? Do you understand?' Tom asked.

'Fuck you,' I said.

'On the count of three.'

We positioned ourselves as well as we could. We were near the perimeter, and I thought, in the far distance, I could see movement. I couldn't tell if it was an animal looking for food, or members of crew, checking to make sure we didn't die.

'One. Two. Three!'

For a few seconds, we all kept pace with one another. As I moved forward, I kept my face slightly turned so that I could see the position of the others. Andrew stumbled almost immediately, zombie-like, shuffling, falling, picking himself up, falling again. Becca was ahead of him, but only by a small margin: she had tried to run, but after a few steps had to slow to a jagged, choppy walk. Tom was racing ahead, and so was I, the two of us neck and neck. I was not soft. I wasn't strong, but I was fast. I was making a strange noise, like the sound a baby makes when they're gearing up to wail, but I couldn't stop. Tom was grunting too, his teeth bared in pain, but his legs still moved, quickly, quickly, and so did mine. Becca cried out in pain, and I saw Tom's head twitch, and then turn to look behind his shoulder. He didn't stop, but he was distracted, and for a fraction of a second he slowed. I pushed forward, the stone before me, almost there, and I heard him grunt again, his arms reaching out, as though to stop me, but I was ahead of him now. I wasn't going home, I wouldn't go home . . .

I made it to the stone and fell to the ground wheezing, every breath an effort. A second after me, Tom slammed his hand on the rock, and promptly vomited on his shoes. My vision was blurry, and my head felt heavy, but I looked up and saw Andrew and Becca, leaning on each other as they staggered across the dusty ground, Becca's face drawn in pain, Andrew with his mouth open and his eyes wheeling around in his head. They were twenty feet away, then ten, and then, without warning, Andrew pulled away from Becca, who cried out and fell. 'I'm sorry, Becca,' he said, and loped forward the final few feet to put his hand on the rock.

Becca didn't try to rush the final stretch. She stood and walked towards us, her limp pronounced, though she moved with a certain dignity that was impossible not to admire. Andrew looked away as Becca took one final stride and sat down on the rock.

The irrigation system came on, and water spouted into the air in great, triumphant streams, silver under the moonlight. We sat and watched it lifelessly. In only a few days the land had become dry and hard, and as the water hit the earth it fell with an audible, drum-like thump.

We helped each other inside, my arm around Becca, Tom's around Andrew. The house was close; it seemed like we would never make it, but then we were standing under the kitchen lights, and it felt like a different world. We smelled of sweat and vomit and blood, and I gagged once we closed the door behind us. We were disgusting. We were vile. Andrew lurched towards the sink, but Tom said, 'Lily won the race. Let her have the first drink.' I didn't stop to consider Tom's distorted ideas on what constituted fair and honourable – I rushed to the sink, no thought in my head but water, water, water. I drank it straight from the tap, and the room was filled by the sound of my gasping and gulping and the water splashing. There were taps all around the house, but I think the others were too tired or injured to get to them. I moved to the side, and Tom took his turn, then Andrew, then Becca, and then I took bottles from the drawers, filled them, and gave them to the others.

'I should go,' Becca said. She was sitting on a chair, and looked terrible – pale and bloody, covered in dust.

Andrew was sitting on the floor. I felt poorly, but definitely better after having drunk the water. Andrew looked no better at all. He couldn't look at Becca. Tom said, 'You can't go out into the desert covered in blood.'

'They need the – the banished person – gone by sunrise,' Andrew said. 'Have a shower and rest for a couple of hours, and then we can take you out.'

'I'll go on my own,' she said. 'I don't need your help.' She hesitated. 'But I do need a shower. I'll take the downstairs one.'

I got up, my joints aching, and helped her to the bathroom. I was ready to go in with her, but she shook her head and closed the door firmly in my face.

We showered and took two bottles of water each with us to bed. I would have slept in the living room, but the truth was I'd grown worried that Andrew might die. I had never seen anyone look so ill. His skin was grey and his lips were chapped to the point of bleeding. Despite everything, I couldn't help but stay close and check on him. I slept fitfully, waking up, looking around me as though in a dream. Becca was still there, and Andrew was still alive, but his breathing was heavy, and each inhalation seemed to go on forever. Tom was snoring: he had fallen asleep first. He had vomited copiously after his second bottle of water, and then had stayed outside, sipping a third bottle slowly.

When I did sleep, I had strange dreams, of ghouls, white and ghastly, dripping saliva and reaching out their translucent hands, and Tom, looming over me, his hand on my throat, asking me if I was all right.

I woke suddenly. It was only a slight noise that woke me, but I jerked upright as though an alarm had rung out. It was Becca: she was standing at the foot of my bed.

'Becca,' I whispered. She looked at me and raised a finger to her lips. She took the silk belt of my dressing gown and moved across the room. She stood over Tom's sleeping form, slipped the belt around his neck, and pulled. He woke instantly, arms thrown out, but Becca was beyond his reach, and he was confused, pulling at the silk at his throat, his fingers scrabbling but finding no purchase. His eyes were bulging, and he was making terrible noises, now flailing behind him to grab at Becca. His elbow caught her in the ribs, but she kept pulling. Absurdly, I looked at Andrew, as though he might sort the situation out. He was lying on his side, on top of his covers, mouth moving, but still asleep.

Above Tom's strangled sounds, I heard something I had not heard in months – the sound of a car, screeching to a stop outside. The sound was a livewire through me – jarring beyond reason, a siren warning that someone was actually dying, and a reminder that although the rules were gone we still lived at the mercy of others. The rational part of me knew that if they were here, it was to help – but at the sound of the car, I felt pure, unadulterated terror. A car door slammed, and there were quick footsteps on the patio.

'Becca, stop!' I cried. 'They're here! They're here!'

I threw myself off the bed to run towards them. But just as I had my feet on the floor, the silk cord around Tom's neck snapped, and the room filled with the sound of his wild gasps.

Becca fell to the ground. The footsteps outside stopped, and came no closer.

Tom wasted no time. He turned to Becca and jerked her to her feet, his hands wrapping around her arms, tiny in his grasp. 'Stupid – fucking – bitch – this, after you left us for dead with no water! After I kept you safe for *months*! Ungrateful bitch – spiteful, pathetic *cunt*! What have I done, but keep you safe?'

She cried out, and I thought the bones in her arms would surely snap. He kept one hand on her arm and brought the other to her throat. I tried to prise his hands from her, my nails sinking into his flesh, but he only released her arm briefly to shove me away. His strength was, even now, shocking, and I careened backwards and onto the floor. I could hear more footsteps, and shouting, too, and the door to the kitchen opening. 'Tom,' I said. '*Tom.*' Becca was clutching at his hand, turning purple. 'They're here. Tom. Listen! They're downstairs!'

'Who?'

'*Them*!'

He looked perturbed.

'She tried to kill me,' he said.

'Look at what you're doing! Let go of her!'

He dropped his hands, and Becca at once started spluttering and gasping, stepping backwards, her hands clutching her throat. 'You're banished,' he said to Becca. 'Now. This minute. Into the desert.'

She took in rattling breaths. 'Let me get my things,' she rasped.

'Now,' he said.

'I'll go with you,' I said.

'No,' he said, swiftly, and without room for argument.

'At least let me get her a coat,' I said. 'For God's sake, Tom, it's freezing out there.'

He hesitated, then picked up one of his own jumpers and pulled it over Becca's head, careful of her injured nose. Her arm got stuck in the wrong hole, and he helped her, then fixed her hair with surprising gentleness. She was shaking, breathing unsteadily. Tom glanced at Andrew, who was still deeply asleep; he looked paler than he had a few hours ago, and his head was moving on his pillow. 'You stay with him,' Tom said to me. 'You might have to wake him up and give him more water.'

He put his arm around Becca's shoulder and walked her out of the room. There was no time for a goodbye, though I wasn't sure if she would have wanted one.

Now I was the only girl left. For all of our scheming, how depressing it was that Becca and I had been foiled by such a thing as brute strength. I wondered if we were always doomed to fail, because they were strong, and we were weak. Was this how it was always going to turn out? If I stayed here, would I always be under the threat of their strength, the end to every argument, the solution to any problem? Even dehydrated and weak, Tom had knocked me about like I was nothing. Andrew, too, hadn't hesitated to become a brute when he needed to. But hadn't I done the same, by helping Becca to keep the water hidden? If I had their strength, would I not use it?

Andrew started to talk in his sleep, sounding distressed. I pressed his shoulder and said his name, as I had done a hundred times or more in the months that we had lived here. He wasn't easy to wake, and I had to shake him gently before he opened his eyes.

'Lily,' he said. His voice was faint. 'Are you okay?'

'I'm fine, Andrew. How are you feeling?'

His eyes moved around, and he muttered something that I couldn't understand. I felt his forehead: he was burning up. 'Lean forward a little,' I said. He didn't, so I cupped the back of his neck, lifting his head gently, and with my free hand took the bottle from his nightstand. 'Open your mouth,' I said. 'Some more water and you'll feel much better.'

I fed him the water slowly. Swallowing seemed painful for him, and he closed his mouth after a minute or so. He put his head back on the pillow and closed his eyes, but when I got up, his eyes opened again. 'Where are you going?'

'I'm going to get you something for your fever.'

'Fever?' he asked, bewildered. 'Where are the others?'

'Outside.'

'What, all of them?'

I wiped some of the sweat off his brow. 'I'll be back in a minute. Try and drink some more water, if you can.'

I went to the downstairs bathroom and got some ibuprofen. I drenched a towel with water, returning as quickly as I could. I glanced out the window, but there was nothing to see, only darkness.

Andrew had fallen asleep again, and it was more difficult to wake him this time.

'Oh, Lily,' he said, vaguely surprised. 'Where's Sam?'

'Open up,' I said. 'I have something to make you feel better.'

He looked around, agitated. 'Where's Sam? He's not in your bed.'

'Sam's in the garden,' I said. 'He wanted to check on the vegetables one more time before he went to sleep. Now, open up for me, Andrew, okay?' He opened his mouth. His tongue was white. I placed the ibuprofen on it and poured more water into his mouth. He fell asleep again shortly after.

I placed the wet towel on his forehead, and dribbled some water on his lips, which were still raw and bloody. The towel seemed to heat up in a very short space of time.

A noise. I looked up and found Tom. He sat heavily on

the bed. He looked exhausted. 'Well, she's gone,' he said. I said nothing and wiped at the sweat gathering in the nape on Andrew's neck.

'How is he?'

I shrugged. Tom came over to look at him.

'Thanks for looking after him,' he said.

I turned my back to him.

'I forget, sometimes, how young you are, Lily. Well, look at you now. Final three.'

I kept my back to him, not saying a word.

He got into bed, and I continued to mop Andrew's face, and waited for the fever to break. I hated them both, but I didn't want Andrew to die – I stayed awake as long as I could, waking him when I could to pour more water into his mouth. I must have fallen asleep at some point, for I woke later, in my own bed, though I didn't remember moving from Andrew's side. I didn't wake of my own accord: it was the sound of the voice that pulled me from my sleep.

'Good morning,' it said. 'Andrew has been temporarily removed from the compound in order to receive medical treatment. He has not been banished and will return as soon as is medically advisable.'

I thought I might have been dreaming, but Andrew's bed was empty. Tom was lying in his bed atop the covers, the sunlight through the skylight shining on his scars and burns. He didn't move, but I knew he was awake.

Seventeen

Tom didn't leave his bed for most of the day. I knew that he was wiped from dehydration, but I thought he might also be moping over Becca's departure.

I left him there, and checked all the taps and lights and air conditioning, paranoid that something else could be turned off. I would have liked to spend the day in bed as well, but I was frightened of Tom, and frightened, too, of the next thing that might be taken from us, or the return of the producers. Though of course the producers had been nearby the whole time, their presence now felt ominous. Watching Tom sleep, I wondered at what point they stepped in; how much pain could be inflicted before it was deemed too much?

We passed the majority of the day without seeing much of each other. I added to my little nest in the linen room, where I'd begun to cache bottles of water and food, some clothes and other essentials. I checked the big screen compulsively, but it remained turned off, as it had been during my first days here. It might have been because Andrew was absent, or it might have been because Tom and I were being given a brief reprieve. Although I was glad of it, it unnerved me to see it blank.

I wandered into the dressing room, where I could still smell the other girls' perfumes. My little screen was glowing softly. I walked towards it, as though in a trance. I had been neglecting my Personal Tasks for weeks, but now that I thought to do them again, I felt a terrible, compulsive need to do as many as I possibly could. In the final three, the rewards were usually incredible, and after our experience with the water, I felt that I had to take everything that was offered. I was determined to win, but I knew that Tom was equally driven; if he did best me, I wanted to depart with a sickening amount of rewards, riches that would make leaving bearable. But they seemed to know that I was desperate for a reward: the task read *Give Tom a compliment*. Upon seeing it, I threw a shoe at the wall in a fit of anger. I thought, for the first time in a while, about the people watching, how stupid they must have thought that I was. I imagined them laughing at me, trapped in the house with Tom, like a rabbit living with a lion. How silly they would think me, simpering up at him and telling him that he was brilliant.

But the reward was diamond earrings.

I found Tom in the gym. He was lifting dumbbells, the ones that Ryan had earned a long time ago. I thought, again, of how things might look as a viewer: when I had regained my strength, I returned to doing Personal Tasks; when Tom had regained his strength, he went to work out.

'You okay?' he asked when he saw me. I nodded, and when I didn't say anything he went back to lifting.

'How heavy are those?'

'Thirty k each.'

'Can I try?'

'Sure.'

I took hold of one, and though I braced myself I could barely lift it. Tom watched me, pitying, but a bit pleased, too. I put it down again.

'Wow,' I said. 'It's heavy.'

'It's not too bad.'

'You must be very strong. You're really strong, Tom.'

'I must be, Lily, I must be.'

I turned to leave. He called my name and I paused. 'Where are you going?'

'Back to the house.'

'Why don't you stay in the house, for today? Better you don't go wandering off, again.'

'Don't tell me what to do.'

'Stay in the house, Lily. I'm warning you.'

I went to my postbox, my hands trembling with excitement. The box was small and velvet, the brand's name stitched in silver thread. I opened it and found two perfect square-shaped diamonds nestled in a silver backing. I took them out and held them up to the light, delighting in their sparkle. They were beautiful, finer than anything else I owned – though I had envisioned dangling earrings, the diamonds huge and oval shaped. But it was a good sign of what was to come, once Tom and Andrew were gone.

That night, feeling too confined by the linen closet, I settled into the living room, bringing my blankets and slippers as well as my night clothes. If I could have, I would have spent all my time on the L-shaped couch. Besides the garden, it was the spot that reminded me most of Sam, and I fancied that I could even smell him there, a little. I was lying there, thinking of Sam, of lying in the crook of his arm, his hand stroking my hair, when Tom knocked on the door and walked in without waiting for my answer.

'Get out,' I said.

'I thought you might want to sleep in the bedroom tonight.'

'I definitely do not want to.'

'Be that as it may, you'll need to sleep in the bedroom.'

'Why?'

'Because Becca tried to strangle me last night, and you stood there and did nothing. I can't trust you.'

'You think I'd strangle you in your sleep?'

'No. But then, I didn't think Becca would either.'

'I'm not sleeping in the bedroom.'

'Fine,' he said, and left. He came back a minute later, with blankets and a pillow. He settled on the rug.

'Absolutely not,' I said.

'I don't want to sleep on the floor either. But I need to keep you in sight until I decide what to do with you.'

I lay still, as though to avoid being seen. My heartbeat picked up. 'What do you mean, "what to do with" me?'

He didn't say anything. I got up and went to the bedroom, taking my things with me. He followed: I heard his step like a lumbering dog behind me. I went to my bed, and lay very still. I kept my sheets tucked low, so that I could see him clearly. My heart was beating loudly.

'I have a knife,' Tom said. 'If you get out of bed suddenly, I will use it.'

I stared at the ceiling and thought of home. It seemed a hazy thing to me now. Was it better than this, or worse? I wondered if Sam was watching. I wondered what he thought of me now.

'I think,' Tom said, after a long stretch of silence, 'We could live together, for a while. We could keep to ourselves. We wouldn't have to see each other.'

I wasn't sure if Tom actually meant this, or if he wanted to lull me into a false sense of security. I thought uneasily of Becca, how he liked to have her around, even when she openly despised him. I wondered if Tom felt better about himself if there was a girl always on the periphery, asking him for help and telling him he was capable and strong. 'Tom,' I said. 'I fucking loathe you. You're a psychopath. I don't want to live with you. As soon as Andrew's back, we're going to banish you.'

Tom didn't say anything for a moment. Then: 'Do you think Andrew would choose you over me?'

'Didn't you and Andrew have a fight in the desert? Over who would be the one in charge?'

'You don't understand the laws of men. It's easier to sort it out in the desert, where a man can be a man, rather than in here.'

'I heard you were like a pair of animals. You don't actually think you could live with Andrew?'

'No,' he said, 'I don't. I'd make sure he was banished, soon.'

'That's nice,' I said. 'The laws of men, right?'

'When you went into the pool naked all those weeks ago, did you do it for me?'

I turned to him. In the dark, I could only see his enormous outline. He was looking up at the ceiling, I thought, but I couldn't make out the expression on his face. I felt a brief, terrible sense of pity for him, along with revulsion.

'No,' I said. 'It was for a personal challenge. I didn't realise you were there.'

He was quiet for a moment. 'I don't like you, Lily. But I had wondered. I thought that maybe . . . the skinny-dipping, the parading around in your tiny shorts and bikinis . . . And when you broke my record player, I was angry, but I wondered if you did it to get my attention, like a girl in the schoolyard. You are very girlish, you know. I think that's why so many of the men looked out for you. Well, I'm glad that you don't like me, that you weren't attracted to me, because I never liked you like that. The truth is, I don't really like girls generally – not to be around, at least. I like them in my bed: I liked Vanessa in my bed. Becca was a good girl, I thought, but I was wrong about her. You never are good girls, are you?'

I rolled away so I wouldn't have to look at him.

How was Tom still here? A couple of seasons ago, there had been a woman on the show who was a pathological liar, and we, the viewers, all hated her; there was enough public response that the producers listened. Sure enough, there were challenges designed to out her secrets, to expose her, and she was quickly banished. Another year, there was a man who was so obnoxious and so boring that we said over and over that we wanted him gone, and then, the following week, he was banished, too. Mostly the residents had control, but sometimes if the public disliked someone enough, the producers would figure out a way to nudge them out. Thinking of Candice, how she left almost immediately after the challenge that revealed that Andrew was cheating, I wondered if the public didn't like her – if the challenge had been orchestrated to banish her.

But why was Tom still here? There was likely a group of viewers who disliked him – but there must have been another group of people who wanted him to stay; people who agreed with him, who saw something in him that they liked.

Why was I still here, then? Pretty and guileless: no one to even do make-up for any more.

I woke up the next morning, the sun at a low angle through the skylight, Tom still snoring, and I knew what to do: a plan already perfectly formed in my head, dropping from nowhere, like a reward.

We kept to ourselves for most of the morning, Tom in the grey room and me loitering outside. I was bringing things into the house as covertly as I could, glancing at the door to the grey room in trepidation. In the afternoon, I knocked on it.

'Enter,' he said.

He had taken the rug from the living room and put it in the

grey room, his room. The nice lamp that had been in the boys' dressing room was in there too, black and brass. It clashed with everything else he kept there, but I could see why he wanted it: it was the nicest light in the house by far. He had found accoutrements to put on his desk to disguise the fact that the desk had no purpose: he had no laptop or writing materials or books, but he had a map of a distant territory. With some bitterness I reflected that Tom, like Mia, would be bringing home with him not just his own rewards, but things we had gotten from Communal Tasks. He was strong enough, too: he would be able to carry twice as much as I could, maybe more.

He looked at me expectantly.

'If I cook dinner,' I said, 'Will you fix the window that Sam broke?' Sam had covered it with a tarp, but it needed to be properly fixed.

'I don't have the right materials. There's no glass to replace it,' he said. I waited, shifting my weight from left foot to right foot. 'But, I suppose I could board it up,' he said. 'It wouldn't look great, but it'd be better than nothing.' He threw an irritated look out the window. 'All of my Personal Tasks recently have been related to renovation or construction. It's starting to annoy me.'

That surprised me a little. Tom wasn't particularly good at construction. Nearly all of my Personal Tasks had involved me speaking to someone, and generally making a fool of myself, or doing silly things that I didn't want to. I wondered if people wanted to see Tom at work, and to see me humiliated.

He thought for a few more moments. 'What will you make?'

'Steak,' I said. 'You can have it when you're done.'

We had been saving the steaks for a special occasion. They would have been nicer on the barbeque, but it no longer worked after the fire. There were ten steaks; I cooked two and put the rest back in the fridge. While Tom banged away at the window – even I knew that he was taking too long to do a relatively simple job – I made potatoes, salad and coleslaw, using some of the fresh produce that had just come in one of our recent deliveries. I used the nicest dishes, folded napkins in the waterfall style, and, in the absence of flowers, took the plastic plant I had won as a reward and placed it on the table outside.

I knew that he was done because I had seen him go out a couple of times to admire his work from a different angle. He came into the kitchen and offered to take the food out, but I told him I could do it. He looked pleased.

I couldn't help but feel pleased too, as I laid everything out on the table. For the last couple of weeks we had been eating the simplest of foods: noodles, pasta, sandwiches. It felt like a luxury to do it right. Tom sat down, and then stood a moment later, saying, 'Just a minute.' While I waited for him to come back, I had the urge, for the first time in a long time, to take a picture. The table looked so good: the steak, the salad, the glasses with perfect cubes of ice. I poured pepper sauce over my meat but waited for Tom before eating. He returned with a bottle of champagne and two glasses.

'Personal Task,' he said. 'I got it a couple of weeks ago. I was going to wait until I made it until the end, but might as well have it now.'

He ripped off the gold foil with his teeth, quickly and methodically. Then he removed the cork, the *pop* like gunfire, champagne at once spilling over and onto the table. In a businesslike manner he wiped the excess off the table and filled our glasses. 'To teamwork,' he said.

I clinked my glass against his and drank. It was warm, but everything was warm.

'You should have put it in the fridge,' I said.

'Couldn't do that, could I? You don't have a good record for sharing.' He wasn't smiling, and his tone was admonishing, but I think he was trying at banter.

I piled salad onto his plate. There was a faint wind, pleasant and smelling richly of the desert. 'I'm sharing now, aren't I?'

He smiled, looking over my head, at the landscape beyond him. He smiled like it pleased him, though I can't imagine what there was to see. For my own part, only the pool inspired some reaction in me, aesthetically. It had been filled again, some time during the night. The pond, too, was full, and new fish swam happily in its depths.

I ate my steak with relish. Tom moved his food around on his plate for a few moments.

'Worried it's poisoned?' I asked.

'No,' he said. 'I know you wouldn't poison me. I'm more worried that you're a terrible cook.'

'How can you be sure I wouldn't?'

'Because then you'd be on your own. And you wouldn't fare well on your own. You know that, too, I think.' I kept my eyes on my food. I knew Tom's weaknesses, but he knew mine, too. He cut his meat into small pieces, his fork scraping against the plate, and ate. He chewed slowly and gave no indication whether he liked it or not. I wasn't a good cook, Tom was right. It was overdone, but I still thought it was nice.

'I'll fix the fence soon enough,' he said. 'I've become quite handy. Did you see the window?'

I'd inspected it while he washed up for dinner. It was boarded well enough: from the outside it looked smooth and sleek, but from the inside it was a mess of nails and overlapping wood.

'I did. Where did you get the wood?'

'I broke apart one of the unused beds. No use for ten beds now that there's only two of us.'

'Three,' I said. 'Andrew will be back soon. Probably tomorrow.'

'Right. We'll save him a good cut of meat.'

We ate for a few minutes in silence. The evening cold hadn't yet set in, but the temperature was dropping bit by bit.

'What is it you do, again? Something in finance?'

He flicked a look at me, as though checking to see if I was serious. 'I'm a financial analyst.'

'Right.'

'It's a big job. A lot of responsibility. It's too complicated to explain, so I won't bother.'

'Do you miss it?' I persisted.

He kept eating, methodically, not looking up.

'I miss it a great deal.'

'Will you go back there, when you leave?'

'What's with the interrogation?' he asked, waspishly.

'Just trying to get along.'

When he was finished, I cleared the table and brought out dessert, a bowl of strawberries, blueberries, sliced apple and pear, mango and raspberries. I had a separate bowl of cream, freshly whipped, and a tub of ice cream.

'This is nice, Lily,' Tom said. He was more relaxed now, trying, I think, to be pleasant.

'Thanks,' I said. 'There's too much fruit for only two people, anyway. It'll go bad in a day or two.'

I ladled fruit into his bowl, and then offered the cream and ice cream.

'Usually I wouldn't,' he said. 'Very fattening. But we're having a nice night, aren't we? The final two.'

'Final three,' I corrected, and added a generous portion of both cream and ice cream over his fruit. For myself, I picked only the strawberries and raspberries out of the bowl, alongside a mountain of ice cream.

'I got fired from my job,' he said. 'After working there for eight years.'

I picked a strawberry from my bowl. 'What happened?'

He moved his shoulders in a gesture of discomfort. 'There was an issue – anger management, you could say. I'd networked extensively, and when I lost my job, I got in touch with my contacts. Well, word had got out, or someone had bad-mouthed me, had deliberately spread damaging information, and there was no one who would hire me. I went to my friend who I had gone to university with, Leo. We'd lived together for three years, and had been friends for longer. He had a high-up position at a company similar to mine. He could have got me a job, easy. He had told me, not long before, that they were looking for someone. We had lunch, our favourite place, and he told me that the job wasn't available any more. It was bullshit. We both knew that it was bullshit. Even my best friend wouldn't help me out.' He put his fork down. 'Christ, I'd like a cigarette.'

'What happened next, then?'

I didn't expect him to continue, but he said, 'I didn't have as much to do with my days as I would have liked. I decided to visit my girlfriend, Amy. Ex-girlfriend. She had depended on me a lot. She always needed someone to change her tyres, or to fix the leak in the sink, or to put up a shelf or something. So I dropped in to see if she needed help. I know how she struggled to get things done.'

'And then?'

'And then she filed a restraining order. Then I applied to be on the show. I was here a month later.'

I glanced at the sky above me. It was darkening, but not yet dark. I needed more time.

'I was nearly fired from my job, too,' I said. It occurred to me, with a drum of sadness, that I would tell Tom this story, but had never told Sam. In some ways, however, it was easier. Tom already knew the worst parts of me; I suspected he had seen them before anything else.

'You're a – hairdresser or something, right?'

'Shop assistant in a department store. Make-up section.'

'Right. You like it?'

'I mean, I did. Until I thought I was getting fired. I haven't really enjoyed it since then.'

I could tell that Tom was struggling between being polite and telling me he didn't care. He made a gesture with his hand, which I took as a signal to keep going.

'I'd been there for a while, and eventually they trusted me to do the cashing up in the evenings. We took in more money than you'd think in a day. I got a commission too, which was nice. If a girl came in on her own you could usually make a little sale, if you did their make-up nicely and complimented their skin. It was better if a man came in, because they never had a clue, and if you shook your head and gave them a certain look they'd be shamed into spending more. But the best was when a girl would come in with her man. I always took my time then, when I did her make-up. I'd pick the nicest colours and blend it so carefully; it looked like a second skin. And she'd look so beautiful when I was done, and her man would look at her and pay whatever she wanted. Mind – I think it wasn't that he handed over the money because of how good she looked. I think it's because a man will do a lot if they think that a girl can't do without them: the girl *had* to have the make-up, and he had to be the one to give it to her.'

'Could you get to the point, please.'

'Well, as I said, eventually I was allowed to cash up at night.

At first, I did it with someone else, and then I did it on my own. Sometimes it was fine, but sometimes it was wrong – the numbers weren't right. I'd stay there for ages after closing, trying to make it right. Well, eventually I stopped trying to sort it out. Nothing seemed to happen either way. Wasn't that stupid of me? After a couple of months, the accountant rang the manager and said they'd noticed that the figures were off when I was closing. The manager accused me of stealing from the till. I was outraged at the accusation and threatened to quit. Then they looked at the camera footage, and said that they knew I wasn't stealing. But they couldn't understand why the numbers were consistently being filed incorrectly. The manager, owner, and accountant made me go through exactly how I did it, with a calculator, and I was talking for ages, going through it step by step, and when I finally looked up, I saw that the accountant was staring at me, and the others just looked embarrassed. I'd been adding up the numbers wrong, you see. Some of the numbers the computer does automatically, and some you need to add up yourself, with the calculator. But I had been adding up those ones wrong. Simple stuff, too. Simple enough that I didn't realise I needed a calculator. I thought that six plus seven was fourteen, and I thought that eight and nine was sixteen. The accountant had to tell me that my addition was wrong. I asked if I was in trouble, and they said no, but I'd better stick to only doing make-up. The seventeen-year-old school dropout does the cash instead, now. Well, isn't that embarrassing?'

He looked uncomfortable. I finished my glass of champagne. I dearly would have liked another glass, but I wanted to stay as alert as possible. He held his half-full glass in both hands, as though worried that I might reach across and take it from him. He filled his own glass and not mine, then ate a few more bites of his dessert. Then he said, 'I'm going to check and see if the big screen is back on.'

He was gone for only a few seconds. While I was telling my story, the sun had set, and the temperature was dropping rapidly. We would have to go in soon. He returned, but didn't take a seat, and instead took his glass of champagne and drank it, standing. 'Well?' I said. 'Is it on, yet?'

He nodded. I tried to keep my face neutral.

'What's the task?'

'Guess to the nearest hour how long until Christmas Day. Stupid, isn't it?'

'What's the reward?'

'Warm clothes, it said.'

I ate a strawberry and thought about it for a while. When the taps were turned off, we were offered water. If we were being offered warm clothes, the weather was set to turn.

I only had to guess the closer number, and he would be gone. But – a maths problem. I had walked into that one. We both looked at each other, thinking. It was clear enough, then, who they wanted to win.

'How long is it until Christmas, do you think?' I asked.

To my surprise, he laughed. 'Do you think I'm going to answer, just like that? And you give an answer that's closer, and I'm banished before I know what's what. You're funny, Lily. You're very funny. I'll bring the dishes in, you can clean.'

Once the dishes were clean, I took my time wandering around upstairs. Tom showered every night before bed for roughly twelve minutes. The shower was high-pressured and extravagantly loud. I could go out then, but not a minute before.

While I was waiting I put the rest of the steaks in a plastic bag and left them on the counter, ready to go as soon as I heard the water turn on. As quietly as I could, I moved from room to room and closed each window. I found Jacintha's garden shears, and left them out on the counter too.

While I was waiting, I thought about months and days and hours. What date had Becca said that it was? And how long ago had that been? How could I not know when Sam had left? I had a vague idea, but the numbers became confused in my head. If it was early October, and there were, say, twelve weeks until Christmas, then that would be twelve multiplied by seven, which would then have to be multiplied by twenty-four. I couldn't think of it: I was too nervous, jumping at every sound from overhead.

At last, I heard the shower turn on. I grabbed the bag of meat and the shears, and ran.

I went out the back, locking the door behind me. I hurried past the delivery area, the tennis court, and on to the southern perimeter. Despite my momentum, despite the blood rushing in my ears like a soldier's song, I hesitated at the boundary. I didn't know how far I'd have to go, and I worried that I would be considered banished if I went too far. Hadn't Susie done it? Couldn't I, then?

Using the shears, I cut the barbed wire in a number of places, making as wide a gap as I could. In my haste I cut my hand on one of the barbs. I cried out, and tried to swallow any further noises, but it hurt, and I looked at it with panic. The blood fell steadily from my palm, and I thought for a moment, then clenched my jaw and reached out with my other hand, slicing it open on the barbed wire, too. Blood fell in great drops from both hands now, and I ducked out under the wire. The desert beckoned before me, the orange moon glowing softly overhead, casting the sand in gold.

Eighteen

Out in the desert I saw no creature at all, nor any trace of any living thing. Sam had walked this way, and Jacintha, and Ryan, and all the rest, but there was no evidence that they'd ever been here. I ran, using the moon as a guide, trying to count the minutes that went by. I didn't go far: better to be early than late, and have Tom hear me coming back in. I dropped most of the pieces of meat as far out as I dared, left the shears at the perimeter, then dashed back to the compound, leaving a trail of blood behind me. I placed the last few pieces of meat around the side and front of the house, where Tom and I had just sat for dinner.

My hands were throbbing, still dripping blood. When I came in through the door, the shower was still humming.

'Tom!' I shouted, running up the stairs. 'Tom, come quick! Tom!'

The water stopped at once. I heard the shower door slide open. I was standing outside the bathroom door.

'Did you call me?'

'Come quick! Please!'

He wrenched the door open, a towel tied around his waist.

'What is it? What's happened?' He looked at me properly, my hands red with blood, my face stricken. '*What's happened?*'

'Outside, please!' I let my voice be swallowed by sobs. 'It's outside!'

He ran down the stairs, his feet flying. 'Stay here!' he yelled.

I checked the bathroom. He had left his knife sitting on the ledge. I took it, holding it behind my back, and followed him down the stairs. When he was through the front door, I closed it behind him. There was no lock on it – we hadn't anticipated needing one – and so I dragged a cabinet from the kitchen and placed it in front of the door. It was heavier than I had thought, still full of random objects, and I struggled for a few moments, adrenaline soaring through me, teeth gritted, before it covered the entrance. I then quickly gathered the heaviest objects I could find – cast-iron skillets and a few pans, plus the weights Tom had been using earlier – and added them to the lower shelves for ballast.

'Grab a light!' he shouted. 'I can't see anything out here!' I kept my back against the cabinet, my heart knocking against my ribs. I heard him moving around, and then he said, 'It's too dark – what was it you saw?'

I said nothing, didn't move an inch, and he sounded more urgent now. 'Lily, can you hear me? What did you see? Lily – what's out here?'

I sat on the floor. September twentieth, Becca had said: the day Sam left. How long ago had that been? Less than a week? More? Without work, without a schedule, I had no reason to mark the days, and had been living in a strange, timeless limbo that now horrified me. How did I not know what day of the week it was? I closed my eyes and went through the weeks, counting on my fingers. Twelve weeks. Twelve by seven. That was doable, I reasoned. Seventy plus fourteen. Eighty-four. I knew that, at least.

'Lily! Can you hear me? Fetch me a light!'

Eighty-four by twenty-four. I clutched my head. Without a calculator was one thing, but without pen or paper was another.

Tom was at the door. It rattled, but didn't open. 'Open the door, Lily; there's nothing out here. It's fine.'

But was I even sure that I had the number of weeks right? Had it really been a week since Becca told Sam the date? How long since Sam had gone? Forever; forever!

'Open the *door*, Lily,' he repeated. The door rattled again. Behind me, the cabinet stayed where it was. He cursed loudly. I heard his footsteps move around the house, towards the back door.

Becca had left yesterday. Was it yesterday? No, two days ago. And we had gone without water for two days. Three days? Two days. But how long before that? Did Tom know what day it was? Had he seen Becca's record, or had he kept his own?

I heard the back door handle shake, and Tom's heavy tread around the outside of the house. He was checking for open windows. I heard him go to the downstairs bathroom window – closed – and then the other spare room – closed.

I shot to my feet. The window in Tom's room; I hadn't checked it. I ran as quickly as I could, my feet loud on the wooden floors. His lamp was on in the corner, and I could see the top window, just slightly ajar. When I got to the window, I screamed: there was a figure in the window, covered in blood. But it was me, it was only me, my reflection catching me by surprise. I must have touched my face with my bloody hands; there were smudges of scarlet across my face. My arms, too, as I reached up to close the window, were covered in lines and streaks of blood. I had cut my left leg on the barbed wire in my hurry, and there were small rivulets of blood there, too. My hands had only just stopped bleeding.

The handle of the window was high up, and I stretched towards it, my fingers reaching, reaching, when Tom appeared on the other side. His face was twisted in rage; mine, I could see, was open with shock. I could almost reach the handle to close it, but not quite. If I turned to get the chair, Tom would have time to open it further and wrestle his way in before I could stop him. He seemed to realise the same thing at the same time: he jumped up, his fingers brushing the bottom of the window but not quite finding purchase. I scrambled onto the windowsill, pressing myself close to the windowpane, and grabbing the curtain rail so I wouldn't fall. I grabbed the inside handle on the window just as Tom got hold of the frame. I pulled, hard. His hold was slipping: he wedged his hand in, but I pulled harder, crushing his fingers, and he screamed in pain and removed his hand. The window closed with a resounding bang.

'Let me in now, and I won't hurt you, Lily. I want to live peacefully together, I promise.'

I stared out, my reflected face clear and pale before me, his shadowed and out of focus. Suddenly, his face came into focus as he leaned close against the glass. His hand slammed against the window with enough force that I flinched. 'Let me in!'

I examined the glass, looking for cracks, but it had stayed intact. 'Do the challenge and I'll let you in. You say your answer, then I say mine.'

I tried to see past my face and see his instead. I couldn't make out much. He spat at the window, right between where my eyebrows were reflected.

He stepped away and disappeared into the night.

I sat by the front door, Tom's knife resting in my lap. I thought maybe fifteen minutes had passed, possibly more, since I had locked him out. I could hear him walking around the house, banging at the boarded window and trying to budge the front door. I tried to tune him out as I did my calculations. I was sure I could do it if I was at ease and had some paper. But I jumped at every noise and kept getting up to check on the windows. In the struggle with the grey room's window, my right hand had started to bleed again. I couldn't keep the numbers in my head, and eventually wrote out the sums in my blood on the floor.

The problem, of course, was that I was bad at maths, and he was good at it. The task catered to him – but hadn't the last one, the race, been suited to him, as well?

It was possible that Tom knew exactly how long it had been, but I thought that he wasn't sure, otherwise he would have suggested that we do it right away. How many days were in November? Every time my mind reached for an answer, my hand itched for my phone.

Suddenly, I heard Tom shout out. He was, I think, somewhere near the side of the house, near the patio. He shouted again, louder, wilder, and I resisted the urge to get up. This, I knew, would be the difficult part.

'Back!' he yelled. 'Get back – get back!' Suddenly he was banging on the blocked front door, just inches from me.

'Let me in! Lily, let me in! There's something out here! Lily, open the door! Lily! There's a – I can't see, but there's something out here! Let me in – *let me in!*'

I could feel the door shaking, but the cabinet was large and bottom-heavy and the barricade held strong.

'Answer the question,' I shouted. 'How many hours until Christmas?' My voice was not as steady as I wanted it to be.

'There is *something out here!*'

Silence fell for the space of a couple of heartbeats. I heard a crash, and though I had promised myself that I wouldn't look, I found myself rising from the ground and crossing to the living room. I kept the light off, and watched from the corner. Tom had broken apart a chair, and had one of its legs in one hand and the seat in the other. In the dark, two eyes glowed.

'Get back!' he bellowed. 'Back!'

It advanced on him, its front paws criss-crossing. Tom was panting; I could hear his breath sawing through the distance between us. I could see that it was a four-legged animal, some kind of wild dog, perhaps a coyote. It paused, not taking its eyes off Tom. He was standing by the table, under which I had hidden chunks of meat. I thought that it probably wouldn't attack, only wanted the meat. But Tom was adjusting his grip on the leg of the chair, and he was leaning forward, his breath leaving him in white puffs. The creature slunk forward, just an inch or so, and Tom struck out, slashing the air in front of it. Even with a wall between us, I could hear the *whoosh* of the chair leg as it cut through the air. The animal moved closer still, crouching low to the ground as if ready to spring, and let out a sharp growl. In response to the animal's growl Tom let out a shout, and lunged towards it once more. This time his aim was true, and the chair leg hit the coyote with an audible thud. The animal moved with devastating speed, and I saw its teeth flash, but not much else. Tom's piercing cry broke through the night. I pressed myself against the window, and saw that the coyote had sunk its teeth into Tom's hand. He seemed frozen, lost in the pain for a few moments, until he brought the chair leg down on the coyote's back. It howled and moved away, but kept its teeth bared, a low snarl spilling from its mouth.

Tom had dropped the seat, his makeshift shield, and was brandishing the chair leg in his uninjured left hand, making a wild noise in his throat. It was then that the second coyote appeared at the other's flank. The newcomer turned its head to look directly at me. Tom's head twitched around to follow its gaze; when he saw me, he turned his head fully, keeping his body facing the animals. The fear on his face wasn't pleasant to see – but it wasn't unpleasant either.

'Let me in!' he shouted, his voice a frenzied rasp. 'Let me in!'

His hand was mangled and bloody; but then again, mine were too.

'There's meat behind you,' I called. 'Under the table. They don't want to attack you. They just want the food. Throw them the meat and get away from there.'

The coyotes had moved no closer, but the second one was growling now, too. Tom's head snapped back towards them.

I wondered if the crew were nearby. I wasn't sure at what exact point they stepped in, how they determined the moment that a life was in danger. Was Tom safer now than he had been when Becca had a rope around his neck? Safer than Becca was when he had forced her head beneath the water for sixty seconds? Was it solely the risk of death that they measured, or did they weigh it against the relative entertainment of the scene?

Then Tom let out an almighty cry, a loud, bellowing roar. He rushed forward, arms thrown out, driving the coyotes back. He chased them backwards again, and again, until they were past the reach of the lights and were hidden from my view. I could hear them, though: they weren't growling any more, but making yipping noises, and Tom was making that same bellow, though it cut off abruptly, and one of the coyotes growled, then howled. The sounds faded. He might have chased them into the garden, or he may have gone all the way to the desert. When I couldn't hear them any more I stepped away from the window.

I went back to the front door and did my calculations again.

On the floor my bloody numbers had dried. I had two thousand five hundred and eighty, but I needed to adjust based on the current time. It was dark, probably half an hour after Tom's shower, which I had always imagined to happen around eleven: Tom went to bed late and woke early. Was it twelve, then?

There was no noise at all, the house silent, waiting, and then a sudden, violent crash at my back. I jerked forward, my heart in my mouth, skidding on my hands and knees. I turned to the cabinet blocking the door, still sprawled on the floor. An enormous thud again, and the sound of Tom's grunt. He was throwing his entire body at the door. I knew, with some certainty, that if he managed to knock the cabinet down and get inside now, he would surely kill me. He launched himself again, and though the door rattled, it remained shut. Even in my terror, the thought crossed my mind that he should have gone for the boarded up window: Sam had made the door, and it was a sturdy thing. The window was all Tom, and was clearly shoddily done.

He slammed against the door again, and this time the cabinet was pushed forward, just an inch. I sprang to my feet at once, but he must have known that he'd gained some ground, as he hit the door again, quickly. I barely had time to scramble out of the way as, with a groan, the cabinet fell over heavily, spilling all of the odd accoutrements and detritus that we had placed in there over the past months and the heavier objects I had loaded into it.

I climbed over it and threw myself at the door, reaching it at the same time he did. We collided painfully on either side. He pushed, and I wedged my foot desperately at the corner, but he had the momentum, and the strength. The door opened another inch – another – another – until I could see the angle of his jaw, the scruff of his beard. We both knew that he would force the door open, that I would be bested, just as Becca had been: beaten and humiliated.

I was half crouched, low to the ground with my shoulder against the wood. Some of the cabinet's contents had landed within arm's reach. I knew its contents well enough. It was where we put random objects and bric-a-brac which we had found no other place for. We generally put the cleaning materials under the sink, but sometimes, if I was lazy, I would throw them into the top drawer of the cabinet.

I kept my foot at the door, my shoulder pressed hard against the wood, and reached back with the other hand, my fingers stretching, seeking. My foot slipped another inch, and the door opened wider. Tom's teeth glinted white in the dark.

I had a sudden, clear image of the girls I had worked with in the shop watching me, howling with laughter.

My fingers found a bottle of detergent. I wedged myself between the cabinet and the door, at the limits of my strength, and fumbled with the cap, my fingers struggling to twist it off. I could see his hand, and then his arm, wedging themselves in the crack of the door. I removed the cap – his hand grabbed my shoulder. He wrenched the door open, lunging at me, just as I threw the contents of the bottle in his face. He reared back at once, his hands flying up to cover his eyes, a terrible cry ripped from his mouth. I didn't hesitate: I shut the door, heaved the cabinet back up against it, and stood, waiting, my limbs trembling, the bottle twitching in my hand. It was made to be used on stubborn kitchen grime. There was a picture of a shining oven, twinkling with ethereal cleanliness. The label told me that it was the nation's favourite kitchen cleaner. *No fuss, no muss*, the slogan read in pink, cheery letters.

Outside, Tom was still making terrible noises. I let the bottle drop to the ground.

After a very short while, there was a knock on the door, a single thud.

'Let me in,' Tom said, his voice a quiet rasp now. 'I can't . . . Lily, let me come in. I need to get inside.'

I waited. I clutched the edge of the cabinet. Then he said, 'Two thousand, five hundred and twenty.'

I moved the cabinet and opened the door. He fell in, his eyes red and streaming, his towel gone.

'Two thousand, five hundred and ninety,' I said.

He sat naked and bloody on the ground. 'Check the big screen,' he said.

I went in: it was green. While I was there, the voice rang out. It said, 'Good evening, residents. The answer is two thousand, six hundred and eleven. Tom, you are banished.'

When I returned, he was still sitting on the floor. 'I need help,' he said.

I stayed where I was, at a safe distance. The knife, which I had dropped in the struggle, was beside him now, not quite within arm's reach, but close enough that he could grab it before I could run.

'No,' I said.

'Please,' he said. 'I can't see.'

I stayed where I was, looking at him. His eyes were a vicious red. He wasn't looking at me, but to the left of me.

'I need to wash my eyes out. I can't see anything. Lily. Please.'

I inched towards the knife, as quietly as I could, my eyes not leaving his face. His gaze stayed fixed in the same spot. I picked up the knife and pointed it at his face, an inch from his eye. Still, he didn't move.

'I have the knife,' I said. 'If you try to hurt me, I'll kill you.'

Wordlessly, he held out his arms. I realised, after a beat, that he wanted me to lift him. I took one of his wrists and hauled him to his feet. He cried out, and I saw that his ankle was a raw and bloody mess. I led him to the kitchen, his weight heavy on me, brought him to the sink and ran the tap. I stepped back and let him figure it out himself, unwilling to stay close by him. He cried out as the water hit his eyes and stayed hunched over the sink dabbing at them for some time. When he straightened up, he faced out the window, where I could see the moon hanging high in the sky, luminous and brilliant.

'Well?'

'Nothing,' he said. 'I can't see anything.'

I waited for some feeling of guilt to come over me, but it never came. We stood there in silence for a few moments. Then he turned to me, his eyes wheeling restlessly. 'Help me get my things?'

He slipped a little on the stairs. Neither of us mentioned it. I threw his things into a bag while he put on a T-shirt and shorts I handed to him. He became agitated, asking me if I had included different items he wanted. 'The navy polo shirt? The watch – the one I wear in the evenings?' I told him yes, I had put everything in, but I wasn't entirely sure if I was packing his things or Andrew's. When we went downstairs to the grey room, he was silent as I packed up the broken record player and the map, the leather wallet and the bone. I filled three bin bags in total. I tied a knot on each one and placed them into his arms. His face fell. 'This is everything?'

'I think so.'

I looked at him closely and, for the first time in a long time, entirely without fear. I didn't know what he was waiting for: I don't know if he thought I might show him some mercy and let him stay until sunrise, in the hope that he would recover some of his sight. We were silent for long enough that he said, 'Are you still there?'

'Yes,' I said.

'Will you bring me out to the boundary?'

'If you want,' I said. I owed him that, at least.

I led him through the house and across the compound. The night was cold and silent, and I could hear the catch of his breath, the gasps of pain.

'You were close,' I said. 'You nearly had the right number. Did you see Becca's calendar?'

'Becca's what?'

'She had been keeping track of the days.'

'No,' he said. We walked slowly, nearly at the boundary. I knew that it was fear as well as pain that kept his pace so slow. 'I had scratched a tally onto the wall in my room. It was my girlfriend's— my ex-girlfriend Amy's birthday in August. I had planned to go home by then, but when the time came, I didn't want to. A month ago, I could have told you the minute and the hour and the date at the drop of a hat. It was the first thing I thought of when I woke up. But I'd forgotten about her. I didn't think I would, but I did.' He paused. 'You left a trail around the compound?'

'Leading from the desert.'

'You went past the boundary?'

'I did.'

I brought him to the southern entrance, to where I had cut the barbed wire, and where the animals had come in. 'We're here,' I said.

He looked, unseeing.

'Where—? I don't—'

'We're at the southernmost point. It's where you came in. If you keep going straight, someone will be there to meet you.' I didn't know how that part worked – they never showed it on television. I didn't even know if it was true.

A wind blew across the sand, cold and sweet-smelling. The weather was changing: I could feel it.

I had stepped back, but he turned and moved towards me, his hands stretched out, pawing at the air between us. When he reached me, he grasped at my hands, and I thought, for a moment, that he was trying for some kind of tender goodbye. But he only took the knife from my hand, turned, and walked across the boundary without a word. I could see him for a few seconds, his arms outstretched, the terrible glint of the knife clutched in his hand, until he was swallowed by the night.

I went to bed. I had been struggling to keep my eyes open all night, but now I couldn't sleep. I drifted off for brief periods, and then would jolt awake, imagining sharp teeth and snapping jaws. I went downstairs and fetched the chair leg that Tom had used earlier. He had left it in the long grass, but I found it easily enough. It lay glistening in the morning dew.

I was both terrified that someone might appear, and desperately, desperately lonely. At turns, I longed to wake up and see Sam's face on the pillow beside me – but just as much I wanted to talk to my mother, and have her tell me that I would be all right. I didn't know how I had got here, lying bloody and alone in a dishevelled bed, clutching a makeshift weapon, jumping at every noise.

I woke again a short while later. I heard a noise from outside and lay for a moment, limbs stiff and unwilling, before I swung my legs out, stepped quietly across the wooden floors, and crept down the stairs. I stopped at the bottom of the stairwell, the leg of the chair brandished in my hand. Andrew stood before me. His hand went to his face in what I realised, after a moment, was horror.

'What happened?' he said.

I looked down at myself, covered in my own blood. It was on the floor in front of him too, some streaks, and other more definite patterns, numbers and symbols.

'Tom's gone,' I said.

'When?'

'Not long ago.'

He looked distressed. 'Didn't he want to say goodbye?'

I wondered if Andrew really didn't know that Tom loathed him. His face was pinched and forlorn, and I was reminded of how he looked in the throes of fever, his face so warm under my hand. Despite what I had told Tom, I hadn't really believed that Andrew would be back. I was sure that he had died, and they were only telling us otherwise so that we could keep up the charade that we were safe and looked after.

'He told me to tell you goodbye,' I said. 'He was sorry to go, but it was his time.'

He nodded, resigned.

'I thought you were going to die,' I said.

He smiled, soft and kind. 'Didn't I say they wouldn't let us die, Lily? Didn't I say that all along? They took such good care of me, you wouldn't believe it. Really, you wouldn't. They nursed me back to health. I feel strong again, and excited too, to be back.'

'I'm glad you're back, too, Andrew.'

'They looked after me so well, Lily. Was Tom very upset? I wish I had said goodbye. He said to tell me goodbye, you said?'

'He said that he'd miss it here, and that he appreciated everything that you did.'

He came forward and hugged me, holding me tight. He smelled clean and fresh: not like the desert scent that we'd all smelled faintly of for so long. His breath tickled the back of my neck and lifted my hair.

'I knew they were looking after us,' he said.

I went back to bed, and he went outside to watch the sunrise.

Nineteen

The bedsheets were ripped off me, wrenching me from sleep. I screamed, but it was only Andrew.

'Time to wake up!' he cried. He was leaning over me, his eyes bright, freshly showered and smiling. He handed me a coffee, made in the mug I had won some months ago. Looking at it, I saw that it turned pink in hot water. I hadn't realised, as I hadn't actually used it. I had this idea that it was too nice to use. In my hand, the purple disintegrated into pink, dreamlike and fantastical.

'It's still early,' I said, glancing out of habit at the slant of pale grey filtering through the skylight. I made a grab for the sheets, but Andrew threw them to the floor. He sat next to me, and I sat up so that my back rested against the headboard.

'There's so much to do,' he said. 'Another day, another dollar.'

'I don't want to do anything,' I said. 'I want to sleep.'

'Sleep!' he laughed. 'No, no, no.' He was still smiling broadly. I shifted uncomfortably.

'Aren't you tired? You were so sick, before . . .'

'Oh, they fixed me right up. I feel fantastic, now. Fan*tas*tic.'

When he had first arrived back, he had seemed strange, but I figured he was maybe loopy on medication. Now, in the light of morning, he seemed manic, frantic. I reached for the throw that had pooled at my feet. I pulled it up to my chin and cradled the mug of coffee in my hands. From the smell alone, I knew that it was a luxury brand. It was Andrew's coffee. When he did a task, he nearly always received a luxury item.

'So, I've been thinking,' Andrew said, shifting closer to me. 'All night I've been thinking. And you know what I've been thinking about? Legacy. I want to make sure that people remember us. We need to put our mark on this place.'

'It's a television show,' I said. 'They'll remember us.'

He looked at me with mild distaste. 'I mean the future residents. The people after us. I want the people who live here next to think: wow. Those guys really lived.'

I decided to humour him. 'Okay. How are we going to do that?'

'I think we should build a monument. Something impressive. Something that screams *legacy*. I think it will impress a lot of people. And I think it will impress *them*, as well.'

'Who's them?'

He gestured around us. '*Them*. The producers. The people who make all of this possible.'

'Andrew,' I said, 'Are you okay?'

'A monument would make a great impact,' he said. 'People would really get a sense of the life that we have here. So I think I'm going to make the monument, and you should work on getting the house in shape. And you could probably do the cooking and things, too, right?'

'I'm not really much of a cook.'

He looked at me in astonishment. 'That's not true. That's not true at all. You and Carlos used to make such wonderful meals!'

'That was Candice and Carlos,' I said. 'I did the cleaning. I cleaned the kitchen.'

'Really?' he said. 'Well – I have faith in you.'

'I don't know . . .'

'Look at this place. Look at all that possibility. Don't you want to be part of something bigger than yourself? Lily,' he said, using his serious, thoughtful voice. 'Let me ask you something. What do you want your life to look like?'

The question alarmed me. It was the one I didn't want to answer, and the one that pressed most frequently on my mind. I knew what I didn't want: I didn't want to go back to work, and do little jobs that didn't mean anything. I didn't want to force myself out of bed every morning, and feel like my soul was being pulled from my body. I didn't want to live with my mother, but I didn't want to try to find somewhere else to stay. I wanted to be free from the daily confrontation with the slow decay of humanity and everything we had built. I wanted to be left alone. I wanted quiet. I wanted to stop pretending that I cared about things.

'I suppose,' I said, 'I'd like to take life at a slow pace. For a little while.'

He nodded. 'I get that,' he said. 'I understand that, Lily. I really do. I think that's really avant-garde. Now let me ask you another question, and I want you to think about this carefully.' He paused, seeming to want confirmation, and I nodded. 'Why do you reckon the two of us made it this far?'

I thought for a few moments. It seemed obvious enough, depressing though it was. I was there because I thought that this was what I was supposed to want: the house and the rewards and all the nice things. Andrew was there because he had a need to exert control coupled with a crippling fear of loneliness.

'Because we both wanted it,' I said.

'Because we both wanted it,' he echoed, nodding. 'You're right, Lily. Well done. But I think there's more to it, don't you? People must have *wanted* the two of us to make it this far.'

'I don't think they want me to win,' I said. Hadn't they tried to hunt me out again and again? I was still there because Tom didn't think that I had that same viciousness in me that he had in him. I hadn't been sure either, until I had crossed into the desert, bait in hand.

'I didn't say win,' he said. 'I mean making it to the last two. That's a far worthier reward than being the last person remaining, don't you think? Because this way, we can work together, help each other out, right?'

'Right,' I said. I felt myself falling into old habits. There was always a part of me that wanted to impress Andrew; to play along by his rules. He had so many ideas, and I didn't mind being told what to do.

'You know I've always had a soft spot for you, don't you? You're really special, Lily. I've always thought so.' He leaned forward so that he was resting on his elbow, his face close to mine. He was looking at me with a strange intensity. I could feel his breath on my face. 'Isn't it likely,' he said, 'That they want us to be together? Why else would it be the two of us left?'

'I don't want you,' I said. I let the words leave me without thought. 'I want Sam.'

'I wouldn't worry about that too much. I think you're great, Lily, but I don't particularly want you either. Not that I don't think that you're beautiful. Of course, you're a great girl and all that, only . . .' He trailed off, and we both looked away from each other. 'But I think we should give the people what they want, right? If they want us together, then who are we to disagree, right? We're only here on their good graces.'

'I don't think I want to do that.' Unnerved, I tried to inch a little further back from him.

He stared at me until I met his eye again. I could see the specks of green around his pupil. Whatever beauty Andrew had didn't move me: not at all. He lifted a hand and tucked a piece of hair behind my ear. He kept his hand there, behind my ear, holding my head in place. I tried not to flinch. I looked at him, and he looked back at me, his hand on my hair. We stayed locked in a lifeless embrace for some time, staring at each other as though waiting for the other to break.

'You wouldn't have to do anything you don't want to,' he said. 'It would just be pretend. None of it would be real.'

'All right,' I said slowly. 'If you think that's best.'

'Oh, now that's brilliant.' He let go of my hair and lifted himself off the bed. 'Well, I'm going to go get started on the monument, and why don't you get started on cleaning downstairs? I don't know what you and Tom got up to, but you're going to need to sort out that mess by the door, Lily.'

'Okay,' I said.

'Now would be good,' he said, and, reaching over, plucked the cup of coffee neatly from my hand.

He disappeared out of the room, and I lay on the bed, trying to will energy into my limbs. I could hear him singing downstairs as he rummaged through cupboards, out of key and strangely pitched. I moved when I felt the chill steal over me. I had been very nearly naked under the sheet, wearing only underwear. I don't think that he had noticed.

In the days that followed, Andrew got to work outside, and I cleaned the house. I didn't mind the cleaning. I enjoyed it, actually, in that it gave me something to do. As I worked, I thought mostly of Sam. When the work became tedious, I imagined that he was in the next room, and that I would speak to him once I was finished.

Often, I didn't see Andrew until the evening, when he came in for dinner. I always wore a nice dress and tried my best with the cooking, but Andrew was happy with anything.

While it wasn't the situation I had imagined for myself, I had the comfort and safety of Andrew, while getting incredible rewards – everything was designer, expensive, the best of the best: a leather reclining chair, a rosewood sideboard, a chandelier made of Murano glass, an LED face mask, a cashmere cardigan, the cosmetics I had sold but couldn't afford. I had never looked better.

Andrew rarely did Personal Tasks – a couple of days after his return, he received a jersey of his favourite footballer, Maximo Igale. He seemed content with the reward, and wore it most days, but otherwise, he didn't bother to check his little screen. He spent most of his time outside, mostly working on his monument, which seemed to be an immense pile of rubbish which towered higher each day. There was the packaging that my rewards came in, and other items that people had left behind, and things around the house that had broken, and unidentifiable lumpen objects that had survived the fire. It looked hideous, but I didn't have the heart to tell him so. For the rest of the day, he puttered about, sometimes trying to mend the fence around the perimeter, and sometimes, worryingly, walking around and talking to himself.

I couldn't pretend not to notice that Andrew had become strange since his return. His moods were erratic, and while he was sometimes kind and considerate he was more often distracted and agitated. He came to bed later and later, and slept little, always awake and at work before I had woken. He was irritated by any kind of mess and snapped at me to keep the house orderly. He would always apologise afterwards, wringing his hands nervously.

We tried, with excruciating awkwardness, to appear like something resembling a couple. This mostly involved him holding my hand while sitting next to me on the sofa in the evenings, telling me about how his day had gone. Andrew liked to talk about what he was going to do the following day, but most of all, he liked to talk about how well he had been looked after by the producers and production team when he had been sick. He could talk about them for hours. I felt that I had no choice but to stay quiet and listen to him, his hand soft in mine. Mostly, I tried to disassociate and think of other things.

One night, when he had run out of things to talk about, and we were sitting in silence, I asked him, 'Do you think Sam would want to see me? On the outside?'

Andrew didn't look at me. 'I don't know,' he said. I nodded and worked hard not to cry.

'Do you think Candice would want to see you?'

'No,' he said. 'She wouldn't.'

'But how do you know? She might be happy to see you, when you get out.'

'Why would she be? I chose this over her. She wouldn't want to be second best, and I wouldn't expect her to, either. And anyway, we're not going to leave, either of us. We're going to stay for longer than anyone has: six months, maybe a year. We'll make a great place for ourselves, and when we finally do leave, the next contestants will be so impressed with what we had.' He took my hand and rested his cheek on the crown of my head.

Though our forced attempt at a relationship was ridiculous to me, there must have been people at home who either enjoyed the sham we presented, or who wanted to torture us further.

Some of my Personal Rewards were now faintly erotic: lily-scented perfume, designer lingerie, jewel-encrusted handcuffs. They embarrassed me: I added them to the pile of items that made up Andrew's monument and hoped that he didn't notice.

Andrew seemed content enough as we were, and never brought up the possibility that one of us might leave. I really don't think that Andrew wanted to win: I think he didn't want to leave, but needed someone around to validate him. I knew that eventually I would have to consider how I might get him to leave, but the more established our routine became, the easier it was to put it off. Another few days, I told myself every week, the air becoming cold and crisp, the evenings rapidly drawing in.

As we spent our tense evenings sitting next to each other in the living room, the screen was lit before us, our current task casting Andrew's face in a faint blue glow, unchanging for as long as we didn't do it. In the show's familiar blocky font, it stated that the reward would be a key, though what it would unlock we didn't know. We never discussed the screen, though it loomed in front of us, unmissable. *Task*, it read, and then, simply: *Kiss the other resident.*

One night Andrew didn't come to bed at all. When the moon had drifted from the view of the skylight, and I had lain stiffly for what was surely hours, sleepless with worry, I went outside to look for him. I felt a thrill of fear the moment I stepped outside. The nights were now bitterly cold, a biting, brutal chill unlike anything I was used to. My breath was visible before me, and I stood in the doorway for longer than I should have, reluctant to leave the warmth of the house. Some instinct told me not to leave, to go back to bed. Then I saw Andrew, standing by the northern perimeter, a torch in his hand, looking out over the desert sands. I called his name, but he didn't answer. I grabbed his coat that he kept by the door and went out to join him. Though I called his name repeatedly, he still startled when I reached him, looking at me with a confusion that reminded me of how he had been in the throes of fever.

'What are you doing out here?' I asked. 'It's freezing.'

'I'm just keeping an eye out,' he said.

'For what? You can't stay out in the cold,' I said. 'You'll get sick.'

'Oh, well,' he said, 'If I did get sick, they'd come and look after me.'

I wondered, with a drop of dread, if Andrew wanted to get sick.

'Let's go inside,' I said, putting my hand on his arm.

'Just a little longer.'

'No, Andrew. This is stupid. Let's go inside. You need to sleep.'

'I think I'll just work on the monument for a little longer.'

Losing patience, I said, 'It's the middle of the night. You're being ridiculous.'

He turned to look at me, swinging the torch, the beam breaking up the night. His face was grave. 'You're not angry at me, are you?'

'No, I'm not mad. I just think we should go back inside.'

'You're sure you're not mad? You're not thinking of – of going, are you?'

'No, I'm not thinking of going. I'm going to stay here for a very long time.'

He turned to face out into the desert again, the light of the torch swivelling along with him. 'I didn't realise until they took me away how close they are. That's how they were able to come so quickly. To us, it just looks like sand and nothingness, but there's vents connecting us to them, just beyond, I think. It's an incredible set-up – they have everything out there. Of course,' he said quietly, 'it's not as nice as the compound.'

'We've made the compound special,' I said. 'We've made it our home.'

'They're so close,' he said, moving his torch slowly back and forth, like the beam of a lighthouse. 'They're just out there.'

He was really starting to unnerve me, but before I could answer, he pressed my shoulder. 'I'm sorry. I'll go inside, okay?'

I took him by the arm and led him back towards the house. As we crossed the great expanse of nothing, we passed by his monument, immense now, a pile of all kinds of odd things from around the compound. 'The monument looks great,' I said, squeezing his arm.

He turned his face to mine, his features alight. 'Doesn't it?'

When we reached the entrance, I stopped. There was a lock on the door. I reached out and tried it, but the door remained closed.

'What is it?' Andrew asked.

'It's locked,' I said. 'They must have come when I was looking for you. We're locked out.'

Andrew's head whipped around. 'They might still be here,' he said, almost shouting, and ran off towards the northern perimeter. I went around the house, checking the windows, but I knew that it was no good. When I finished, I sat on the step by the back of the house, the warm glow of the house behind me. I shivered violently, even in Andrew's jacket. I didn't feel particularly shocked or angry by the new development. In a way, I had known that I wouldn't be able to get away scot-free from what I had done to Tom. I supposed that they were laughing now – when I had locked Tom out, he had battled desert animals and knocked down a door to get in. I was just sitting there, trying to pretend it wasn't happening. They knew how to humble you, I could give them that.

I called Andrew's name until he returned. 'No sign of them,' he said.

'Come here for a minute,' I said. He sat beside me, and in the faint light from the house, I could see the deep, dark circles under his eyes.

'We need to decide who's going to kiss who,' I said. 'So that one of us can go inside, and the other can go.'

'Go?' he said. '*Go*? Neither of us are going, Lily. Don't be silly.'

'We can't stay here all night,' I said. 'It's too cold, and there are things out there in the desert.'

'Well, I'll protect you.'

We sat in silence while I tried to think of something to say.

'Wait there for a minute,' he said, and then disappeared into the darkness. I sat, shivering, wondering if I should simply throw myself at him and kiss him. Could I do that to him? Would it be right?

I didn't hear him return, but I felt him take my hand. I looked up at him guiltily. Then I felt a cold bite of metal on my wrist and looked down. There was a handcuff on my wrist, the one that I had won as a reward, jewels sparkling along the cuffs, and Andrew was fastening me to a pipe that jutted out of the house. I shouted out, twisting my face so that my lips weren't exposed to him.

'I'm not going to kiss you,' he laughed. 'I don't want to get rid of you. I just need to make sure you don't leave.'

I stared at him. 'What are you doing? Let me go! We can't stay out here all night. Andrew – let me go!'

'We'll be fine,' he said. 'If anything were to happen, they'd look after us.'

'Andrew,' I said. 'Please!'

'Although,' he said, 'they'd come quicker if we were actually sick or injured.'

'Wait,' I said. '*Wait—*'

I watched as though underwater as Andrew looked around him. He considered for a moment, and then, in a quick, sharp motion, bashed his head against the wall. I screamed, and he rebounded, clutching his head and groaning. I called his name, and he tottered for a moment, then turned to me, blood already gushing from his forehead, his nose out of place.

'Is it bad?' he asked. 'Is it bad?'

'Oh God,' I said. 'What is *wrong* with you? Why did you do that?'

'I'm injured,' he said, blood dripping onto his chin. 'They'll come and take me in and get me better. They won't leave me out here like this.' He put his hand to his forehead and checked the blood on his hand, wincing. 'All right,' he said. 'Now you.'

'What?'

He searched around for a moment, then found a rock in the debris near the bins. 'You need to injure yourself too, so we both can be taken care of.'

I stared at him. 'You're joking. You're insane.'

He looked at me in bewilderment. 'I'm not going to leave you here on your own, Lily. They'll take us in and patch us up, and then when they return us, we'll be so much better, and we can sort out how to get inside. To be honest, I think if we just asked them for the key they'd give it to us. They're resplendent like that.'

I started to pull desperately at the handcuffs, but the metal only bit into my skin. Still, I pulled, yanking with what strength I could. Then Andrew took a step towards me, the rock in his hand, and I screamed as loud as I could, as though there were someone around to help me. The sound seemed to frighten him, and he dropped the rock and skittered away from me. I kept pulling at the handcuff, crying now. He returned and stood a few feet away from me. 'I wasn't going to force you,' he said sullenly, his face red with his own blood. 'I'm not like Tom. I'm nice.'

I continued to sob, and his face grew soft as he watched me. He sat down behind me, and I twisted desperately, trying to keep out of reach. 'Lie down,' he said. 'It's cold. We'll warm each other, okay?' He forced my body into the foetal position and curled behind me. My hair was wet, and I knew that it was with his blood.

'Now, isn't this nice? Let's just stay like this for a while and keep warm, and in no time they'll be here. I'll make sure they take you too, okay? They'll take such good care of us, you won't believe it.'

'You're bleeding, Andrew. You need help. Let me help you.'

'Shhh,' he said. 'They'll be here soon.'

I continued to cry, my body convulsing with sobs and violent shudders. Even through my fear, the cold tore at me insistently. After some time, with Andrew pressed against my back, his blood seeping into my T-shirt, he said, 'Would you do me a favour? I don't want to make you feel uncomfortable, but . . .'

'What?'

He tightened his hold on me. He spoke quietly, though his voice was the only sound in the compound. 'Could you pretend to be Candice for a few minutes?'

'Andrew . . .'

'I just mean— I used to stroke her hair, to help her get to sleep. Can I stroke your hair and pretend?'

I said nothing. I only cried, and pulled at the handcuff. My face was wet with tears and numb with cold. I felt Andrew's hand reach out and rest on my head. He stroked my hair from the crown to its ends with a terrible gentleness. 'It's okay,' he said. 'They'll be here soon.'

I don't know how, but I somehow drifted into sleep. I woke up some time later, the dawn a fantastic purple around me. I lurched upright, and twisted to face Andrew. I thought he was dead, and I screamed. He wasn't dead, but he was pale and caked in blood. I reached out and pressed a hand to his forehead. It wasn't actually that bad, his wound. He hadn't done a particularly good job of injuring himself. His eyes opened, and he sat up. He gazed around, looking a little like Tom had the night of the fire, when he watched the shed burn to the ground.

'They didn't come?' he asked. I shook my head. 'I was sure that they would come.'

'Andrew . . .' I didn't know how to say it to him. I think that he knew then, in the biting morning air, with his blood dried in a shallow pool on the ground, that there was no one here who cared about him. It was worse than Tom knowing that he had been beaten. I took no pleasure in it. I saw him look around the compound with a kind of sadness that moved me. He hadn't really done anything in the past few weeks. Despite all of his plans, he hadn't fixed anything, or improved the compound in any way. There was a part of me that wanted to protect Andrew from the knowledge that was finally dawning on him: he wasn't actually good for much. But my mind shied away from the thought, both for his sake and for mine. If Andrew was of no real use to the compound, then what did that say about me?

'All right,' he said, after a minute. 'Yes, all right.'

'Let me clean your wound. I could try and fix your nose, maybe.'

'Never mind that,' he said. He reached into his pocket and took out a key. He unlocked the handcuff, and I wrenched myself free, scrambling backwards. Before I could get far, he reached out and took my face in his. I tried to twist away, but he held me firmly.

He crouched beside me and smiled. 'Now, you be good, all right?'

'Wait,' I said. 'No.' He held my face firmly in his hands.

'Kiss me, and I'll go,' he said. I tried to shake my head, but I was caught in his hands. He squeezed a little tighter, not enough to hurt me, but I cried as if he had. I closed my eyes and kissed him. I could taste his blood.

'Andrew,' the voice said. 'You are banished.'

'It's all right,' he said. 'You'll have a nice time here. There's enough wood and fuel to last you through the cold months. And you can always ask for more, if you need it.'

I shook my head, too numb to do much else.

'I suppose,' he said, then took my hand, as though out of habit, 'I suppose I don't really know what I'm doing. And if I'm getting into it all – I suppose I'm not very happy, either. Well, I don't suppose anyone's really happy, are they? But you know what? It was worth a try. And it was good, wasn't it? Didn't we have fun? It's been really special,' he said. He put his hand on his heart and looked out. 'It's been completely magnanimous. I feel very lucky.'

I reached across and hugged him tightly, too tightly. He had to pry my arms off of him. 'Don't walk me to the perimeter,' he said. 'Go get the key from the delivery area and get inside. Go straight to bed, and things will be better when you wake up.'

'I don't want you to go,' I said. Despite everything that I had done to reach this very moment, I suddenly couldn't stand the thought that I would be completely alone.

'Now, now,' he said, fondly. 'You can't go on like that, or I'll cry, and how would that look? When you leave, whenever that is, will you bring my things? I can't bear to go inside, or I know that I'll never go. Pack them up and bring them, and I'll come and pick you up from the meeting place, whenever you decide it's time, okay?'

The compound, all to myself; I couldn't imagine it. I didn't want it. Why had I ever wanted it? 'Please don't go,' I said. 'Please don't leave me here.'

'You won't be alone,' he said. 'We'll be watching you, at home. We all will.'

He looked at the house one more time, and then he turned and walked, until I couldn't make out his shape from formless shadow. I stayed where I was, sitting on the step, as though waiting for someone else to arrive.

Twenty

It took me a while, to get inside. There was no key, but a selection of odd items: a clothes hanger, a screwdriver and a hair grip. Clearly, I hadn't kissed Andrew with enough conviction for the producers. I spent a long time trying to pick the lock, my hands numb, switching from the hair grip to the screwdriver over and over. Several times I considered simply bashing a window in, but I remembered, with a distant sense of surprise, that there would be no one around to fix it for me. When I at last unlocked the door, I felt a surge of satisfaction that dissolved almost at once when I went inside the empty house. I wandered around as though it was an entirely new dwelling. I turned the heat on, and heard the house come to life. In the living room, the screen had lit up green. As I approached, writing appeared in large, white letters. *State what you want*, it said.

'Slippers,' I said.

I pulled on a coat – Andrew's coat, which he wore when he was trying to get work done outside – and went to the delivery area. My slippers were there, fur-lined and perfect. I had seen a picture of an actress wearing the same ones as she sat in her make-up chair, reading her script. I had lusted after them for years. I wondered how they knew I wanted that exact pair.

You didn't have to work for the rewards, but you still had to thank the brand.

'Thank you, Corst,' I said. 'I'm glad to be the proud owner of a pair of your limited-edition suede slippers.'

I slipped them on my feet and returned to the big screen. I left my old shoes outside, by the delivery area.

State what you want.

'I want an electric milk-frother,' I said. I thought for a few moments. 'And I want an oil-based cleanser. I'd like heated hair-rollers. And heart-shaped sunglasses, and really soft toilet paper, and an ultra-fast food blender and a sheepskin rug. And I'd like nail clippers and a hand-held hoover and a label maker and giant matchsticks and a jasmine-scented candle. I'd really like a black dress that covers my chest but hugs my ass, and a wide-sleeved striped sweater. And a yoghurt that promotes gut health and a motorised inflatable for the pool.'

When I had thanked all the brands, I went back to the big screen and asked for a wheelbarrow. When that arrived, I loaded up my rewards and wheeled them into the house. I wanted to take them to the bedroom – *my* bedroom – but it would have taken too long, so I went to one of the empty rooms on the bottom floor and left them there. I dragged a mattress into the room and sat cross-legged, sifting through all my new things, and ended up falling asleep where I was. I woke in the middle of the night and started violently, thinking that there was a figure beside me, looming over my bed. But it was only the wheelbarrow full of rewards, and when my heart had returned to its regular rhythm, I drifted back to sleep.

*

I asked for an assortment of alcohol, mixers, fruit, syrups, straws and little pink umbrellas, and spent my days drifting around drinking cocktails. It was too cold to swim in the pool any more, so I wrapped up in warm clothes and lay on my motorised inflatable and drifted in the pool for most of the afternoon. When I wanted something I asked the big screen, and I spent the rest of the time thinking about what else I might want. After a couple of days, it became surprisingly hard to think of anything beyond what I already had. On the third day, I ordered a pizza, and had been on my way inside when the voice rang out. 'Good evening Lily,' it said. 'Please remember to thank the brand.' I jumped at the sound, dropping my pizza. I stood, shaking. I had forgotten about the voice. I had thought, somehow, that it had left along with everyone else.

'Thank you, Gourmet Gals,' I said. My voice was slurred, and I felt overtaken by a great wave of shame. I put my pizza in the bin, and thought, distantly, of the empty pizza boxes I had seen on my first day there, left over by the previous residents. I'd assumed that they left in a hurry, perhaps after some conflict, but I wondered now if they hadn't left quietly; just finished their meal and left.

The sound of the voice had rattled me, and I went upstairs to my bedroom and hid beneath the blankets for a while. I had forgotten that people could still see me. Once there was only one person left, they only aired an episode weekly, rather than daily. It was just a cursory check-up really, showing the embarrassing or interesting things that they did. Viewers weren't really invested at that point, but they still had a faint interest; it was like checking up on a friend you hadn't seen in years. Dropping the pizza on the ground while visibly drunk would probably feature. The moment from the day before when I had cried because I couldn't get my jumper over my head – that would probably feature too.

I didn't drink the following day.

I continued to struggle to think of what to ask for. It wasn't that my desire for things had faded, but rather that I felt overwhelmed by choice, panicked that I was forgetting something that I really wanted, worrying that there was always something better that I just hadn't thought of yet. I was frequently anxious, feeling as though whenever I wasn't requesting something I was wasting my opportunity.

Having been in the compound for so long, I found it increasingly difficult to distinguish memories of my own life with the recollection of previous contestants on the show. Although I had never met any of the people from the seasons before me, they seemed more real to me than the people who had made up my life before. I sat by the lake, and thought about Brittany and Donna, generally agreed upon to be the most successful contestants in the history of the show.

Brittany and Donna were friends who had made it to the final two. They had been close from the beginning, and while they each had had boyfriends in the compound, they didn't seem that bothered when they left. They were friends in the truest sense: they defended each other to the death, were honest and kind to each other, and each thought that the other was the funniest person they had ever met.

Although neither of them actually 'won', they had stayed for the longest time. They didn't get unlimited rewards, but they worked well together, and did enough Personal Tasks to have a steady stream of supplies. Curiously, the tasks rarely took a sinister or malicious edge for them: they were so committed to having fun that the tasks only heightened their potential for goofing around, or for making each other laugh. Occasionally there was a task which was designed to make them create conflict – *tell Donna what you dislike about her* – but if they didn't like the task, they simply ignored it. They seemed content to just enjoy themselves. They filled the bathtub with champagne that they had won, but had never drunk. They both got into the bath, fully clothed, and shrieked with laughter, getting drunk on the bubbles they splashed around in. They did all kinds of silly things, and everyone loved watching them. We kept waiting for one of them to turn on the other, to take the prize for herself, but they never did. They stayed for six weeks on their own, and they seemed to enjoy it immensely. Then Brittany won a kite in a Personal Task. They were both giddy, eager to fly it. It was a beautiful royal blue, I remember, with a golden string. They threw the kite up into the air, over and over, but there was no wind, and it fell back down every time. They tried for a while, the blue of the kite thrust against the blue of the sky, again and again. When it fell once more, they left it on the ground and looked at each other. They didn't speak – it was impossible to know what passed between them – but they went inside, packed up their things, and left within the hour. The next day there were new contestants in the compound. They binned the kite without a second thought.

That evening, I let myself dissolve into tears: loud, ugly, wailing sobs. I spent the next day in a similar way, crying on the tennis courts, crying in the kitchen, crying in bed and crying while walking around outside. I cried while I ate my breakfast and when I showered. When I wasn't crying I lay in bed, or sometimes the couch. After a few days of this, when I was collecting a latte in the morning from the delivery area, I found a small phone, sleek and shining.

I sat by the lip of the pool, phone in hand. It was disgustingly dirty, a murky grey-green, filled with ash and sand and debris. I might have ordered a new filter, but I didn't feel up to the work involved.

I called my mother, the only number I knew by heart. It rang for a long time, and I thought that if she didn't answer, I would just tip myself forward and drop into the pool.

'Hello?' came her voice in my ear.

'Hello? Can you hear me?'

'Yes – is this Lily?'

'Yeah, it's me.'

'Oh. Oh, very good. You're finished with the show, then?'

'No, I'm still here.'

'I thought they didn't let you talk to people on the outside.'

'They don't, usually, but I'm the last one here, so I guess they let me.'

'The last one, you said? Why are you still there, then?'

'I'm the winner,' I said, irritated. 'I get to stay as long as I like.'

'Oh,' she said. I could hear the sounds of our kitchen: the splash of water in the sink, the rumble of the kettle.

'Have you not been watching the show?'

'I watched an episode or two. It wouldn't be my kind of thing.'

I can't say how I'd wanted the phone call to go. I felt a little as I had when I was a teenager, terribly drunk at a party, calling her to collect me. I remembered the feeling exactly: standing outside, wobbling in my heels, knowing she would shout at me, but thinking it seemed worth it if she would just come and get me.

'What about that boy you were with? Ryan, was it?'

'Not Ryan. Sam.'

'Sam, okay. I thought you got yourself a man and coupled up together. Is that not how it works?'

'It's a test,' I said. I felt dreamy; I felt separate from everything around me. I couldn't reconcile my mother's voice in my ear and sitting in the compound, my feet resting just beside the scum at the surface of the pool. 'You find yourself someone you want to live with, and you couple up. If you really like them, you'll stay together, and resist the temptation of infinite rewards.'

My mother was quiet for a few minutes. I heard a faint scrape, and a slight creak of wood. I could picture her perfectly, settling down in the red armchair by the kitchen door. It was worn and tired, and had been there since I was born.

'You're not exactly a winner, then, are you?'

I knew, then, that my mother wouldn't be there at the collection point, wherever it was. Andrew had said he would come, but I didn't want to see him. He would be so disappointed in me, to see the mess I had made of the compound: how little effort I had made to keep our home as it had been.

'I might come home soon,' I said. 'How are things on the outside, anyway? Has there been any trouble?'

'Oh, I don't know, Lily. Things are the same, I suppose. The best you can hope for, with the way things are.'

I paused, then asked, 'Any word on Dad?'

'No,' she said. 'Still nothing.' She sounded weary, either from listening to me ask that same question again, or because she had to give the same answer.

I used to think that I had tried that life, and was sick of it. I thought that because I didn't want my little slice of life – sitting in front of the television, trying not to take up too much space in my mother's house, avoiding the news yet waiting for an update on my father – that I didn't want any of it. But in that moment, I suddenly wanted to go to a city, and have total strangers walk right by me; I wanted to go to the sea, and let my hair be thrown about by violent, salty winds; I wanted to find Sam, and lie beside him on a tiny bed in a tiny room, and make plans for the weekend together. 'Do you think I should stay here, then?'

'Stay there? And do what?'

I picked at the laces of one of my shoes. They were white and gleaming, fresh from the box. 'I don't have to do anything here. I can just live in peace. No one disturbs me. The house, the whole compound, it's mine to do with as I want. If I choose to leave, the next group of contestants can come and start over, like we did.'

'And what if you decided to stay? What happens then?'

'What do you mean what happens then? I can stay here and get whatever I want just by asking for it.' There was silence for a moment. 'The house, the compound, the rewards: it's all mine. No one has stayed longer than six weeks. But I think I'll be the first. The longer you stay the more famous you become. No one remembers the people who only stay for a few days, but everyone remembers the two girls who stayed for six weeks.'

'Well,' she said. 'If that's what you want.'

'Hey,' I said. 'Do you know – have you heard – if people, ah . . . like me?'

'I wouldn't know. I really haven't been paying much attention. I'm sure they like you. Why wouldn't they? I did mean to tune in a bit more, but you know how things are with work. I come home so tired, I don't want to do anything. In fact, I'd better go, it's about time I got ready. I don't want to be late.'

'Okay,' I said. 'I'll talk to you soon.'

'All right. Thanks for calling.' I stared unseeing in front of me, feeling hollowed out.

As soon as I hung up, the phone died. I looked at it in my hand, small and dark, like a cockroach. I hadn't ever seen a version like it, and thought that a new model must have been released while I had been in the compound.

I went to bed, though the sun was still up. I was cold, and wanted to cocoon myself in blankets and stare at the ceiling.

I wasn't sure what time it was; I could have requested a clock, but I had a vague dread of seeing the slow movement of time. I didn't want to be reminded of how much of it had passed, and how little I had achieved. I wondered if they would kick me out when it became clear that I wasn't going to do anything entertaining, or if they would continue to watch me as I slept in later and later, and let myself and the compound go to ruin.

There was a shrill beeping noise from beside me. I screamed, then immediately felt embarrassed for having reacted at all. I looked around to see where the noise had come from. On the other side of the bed were a number of the rewards I had requested from the past few days: eyelash serum, and batteries, and a swimming hat, and a jigsaw that I hadn't opened, and a packet of jellybeans and a tanning glove. I had thrown the phone in the midst of it all without really registering it. I fished it out from amongst the mess and stared at the screen, lit up with a single message. I wondered if it was my mother, remembering to tell me that she missed me. *One new voice note*, the screen read. I looked at it fretfully. I held it in my hand for a while and stared at the ceiling. I pushed some of the things aside so I could lie comfortably on the bed. I pressed play.

'Hey,' a voice said. I paused the voice note to let myself cry, but only for a minute. I pressed play again. 'It's Sam. I don't know if you're hearing this in the compound, or if you're home again. I'm not really sure if you'll get to hear it at all. I wanted to get in touch, but the producers said it wasn't possible – then they sent me this number this morning and said that maybe you'd like to hear a familiar voice. I hope that's okay with you. I tried calling, but I don't have much reception where I am. I'm hoping this message gets to you anyway. I'm travelling at the minute – I'm on a boat, actually. I'm visiting an island I read about in a story when I was a boy. I didn't think it really existed, but I was looking at flights a couple of weeks ago, and I saw that it was only a five-hour journey from where I live. It was weird, going home after the compound. I thought I was looking forward to it, but I felt pretty numb for the first few days. Someone from the show called me a week after I got out to check up on me. I said I was okay, but didn't really feel entirely connected to reality. They told me that was normal, that all contestants feel that way when they come out. Anyway, I thought that it might be good to have a change of scenery, so I sold some of the things I won – I didn't realise how valuable some of the rewards were. It was enough for a plane ticket, so I booked a flight and then a boat, and now I'm almost there I think.

'I'm going to travel around for a bit, and then I might work on a vineyard for a little bit. It'll be good for me, I think. I miss the heat of the desert: I'm cold all the time now. I'd like to work in the sun again. I miss going inside to the shade after working outside for a long time, and your muscles are aching and there's sweat on your face and on your back, and that feeling when you take the first drink of ice-cold water.

'I miss waking up to you beside me. Sometimes I wonder if I imagined it all, especially now, when I'm somewhere new. I miss you so much I sometimes don't know how I'll get through the day.

'I'd been feeling poorly for a while, even before I went on the show. I didn't know what I was doing with my days. I found it hard to plan for the future. I kept thinking, why bother when we'll probably be dead in twenty years, maybe fifteen. I think probably all of us must have been very unhappy, otherwise why would we have done that to ourselves? I know we told ourselves that we wanted to live peacefully, but I think we were looking for new ways to make ourselves miserable. I did enjoy it, for a while. I was happy when I was with you.

'I'm sorry about how we left things. I've replayed it a thousand times, over and over. I'd do anything for a second chance with you.

'I don't think I'll go home for a while. But I'd really like to see you. I don't know what's been going on with you – you told me not to watch, and I haven't been on my phone much. Or I could come and see you, when you're out. It's a frightening journey, going from the compound to the pick-up point. But maybe you don't want to see me, or maybe you're planning on staying there for a while. I hope you're happy, whatever you're doing.

'Okay, I think I've said enough. I'll keep my phone on for a few days in case you want to get in touch. I love you. Bye.'

I sat in silence for a while. I pushed the things off the bed and stood up. I stretched, and looked up at the skylight, where I could see a little patch of dull blue.

I went to the screen and ordered one final thing: a sled. Drunk one day, I had requested a car, but it was denied. A sled was the only thing I could think of big enough to hold both all of my things and Andrew's. It took hours to pack. I included some pieces that other people had left behind, too: Candice's gossamer scarf, Jacintha's perfume and Sam's telescope. I threw the dead phone onto Andrew's monument; it was quite literally the ugliest thing that I had ever seen in my life. I couldn't fathom what the next group of residents would do with it.

Hauling the sled through the desert was, without question, the hardest thing I had ever done. My arms ached as they never had before, my back tense and cramping. Though it was cold, sweat poured down my forehead, and clung to my hair.

Day turned to evening, and evening turned to night. I could see the puff of my breath before me, and little else. I was horribly tired, but not afraid. I stopped often, and looked around, but there was nothing to see except for the shape of the enormous sled behind me. I didn't know what direction I was going in, or if there was a landmark I could use as a guide. When the temperature dropped further still, I stopped, shivering, terrified that I had passed the collection point, and that there was nobody there to get me. I had never seen this part of the show before, and wasn't entirely sure that it existed. Although rationally I knew that this wasn't going to be shown, I kept imagining people watching me search for someone who wasn't there, stumbling blindly, clutching my rewards. What brilliant viewing that would be, I thought with something nearing hysteria – what excellent, excellent television!

And then: a voice called my name. A hand lifted, in greeting, or as though to ward off a skittish animal. I raised my hand, returning the gesture, and stepped forward, the sled dragging heavily behind me.

Acknowledgements

A very warm thank you Rachel Mann, without whom this book would not have been possible: I'm so grateful for all of the work that you do, and most of all for your unfailing kindness and wisdom.

Thank you to my family for their support; thank you to Felim for letting me paint the walls in your house as I wrote, and to Bernie for being one of the first readers. A particular thank you to Deirdre and David, to whom this book is dedicated, for your unwavering support and enthusiasm. In the lottery of life, I got lucky to have you as my siblings.

Thank you to Aisling Grennan, for always being there, and for teaching me to drive.

Thank you to my editors on both sides of the Atlantic: Caitlin McKenna, Miriam Khanukaev, Suzie Dooré, Beth Coates, copyeditor Simon Fox and proofreader Rhian McKay; I'm so grateful for your insights, kindness and consideration.

Thank you to everyone at CAA, particularly Mollie Glick, Via Romano, Sarah Harvey and Yasmin McDonald. Thank you to everyone at Random House, especially Naomi Goodheart, Alison Rich, Maria Braekel, Windy Dorresteyn, Erin Richards and Madison Dettlinger. Thank you, too, to everyone at The Borough Press, particularly Jabin Ali, Jo Kite, Emily Merrill and Maud Davies. For the art and cover designs, thanks are due to Carrie Graber, Sarah Horgan, Greg Mollica and Anna Morrison.

Thank you to Cathal and Ciara Lee for letting me finish my edits in Carcassonne; thank you particularly to Meadhbh and Cliodhna for your invaluable help, and for waiting for me to finish before you got into the pool.

I'm grateful to all of my students, but I'd like to extend a particularly fond thanks to my 2023/24 TY High School class for your enthusiastic and stimulating conversations on consumerism and late-stage capitalism which helped to form some of the central ideas of this book.